Her Maiden Scandal

From her hiding place in Clinton Bell's bedroom, young Laura DeWitt Dahlgren blushed at her own shameless behavior. She had flirted outrageously with Clint to persuade him to harbor a runaway black man with a price on his head. And here she was—for the first time in her life—in a man's sleeping quarters.

Now, she listened tensely to the voices in the next room. The voices belonged to Ruth Ann, Laura's older sister, and to Fremont Hunter, Clint's distant cousin and Laura's self-styled suitor.

"The point is, cousin," said Fremont accusingly, "there is a nasty rumor afoot tonight, linking Miss Laura with an escaped Negro, and, as she isn't in her room at this late hour, and as we know you and Laura are, ah, friends, we couldn't help wondering if she was with you."

"No!" Clint said, the lie choking in his throat.

Then, from the window, Laura saw a new menace entering the fray: Clint's landlady, the town's most vicious gossip and snoop.

Laura knew then that there was but one way she could save black Amos from discovery.

Unlacing her chemise so that it exposed the upper swell of her full young breasts, she stepped, heart pounding, into the outer room . . .

The FREEDOM FIGHTERS *Series*

The Turning of the Tide

Jonathan Scofield

A DELL/BRYANS BOOK

Published by
Dell Publishing Co., Inc.
1 Dag Hammarskjold Plaza
New York, New York 10017

Dell ® TM 681510, Dell Publishing Co., Inc.

ISBN: 0-440-08490-3

Printed in the United States of America

First printing—September 1981

Autumn, 1863

THE AUTUMN AIR of the Hudson River valley was as heady as wine. Winter still seemed a long way off . . . the war even farther off.

The fighting hadn't seemed so far off to Laura Dahlgren when it had been at Gettysburg. But that had been a hundred and ninety-two miles southwest, way back in July, almost ancient history to her young mind.

Now the scarlet and purple glory of the wooded valley fired Laura's imagination. Her heart beat with new life. Within the month she would turn eighteen.

"As old as that," her neighbor Marvin Carson kidded, shaking his head thoughtfully. "My Mildred and I should be thinking of having a party for you . . . unless your mother would be having objections."

Laura grinned at the scarecrow-thin man and wrinkled her nose. They were both well aware of the objections that Lucille Dewitt Dahlgren could raise. They had been raised and raised, for going on three solid years now.

The main objection had been raised once again that very day at the breakfast table.

Lucille Dahlgren had cleared her throat ominously, and

stared rigidly at her daughter. "I try, Laura. The good Lord knows how I try to understand your compassion for the valley people, but must you go again to sit with that invalid woman?"

"I promised, Mama. Mr. Carson has another . . . he has business again in Peekskill."

Lucille inclined her head in severe disapproval of Marvin Carson's business.

"It just makes my skin crawl to think of you associating with a man who touches the death of others for a livelihood. Just makes it crawl."

Clarence Dahlgren, who had intimate acquaintance with his wife's views on all matters, said nothing, but sank further behind his newspaper.

"Mama," Laura insisted, "it is Mildred Carson I _associate_ with, while Mr. Carson has to be away. If you ever went down to town you would realize that the undertaker's shop is quite separate from their home. Besides, I feel I'm doing a bit for the war effort in that way."

"I also love my country," said Lucille in tones of noble anguish. "But I hardly see how sitting with an invalid while her husband carts dead soldiers home to their poor families has anything to do with the war."

"Ah, perhaps not," breathed Clarence, from behind his newspaper. "But someone must do that task and Mildred Carson can't be left alone."

Lucille gloomily considered this for a moment, then, after a sadly sardonic glance of acknowledgment at the unseen man for his unsolicited comment, she shook her head, bowed her triple chin on her heavy bosom, and sighed.

"I hope such an influence does not come back to haunt us, Mr. Dahlgren," she said, in a fatal tone. "There are valley women who could care for her. It shouldn't be left to a Dahlgren. After all, we are doing more than our share for this senseless war. This calamity would never have befallen us if we still belonged to _our_ proper country."

She sank into melancholy. Clarence Dahlgren lowered his paper. He knew what feeling she intended to convey to him: ferocious pride and long-suffering devotion to a heritage that was no more—although Lucille had the knack of making 1776 sound as though it had happened just the week before. But almost a quarter century of marriage gave him insight into what she was really feeling: sullen, envious resentment that the titled status of the DeWitt family would be no more. He knew his wife to be a woman who felt she had lowered herself in station by marrying a Dahlgren.

"You are a busy lass, Laura," he murmured, leaning toward his daughter with deep love. "And I'm not one to discount your work as charitable, so be running along. I'd like to 'ave a word with your mother about certain household matters before I am off for the day."

Lucille lifted her head. In the frigid cold of the room, her little blue eyes slitted with eager malevolence. She pressed her lips together and prepared for the age-old battle.

"Ah, yes, certainly run along, Laura." She hesitated elaborately, then, with an air of determined courage she said: "Leave your poor sister and me to do all the work for tonight's dinner party. The care of Mildred Carson is far more important than your family obligation."

Clarence quickly waved Laura away. This session, he perceived, was going to be even worse than he had anticipated.

"We cannot afford to go on this way," exclaimed Mr. Dahlgren in a tone of strong consternation, as soon as his daughter had cleared the room. "Woman, once again you have me near the point of bankruptcy."

She compressed her lips until her mouth was a mere slit in her florid face. She regarded her husband grimly.

How I've come to loathe you, she thought. What happened to the aspiring young man I married? You've grown bald, stoop-shouldered, thin as a rail. That suit is a baggy disgrace—and push those horrible glasses up from the tip of your nose. Really, must you always look like a common bookkeeper?

"Scarcely bankrupt, Mr. Dahlgren. That is, unless you have allowed the army to cheat you once again. Had you not offended your brother, we might not be in this sorry state of affairs."

Clarence was in awe of her ability persistently to twist facts to cover up her own misdeeds.

He had not offended his brother John—she had. As

chief of the Navy Bureau of Ordnance, his brother had invented a cannon that bore the family name, and which should have been a thing of family pride. Instead, Lucille had turned it into a thing of bitter dispute. When a gun factory was built to foundry and test the massive new weapon she had felt that Clarence should be included in the project—and the profits. But there would be no profits for the naval officer, and the manufacturing contract had been awarded to Gouverneur Kemble's West Point Foundry at Cold Spring. For a year John Adolphus Bernard Dahlgren's name was forbidden to be mentioned in Lucille's presence. Then, in 1861, when John became an unofficial aide to President Lincoln, Lucille suddenly put all of the blame on Clarence's shoulders. The Dahlgren name was beginning to mean something—if not financially, at least socially.

"And I may be able to rectify your mistake with Mr. Kemble," Lucille resumed. "Ruth Ann has been able to learn from one of the young officers at the academy a most interesting fact. I fully. intend to discuss it with Mr. Kemble this evening at dinner."

"You haven't invited him?" said Clarence, in a concerned voice. "He's snubbed every one of your invitations to date, ma'am, and I doubt he's forgiven your uninvited intrusion on his picnic party last summer."

"When one is in a higher social class," Lucille remarked, with a swift toss of her head and a sniff, "one need not stand on the ceremony of an invitation. Besides, Ruth Ann had an invitation through a young gentleman and I felt duty-bound to escort them as a chaperone."

"Let's return to the point," Clarence groaned, "and look at our financial picture realistically. Mrs. Barker was up from Peekskill yesterday. A small matter of five gowns for Ruth Ann—unpaid these past four months."

Lucille smiled darkly. "I assure you they were of such poor quality that I may just have to let Laura wear them for everyday. Had you allowed Ruth Ann to go into New York City and shop properly, I wouldn't have been embarrassed in stalling the woman for money I hardly feel that she honestly earned."

Clarence shook his head over and over to himself, as if he was too aghast to speak immediately.

"I paid it," he finally murmured. "You forget that Mr. Barker is my biggest supplier of undergarments and socks for the academy. He allows me no credit line and I demand you not ask for one from his wife and her seamstresses."

Lucille turned her head to him alertly and smiled.

"I have no intention of ever using the woman again, Mr. Dahlgren. Ruth Ann is a lady of breeding and family and shouldn't have to wear such rags. Now, if she could just go and spend a week with Laddie to acquire a fall and winter wardrobe . . ."

Clarence winced. Any mention of Lawrence Alastair Dahlgren set his teeth on edge. In his heart his son was all but dead. Bringing him into any discussion was Lucille's secret weapon to close off debate and make her husband flee from opening yet another old wound.

"We have not the money," he sighed, studying his breakfast plate mournfully.

Lucille cleared her throat. "How can that be, Mr. Dahlgren? We had the contract to supply beef, pork and produce to the academy for the whole summer."

"As most of the cadets so frequently seem to find their way to our dinner table, the quartermaster's gain is our constant loss. Lucille, I beg of you, no more."

"And I beg of you," she said flatly, "to consider your daughter. It is our duty to see that she is afforded the opportunity to marry into the proper social class."

He rose. He could never win against the woman. He tried to bow his way out, but Lucille lumbered to her feet and blocked his escape.

"I have yet another matter," she said, as though she had been the one who initiated the whole conversation. "This place is like an icebox. Your men have been most derelict in supplying me with firewood. It must be delivered today. You know Fremont cannot stand the cold. And I know that you are going to frown, so don't. Fremont is the one who has given Ruth Ann the information that will make us a fortune."

He did not wish to discuss Fremont Hunter. He did not really care what information the senior cadet might have come across. He found Hunter boorish and quite rude. Nor did he care if the cavalier caught his death of cold in the house. The house was always cold—in personality, personnel and structure.

In both name and appearance, Highcliff-on-the-Hudson was an affectation of Lucille's fierce clinging to her ancestry. It perched on the cliffs overlooking the river valley like a block of medieval gray granite, buttressed and turreted like the DeWitt castle must have been in the old country—and probably just as draughty as the original.

And Lucille maintained it as though it were still an important arm of the English court. The majority of her household expenses went for a cook, a maid and a quasi-butler—just because Gouverneur Kemble maintained a similar staff at his Cold Spring mansion. The great, ugly stone pile actually required a staff five times as large, but Lucille wouldn't lower herself to hire local cleaning women. And if truth were told, none cared to work for her.

Clarence stepped around his wife. "I barely have enough money to pay the men this week, let alone pay them for wood. You had best cancel your plans and we shall spend the evening in the kitchen."

"You cannot do this to your family," Lucille warned, her tone savage.

She spun, her wide hoops swaying stiffly about her as she stalked to the parlor. She had quite another means open to her that day to put her hands on ready cash. However, it riled her that she was constantly put in the position of having to pull the family chestnuts out of the fire.

The parlor was hardly less chill and gloomy than the dining room, and as sparsely if elegantly furnished. It was Lucille's "entertaining" room and had been furnished before any of the other rooms.

"Kitty, you may finish your cleaning in here later. Has a Mr. Garth Wilkins arrived?"

"He's waiting in the foyer, mum."

Lucille eyed the pock-faced dumpy girl. Really, she thought, the girl is impossible.

"Well, Kitty," she sighed, "please show the gentleman in."

The girl curtsied, and despite herself, Lucille began to laugh.

"Is there something else, mum?"

"Nothing." Suddenly Lucille was all smiles, the perfect hostess.

"Ah, Mr. Wilkins, please enter . . . and kindly pull the door to as you come. I am Mrs. Clarence Dahlgren."

Garth Wilkins approached her warily. The rangy, hawk-faced man had come up from New York City on the morning train. Upon viewing Highcliff-on-the-Hudson he had begun to get a feeling of foreboding about this visit.

Lucille studied him like piece goods to be matched for a quilt. He was not what she had expected. Hat and gloves elegantly in hand, his cane tucked under his arm, he bowed and frowned his way to the chair indicated.

When it came to business Lucille did not believe in a long preamble.

"My son, the former Captain Lawrence Alastair Dahlgren, is the one who learned of your services for me, Mr. Wilkins."

"Former?" he asked on a note of confusion.

Lucille laughed, regally placing herself on the edge of a Lady Anne chair.

"Former, sir, as a captain in the service, but not former in life. He served until Shiloh, where he was wounded. After being highly decorated he was returned to us."

"I am sincerely happy that he was returned safely," he said.

"Which will underscore the purpose of your visit," said Lucille in a slightly theatrical voice. "What my son suffered, while others get away with . . . well, to the point, sir. My son tells me it is your business to bring to bay these criminal elements who bounty jump."

"That it is, Mrs. Dahlgren. It is a most horrible disgrace. The figures are staggering."

Lucille did not need to be told the figures; she was an expert on the matter. But she painted an expression of interest on her face as he recited facts and numbers with which she was already familiar. She did not wish to inform Mr. Garth Wilkins that he was not the first bounty hunter that she had done business with.

"Thank you," she said sweetly, when he was finished. "I believe the case I am about to bring to your attention will be most similar. This man participated in the draft riots down in New York City, which caused the deaths of those seventy-six unfortunate people. He returned to this area and awaited this money-wasting bounty enlisting system. I have firsthand knowledge that he received nearly a thousand dollars for enlisting down in Peekskill. Four months later he was back here as a deserter, enjoying his evenings in the tavern, and then he marched himself off to Albany to re-enlist under a different name, his profit now being close to two thousand. I'm sure the man will try the scheme over and over again."

"Oh, I agree with you perfectly, Mrs. Dahlgren," said Mr. Wilkins, with a knowing look, his hope of monetary gain growing. "One can't help but think of the greed of some in the time of war. You are most patriotic, to say the least, as I always say. Now, if ye'll be giving me the nature of the man's name and latest whereabouts . . ."

Lucille inclined her head with approval of the worthy sentiments.

"I have it all on the tip of my tongue, sir. But did my son mislead me—telling me that such information would be rewarded?"

Wilkins nodded grimly. He thought he had smelled her out as a cunning one, but he wasn't yet sure just how cunning. His best information often came from posh houses like this.

He and his men cared not if they hunted down Union or Confederate, black or white. Their allegiance was only to the gold they could make. They could smile and be sympathetic to either cause.

"It all depends, Mrs. Dahlgren, on the circumstances and how long it takes me to track the man down and bring him in."

Carefully rising, Lucille smiled. "The man in question, sir, is the undesirable boyfriend of my maid Kitty. At this very moment, if I am not mistaken, he will be sitting in my kitchen partaking of free coffee and breakfast. Have I not made your job most simple?"

Now Mr. Wilkins was truly amazed at the cool regard she had shown in the matter.

"But, ma'am, if that be the same lass who entered me . . ." He gulped. As cold and heartless a business as he was in, this woman was a marvel to him. "Will she not suspect you of turning in her lad?"

Lucille winked ponderously. "Ah, but you have much to learn about well-mannered servants. They would know that on such a matter as this the lady of the house would be quietly approached to save her embarrassment among her peers. The man's name is Wilf Jamison. There will be no commotion from my servants, I assure you."

Wilkins shrugged and reached for his wallet. He considered it wise to pay a woman of this nature in advance. He vowed that he would never want her as his enemy. He counted out five pieces of paper from the leather wallet and handed them to her.

Lucille looked puzzled. "And what manner of payment is this, sir?"

"This is the new government issue of paper money, Mrs. Dahlgren. They're called 'greenbacks' because of the ink."

"But is it real money?" she gasped.

"Says right on it that they're legal tender. Had no trouble with them in New York City. Coin is hard to find these days. I've given you five bills, each of a ten-dollar denomination. Most reward information is only worth a good five- or ten-dollar reward. I'm making it more, because we may wish to do business in the future."

Lucille was astonished. She had received only ten dollars for the runaway slave. Yes, she would become more alert than ever now. She fully intended to do business with Mr. Wilkins in the future.

2

EXCEPT FOR THE PALE SMOKE in the sky one would never have guessed how close the two villages lay— West Point, a sleepy little hamlet, and Cold Spring, a beehive of foundry activity. Even though women like Lucille Dahlgren classified them all as "valley people," here too was a social hierarchy. The people of Cold Spring were considered newcomers, although many newcomers lived in West Point. West Point owed its sixty-two-year existence to the fieldstone buildings and battlements perched on the west bank plateau. One would have thought that having the United States Military Academy as a neighbor would have given them a sense of being near the war. But in fact life was little changed. The war seemed far off.

The country smelled of harvest fields in the fall and of sugaring in the spring. Laura Dahlgren loved it all dearly. The spirit of freedom born of the fields and woods had grown into something more than an attitude of mind. In the valley she could be natural and herself—not constantly play-acting like her mother and sister. Among the valley people she was automatically accepted and did not need

Ruth Ann's clothing or Lucille's looking glass to tell her
that she was beautiful. It was something that radiated
from the inside out when she was among friends. She was
just naturally in love with life and with people. To the
chagrin of her mother, Laura knew almost all of the valley
people, and loved all of them that she knew.

That morning, because Marvin Carson's sad consign-
ment was not yet ready in Peekskill, she had been relieved of the duty of sitting with Mildred. She would be
required that evening, and that was a worry. She was also
required to be in attendance at each and every one of
her mother's stuffy dinner parties and social evenings. And
having been relieved of sitting with Mildred she knew
that she should get on up the path to Highcliff-on-the-
Hudson to help out. She didn't like to disobey her mother;
but she just couldn't let such a glorious day slip away from
her. An adventuresome thought came to mind.

"That's what I'll do. I'll go toward Cold Spring and
gather walnuts, hickorynuts and chestnuts. Mama can't
scream at me for putting my time to such industry."

But the morning seemed to slip away without her ever
getting out of the hamlet and onto the Cold Spring road.
There were just too many people to greet; too many little
unexpected errands to do for them; too many babies to
hold for just a minute while their mothers saw to other
matters.

As she rounded the schoolhouse on her way to cross the
village green, the bell clanged and the yard instantly filled
with eager children on their way home for lunch.

"That's where I should be," she said aloud, "if only I
were younger."

"And where is it you should be, Laura Dahlgren?"

"Clinton Bell!" she gasped, turning. "Why aren't you at
the foundry this time of day?"

Clint Bell swung a tin lunch pail from off his shoulder
and patted it lovingly. "It was too glorious a day to be
eating my fare with coke soot in my lungs, so I hiked over
to have it on the green. Would you join me, Laura Dahlgren?"

Laura frowned. His clothing did not suggest that he had
been at the foundry at all that day. His square-jawed face
was free of soot and his sandy hair was neatly brushed.

"I might consider it," she said, "if you'll tell me the truth."

Nineteen-year-old Clinton Bell laughed—a rare sound from the serious young man. Wide-shouldered and thick-limbed, built as square as his jawline, he dwarfed the other foundry men in breadth if not always in height.

"It's a holiday present from Gouverneur Kemble himself. Been the whole morning with him, I have. Tomorrow, if I'm not sleeping and dreaming this all now, I'll be going back to the foundry as a foreman."

"Oh, Clint!" she cried with glee, "how wonderful! I'm so pleased for you."

Clint was pleased for himself. Because of his experience as a cooper he had been apprenticed to the foundry owner and brought from Connecticut at the start of the war. To be elevated over men twice his age was an embarrassment but exhilarating. And what a great stroke of luck this was! There was no one in the world he would rather have shared such news with than Laura.

"Will you share my lunch?" Then he blushed. "It ain't a lot, mind you. Mrs. Rivers is still a little unsure she should be giving me board without room."

"I'll be glad to," Laura said quickly. Nettie Rivers was one of the few people she could not abide. Gossip offended Laura, and Nettie Rivers and gossip went hand in hand. The widow woman had turned her home into a boarding house before Clint's arrival. She had taken in ten foundry men and said that was her limit. To her chagrin her own words became a local joke and so she had allowed Clint to fix up a portion of the carriage shed as private quarters. Because of his youth he was allowed to sit at her boarding table and help safeguard her reputation.

She never showed favoritism at her dinner table—only in the various men's tin lunch pails. Her temper would have flared to hear Clint say that his pail was not 'a lot,' and in truth there was plenty of food for the two of them. There was cold mutton between fresh breakfast biscuits, wedges of salted cucumber, slabs of walnut cake, red apples and a hunk of homemade taffy. Laura ate as though she hadn't seen food in a month. In the open air everything tasted so much better.

Clint never took his eyes off her once. By the oddest

happenstance they were lunching very near the spot on the green where they had first met just a year before.

It was bazaar time. The village green was crowded with people and brightly decorated booths. Clint, a loner, had avoided it his first two years in West Point. He had also avoided, except for a rather embarrassed first meeting, the fact that he possessed a relative in the cadet corps, although he and his cousin from the South were only very distantly related.

But Nettie Rivers enjoyed showing off her prize boarder. Throughout the day she kept Clinton running hot scones from her kitchen ovens to her bazaar booth, to be split, stuffed with a generous spoonful of whipped butter and a portion of her homemade strawberry jam.

Clinton saw the girl at the booth on three of his various trips, eating her heart's content of the delicacy. Each time he stared in disbelief at her beauty. Clinton had never before paid attention to girls. He might easily have kept his nose in the Bible and become a staunch moralistic preacher, marrying, in time, just as staunch and moralistic a bride. But this girl he measured against every Biblical heroine he had ever read about. She was fair, comely and possessed a God-given smile that held him in awe. He feared he would never meet another like her. He dared not even ask Nettie Rivers who she might be.

As he stared at her for the third time, his revery of her was interrupted. "What ho! Cousin Clinton, is it you?"

Clinton spun, embarrassed, recognizing the voice at once. The intrusion meant one horrible thing. Now I shall never see her again, he told himself immediately.

He saw there had been no change in Fremont Hunter. The cadet captain was still slim and blond, with hair not two shades darker than that of the annoyed young lady on his arm.

"Yes, it is you," Fremont said, impatiently. "And where have you been?"

"Here. Working in the foundry."

"Well, I feared they had carried you off in the draft. I informed father of our meeting, but letters back from him are hard to come by, especially now that he has a new bride. Is your own family well?"

Clint nodded. Young Hunter's voice was unexpectedly rich and deep. Far more Southern than Clinton remembered. He looked at him, bemused. Could they have come from the same blood line? Fremont's hands were clean, slender, manicured. His own were broad and hardened by work. Still, he was forced to revise the impression he had first formed of his cousin—an impression of effeminacy. True, Hunter was all grace and dashingly handsome beauty, but it was a grace and beauty of a generation pampered with little more than fox hunts, cotillions and lavish garden parties. He was a coddled product of a short-lived courtly period in American history. But grace and manners he would always possess.

"Cousin Clinton, may I present my companion, Miss Ruth Ann Dahlgren, and the girl trying to buy out your booth, her sister, Miss Laura Dahlgren."

Clinton tried to bow to each, but felt clumsy. Ruth Ann tried to ignore him as though he were beneath her notice, but Laura stared in utter amazement. It was as much an amazement to her that the two men were cousins as it was for Clinton that the two young women were really sisters. Ruth Ann's beauty was contrived. That is not to say that she was not lovely—but it was a hard, calculated loveliness. Not a blonde hair was out of place, the lips and cheeks had been pinched or rouged to a deep rose, and the eyelids given a dash of color to bring out the sea-blue of her eyes. She was slender and high of bosom, but her carriage suggested whalebone stays and not natural posture.

Unlike Ruth Ann, Laura's looks and demeanor were entirely natural. She stared openly at Clinton and exclaimed, "Your cousin? I can't believe it!"

Seeing the expression of wonder on her face, Fremont burst into laughter. "Quite true! Sometime in the past, a past which neither family cares to discuss, Clinton's great aunt Deborah married my great uncle John Langley Hunter. The begats in between we need not bore you with."

"Thank God," Ruth Ann said, not hiding her sarcasm.

"I think it is utterly fantastic," Laura said. "I must hear more."

Ruth Ann had heard all she wished to hear. To her Clinton was a gnarled, rough workman, easily ignored—

although he did perhaps have a certain animal appeal.

"Come along, Fremont, will you!" Ruth Ann said, her voice genuinely angry.

Fremont ignored her, casting his eyes at Laura, which only increased Ruth Ann's ire.

"Cousins?" Laura went on, as though nothing had happened. "I think that is very nice."

"You do?" Fremont smiled. "Well, if it is so nice, perhaps you'll be inviting us all for tea."

Laura was all for the suggestion, much to Ruth Ann's ill-disguised disgust. But Clinton suspected Fremont's real motive in making the suggestion. So, he said to himself, Fremont's in love with the one and squires the other around. He found the idea unusually disquieting. He didn't know if he wanted Laura for himself—though he knew he didn't want Ruth Ann. But it seemed a little unfair for Fremont to have both.

He had been invited to Highcliff-on-the-Hudson once only—a fact that still haunted him now, nearly a year later.

"What is it, Clint?" she said. "You look so troubled."

"It's your mother," Clint said after a silence. "You aren't going to get into trouble having lunch with me, are you?"

Laura put out a hand and let it rest atop his own. It was the first time they had ever touched and the feel of her cool hand on his gave him a great deal of pleasure.

"No, Clint," she said. "What harm can she see in my having lunch with a good friend right out in public view?"

His heart sank again. He had begun to think about her almost constantly and wished he knew a way to change their relationship into something more than just friendship.

"I hope you're right," he said. "She probably wouldn't say a word if you were having lunch with Fremont."

Laura pulled her hand away and looked at him, her eyes filled with sudden mischief.

"So, Mr. Clinton Bell," she teased, "I do believe you are a mite jealous of your cousin. What makes you think I would even consent to have lunch with that stuffed shirt?"

"Careful," he grinned. "You're talking about my cousin, you know."

"Is he?" she said merrily. "Is he really, Clint? I've never

heard you talk of your family and yet that's all that he seems able to talk about. You would think that the Hunter family had founded all of the South, to hear him talk. And brag? There isn't a time that he's at our dinner table that he doesn't have to recount the fact that Custis Lee was his platoon leader his first year at the academy. He seems to think that Robert E. Lee was the only worthwhile superintendent that the school ever had. I'm amazed that such talk doesn't get him into trouble with his fellow cadets."

"You've got to look at it from his point of view, too," Clinton said earnestly, feeling a little strange standing up for a man whose background he knew only from family chitchat. "We're really not all that closely related. And the Hunters . . . well, they've always relished their freedom and when someone comes along to challenge it, they're more than ready to fight. It was very rough on him to forsake his family and Southern tradition to stay and finish his military schooling."

Laura frowned thoughtfully. "I don't know. I once heard him tell my father that he had erred. He stayed because he thought the South would win the war in a matter of months and now he was stuck with his decision for the duration."

Suddenly they heard angry voices through the fall-colored trees of the village green. One was Sheriff Addison's, while the other Laura recognized after a moment as that of Wilf Jamison, their maid's boyfriend. She did not know the third man.

"They have Wilf shackled," Laura whispered, her eyes growing large and fearful.

"You know him?"

"Yes." She hesitated, then the truth came bursting out. "He went to war in my brother's place. Wilf would do no wrong. I must find out what this is all about, Clint, and report to father." Then she gasped. "Oh, I'm a clappermouthed fool! Please, Clint, don't ever repeat what I just said. Mama would skin me alive."

"I'd do anything you ever asked of me, Laura."

She hardly heard his heartfelt declaration. She was already racing across the green toward the stone jailhouse.

* * *

Garth Wilkins wanted the man held in custody until the afternoon train. He wished him turned over only in New York City, where he had military friends.

Sheriff Alfred Addison didn't like it at all, but the law required him to give all necessary help and assistance to a legally registered bounty man. He could find nothing wrong with Wilkins's papers, but silently vowed to walk down to the warehouse and discuss the matter with Clarence Dahlgren as soon as he could.

Addison's face was furrowed with a deep frown when Laura entered the jail office. Garth Wilkins stood with his back to her, speaking sternly as he concluded his conversation with the sheriff.

"The man is sly and cunning, Sheriff Addison. Twice and possibly more times he's received bounty pay and then deserted. Keep him locked securely. Now, where might I catch a bit of lunch?"

"Tavern or Nettie Rivers's boarding house," Addison answered shortly.

"I abstain when on duty, sir, so I'll try the latter."

He touched cane to hat as he brushed past Laura.

As soon as Wilkins's back had turned Sheriff Addison had warned Laura to silence until the door closed. Now she blurted out, "What does he mean by 'bounty pay'?"

The thin mouth made a cavernous O in the sheriff's craggy face. "Something I've a mind to discuss with your father, girl."

"Why not with Wilf? He's the one who has been accused of whatever it is."

"Your logic, my dear, is most feminine." He laughed, then sobered. His respect for Laura Dahlgren was monumental, but held quietly to himself. Most thought he did very little to earn his pay, because there was very little to do. But very little happened between Peekskill and Cold Spring that Alfred Addison didn't know about. He had lived in the valley for all of his sixty-seven years, coming out of retirement when the young sheriff had gone off to war. He knew Laura Dahlgren for being a very closed-mouthed creature and saw where he might put her to his own use at that moment.

"But, perhaps, very good logic. Would you talk with Wilf while I go down and see your father?"

"I . . . I only know him as Kitty's boyfriend . . . but I can try."

"Good girl!" he said. "That's the spirit! You'll find him in the back. It's the only lock-up cell we possess."

The twenty-two-year-old man sat on a three-legged stool brooding, his bad leg jutting out at a strange angle.

Laura stood there a long moment before he looked up and noticed her. Then his anger burst upon her ears.

"What in hell do you want?" Wilf roared. "Haven't I had enough damn trouble from your family?"

"I would hardly know about that."

He glared, his face and eyes taking on the semblance of a cornered animal measuring an enemy. "Then why are you here?"

Laura stepped up to the barred door. "I was on the green when I heard them bringing you in. What did that man mean by bounty pay and saying you had deserted?"

The hardness in his expression melted and his face grew very pale and boyish. Suddenly he saw the whole horrible truth behind his arrest.

"I fear telling you, Miss Dahlgren," he whispered, "for I don't like being called a liar."

"I have no reason to call you a liar," declared Laura, "nor do I know what you mean by trouble from my family. Has all of this something to do with you serving for my brother?"

He gasped as he struggled up from the stool. "No one knows of that but your parents and brother!"

Laura slowly shook her head, a grim smile lighting her dark blue eyes.

"I seem to have the knack of overhearing conversations right at their end, Wilf. I heard my father arguing with my mother about sending you to war in Laddie's place. Father was quite upset about it and moped for weeks after you left. And I heard the last of a heated fight between my father and brother when Laddie came home a war hero."

Jamison's voice again rose to a frenzied roar. "War hero!" he cried. "He has taken all of the glory and I'm

unable to get even a dirty dime for this leg I'll be forced
to drag along forevermore!"

"Sit down," she said gently. "You will find that my father
is not an unreasonable man. If a wrong has been done, let
us help to right it."

Jamison buried his fingers in his muttonchop whiskers,
unconsciously yanking at them as he shook his head in
despair. "I know you mean well, miss, but it will do no
good. I know your father tried. He's been uncommon good
to me. But he had no voice against her before and won't
now. She's got me and got me good. Even this bounty
hunter says she's the one turned me in. She'll lie through
her teeth to save your brother."

Rage mounted up and beat about Laura's ears. She
knew how cruel her mother could be at times—except, of
course, when it came to Laddie and Ruth Ann. But to
treat someone this way was unthinkable.

"Perhaps she will," she said softly, "if you allow her to
get away with it."

"Girl," he ranted, "get it through your head! It's your
own mother I'm speaking about!"

Laura nodded. "And I'm speaking about why she might
have had you arrested. I can't help unless I know the
whole story from the beginning."

"You'll not be liking it," he insisted.

"I don't like parsnips or carrots either, Wilf," she said,
grinning, "but I'm forced to eat them twice a week."

He slumped back on the stool. It was wrong of him to
tell her all, he knew. She was so young and innocent, and
according to Kitty the only decent person in that whole
horrible household. Perhaps he could put his trust in her.

"Well, miss," he started slowly, "back when they announced the draft a man could buy an exemption for
$300 or hire a substitute to serve in his name. Most folks,
though, kinda looked down on a man who just outright
bought an exemption. I was just twenty and taking up
with Miss Kitty at the time. You probably don't even recall me."

Laura puzzled. "Weren't you our gardener for a summer?"

"The very summer I speak of, miss. The very summer
your mother approached me. Seein' as how I had my heart

set on taking up house with Miss Kitty, I thought the offer most fair. Five hundred a year, and I could keep my army wages, if I went to serve under your brother's name."

"Under his name? What was he to do for a name in the meantime?"

"According to what your mother told me she was going to set him up in business down New York City way and the name didn't matter. But from what I now hear from this Mr. Wilkins, a Wilf Jamison has been collecting money for enlisting in the northern army, then deserting and enlisting elsewhere for more money. I'm sorry to say, but I now strongly suspect it was your brother using my name."

Laura turned the thought over in her mind. It was not at all unlikely. Her parents were always fighting over Laddie's business failures and need of money. Then, suddenly, from out of nowhere he would come up with enough capital to start anew—and it did not come from her father.

"That may be true, but can't you prove that you were in the army at the same time that this person was collecting the money and then deserting?"

"How can I prove it?" Jamison said coldly.

"But you have the money my mother paid you and your army pay as evidence."

His laugh was cruel. "Ain't had either. Don't get no pay while a battle is raging, miss. Comes after. I wasn't there for after. We were way out in Mississippi, you see. They called the place the Wilderness, and it was that. A tangle of woods broken here and there by small farm houses and fields. We had more than twice the numbers as the Rebs, and nearly three times as many big guns, but even an inexperienced man like me saw that artillery would be practically useless. How you going to use four hundred big guns in such woods? It was going to be a fight between the infantry at close range."

He paused for a moment, the scene coming vividly back to his mind.

"Had been in a few small battles up to then, but nothing like this. We had begun to bivouac for the night. The next day was really gonna be something. A flock of quail were suddenly startled out of the woods and flew over our heads. My captain drew out his revolver and potted one for his supper. Gave me a queer feeling all over—like his shot had brought about a thousand eyes peering at us from the woods. There were, but we didn't know it then. Seems Gen'ral Jackson had slipped his men up the slope in two long battle lines, with the rest of his columns in support. Miss, I hope you never have to see what I saw then.

"Worst sound in the world is a bugle when you're not expecting it, and then that devilish Rebel yell from the greys. Our rear was unprotected and the killin' just swept down on us. Before we could even take a breath a whole regiment was blown to bits. Twenty regiments, pointed all wrong. Our backs were to them in the trenches. My captain was so green to battle that he just stood there shaking the dead quail at the Rebs. There was nothing but panic as we grabbed for our guns and tried to fight back. We had no support. Sickles's division was ten miles away and there was a whole mile-wide gap for them to enter and scatter our lines. No man alive could have counted fast enough to keep track of the falling."

He stopped short, a look of anguish sweeping his strong young face. "That's when it all happened."

There was a long silence between them. Breathlessly, Laura heard herself ask, "When what happened?"

He stared down at his leg. "That's when I found myself suddenly on the ground. A cannon ball had torn most of the leg away. Funny, there was no pain until my captain came and tied his handkerchief around the mangled part, twisted it into a knot to stay the blood and hauled me off to behind a tree. Last time I ever saw him. For 'most an hour I lay behind the tree, knowing I was gonna bleed to death. Minié balls struck the tree so often that I was fast losing my shelter. In the din I didn't hear the call for the blues to retreat. Hell, all I could see were fresh regiments of greys attacking. I stared at 'em so hard they must have thought my eyes was frozen in death. But I was damned if I was going to die without taking a few of them with me."

His voice now took on a fierceness. "I'd fire, then freeze. They didn't know where the shots were coming from. Then I'd have to reload when they weren't looking. But I was almost out of shots. Then this Reb colonel rode up. The blues must have just got their cannon turned, for a shell exploded squarely on top of him. It nearly shattered my ears and all I could hear was the pitiful cry of the dying horse. Doesn't sound pretty, miss, but all that was left of the colonel was the hand he had been holding up with a revolver."

Laura shuddered at the grisly description.

"That revolver gave me six more chances to keep on living. And each Reb it dropped gave me another gun and even more chances. Somehow, without knowing it, I was using my leg to get from new gun to new gun. It was me or them, and that's all I thought about. But the big guns of the blues were finally booming back. The field beyond the Chancellor House was again turning from grey to blue. As a Northern regiment went by me at the double-quick, their colonel pulled his horse up short right beside me. The reins of the horse were wound about the pommel and he commanded the beast with his knees and heels. In one hand he held a spyglass, and a saber in the other. The saber was dripping with blood but he still touched the sword down to my shoulder.

"He asked for my name and I automatically gave him your brother's. Then he shouted for me to get along with his men. I guess I must have done exactly as he ordered. I don't remember sundown or the hours thereafter. Somehow I do recall a whisper that went through the ranks that Jackson had been carried from the field fatally wounded. Nobody cheered. After an evening like that nobody cheers the death of another. But many of the living were still to die that night. For three hours after midnight the lines fired at each other until the blazing muskets made the darkness seem like a scene right out of hell. But darkness came sooner for me than for most. I guess I had just lost too much blood and fainted away like a swooning woman."

"Swooning woman?" Laura protested. "I'm amazed you stayed upon your feet so long. Praise be that you did so they could finally get you out of the battle."

Wilf Jamison chuckled drily. "Or put me square into a new one. The next morning the Confederate artillery was regrouped and able to reach General Hooker's headquarters and the old Chancellor House, which was being used for a hospital. It was knocked to pieces and set afire while the doctors were working on my leg. There were hundreds of wounded in the yard and blues and greys alike rushed down to pull them out of the line of cannon fire. Then they went back to battle each other. I don't remember, but they say I went along for the rest of that day. Don't remember much, except they say the Rebs won that battle at Chancellorsville."

Laura was suddenly dubious. "I thought you said you were in Mississippi."

"I was."

"But Chancellorsville is in Virginia."

"You sure, miss? I was told the battle of Shiloh was in Mississippi."

"Shiloh!" she protested. "Why that was in Tennessee, and 'most a year before Chancellorsville. I know because I . . . well, because a friend keeps me informed."

Had she been fed a pack of lies? He had sounded so convincing in the tale, but she now had great doubts. For many good reasons Marvin Carson kept himself well informed on each and every battle.

"Why were you told it was Shiloh?" she asked.

"I don't know why she told me that, miss," he said on a shrug.

"My mother again?"

He nodded. "When she came to fetch me home from that hospital in Pennsylvania. Said she and Kitty would care for me, which they've done, until lately. Your mother, that is, not Miss Kitty."

Laura was looking at him with wide-eyed growing wisdom.

"How lately is lately, Wilf?"

"The past month."

"After my mother came back from her trip to New York?"

"Yes, that's about it."

"And your decorations?" she prompted gently. "She kept them?"

"That's right. It was part of the deal as long as they were in the name of Lawrence Dahlgren."

He could see the excitement in her face, but he did not guess its cause.

My mother thought she was picking a fool, she thought, *without knowing he would stumble onto the hero's field.*

Now, to make Laddie look great, Lucille Dahlgren was misleading the man to make him appear a liar. Who would believe him?

"One more thing, Wilf. Why have you stayed around this month?"

He looked at her as though she hadn't heard a single word he had said. "For the money, miss. Each day she promises it so Miss Kitty and I can set the banns for our wedding."

Laura's worst fears were instantly realized: her mother had methodically plotted out the whole thing. Who would question the word of Lucille DeWitt Dahlgren over this man?

"Wilf," she said slowly, "are there not other soldiers and officers who would remember you from that battle?"

"No," he said grimly. "When your brother talked to me about the battle he said that we had lost seventeen thousand and the Rebs thirteen thousand."

"And you told him all about your experiences?"

"Sure, why not?"

Laura's heart sank. Her mother and brother had planned well. She felt sick.

"Talk to Kitty," he suddenly added. "She'll tell you just about the same."

Laura got up slowly, filled with sick horror. "I'll do what I can."

She left Wilf Jamison's cell feeling miserable.

"Dear God," she whispered, "give me strength. This is my mother and brother who have brought this about. It isn't fair. But what am I to do?"

She fled the jailhouse and right into the arms of Marvin Carson.

"Ah, Laura, lass," he said, "I've been looking everywhere for you. The word is up from Peekskill. I must be off by nine at the latest. Will you help me?"

Laura frowned as she nodded agreement. The truth of the matter was that he had just given her an excuse to escape from this whole problem—for a time, at least. Marvin and Mildred were her real family. In their house she received love and acceptance; in her own, nothing but abuse and ridicule.

Marvin raced off in one direction as Alfred Addison sauntered up from the other, shaking his head.

"Your father was too busy to see me. How did you make out?"

Laura merely shook her head. "I must be getting home now." Then, without daring to look him in the eye, she turned and started up the street.

Sheriff Addison stood scratching his bald head. "Funny bunch of worms starting to crawl about in this can," he said to himself. "Best way to make them crawl out is for me to get lost with the jailhouse keys until after the 5:10 passes through."

3

T HAT EVENING when Clarence opened the door to his
wife's dressing room, he said one word only:

"Why?"

"To protect our son."

"Protect—protect from what?"

"No, the next question is mine. What do you know and
who did you learn it from?"

Clarence looked at her in distaste.

"I know only what Nettie Rivers told me when she
accosted me on the street, not five minutes ago. She's
having to put up a bounty hunter who arrested a man in
this house today."

"Overnight!" Lucille gasped. "I thought he was taking
the evening train south."

"He's not!" Clarence growled. "But I have been subjected to a weepy-eyed Kitty at the door and Sheriff Addison camped at my office most of the afternoon."

"I'll fire the slut!" Lucille said, her jaw setting in anger.

Clarence's knees buckled suddenly, so that he might
have fallen if he had not had a chair close at hand. As

it was, he sat there a long time, wiping his face with a large handkerchief.

"What will it cost us?" he finally whispered.

"Cost? Nothing! I've actually made money on the deal."

"You've made nothing!" Clarence said suddenly, fiercely. "That clapper-mouthed woman will eat away your profit with gossip."

"Let her." Lucille scoffed. "She's always been a jealous old peahen, and doesn't worry me in the least."

Even though the pain inside his chest was like fire and brine, his words were softly spoken.

"Well, she worries me, Lucille. All of our government contracts come due in the next three months. We can't afford the least hint of scandal. And what you're doing to Jamison is unconscionable."

Lucille scoffed again. "How could scandal touch us, husband? We have a hero for a son and friends in high military positions."

"Fiddlesticks! Our son is a draft dodger for whom you have bought fame and medals while the real hero is unacknowledged. And our military friends are vultures clutching at my throat daily for more and more payoffs. I can't take it anymore, Lucille. I *won't* take it anymore. We're at the end of this rope. How much? How much is it to cost us for your latest folly?"

Lucille sat back, carefully powdering her face.

"If you had—" she started, but he cut her short.

"How much?"

He was staggered when she suggested buying Wilf Jamison's silence, and even more staggered by the sum she suggested. Jamison would never ask for that much, Clarence knew, which could only mean that Lucille meant to pocket some of the money for herself. But because it was for Wilf, who had been so badly used—more badly than anyone but Clarence knew—he agreed without protest to pay it. Besides, he wanted to hear no more on the subject.

"Make my excuses to the guests," he said dully. "I will try to raise the money, see the bounty man and try to straighten it all out."

"It is a horrible waste of good money," she declared hotly.

"My whole life," he said sadly, "seems to be a waste of good money where you are concerned, Lucille."

She ignored him and went back to powdering her face. The matter no longer concerned her.

Fremont opened the evening on a discordant note for both Laura and her sister.

"Why, Miss Laura," he said, "I do believe that you make Miss Ruth Ann's dress more of a delight than when she first wore it."

Ruth Ann took immediate offense. "Why, Fremont Hunter, you are a cad! I've twice the figure for that dress. Laura's nothing but a puny little stringbean!"

"Miss Ruth Ann," he drawled sweetly, "I'm too much a gentleman to comment publicly on your natural gifts. I was commenting on the fabric and color. They are pale —fittin' for Miss Laura's blondeness. You be fire and lightning."

Ruth Ann batted her eyelashes until Laura thought they would break off and fall into her soup.

Throughout the greeting of the guests Laura had kept looking for her father. She was dashed when Colonel Arnold Beetle took her father's chair at the table. She was uncertain when she would be able to see him and share the burden of her heart—if she decided to share it. She was still undecided as to what she did wish to do about Wilf Jamison.

It was obvious from the first of the evening that West Point, rather than the war, would dominate the conversation. And it was obvious that Fremont was determined to include the Lee family in every sentence uttered.

"I grant you," Colonel Beetle said, "that the gentleman did labor steadily, changing rules and adding much needed buildings. But, Cadet Captain Hunter, are you not being a little bit swayed by having served with his son Custis?"

"Excuse the correction, sir, but I never served with, only under Custis Lee. It was Rob—Robert E. Lee, Jr.— that I shared quarters with."

Colonel Beetle smiled, but thought: What an insufferable prig! Who cares which Lee shared his life? All the Lees are rebels now and I'd love to be fighting the lot of them. If only Lincoln would recognize that the talent for running the army is to be found where the army is being trained.

Laura's thoughts were troubled. Why must everyone keep giving me false bits of information that I have to sift through for the truth? Everything seemed false that evening. Kitty was serving the dinner, smiling as ever. Her mother was bubbling as though she had not falsely condemned a man to prison that day. The cadets and officers, their wives and ladies, talked about the placid academy grounds sweeping back from the Hudson. It was as if the horrible war had nothing to do with them. She wanted to scream at each and every one of them.

"Laura," her mother interjected, "are you all right, child? You've grown pale as a ghost."

She hung her head. "Mama, I'd like to be excused to my room. When will Papa be home?"

"You may be excused, child, but I can hardly answer your question. The war keeps him working hard hours to keep food upon our table."

Laura bit her tongue to keep the acid retort from escaping. The food being served to the ten extra people at the table would have fed the Dahlgrens nicely for over a week.

Without another word she turned and stalked out. She had her own war to wage and knew none of those people could help her. She was amazed as she passed the hall clock to see that it was nearly nine already. She would have no choice but to change her clothing at home, rather than at the Carsons'.

Because everyone was still preoccupied in the dining room she didn't even take the precaution of locking her bedroom door. In her haste she tore a sleeve out of the dress as she pulled it over her head. That's the type of day it's been, she mused, knowing the scene it would cause for the next day. She removed everything but her cotton chemise and then began piling her shoulder-length hair high upon her head, securing it tight with pins.

She hardly recognized the face peering back at her as she smoothed and tucked up the hair. The plump cheeks, which normally matched the shade of early ripening peaches, were pale and ashen. The deep blue-green tint of her eyes was darkened. The smile that brought about deep-set dimples and showed white even teeth wasn't to be seen.

From deep within the clothes press she pulled forth an odd bundle of clothing. She donned the cotton flannel shirt and buttoned the front all the way to the neck. Then she stepped into the homespun bib-overalls and fastened the straps across her shoulders. Next came heavy, cumbersome-looking brogans, badly scuffed and unpolished. But the greatest transformation came with the donning of the floppy, misshapen old felt hat. Its brim cast a deep shadow over her face and gave her the look she was trying to achieve. No one, she was sure, would take her for being anything but another farm lad. It was a disguise that had been most successful for two full years.

Her escape route, when it had been required, had always been successful, and this night was no different. No one was about on the back stairs, the cook was asleep in her rocker and Kitty was slaving over a mountain of dishes. Neither heard her slip through the pantry and down the stairs to the fruit cellar. Experience had taught her the path through the racked aisles in the dark, so she could exit to the yard unseen.

But this night other eyes did see. A man stepped quickly back into the shadow of the trees and watched in puzzlement as she darted down the path to the valley. At first he thought it most peculiar for a servant boy to be leaving in such stealth and in such a rush. Then his methodical mind began sorting over a gnawing thought. He had seen the face but a fleeting second in the moonlight, but it was oddly familiar. Try as he might, Garth Wilkins could not place the face in his memory. Then he shrugged. He had more pressing matters at hand. He was furious that the train had been missed, and suspected a scheme to thwart him. Information he was now being given by Sheriff Addison and Clarence Dahlgren was in deep conflict with what he had learned from Lucille Dahlgren. He would get to the bottom of the matter with the woman, or know the reason why.

Mildred, sitting upon her heaped and ruffled pillows, uttered an exclamation of pure delight.

"Oh, child, we'd most given you up for the night."

"Another of my mother's dinner parties," Laura said with a scowl.

Mildred shook her head, a smile on her lips. "Even though you make them out to be most boring, I would love to serve company again."

For the moment Laura's smile returned and the dimples dropped into deep valleys. She knew that company never came to the Carson house and it had nothing to do with Mildred being in a wheelchair. People just found it very hard to socialize with an undertaker. Laura had always felt that such ostracism was ridiculous, especially when it concerned a woman of as sunny a disposition as Mildred Carson. Mildred's moon face was gentle and sweet under the white night-cap. She was always rosy, plump and sweet-smelling. The blue eyes were always filled with mirth and the little mouth ready at a moment's notice to break into a hearty laugh.

"Himself is hitching the horses to the hearse," Mildred went on. "This won't be getting you in dutch, will it, child?"

Laura smiled even more. She lovingly tucked the quilt about Mildred's useless legs. "Well, this time I didn't have to use the excuse that I was sitting with you."

"I feel so guilty sometimes, my dear, making you live a lie. But when you're with Mr. Carson I feel so much more secure."

It was also Mildred Carson's lie. If the truth were known, she was far more capable of taking care of herself and her husband from a wheelchair than most women were with two legs. But to help protect Laura she played the part of the frail invalid for the eyes of the valley people, and Laura was loved all the more for seeing after the woman. Invalid or no, it just gave people a creepy feeling to call upon an undertaker's wife.

"That's his whistle, child. Take care, both of you." Then as she wheeled the chair after Laura, she said casually, "Are you all right, Laura?"

Laura hesitated. Mildred Carson was the sort of woman before whom one could lay the troubles of the world and gain solid, constructive advice. But Marvin's second whistle told Laura she did not have time to reveal the story.

"I'll look out for him," she said and darted from the house and across the yard to the undertaker's shed.

Halfway to Peekskill Marvin Carson repeated his wife's question. Laura was usually full of the spirit of adventure on such nights, but she had been dour and silent this whole trip.

It had been in her mind to raise the subject with Marvin, but she had not been able to find the right words to begin. Now, instead of delving into the matter of Wilf Jamison she said:

"Remember the first trip I took with you, Mr. Carson?"

Marvin chuckled drily. "The time my arm was busted and you had to handle the team? Still can hear ol' Nettie Rivers screaming at Mildred about letting a wisp of a girl in pigtails drive a hearse through town with a coffin in it. Now she thinks I got a country lad to help out."

Laura giggled. "Funny she's never found out what you sometimes carry in the coffins."

Marvin frowned. "Wouldn't be able to carry them any longer if Nettie ever found out, child. Trouble enough having to talk some of them into the type transport we've got to offer."

"Surprised me at first, too."

Now the booming laughter came up from the pit of Marvin's stomach. "It was the man and not the transportation that surprised you. I'll never forget how you stood rooted to the spot and asked who he was."

"It's not my fault I'd never seen a negro man before. I wasn't even sure what Africa was. I'm glad he was our first—my first. He may have been black as coal but he was at least jolly. Quite a difference from those two men we had to take to Poughkeepsie last week."

"It takes all kinds, child, all kinds. They were just afraid the bounty-hunters would catch them and take them back. What puzzles me beyond all comprehension is how those two could be so afraid and yet so hateful to us for helping them."

Marvin Carson had been doing work for the Underground Railroad since before the days of the war. He wasn't sure anymore how many black men, women and children he had helped escape from slavery. Most were happy to be escaping, and approached the border into Canada with both fear and anticipation. But these men, who had talked to each other in a strange tongue, had been sullen and distrustful. Then, in repayment for his kindness, they had stolen one of his horses and made off in the night.

"Marvin, I've often wondered. Why do we have to come down here to Peekskill to fetch them?"

He shrugged. "It's just the system, little lady. I'm not told how they get to Peekskill and I know little about where they go to after Poughkeepsie—except that it's to Canada."

"That's what's always amazed me. A faceless society of people who really don't know each other and yet they can transport thousands of former slaves."

"Well," Marvin drawled, "there be some who know the whole underground system or it wouldn't work." He frowned anew. "Got to be faceless, though, because it's got as many enemies here in the North as in the South. That's why it's dangerous for us to take more than one or two at a time."

That statement, and what they found in Peekskill, washed Wilf Jamison from Laura's mind for some little time.

"You shouldn't have accepted so many," Marvin objected. "I can't take this many people in one load."

Hazel Faraday was unperturbed by Marvin's obvious irritation. "God made the number grow, Marvin," she said calmly. "Ten when they arrived, but a child has been born."

"What are they thinking about down the line?" Marvin exclaimed.

"Not us, that's for sure," Michael Faraday snorted. "Had to keep 'em a whole extra day 'cause of the birthin'. Can't afford such food costs, man. Take what you can and I'll be turning the rest out into the woods."

The light entirely left Hazel's pinched little face, but it retained its calm. She continued as if her husband had not spoken. "They would not be sending so many at once unless they had good reason, Mr. Carson. They just failed to inform us of the reason. Is there no way?"

The door opened violently to admit a towering black man. His dark face was distraught and his black eyes, as they flashed on Mrs. Faraday, smouldered with misery.

"There be troops on the river road!"

"That decides it!" Faraday flared. "Out to the woods with the lot. I'll not have them found here to be taken back!"

"Ain't goin' back," the black said. "Word all over the south is the plantation owners is aimin' to kill the niggers rather than turn us over to the new Yankee owners."

No one said anything. Laura turned. She had been standing near a very young negro woman at the side of a baby crib. Throughout the discussion she had been looking down at the first black child she had ever seen. Her smile, now toward Marvin, was beseeching.

"Couldn't we get them all in . . . somehow?"

He turned to her abruptly, knowing that Laura was thinking as his wife would have thought.

"Faraday," he said after a moment's consideration, "I'll have to leave the coffin with you to make room. Just pray they don't stop us and want to see behind the funeral blinds."

"Fair exchange," the Peekskill farmer said drily.

Even when the casket was eliminated, some among the two men, three women, and six children balked at being transported in a hearse. The big black stilled their protest with a flickering of fire in his eyes, packed them inside and dropped the satin side curtains over the viewing windows.

"What about you?" Marvin asked of the man.

Without a word, the black climbed under the hearse and up onto the undercarriage.

"But it's over an hour's ride," Marvin protested.

"Amos Mobley be all right," he called back. "Amos Mobley got strong arms and legs."

That he would be spotted was the least of their fears. The baby, cramped in the nearly airless quarters and frustrated with the young mother's inability to produce proper breast milk, was bawling constantly. Fortunately, the troops that raced past payed little attention to the slow-moving hearse and didn't get close enough to hear the child's wails.

Only when they creaked into the outskirts of West Point was the child heard.

Sheriff Addison surveyed the vehicle with his pale blue, watery eyes. It was near midnight. He had just returned from delivering Wilf Jamison to Highcliff-on-the-Hudson.

He repressed a laugh at the spectacle Laura made sitting next to Marvin Carson. He had long been aware of their missions and had chosen to look the other way. He was useful to them. He could always tell a bounty-hunter, the moment one stepped from the train or rode into his territory, and he made sure that Carson was warned.

He turned and strode back toward the path up to the plateau. If Garth Wilkins had finished with his verbal battle with Lucille Dahlgren, Addison felt it his duty to stall him along the way until the hearse was out of sight and Laura safely home.

But all Alfred Addison saw was Laura scurrying up the path a half hour later.

Near the top Laura stopped in alarm. Nearly every window of the second floor was ablaze with light, although the rest of the house was quite dark. Not knowing exactly what it all meant she was tempted to flee back to the Carsons for the night. But that would have been even more of a burden on Mildred and Marvin. Normally, the family parlor in the undertaker's shed accommodated the "overnight guests." Tonight, however, it was cramped quarters for the two women and the three female children, and the barnlike casket factory had to do for the men and male children. Mildred insisted, however, that the young mother and newborn be brought right into her house. Though she had never been a mother, she was quite expert in devising ways to get the child to drink warm milk and to lull it into a quiet and restful sleep.

Garth Wilkins had reduced Lucille to tears. He not only dressed her down, he told Clarence what he thought of him for buying Wilf Jamison's silence. His real anger was over the money he stood to lose in the whole affair. Through her tears, Lucille made a rash promise. It had quieted him, at least for the night.

Her promise had kept the lights blazing in the master bedroom.

"I cannot understand what you are thinking of, woman."

Lucille compressed her lips, waiting until she could speak in a calm voice. "Mr. Dahlgren," she said at last, "you simply do not understand the situation. How can you give that idiot gardener three hundred dollars of borrowed money and me not a single penny with which to repay Mr. Wilkins? I had to promise him something."

"How was I to know that you even had need of the money, Mrs. Dahlgren? You will just have to try and gain some of it back," he said bitterly, wondering how much she had kept of the money meant for Wilf Jamison.

Lucille contemplated the possibilities, and her powdered white face momentarily became uncertain and confused. She toyed with revealing the fact that a good portion of it was hidden away to send Ruth Ann to New York. But in her mind that was money that was already committed.

Clarence continued, "And quickly. I have but two weeks in which to pay Mr. Kemble back the loan, as it is. And keeping houseguests over the weekend is scarcely going to reduce our expenses."

Lucille didn't answer. She had thought that to be a brilliant ploy on her part. Keeping Mr. Wilkins at Highcliff-on-the-Hudson kept his knowledge from the valley people. Keeping Fremont Hunter as a weekend guest kept the children out of the conversation.

Sensing that her silence would last the night, Clarence rolled over and tucked his head deep into the pillow. She was once again making chaos of his life. And once again, he wished he had never laid eyes on her. He hated himself for such thoughts, but would she never learn the value of money? And would she never learn the value of the lives which she so blithely manipulated?

Lucille rose from her dressing table. With bent head she slowly paced up and down the room.

"What manner of scheme might I come up with by morning?" she thought darkly. "Surely there's some way I can buy Garth Wilkins off without having to repay the money."

She continued to pace the cold bedroom floor as if it would give her inspiration.

4

To LAURA's UTTER amazement she had been able to make it down the silent second floor hallway and up the inner stairs to the third floor. She had heard muffled voices from behind the closed door of her parents' room, but still puzzled over why she had seen lights in the other second floor bedrooms. No one was ever allowed to use Laddie's room, and it didn't seem possible that he might have arrived during her absence. She would have been called down to dutifully greet him and a ruckus would have been raised over not finding her.

Climbing out of the boy's clothes and hiding them, she put the mystery out of her mind. She was starved. She had picked at dinner like a bird and now she couldn't get the thought of food off her mind.

She rumpled up her bed, making it look as though she had been in it for hours, then donned night gown and dressing robe and ventured back downstairs again.

This time, on the second floor, the only light shone from beneath the door of Laddie's room. She shrugged and went on down to the kitchen.

Laddie's room was vacant and the bed untouched. In

the next-door guest room Garth Wilkins lay staring into the darkness.

"Does the woman think me a fool?" he mused. "It is now patently obvious who scrubbed the army out of the money and kept deserting. Her son is the scoundrel I should be after. What a strange woman. What a strange family . . . with perhaps one exception . . ."

Garth drew a deep breath. Something more than Lucille's promise had stilled his anger and made him accept the houseguest invitation.

When he first came to this house, he had been admitted by Kitty to the music room to await Lucille. A lanky young cadet lounged in a Morris chair next to the roaring fire and a young lady in a striking gown sat at the pianoforte, playing very badly.

Wilkins did not hear the missed chords. He thought only, "What a ravishing beauty," and bowed with polished dignity. Ruth Ann waved back cheerfully, thinking the man to be a business associate of her father. She didn't give him a second thought. Garth Wilkins, however, had thought of little else since.

"Perhaps," he mused anew, "the woman, overprotective as she is regarding her son, is not so overprotective regarding her daughter. Surely the girl is more intelligent than to have any interest in that pompous young cadet."

In the dark bedroom across the hall, Ruth Ann rose and stretched. The moonlight filtering in through the casement window revealed that corsets, stays and padded gowns were more responsible than nature for her small-waisted, high-breasted figure. In this nude, relaxed posture, she was beginning to develop a waistline that would one day equal her mother's. Her breasts hung limp and swayed as she sauntered over to the dresser.

"Don't be a prude," she said snidely. "All of Laddie's friends smoke tobacco."

Fremont Hunter lay upon her bed, utterly furious. Not so much over her present suggestion, but over the events of the past hour. But he felt compelled to deal with her present suggestion first.

"It's utterly disgusting," he snapped. "Decent women

just do not partake of tobacco products. Only nigger mammies and poor white trash women smoke a pipe."

"If you speak from experience, it means you've been in their bedrooms as well."

"Don't be crude, Ruth Ann."

She giggled, filling the little clay pipe. "I be crude, Fremont? I've not been the one trying to see the inside of this room for the last two years. I was not the one to make all of the overtures tonight."

And what did it gain me, he thought bitterly. Ruth Ann had been the real instigator; his own desire would have been to enter a certain bedroom a floor above.

If the truth be known, it had been Laura's lips that he had imagined touching his in the hallway during the goodnight kiss. It had been Laura's hand that had grasped his and brought it up to cover her rounded breast. It had been Laura's voice that had suggested to him that the bedroom door might be left unlocked. And it had even been Laura's nude body spread suggestively across the bed as he had later entered the brightly lit bedroom.

But once he lay with the lights blown out, the form became pure Ruth Ann. He became just another cadet, she just another of the farm girls across the river that the average cadet sought out for a moment of sensual pleasure. "Mucking in the rack" was their phrase for it, an experience his Southern breeding had forbidden him to taste as a cadet. This had hardly been a rack of straw to be crawled within, nor a dress to be quickly raised. But he knew it had to be nearly the same, even without the straw. She had been the voice out of the darkness—the teacher and experienced leader.

"No, it is not large enough," she had scolded. "How do you expect to give pleasure in such condition? Must I do everything for you cadets?"

Fremont Hunter was no virgin, but he had never encountered a woman like Ruth Ann. She was so forceful, so blunt in her declarations of what she desired from him that she lessened rather than increased his normally rather healthy appetite.

It was not the first of such liaisons for Ruth Ann; nor was it her first disappointment. She had learned to use men, then quickly to cast them aside. To her way of thinking, the war was ruining her life. She was still unwed at twenty-four. She could have had her pick of the cadet corps during the last few years, but neither she nor her mother had felt that any of them had been suitable. From birth she had been trained as a true Dewitt. When she married it would be for a titled station in life. In the meantime the cadets offered the occasional sating of her lust—but this evening had been unusually unsatisfying.

Puffing on the pipe, she came back and sat on the foot of the bed, openly scrutinizing his nude body.

"You look much better with clothes on," she said coldly. "I was never aware that you are really quite skinny . . . everywhere."

"Don't be vulgar."

"Me?" she said coyly. "I've always been trained to tell the truth . . . Oh, dear," she said, feigning sudden dismay. "If Kitty reports smelling smoke in my room, I'm bound to blame it on you."

Ruth Ann, who always appeared to everyone else to be a girl with both feet planted squarely upon the ground, was in actual fact a dreamer. She lay back on her bed, her thoughts drifting back over the day. She now found Fremont Hunter to be almost as prissy as her brother Lawrence, acceptable in name and position only. She wanted someone more earthy. She focused on Clint Bell, until she had his full figure clearly in mind. There was something about his open face, his muscular, stocky frame that she had always found appealing. But the bubble burst, as it always did when she thought of Clinton. She could simply not see him for anything more than a golden rule moralist.

Her mind fixed on Garth Wilkins. She wove him into her fantasy, but the dream caused even less arousal than had Fremont Hunter, and soon it seemed to fragment and fade. Disgusted, she rolled over and dropped off to sleep. She would have to measure Mr. Wilkins again tomorrow to see if he was worthy of future dreams.

"And how," he sputtered, "will you explain my being in your room?"

That was the least of Ruth Ann's worries. "I'll handle

that if it arises. I've never been caught before, but I do like to be prepared." Then she eyed him narrowly. "Don't fear. Mother would never suspect me of bedding the likes of you."

Fremont snorted, for he considered himself to be the apple of Lucille's eye, but he stopped the retort that was on the tip of his tongue. He reminded himself that he was a gentleman; more importantly, he did not wish to ruin any future chances he might have with Laura.

With calm indifference he rose and put on a dressing gown borrowed from Clarence and then strode from the room.

Ruth Ann thumbed her nose after him and went into a sulk. He had not pleased her in the least, although she had for some little time now toyed with the idea of what he might be like. She had found him soft and unmanly, just as she had found most of the other cadets who had passed through her life.

"Mere boys," she scoffed, "tried and left wanting. It makes me question if all mother says is gospel. Noble men are hardly noble lovers. I wonder . . ."

She took another long pull on the clay pipe. She had rarely smoked before, and the tobacco fumes went right to her head, making her feel dizzy and a trifle nauseous. She set the pipe aside and let the feeling pass.

Fremont Hunter could not believe that all of his dreams were coming true at once. The object of his thoughts sat at the little kitchen work table nibbling on a cold turkey sandwich and sipping a glass of buttermilk. For a moment he was not sure which he desired more—the food or Laura.

"The pittance I make as a cadet—I would dole it all out to you," he said breathily.

Laura started and turned to look at him steadfastly, but she knew little about men and could not read his expression.

Fremont continued, in a more hurried and casual tone. "That sandwich looks delicious and I am near famished. Tell me where I might find the ingredients and I will hurriedly join you."

"It would take less time," Laura said on a laugh, "if I made it for you. As Mrs. Kemp is given full power over our kitchen there are certain rules for its tidiness."

"That sounds like home. Before my mother died, she was allowed into the kitchen at Hunter Hill only to present the menus she wished prepared. Of course she had ample staff to see to her every wish. Naturally, the same holds true for my new stepmother."

Laura could tell at once that it was simply a statement of fact and not one of his common boasts.

"Were they all slaves?" she asked.

"Of course."

"That system is hard for me to understand. It seems so cruel."

"I wonder," he said thoughtfully, "if it is any more cruel than your own northern system, which allows your mill and factory owners to use the labor of children and women at wages they are barely able to live upon. At home our darkies are at least properly clothed and fed and medically seen to."

Laura put the food in front of him, her expression serious as she thought over his comments.

"That doesn't mean either system is correct, Fremont. Nor does it mean that every mill owner operates that way or every plantation owner is as caring as your family seems to be."

Fremont rubbed his finger against the thin line of his mustache. The last thing in the world he wanted was a political disagreement with her. He took a huge bite out of the sandwich, winked and nodded his approval.

"I was not aware that we had a house guest," she said.

"Several," he answered, ready to take another bite. "There's a Mr. Wilkins, who looks at Ruth Ann as though he knew what she looked like without a chemise, and a young man that Sheriff Addison delivered to the front door."

The information was both disturbing and pleasing. She couldn't fathom why the bounty-hunter would be there as a guest, but she was relieved to hear that Wilf Jamison was free. But now it was her turn to wish the conversation changed. She was also slightly embarrassed over his comment about her sister.

"Well, I guess it's time for the house to start getting used to guests. Christmas will be here before we know it, and then the house is always jammed with people. That's right. You spent last Christmas with us and should remember. I used to like Christmas, as a child. Now it's just a houseful of Laddie's and Ruth Ann's friends. I'm not much of a party girl, I guess . . . Oh, it suddenly dawned on me. This will be your last Christmas with us—won't it? It's your last year at the academy."

For an instant an inscrutable look passed over Fremont's features. He tried to keep the thought of his graduation in the far reaches of his mind. Eight months. In eight short months he would graduate—and what then? The war just had to be over by then. It just had to!

Laura had stepped around the table to clear away his plate and glass. Instead of answering her, he grasped her hand.

"It's all right," she said, misunderstanding his reason for taking her hand. "I don't mind cleaning up."

"That wasn't it, Laura. That wasn't it, at all. I've wanted to take your hand for ever so long."

"Fremont," she laughed. "Ruth Ann wouldn't like you saying such a thing."

"To hell with Ruth Ann! You're so much more beautiful."

"Thank you," Laura laughed again. Then she sobered abruptly. "Fremont, you're beginning to hurt my hand."

He quickly rose and drew her into his arms. Then his mouth crushed down, pressing hard on her lips. It was all so sudden that it took her a moment to register a thought. Just as she moved her hands to strike him or push him away, he softened his kiss, his arms abruptly less demanding. Now her thoughts were truly mixed. It was her first kiss and it seemed strangely polite, little more arousing than kissing her father goodnight. She had always thought that it would be inexplicably exciting, but she felt nothing—except the nervousness that was rippling through his muscles. He stepped back, took her again by the hand and tried to lead her away.

"Let's go upstairs," he whispered.

"I've got to clean up, Fremont," she protested, grasping at the easiest escape.

"We can come back and do that afterward."

She was suddenly conscious that Fremont was gazing down at her with a most peculiar glint in his eyes. It was a little unnerving.

"Afterward?"

"Don't be a child," he said gruffly. "I think your room would be safer than mine."

Laura frowned, looking up into his demanding face. She opened her mouth, then closed it again, grimly.

"I'm sorry," he said. "I shouldn't have called you a child."

"No," Laura said, "you have every reason to call me a child. I am a child, Fremont, when it comes to what you were suggesting."

Fremont leaned forward, something close to mischief in his eyes.

"Come on, Laura, I bet you've never refused my cousin before."

She was stunned and appalled. "Fremont! Clinton is a perfect gentleman where I am concerned!"

He laughed, his mouth twisting into a cruel line. "That clod a gentleman? I bet he doesn't even have enough manhood to tickle you, much less kiss you."

"Stop it!" she gasped. "I refuse to be a party to this conversation any longer."

Fremont smiled, a slow, quiet smile.

"Then let's move the *party* upstairs." He winked. "After all, no one is going to find out."

"No one but me!"

The words were spoken so savagely that both Fremont and Laura started and spun to their sound. They saw Wilf Jamison rising from a pallet laid behind the kitchen range. He glared at Fremont, who stood with his mouth agape. Wilf's face was grave. In his hand he held a stove poker.

"Look here, you," Fremont stammered. "This is none of your damn business."

Wilf's bullet-shaped head turned to Laura as he calmly answered Fremont's claim. "Seems to me you were asking the young lady to do something she didn't want to do."

"That's between the two of us," Fremont growled.

"Three. Four, if'n you want to include this poker."

"Laura," Fremont insisted, "please tell this ruffian to go away and mind his own business."

Laura looked at Fremont, a smile growing about her lips. "I think, Fremont, the only thing for me to tell anyone, is to tell you goodnight."

She picked the dishes up from the table and took them to the sink to wash them. It was very quiet for several moments. Then she heard the poker drop back into the coal scuttle and knew that Fremont had departed.

"Thank you," she said, turning.

"One good turn deserves another, as my maw always said."

Laura felt suddenly guilty. "Wilf, I really didn't get a chance—"

He held up his hand and grinned. "I figured as much from talking with your paw and the sheriff. But if you hadn't talked to me in the first place, I'd never have opened my mouth to them."

Laura sighed. "Then you're free and everything is set?"

He scowled. "I guess. Your mother gave me all she could scrape up. Seems plenty, but it ain't. I'm supposed to keep my mouth shut about your brother and head on out west."

"And Kitty?"

"There's the rub," he said softly. "She's used to the finer things in this house and is a mite afraid of not having them. Besides, if your paw had trouble raisin' the money for me, how's he gonna pay her up on back wages?"

"I wasn't aware . . ."

He grinned. "Except for Miss Kitty, I 'spect you're the only soul on earth I'd care to let in on what I'm thinkin'— and I think it's a smart plan."

"I'd be happy to hear it, Wilf Jamison."

She cleaned up the kitchen as she listened to his plans. She saw at once that he couldn't be called a fool. The North was desperate for good soldiers, even one with a gimpy leg. He would leave the money with Kitty to put away as a nest egg and make everyone believe that he had gone west and would send for her when settled. But as "Lawrence Dahlgren, war hero," he felt he could get a premium enlistment bonus—more than enough to set up a fine house for Kitty at the end of the war.

Laura thought it was poetic justice for him to gain something out of using her brother's name. She didn't think she could ever look Laddie square in the face again. How could he live with another man's laurels? She just didn't understand. But then, she had never really understood Laddie. The nine years that separated them were an unbridgeable chasm. There were times when she felt as if a gypsy wagon must have dropped her off at the Dahlgren door in the dead of night. Her father was the only person in the family she had ever felt close with, but since the war he had been so strained and preoccupied that even he didn't have time for her. Things will be different, she told herself, when I am eighteen. That is almost grown up.

Then she thought of Wilf Jamison again and was happy. It was nice that one thing had turned out good that day.

The next morning started on a less happy note.

Upon entering the breakfast room, Laura found her mother reading the early morning newspaper. Her father's face was as black as a thundercloud as he listened to her read.

". . . *Daily Sun* reporter, Nathan Ledbetter, risked his life bringing the group from a farm north of Atlanta, Georgia. According to Mr. Ledbetter, the 'underground' kept adding slaves to his responsibility. His main objective, which this paper paid a handsome sum to bring about, was to smuggle the body servant of President Jefferson Davis out of the South. It is our belief that this man, who for the moment will remain nameless, is very knowledgeable on all aspects of the current situation surrounding the Confederate president and could help shorten the war by many months. But this newspaper has been defrauded. These so-called abolitionists . . ."

The newspapers were forever full of news of escaped slaves those days, so Laura had been paying scant attention as she helped herself to kippers, coddled eggs and fresh biscuits at the sideboard.

"Really, Clarence," Lucille pouted. "It is the second time I've read it aloud. You know very well that the man was attacked by thugs and the negroes taken away from him—and right in one of the most fashionable sections of New York."

Clarence shook his head. "It just won't work, woman. It just won't."

"Don't even think it!" Lucille roared. "It will work. Besides the academy superintendent and Mr. Kemble, we're the only family in the valley that gets a morning paper off the first train through. From what this Mr. Ledbetter says, he has good reason to suspect they were brought to Peekskill. Logically, they would be heading north up the valley."

Laura was now listening intently, her fork poised in mid-air.

Her mother went right on. "Mr. Wilkins need not know where I gathered such valuable information, sir. Just think. Ten slaves. Minus what I owe him and the loan from Mr. Kemble, that leaves a tidy little profit of a hundred and fifty."

"It's barbaric!"

"Nonsense! It's a remarkable stroke of good luck for us, Mr. Dahlgren."

"*Mama!*" Laura gasped. "This is unthinkable. You make it sound as if you were bartering for so many chickens."

"Hush, child!" Lucille said sternly. "You just don't understand these things. To a certain degree, they are just like chickens, another man's chickens who have been stolen away from him by thieves in the night. It is our duty, when we learn of such matters, to let the proper authorities know and attempt to return that man's rightful property to him."

Laura stiffened. She had never felt so repelled in all her life.

Lucille was paying her no heed; she was glancing warily at her husband.

"I'll have no part of it," he said ominously. He got up and strode from the room, leaving his cold breakfast sitting on the table.

Laura wanted to race after him and tell him all, but just then Kitty came scurrying fearfully out of the kitchen.

"Oh, mum, whatever will I do?" she wailed, her pocked face screwed up in misery.

"You might start," Lucille said curtly, "by explaining this intrusion!"

"Oh, mum, it's this note and money from me Wilf. He's headed west and will send for me when he's ready and I've my back wages paid up."

Good boy, Laura thought. He was smart enough not to reveal his full plan to the girl.

Lucille's heart skipped several beats seeing the number of greenbacks Kitty clutched fiercely in her hand.

"How much do I owe you for each month?" Lucille demanded.

"S-seven dollar fifty a month, mum," Kitty said in a quavering voice.

"And it will be months before your young man can travel such a long distance and establish himself," Lucille said sweetly. "In the meantime, because of your loyalty in staying, your wages shall be raised to ten dollars a month. But there is a worry on my mind, Kitty. I don't like to have large sums of money kept in the house. Thieves can smell it out too quickly."

Laura looked at her mother in bewilderment. The only robbery she could recall taking place in West Point was when the negro men stole Marvin Carson's horse. Kitty, however, looked at Lucille in astonished fear.

"Whatever will I do with it, mum?"

"Bank it, child, so that it can make more money for you."

Kitty blinked foolishly. "I don't know how to do that, mum."

Lucille smiled contentedly. "Mr. Dahlgren knows all about such things, Kitty, and would be most happy to take care of it for you on the way to work this morning. Just hand the money to me and I'll give it to him."

Kitty quickly agreed, and handed over the cash. Her red face, as she fled back into the kitchen, was a study in joy.

Laura looked at her mother. Poor Wilf Jamison, she thought. He's being taken by this family once again, and I'm helpless to say a thing. But I'm not helpless to warn Marvin about her scheme.

Lucille was so engrossed in her own thoughts that she didn't even see Laura slip silently away from the breakfast table.

"Yes," Lucille mused, "God has certainly answered my prayers this day. And for the moment I don't think it necessary to inform Mr. Dahlgren that I have earned back the Kemble money. It will be absolutely months before we hear from that stupid gardener."

Again Garth Wilkins was given only a fleeting glance of Laura as she pulled a shawl over her head and scurried out the front door.

Now his puzzlement really grew. Was that not the same girl he had seen in Sheriff Addison's office? No, that just couldn't be. That girl had definitely been of the servant class. This one had to be the Dahlgren girl he had not met last evening. The smell of food kept him from thinking again of the boy he had seen the night before.

He was at first greatly disappointed not to find Ruth Ann already at the breakfast table, but Lucille's immediate offering of the fifty dollars owed him revived his spirits. Then his spirits really began to soar as she carefully uncovered the news about the escaped slaves.

"My dear woman, however did you come by such news?"

Lucille smiled coyly. "My dear sir, I *am* a Dewitt and we have always had those who are loyal to such a family name. I'm just sorry that I can't give you the exact whereabouts of the negroes, but I would vouchsafe that they are indeed on their way through the West Point area."

"By train, do you think?"

Lucille laughed, as though it were a delightful joke. "Sir, blacks do not ride the train, except for servants escorting paying passengers."

Wilkins smiled to himself. Either she had smartly sidestepped the trap he had set or there was actually some merit to her information.

"Of course," Lucille said, setting a little trap of her own, "we would be glad to have you stay as our guest while you conduct your search in this area."

Wilkins nodded his thanks. Such an offer could not be refused. He would partake of the excellent breakfast and then go to the railroad station to wire for more men.

There had been a frost during the night. Together with the sun it created a soft gray fog that rolled up from the river and out across the fields.

Laura seemed to float rather than run along. She was so used to the route that she had no fear of an accident. Still, when she came to the split-rail fence she slowed her pace and scanned the Carsons' entire yard.

With a sigh of relief she noted that the hearse was already gone and she skipped the rest of the way to the kitchen door on the back porch. The pungent aroma of cinnamon rolls and coffee wafted out the door as she slipped through. Then she stopped short.

"Mornin', Laurie," Sheriff Addison cheerfully called. He sat at the kitchen table feeding the black baby out of a strange-looking contraption. "My woman made this thing when our cow died and we had to feed her calf or lose it. Never thought to have to use it again."

"I see," Laura stammered.

"The mother took sick during the night. Mildred's in seein' to her."

Laura stood in indecision, not knowing how much more he might know.

"Glad you got here," he went on, smiling down at the small child. "Those other poor souls could sure use those rolls, coffee and a few bowls of that porridge Mildred stewed up."

"They're still here?" she stammered.

"Had to stay. Mrs. Holbein passed on in the night and Marvin's out in Dutch country fetchin' her back. Told his carpenters to take the day off from the factory."

"Oh, no! Mama read all about them in the paper this morning and she's going to give the information to that Mr. Wilkins."

"Not so loud," he cautioned. "The little tyke is most asleep. And don't you be frettin' none. I always read the superintendent's paper before the cadet rides down to fetch it. Wouldn't have needed it this morning, though. Some sassy captain was banging on my door even 'fore I had my britches on. Everyone under the sun seems to be looking for these folk."

"Is that how you knew?"

"Nope. Saw you all bringing them in last night, girl. Or should I say boy? Now, how about a little help from you, whichever you may be this morning?"

It was three days before Sheriff Addison thought it would be anywhere near safe to move them. Three days in which the two carpenters began grumbling about the lost time and wages they would never get back. One of them was a permanent resident of the boarding house, and Nettie got an earful of his complaints.

"Don't seem like Marvin," she mused. "He ain't ever before kept the factory closed while he handled a funeral. I wonder if Mildred is poorly. I see that Dahlgren girl shagging herself over there most every day."

"Yep. She's there so much it makes a body wonder why. Marvin ain't exactly ready for one of his own caskets, if you know what I mean. Young Bell better watch it or he'll be losing his gal."

"Timothy Caruthers," she snapped, "what ever gave you the idea that sweet young boy had any interest in that girl?"

"No more'n what I see with my eyes. Holding hands and eating a picnic lunch on the green."

"Well, I do declare! Imagine him sharing *my* food with the likes of her. Why, her snooty mother would tan her behind if she knew, to say nothing of the talk about her and Marvin Carson. He should be ashamed, with an invalid wife and all. Poor Mildred. The wife, of course, is always the last to know. Lord sakes alive, I can't recall the last time I had a spare moment to call on the poor, dear woman. This is cherry pie day and I might just take her a slab this evening."

"Won't you be needing extra for all them men you crowded onto your porch?"

"Civic duty ain't crowding, Timothy. It was the least I could do to put up those four gentlemen who work for that nice Mr. Wilkins."

Caruthers chuckled. "You didn't think he was so nice when you learned he was stayin' up with the Dahlgrens."

"He is nice," she snapped. "And he pays their room and board on time—which I can't say for some others of late."

And, she thought sourly, I'll be finding out about Mr. Clinton Bell sharing my good food with that girl and be charging him extra for it. I've had a feeling recently that he hasn't been as sweet to me as before. Well, he won't want to associate with that baggage after I've had a little chat with Mildred. Disgraceful.

"What'cha about?" Sheriff Addison called out, so that anyone within good ear range could hear.

Marvin climbed up onto the first wagon and pointed. "Ole man Holbein paid me in hay. Gonna take it back out to Dutch country and sell it."

Addison rode on into the undertaker's yard and hissed. "Why ain't you off yet? Troops done rode south and Wilkins' men are stuffing themselves with Nettie's vittles."

"Laura ain't here yet to drive the other wagon."

"Are you loaded yet?"

"Yep. Got them all."

"The baby?"

"Quiet as a church mouse, so far."

Alfred Addison took off his hat and scratched his bald head. He didn't like it. He had suggested the plan and put his neck way out to help Marvin get rid of the people.

"You can't wait, Marv. It's darking up fast and people will wonder why you're selling hay so late. Get on up to Beacon. The man's name is Hallensack and he'll have enough wagons ready to split them into three groups."

Marvin didn't like the change in plans, but had little choice. He wanted to get the hay wagon with the negroes hidden inside out into the country before the baby woke from its last feeding. He worried about the sick mother, but it was just getting too dangerous to hold the people in his factory any longer. Day after day, troops and a wide variety of bounty-hunters had been scouring the whole region.

Then, as he was turning the lead wagon in a wide arc, he saw Laura's floppy felt hat come bouncing through the tall grass that rose from the river's edge. He stood and waved, keeping his team moving. She would have plenty of time to catch him once they were off the village streets.

Down the road he nodded politely to Nettie Rivers and didn't give it another thought.

Nettie pursed her lips quizzically, then saw the small figure break from the tall grass and race to the second wagon in the yard. Without knowing why, she stepped off the road into a bramble growth and waited. Thus she didn't see Sheriff Addison wave Laura up onto the wagon and ride off in the opposite direction.

Breathlessly, Laura took the reins and urged the two mules into motion. With one excuse and another, she had avoided a meeting with Garth Wilkins until that night at dinner. He had sat looking amused and puzzled. Either there were triplets in the village, he concluded, or something strange was afoot. He was amused at her sweet, outgoing personality. As the days had progressed he had come to realize the cold, shallow person that lived within Ruth Ann's shell. But this child was an utter delight. If she were sneaking out at night in the disguise of a boy to meet a secret lover, that titillated him greatly. She may have been six years younger than her sister, but she was far more woman. He vowed to satisfy his curiosity about her, but when Laura made her excuses to leave the dinner table, he was not able to follow. Not until Laura already had her wagon moving out of the undertaker's yard was Wilkins finally able to break free from the forceful Lucille.

Nettie Rivers squinted and then gasped. She held her breath until the wagon had fully passed her.

So, she sneered, that's how they get away with it right under Mildred's nose. Pawning her off as a boy so they can go out in the country and . . . Why, it's downright perverted! Just as though he wished to do it with a boy in the first place. Sickening! I hope she hasn't taught Clinton any of her nasty little tricks. And all this time Marvin let Timothy Caruthers think he had a farm boy who came to help him drive. Farm boy, indeed. I've always thought those Dahlgren people were a little weird. Laddie and his lace-panties attitude must have gotten mixed up with this one at birth.

Then, storming into the Carsons' yard, not caring if she crushed the cherry pie or not, she suddenly stopped short.

"Why, Nettie Rivers," she gasped aloud. "Sometimes your agile mind just amazes me. Of course! It would surely require at least two wagons to transport ten niggers. And why else would Marvin Carson wish to keep his workers away from his casket factory?"

She spun about, the overheard tidbits from her boarding house guests now making much more sense. Mr. Wilkins gaining valuable information from Mrs. Dahlgren, indeed! Making the poor man look like a fool when her own daughter was helping in the Underground Railroad system. And right here in West Point! It would give her great pleasure to inform Clinton Bell of the manner of girl he had been holding hands with. He had never held her hand!

The whole lot of them should be lynched—including Marvin Carson. A nigger-lover as well as a wife-cheater! Well, she could handle the whole matter quite effectively. After all, the bounty-hunters were there to keep the North from turning as black as the perverted South. Besides, it was her moral obligation to save that dear Clinton Bell from that depraved girl, who probably knew all about black men as well.

Twenty-two years of handling a hearse had tuned Marvin's ear for the road. People just didn't like to ride behind a "Black Maria" and Marvin had learned to be polite enough to pull to the side and let them pass.

A half hour after turning his wagon inland toward Beacon and leaving Laura to travel slowly up the river road toward the north, he sensed the fast approach of horses before he saw them.

There was no need for panic. When the right opportunity presented itself he steered the hay wagon off the narrow farm road, down into a dry creek gully and back into the deep shadows beneath a covered bridge. Casually, he picked the milk feeding contraption off the seat and pushed it down among the straw to awaiting hands. Then he sat back and waited. In the moonless night the farmland was filled with its own sounds. Marvin heard none of them, his mind and ears awaiting one particular sound.

It was quicker coming than he had expected. The men were pushing the horses hard. The horse's hooves made a fierce echoing clatter as they raced through the covered bridge. It was deafening, but still Marvin was able to determine that it had been just three men ahorse.

Still he waited. Within twenty minutes the riders thundered back through the bridge. Now they were confused. The road to Beacon was empty. They would have to circle back to the road to Fishkill or up the river road. For the moment his passengers were safe.

Not until he was informed that the baby was again sleeping did he urge the horses to pull the heavy wagon back up onto the road.

Near the same time Laura had also heard the distant approach of horses. She felt no need for panic either. Everything was going just as Sheriff Addison thought that it might. Patrolling bounty-hunters would have to split up to keep track of all the roads—and of both wagons if they had accidently seen them leave.

Laura pushed the battered felt hat further back on her head and eased the mules to a slower walk.

"No use letting them tire out their poor horses," she chuckled to the beasts. "They're going to find that we're carrying no more than our hay load."

Laura waited. Let them come! she thought. It's all the better, if they do come now. It will make the night that much longer for them searching for the real wagon.

Two men came riding hard past the wagon, seeming to pay it no mind at all. They continued north, leaving a dust cloud in their wake.

Darn it all! Laura was thinking. I didn't expect them to overlook me altogether! I wonder if they were even bounty-hunters . . . She straightened up on a new thought. They're looking for the other wagon. Then they did see us leave town together. She wished them a long trip down the road, but a mere five minutes later they came riding back, disappointment drawing their faces into villainous masks. They stopped their horses and blocked the road.

Laura calmly pulled the mules to a stop within inches of them and tried to sound like a farm boy.

"If'n ye be highwaymen, ah hain't got nuffin but a hay load."

They didn't answer, but only glared. The tallest one climbed from the saddle and took his rifle from its sheath. He came to the wagon, at first walking about it slowly, carefully, as though listening for the least little sound. Then, with savage purpose, he began to ram the rifle barrel deep into the hay mound. Again and again he pulled forth the rifle and thrust it down until it collided with the wagon bed.

Laura was watching his every motion. She did not see the other man slip from his horse and come to stand right below her. Then, suddenly, he seized Laura's arm and pulled her off the driver's perch.

"Where's them damn niggers?" he demanded harshly.

Still startled, Laura shook her head stupidly.

Then his hands were upon her shoulders, thrusting her roughly back and forth, his fingers iron-hard, hurting her, so the felt hat went flying and the pins began to drop out of her hair.

"Jesus!" he growled, "I think we done found ourselves something better than niggers, Lem."

The man took one look, gave a grimace of disgust and started to move back to his horse.

"Ain't got that on my mind."

The man holding Laura grinned, his yellow teeth gleaming in a leer.

"Always on my mind, Lem, if she don't smell too much of mule shit."

Lem Gunther turned back. "Ain't much to her for both of us. How you want to decide firsts?"

"First?" Herkimer Dayton exploded. "I found her and I get firsts."

Terror started gnawing at Laura's stomach. Her mouth went dry and her hands clammy. Suddenly she kicked backward into the man's shin and swung her arms wildly.

Both at once began cursing and grabbing at her flaying arms and legs. Over their curses she could hear her own screaming. Her strength was no match for theirs and she was quickly grappled to the ground. Rough hands attempted to tear away the bib overalls.

Then she saw the hay mound explode, the straw thrown a full ten feet into the air as a massive figure leapt up and sailed over the wagon's side, falling on the two bounty-hunters like a fish hawk ready to carry off its prey. Great coal-black fists pumped out, delivering blacksmith-heavy blows.

The men staggered back, unsure of what had hit them. Laura was also unsure, but once released she scrambled under the hay wagon. Then she saw who had come to her aid.

Amos Mobley squared off with one of the men, pivoting with the grace of a panther, leaning forward and putting his near three hundred pounds into a blow that hooked the bounty-hunter's exposed jaw so hard that Laura expected to see the head and body divorced from each other. But they remained together as the man flew over the bank and crashed into a tree with a sickening thud.

Herkimer Dayton eyed Amos briefly, then made a dash for Lem's rifle on the ground. The black's long legs crossed the ground in half the time; he deftly brought the rifle up by the barrel and arched the butt into Herkimer's charging belly. The man screamed and careened away into the woods, doubled over in agony. Amos turned toward the wagon, ignoring the fallen man at his feet.

He gently lifted Laura from beneath the wagon and onto her feet. Her face was gradually returning from a pastey gray to its natural rosiness.

"How did you get here?"

Amos pretended not to hear her. "Another horse coming. Let's git."

"But the mules and wagon—"

"They ain't goin' nowhere. We is!"

She followed him across the road and up the slope into a bramble patch. A few feet into the thorny maze he squatted and pulled her down. She knew better than to open her mouth to question him. The new horseman was nearly upon them. And with his approach, Dayton had stumbled back out of the woods.

Even in the darkness Laura could tell who the new-comer was. There was no mistaking his derby hat and raised cane.

"Dayton," Wilkins exclaimed in dismay, "what in hell happened here?"

"She had a big buck with her," Dayton explained, his voice raspy with pain.

"She who?"

"Some gal dressed like a farm boy."

Wilkins smiled to himself with amused contempt. No wonder Lucille Dahlgren had been so well informed, he thought. Or was she? And why would Laura Dahlgren have only one of the slaves with her?

"Wake him up," he snarled, indicating Lem Gunther. Then his thin hands pulled the bottom of the cane from the handle, unsheathing a razor-sharp sword. Just to make sure they had not hidden themselves in the hay he rode around the wagon jabbing at the mound with the rapier.

"Lem did that with a rifle," Herkimer called, "but it seemed like there was no one there."

"Naturally," Wilkins growled, "because you are dealing with a very unusual black man, I am coming to realize. Was he as big as a house?"

"Big as a barn, is more like it."

Wilkins sat silent for a moment. "Up to now I thought it was a ruse on the part of the newspaper. Now, I'm sure that man is worth more than all the others combined. Get Lem on his horse, release the mules and then set the wagon to flame."

"Why?" Herkimer asked stupidly.

Wilkins sighed. "It's very simple. They can't go on without the mules and wagons and so they'll have to turn back. We can capture them a lot easier on foot."

"What if he's just hiding nearby and has heard you?"

Wilkins scoffed. "The man is military trained. He would have headed out the moment he knew the two of you could no longer follow. How long do you figure it's been?"

Dayton was unsure. He had been hit hard enough so that he wasn't certain he hadn't lost consciousness for a while, and he had never been good at figuring time anyway.

"I'd say well over a half-hour."

"Damn," Wilkins cursed. "Then let's get cracking!"

Laura sat like one mesmerized, gazing into the face of the giant of a man as she whispered, "Is he right?"

"Hush!" he hissed, scowling darkly, knowing Garth Wilkins was right on at least one point. He would have to go back. He would have to go back just to make sure that the girl got back safely. No telling what they might do to her now if they caught her alone.

Amos glanced quickly at Laura. This one has never known this much danger, he thought. She could turn pure panic at any moment. He would just wait patiently until the wagon had burned down to its springs before he would move a single muscle. . . .

Laura began to get cramps in her legs before the firelight started to die down.

"They've been gone for some little time," she whispered, and straightened up at once.

"But he'll be waiting in hiding down the road for us," Amos warned.

"I didn't figure we would go that way."

Amos's eyes went round with surprise. "And which way had you figured?"

"Across the river," she said simply. "It's all military reservation over there and we can travel without anyone knowing it."

His black eyes glinted in the firelight and he gave a low laugh. "You had that figured out all along?"

"Yes," Laura said coolly. "At least after what Mr. Wilkins said. Which raises some questions about the other things he said and why you were in my wagon."

She saw at once that he was also deeply worried over the things Garth Wilkins had said. He was worth more money than even the bounty-hunter dreamed possible. The Confederate States of America had a price on his head that would have given Lucille the vapors.

"Let's be going," he said incisively. "I tell you some as we move along."

Obediently, Laura followed him down past the burned out wagon and on toward the river. But she wanted to hear all and not just some. He was not going to tell her anything, however, until they were a lot safer. And suddenly, in his mind, safety seemed a far distant thing. He was looking at the rolling dark waters of the Hudson River, but his mind was on a long-ago memory.

Seeing the expression on his face, Laura said, "I've swum it many times in the summer. The current isn't too bad once you're past the middle."

He nodded as though he were in perfect agreement, and continued to gaze at the water. It was incredibly wide. The cliffs and plateau of the far bank seemed a million miles away. The darkness made it seem wider than it actually was.

"Most like the Mississippi," he muttered.

"Hardly," Laura said, "although I've never seen it."

"I have. Born on its banks after my mammy was brought from Jamaica. Never swam it though, even though Mr. Davis tried his best to teach me."

"Then you were Jefferson Davis's servant," she said on a note of awe.

"Since birth," he answered simply. "Twenty-eight years."

Laura was now a fountain of questions bubbling to get out, but she knew that not a single one of her questions would get them across the river.

"Well, Amos Mobley, if that is your name, there's nothing that says we can't float across. See that log? All we have to do is hang onto it and kick our feet."

It sounded good in theory, but was difficult in practice. The water was already nearly as icy cold as it would be when frozen over. No more than a hundred yards out their legs were already starting to numb. Laura wondered if her arms would be able to grasp the rough bark curve much longer.

"The middle," she gasped through chattering teeth. "We can rest and let the current carry us along . . . if we can just . . ."

"Save your strength. I'll kick. My legs are used to such things. General once made me walk from Mexico back home to Brierfield . . ."

With a mighty effort he made his legs move, driving down his fear by sucking in a tiny breath of air, and then another and another, wheezing in his effort until he felt his legs being tugged sideways by the current.

"Is this the middle?" he panted.

"You bet it is! Now rest." Just the thought of it made Laura feel warmer. "The current should take us in near the bank at the next curving."

It was as she said, but the log could no longer be their vehicle. It had started out saturated with water and was rapidly sinking. Amos was sinking just as fast.

"Use your arms and legs," Laura called.

The old memory came flooding back again. Jeff Davis had thrown him into the river and told him to sink or swim. Amos had sunk. He had fought the water then, just as he was fighting it now. And now, just like the nightmare of before, he felt as though his kinky hair was being torn out by the roots. He opened his mouth to protest and drew into his lungs a strangling chill stream. The blood rushed to his brain in a wild explosion of the terror of death. He struck out madly with his long arms and legs, but somehow realized he was now over on his back and the yanking at his hair more fierce. Then there was a new pain. His heel had kicked something hard, then his elbow was scraped. Suddenly his hair was released. Coughing and spluttering foam and water from his mouth and ears and nose and eyes, it took several seconds for him to realize that he was sitting upright with his torso out of the water.

He saw that Laura was sprawled next to him, drained and weak from dragging him through the river. The cool autumn night air was beginning to make her shiver violently in her wet clothing. Amos saw it and instantly shook off the nightmare. Now there was a new enemy to face. Again it came from a long-ago memory. Jefferson Davis had made his troops march through the sleeting rain. It was either march or die with their uniforms freezing onto their bodies.

He hauled Laura to her feet and started walking up the bank and out of the water.

"Rest," she pleaded, "just let me rest for awhile."

"No! The general says that we march to keep warm and we'll do what the general says."

"Was he really a general?" she asked.

"I'll say he was," he declared, knowing that talk would keep her mind off the cold. "And a lot more than that. He was a hero in the Mexican War under General Zachary Taylor, who was his brother-in-law. He had already been a congressman in Washington City, and after the war they sent him back as a senator. Mr. Jeff later became the secretary of war and later still the president of the Confederacy. Yes, miss, me'n he seen a lot of country together."

"All that moving must have been hard on his wife."

Amos's black eyes dulled. When he answered, his voice was sad. "Miz' Davis died of the fever the year I was born. Guess that's why himself kept my mammy as a housekeeper and me as a body servant. We was family, like."

"And your father?"

Amos chuckled deeply. "Ain't ever known him. My mammy was brought away from the island without knowing I was in her belly. She was just ten, you see."

Laura broke away from his support and stared. "Why, that's just horrible!"

Amos grinned. "Not for me. I'm here, ain't I? And it wasn't horrible for her. She was one right smart and educated lady."

"Was?" Laura had to almost run to keep up with his long stride.

"Well, miss, I didn't mean to make it sound like she was dead, but maybe so. With Mr. Jeff and me in Montgomery, we ain't heard much from Brierfield since the Yankees went through there. That was my plan. Make it across Canada safe and then head down the Misssissippi toward home."

"And that's why you went with me and not the others?"

Amos's face looked uneasy at the question, but after a moment it cleared.

"Thought it best for their safety, miss. More trouble for them if I was caught with the whole group."

"Trouble? Just because you were a servant of Mr. Davis?"

He lowered his voice to a conspiratorial whisper, all the time nearly racing along.

"I don't mind telling you there've been several attempts on my life. Mr. Jeff, you see, graduated from this very ground we're walking upon. He raised me military-like. I was the one he talked to when there was no one else to talk with. He made me learn to read as good as a white man, write as good as a white man, and speak as good as a white man." He laughed. "My mammy, being born and raised in Jamaica, still talks like she was born in England."

Laura giggled. She would have loved to see her mother's reaction to a black talking like a British subject.

"Did I say something wrong?"

"Not in the least. I was just thinking of my own mother, who still thinks of herself as very much English."

Amos's black eyes sparkled. "Does she now?" he said, his speech suddenly clipped and precise. "What would her ladyship be saying about a man who speaks like me?"

Laura stared at him at first and then laughed. "That is incredible. You sounded just like my uncle in Boston. Stuffy and pompous."

Good, he thought, laughter is better than tears. It was keeping her moving and rapidly drying out their clothing. But it also brought a sudden silence between them.

"The academy buildings will start a mile or so ahead. We can skirt them and go to my house," Laura said at last.

"No, I'm putting you in enough danger as it is."

"But you can't go back to the casket factory. Wilkins must know the wagon he burned belonged to Mr. Carson."

"I hadn't even thought of going back there. I'll see you

home and then strike out on my own. I made it all the way
to Atlanta that way."

"Why did you leave Mr. Davis?"

"He sent me away," he said grandly, then sobered. "It
nearly tore my heart out. He's got to make me look like a
traitor and turn-coat, just to protect himself from his enemies. His critics and advisors think I had too much influence on him and blame me for some of the errors of the
war. It was a war that was lost before it was even started."

"If he sent you away," she mused, "then how did you
get involved in this newspaper thing?"

"A clever scheme of Mrs. Davis."

Laura was not sure she had heard correctly. She looked
at Amos, but the big man's expression had not changed.

"I speak, of course, of his second wife. Miss Varina is a
brilliant and witty hostess, but a most jealous woman. She
was a Howell and used her family's money and power to
contact the paper and let them know where I was hidden
on the farm above Atlanta. It was almost too late when I
saw that she was my worst enemy. She thought that bounty-
hunters would kill me along the way for the price on my
head. I saw that Mr. Ledbetter and his newspaper were
going to make a mockery of me and Mr. Jeff. The man is
a liar. I overcame him in New York and took the others
to find the proper underground system."

Laura could believe that, after having seen what he had
done singlehanded with those two bounty-hunters. But it
had not been said boastfully. That she liked. She was
properly awed by his importance, and for the life of her,
she could not repress the feeling that he should never have
been a hunted man.

"What is it really like to be a slave?"

"I really couldn't tell you. I was a servant and have had
manumission since I was twelve."

"Then you are a free man!"

"That's so." He shrugged. "But who would believe me
now?"

"Believe?" Laura echoed. "That's odd, but I suddenly
know where to take you. 'In my Father's house are many
mansions . . .' And one of them better be opened to us
or else."

*   *   *

"But, Laura," Clinton sputtered, "I just can't go along—"

"Clint," she warned, " 'Do unto others as you would have them do—' "

"That isn't funny," he protested.

"I wasn't trying to be funny," she said coolly.

"Oh, Laura," he sighed, "how did you get yourself involved in all of this?"

"Because I try to live the golden rule and don't just spout it to my friends to impress them with my biblical knowledge!" Then she turned pure feminine, softening her voice to a near coo that Amos would not be able to hear back in the bedroom. "Besides, I thought a girl who had certain feelings for a young man could rely upon him in time of trouble."

He blushed scarlet. "Laura . . . I . . . Oh, gosh!"

She knew she had to press her advantage quickly. Calmly, she approached him. When she was close she put a hand to each side of his lantern jaw.

Clint found himself thinking, my God, she's going to kiss me! Then Laura bent forward and found his mouth. She kissed him slowly, lightly, lingering upon the caress. His lips were warm and sweet, a hint of cherry pie still lingering on his breath. The kiss of Fremont came to her mind. But here, the roles were oddly reversed. It was Clinton who was deliberately trying not to kiss back, a line of worry forming between his tightly closed eyes. It was morally wrong for him to have a young lady in his quarters, no matter what the reason—and the kiss was rapidly changing the reason for both of them. But how could he go on denying such gentleness? How could he shun a dream he had harbored for so long?

At last the response she sought was there, the handsome face pivoting on the bull neck, the warm lips moving upon her own with feelings that Fremont had not conveyed, giving, giving until they parted.

They were aware, after a time, that someone was knocking at his door. The pounding had been going on for some time before it penetrated their consciousness.

Clinton suddenly drew away and turned ashen.

"Lord," he whispered, "oh, Lord, we're caught!"

"Hush! It's probably just that busybody landlady

of yours. I'll hide back in the bedroom with Amos."

Nettie Rivers was the last person Clinton Bell wanted it to be. He felt sinful and sinned against. The devil was now going to make him pay for that amorous moment. Slowly, numbly, he turned and went to the door and opened it. His cousin stood before him, flakes of snow in his hair and on his gray uniform greatcoat.

"Well," Fremont growled, "aren't you going to invite us in?"

"It's late," Clinton stammered.

"Bad news doesn't keep time, Clinton. Despite your bedroom attire, we need to know if you've seen Miss Laura this evening. It's urgent."

His reply caught in his throat. He had totally forgotten that Laura had roused him from bed and he was dressed only in a bathrobe and long woolen underwear. He flushed with embarrassment as he spotted the person standing behind his cousin. He stood there a moment longer, looking at Ruth Ann Dahlgren's slim form in a winter coat of silver sable. Snowflakes were landing on the long curls that hung from each side of her head.

"I wasn't aware it had started to snow," he said lamely.

Fremont took it as an entrance cue and helped Ruth Ann in by the arm.

Clinton closed the door. His lips parted as if to speak, but he said nothing.

"We saw your lamps still lit," Ruth Ann whispered, "and Fremont thought we should check."

Still he said nothing.

"I never would have thought of it," Ruth Ann continued, "but Fremont is under the impression that you and my sister are . . . ah . . . good friends."

"I know her," Clint mumbled through his misery.

"The point is, cousin," Fremont said, taking over in a lecturing tone, "there is a nasty rumor afoot tonight concerning Miss Laura. Some have placed her at the scene of some negroes' escape, dressed as a farm boy. Such a lie has Ruth Ann's mother nearly beside herself with worry. Worry, you can understand, that was greatly increased when the girl was not found in her room—or any other portion of the house."

"At first we weren't too concerned," Ruth Ann took

over, "because my little sister has a very nasty habit of wasting a great deal of her time at the Carson house. But Fremont and I have just come from there and Mildred Carson is quite alone. Now we're growing truly concerned."

"I see," he muttered, and couldn't help but think that she sounded far less concerned than his cousin.

"As the hour is late," Fremont went on, "and as your lamp was lit . . . we couldn't help but wonder . . . well, to possibly think that perhaps she was . . ."

"No!" Clint got out, the lie strangling in his throat. He was a man of strong religious convictions, but tonight God would have to forgive him.

It might have stood at that. They might easily have accepted his word and gone in search of Laura elsewhere, but from the bedroom window Laura saw an even greater problem brewing.

Nettie Rivers stood on her back porch, lantern held high, her head a mass of rag curlers. The pony cart's arrival had awakened her and she now stood debating whether to investigate who might be with Clinton in the made-over shed at this ungodly hour.

Laura didn't wait to see what the woman might do next. Her only concern was to protect Amos Mobley at all costs. Her plan might not work, but she quickly prepared to attempt it. Amos puzzled at her doing, but she waved him into silence.

She did not even pause to think further, but went right on through the door and into the outer room.

Clinton stood there, staring as she fumbled to draw the unlaced chemise back about her half-exposed breasts.

She didn't say anything. She didn't think she would have to—at least for the moment.

The silence was broken by Ruth Ann breaking into a violent fit of giggles.

Fremont's rage was instantaneous. He could not help but think that Clinton had been awarded what he himself had been denied.

"Where have you been?" he demanded harshly.

"In the bedroom," Laura said simply and truthfully.

"No!" Clinton croaked hoarsely, "we . . . haven't been . . ."

"Hush!" Laura whispered. "It's none of their business."

The laughter died in Ruth Ann's throat and almost choked her. "Business?" she hissed. "You have the family worried to death over ugly rumors while you're out playing the trollop with this ape-creature, and it's not our business? Get your clothes, hussy. We'll let Mama settle your hash!"

Laura said the first thing that came to mind. "This is all I came out in."

Clinton looked as though he were going to die. His look tugged at Laura's heart, but she said nothing. She had not considered that she was putting his reputation in jeopardy to protect Amos.

It was not necessary for any of the quartet to speak further. The door came flying open and Nettie took in the scene at a single glance. The lean, iron-jawed woman needed nothing more to answer her suspicions.

"Out!" she bellowed. "I do not allow fornication in my establishment!"

Laura began to wail and ran toward Fremont. With alacrity he was out of his greatcoat and wrapping her within it. Wordlessly, he propelled her out the door and toward the pony cart. He didn't even look back to see that Ruth Ann was following in a near apoplectic state. She would never forgive her sister for embarrassing the whole family in front of the worst gossip in town. It would just kill her mother, and that she knew for a fact.

Fremont was almost smiling again as he helped Laura into the cart and wrapped a lap robe about her bare feet. Instinctively he felt that he had arrived just in time to save Laura from a full bedding with Clinton. He was sorely puzzled at the moroseness in Ruth Ann's face as he helped her in beside Laura. She had, after all, gone much further with him the night before. It was snowing harder on their twisting climb up to the plateau and Fremont had to let the pony have frequent rests from the load. No one spoke. Every time Fremont glanced at Laura by his side, his excitement mounted. She had been a mere girl when she had denied him. Tonight she had proven she was capable of being a full woman . . . his. By the time they had reached Highcliff-on-the-Hudson he was actually grinning with desire.

* * *

Clinton was not grinning. Nettie had silently closed the door after their departure and painted a quiet hurt upon her face.

"I can't understand this of you, Clinton," she said quietly. "I wish to believe that you were lured into a situation over which you had no control."

"Thank you for saying that," he murmured. "Mrs. Rivers, I owe you an apology. I never should have had a girl here."

Nettie began to soften. Never had she seen such agony in a male face. He reminded her of a cuddly little boy who needed soothing in motherly arms—her arms.

But there was a great puzzlement in her mind. She was quite sure she had seen that little baggage dressed as a boy and taking a hay wagon out of the Carsons' yard. The last thing she wanted was for one of her boarders to be involved in this nigger business.

"Well," she said slowly, "confession is good for the soul, Clinton, and your soul seems greatly troubled. When exactly did you invite the girl here?"

"I didn't invite her," Clint said, a note of anger creeping into his voice. "I know your rules. She came on her own."

"I was sure that you did," Nettie replied, "but still she was here in . . . questionable attire."

"That's true," Clinton admitted. "I was wrong in letting her in and I'm sorry."

"Sorry doesn't answer the appearance it suggested."

Clinton shook his head, his cheeks a deep scarlet, and slumped into a chair.

"Nothing happened," he said miserably. "Please believe me. I've . . . I've never . . ."

Nettie looked down at him, seeing his misery, his manliness, his desirability.

She bent her head suddenly, resting her cheek on the top of his head.

"Now," she soothed, "I haven't been a boarding house woman all these years without learning a thing or two about men and the tempting powers of certain women. No wonder her poor sister had to search her out in the night. But her clothing?"

For all his moral staunchness, Clinton had certain human weaknesses. His reputation was at stake. His home was at stake, if Nettie Rivers decided to put him out over this incident. He was so rattled that he wasn't even thinking about the primary reason for Laura's arrival.

"I forgot about them," he said. "She must have left them in the bedroom."

"And where were you?" she cooed, stroking his hair and letting her other hand fall lightly onto his broad chest.

"Here. Answering Fremont's knock. She went to hide." Then, realizing how damaging that sounded, he quickly added, "But she had all of her clothes on!"

"I believe you." To add emphasis to her words she patted him on the chest and let her hand fall to his lap. She gave his head a little hug and knelt down beside him, resting her arm along the steely top of his thigh.

"I'm well aware, Clinton," she whispered, desire making her voice crack with emotion, "that men are such that they have certain needs . . . especially young men such as yourself." Her fingers inched toward the robe-covered crotch. "But you must be careful, especially in a small town such as this, about the manner of woman who is selected to . . . ah . . . help you in those moments."

Clinton was truely naive. He thought he was receiving nothing more than a gentle lecture for his near falling from grace. His relief was growing because she was being so understanding.

Nettie's hand began to tremble slightly. It now rested gently upon him and through the robe she could feel that, though there was no arousal, even in a flaccid state he was of amazing size.

"Oh, Clinton, Clinton," she cried softly, grasping him about the waist, and nestling her head and cheek against his crotch. "This night worries me no end. A family will go to great extremes to protect the good name of a daughter. Even though your cousin saw all, they will try to make you look the blackguard. We just can't let that happen."

"No . . ." The tables had suddenly turned. It was he who now found himself wishing to soothe her worries and comfort her. She had been so understanding of his plight. She wanted to help him save his reputation. He patted her head, his hand gentle against the mass of springy rag curlers.

Nettie smiled to herself, her body burning with a strange fever. As though accepting his sympathy she rolled her head from side to side, pressing her cheek close to stir his blood.

The warmth and movement were inevitably having an affect on Clinton, but he was too inexperienced to think evil of Nettie's intentions. As the rubbing cheek stirred him, so did it arouse his embarrassment. He tried to close it out of his mind and will his arousal away, but it was impossible as long as the caressing continued. It was a situation he did not know how to handle.

Nettie's courage increased as the flesh under her cheek grew as firm as the thigh muscle beneath her arm. This moment had been in her daydreams for so long that the reality was more dreamlike than real. At any moment she expected him to fully comprehend her true motive and make some comment or motion that would deny her her quest. But until that moment happened she would bask in the conquest to date. She moved her head so that the robe could fall apart and was disappointed that a wool and bone button still lay ahead.

"You've never been with a woman, have you?" she whispered softly.

"Never . . ."

"Then I can help you."

"H-how?"

Nettie lowered her head and let her lips rest gently for a bare moment on the burning flesh exposed through the slit.

"I can proclaim your innocence from the housetops, if need be. I would do anything for you. Anything that you desired."

Clint's body had gone rigid at the touch of her lips, but still no amorous thoughts entered his mind. A very naive portion of his brain counselled that the woman seemed to be paying no attention to his growth; she was learned on such matters and was therefore not embarrassed. But his answer was not well thought out, to say the least.

"Anything you could do for me would be greatly appreciated."

It worked on Nettie's system like a massive dose of adrenaline. She had heard the statement before, in varying forms from various boarders. It always meant the same. She would be the victor and had only to plot the final battle plan.

"Oh!" she gasped, starting to fall to the side. "I have a cramp."

Clint automatically reached out to break her fall and pulled her back. In his strong grasp Nettie slumped forward, the jostling masking the fact that her fingers were expertly working at the buttonholes. It took but the release of two buttons to release the object of her quest.

Clinton instantly felt what had happened, but his faith in her was still such that no evil was yet apparent to him; besides, his semi-cloistered life to date had kept him innocent of any sensual or sexual matters.

"Oh . . . my . . . God!" he gasped, rearing back in the chair.

The moist warmth had come down on him so suddenly that the natural rearing action had tended to force his length further into Nettie's eagerly accepting mouth. Her hands closed about his waist in a steely grip. She could feel him quiver under her fingertips, further expanding and forcing her jaws wide. But years of experience told her it would be a most short-lived expansion.

His body exploded; body and soul seemed to flow out of him in an exhausting stream. Sensual, animalistic reaction made him rear back again to drive himself to the full limit.

Blackness seemed to close in from the corner of his eyes. His limbs went weak and limp. He could not have moved if the shed was raging with fire about him.

He was not even aware when the woman agilely rose from his side, a mixture of pleasure and frustration upon her face. Nettie was pleased, but only in anticipation. This had to be only the beginning of her on-going education of this pupil. But to protect such a future, she had to protect the pupil. While he sat in stunned silence, she walked to the bedroom door and entered.

A slow, evil grimace crossed her face as she saw the boy's attire scattered about the floor. On the point of Laura Dahlgren being the driver of the hay wagon, she was now quite sure. Her recent experience with Clinton Bell proved without a shadow of doubt, at least in her mind, that he was innocent of any union with the girl. No man, in her years of experience, could regain such a state of excitement that quickly after . . .

The thought suddenly froze in her mind. To scream would not have been a true reflection of her emotions. No question of fear crossed her mind as she spied the man standing inside the room. The light from the open doorway caught him at a strange angle, giving him awesome size and presence.

She stared, while Amos contemplated. He had heard all. The temporary walls in the shed were so thin that he could not have helped overhearing this woman with Clinton, just as he had overheard Laura's frantic attempt to save him from discovery. That had been an innocent attempt, but what he had later heard was far from innocent. It would be a kind of blasphemy not to attempt to protect the person who had attempted to protect him.

Steeling himself as he slowly turned his profile to the woman, he mentally forced himself to renew the arousal that had automatically built while listening to them. This was not a new experience to him. He had many times stimulated himself mentally while being forced, in his teens, to serve as a studman on the Davis plantation. It had been little more than a matter of survival. He could do such a thing again for survival—for himself and others. He prayed he was measuring this woman correctly.

Nettie continued to stare as he turned to the side, her eyes frozen on him. She had just been with a boy; this was a real man.

Her frustrated desires from Clinton were now in full command of all her senses. She watched him walk to her as though in slow motion. She allowed him to take her hand and lead it to the point of her stare. Never had she felt anything so exciting. This was the most victorious night she had ever experienced. At his touch, she knelt quickly and eagerly.

5

THERE IS in the make-up of many a mysterious urge to commit calumny to overcome their own feelings of guilt.

Such was the case for many during the remainder of that night and into the next day.

Laura prepared for bed as though her father were not in the room. Her mother had refused even to see her. Ruth Ann had made her report as sordid as she could manage and a mortified Lucille had instantly taken to her bed. How could she ever look Mr. Wilkins in the face again? How could she ever look anyone in the face again? Nettie Rivers would have the whole shameful scandal spread wide by sunup.

"Mr. Wilkins," Clarence continued, the darkness of his smile increasing, "points out that two of his men were badly beaten by the black."

"That was to protect me, Papa."

"Then you do admit helping the man to escape?"

"Yes, Papa," she said in a low voice. "I didn't know he was in the wagon, but I'm glad now." She shivered. "He saved me from what those two wished to do to me.

Then I had to save him crossing the river because he couldn't swim." She paused. Her beautiful and open face tightened. She continued, in a lower but firmer voice. "That makes us even, I hope. But I did do a wicked thing tonight, I now realize."

For an instant a look of dread passed over Clarence's features. But he said nothing just then.

Laura continued, as if recounting a scene of indescribable horror to herself.

"To keep everyone from knowing that Amos was there I had to make everyone believe that Clinton Bell and I had been . . . bedding. We hadn't, Papa."

"That's some lie to tell just to protect a black man."

"He's more than just a black man, Papa. He's educated and refined and a gentleman. I hope Clint will forgive me for what I said."

Clarence was looking at his daughter with wide-eyed admiration.

"If *he* is a gentleman, he shall, my dear. Now let's forget this until the morning."

Fremont Hunter was waiting for him in the hall.

"Is she all right?"

"I would pray so, sir."

Fremont drew a deep breath, as though greatly relieved. "That's a blessing . . . Oh, that Mr. Wilkins is still waiting for you in the study. He's most curious to learn if Laura has told you anything about the slave. I hope you don't repeat it if she has."

"I hardly would have taken you for an abolitionist, Fremont," Clarence murmured sardonically.

A dull flush crept under the smooth parchment of his skin. Listening to Garth Wilkins tell about the man, he had developed a personal motive concerning Amos Mobley. He drew up haughtily. "I am no such thing, Mr. Dahlgren, and never could be. I just consider this is a matter that would be better handled by the military than bounty-hunters. Now, if you will excuse me, I must return to the academy."

Clarence nodded his farewell. Despite the late hour he did not urge the young man to stay the night. The fewer strangers about, the better chance he had to cope with his wife.

If this incident had not occurred Fremont would have continued to take advantage of his overnight pass. Now he would use the situation for his own benefit. This was news, he was quite sure, that would put him in a most favorable light with Colonel Arnold Beetle. He was even prepared to chance the commandant's disfavor by awakening him at this ungodly hour.

Dawn came too soon for some and not fast enough for others.

Clinton Bell felt as though he had not slept a single wink—would never sleep again as long as he lived. He purposely departed the shed before dawn to avoid the sleeping black man—and to be at the boarding house breakfast table and gone before Nettie's arrival.

The first snow of winter lay heavy upon the ground. It would cause Clint more time in walking to the foundry and so he turned to the road instead of crossing the back yard to the boarding house.

From the kitchen window Nettie saw him depart and she boiled with rage. She had prepared him an extra-fine breakfast and lunch to carry along. She marched through the kitchen with his heaping plate and out into the dining room. She stopped there, thinking of all the things she had to say to Clinton Bell. It would be beneath her dignity to run after him in the snow like a thwarted young belle. She eyed the three men already at the table and plunked the breakfast plate in front of Timothy Caruthers.

It was a surprise to all, because Nettie had put Timothy on very short rations until he caught up with his room and board. The breakfast was good, but Timothy could not eat. He sat brooding miserably over the hot rolls, coffee, sausages and cake. Nettie saw his mood, but didn't comment until the other men had left the table.

"You look about the way I feel this morning, Timothy."

"I bet he blames the snow today for our not working."

"A man can't do day work when he's out most of the night on questionable errands," Nettie scoffed.

"How do you know that?"

Nettie pulled a chair up close. "I saw with my own eyes. He was taking a hay wagon out of the yard."

"Whatever for?"

"Oh, Timothy, it just breaks my heart to think such a thing but I'm quite sure that under the hay he had . . . had . . ."

"Slaves," Timothy supplied gently. "I've been thinking the same."

Nettie could see the excitement in Timothy's face, and she made her eyes look very sad.

"But one of our own is involved and it has me near frantic. Last night I heard Clinton coming back late. He snuck a nigger into the shed. I'm a manless woman, Timothy. What am I to do or say?"

He bent forward, looking at Nettie as though she had just presented him with a bag of gold.

"You just leave everything in the hands of Timothy Caruthers."

"Oh, Timothy, I'll never know how to thank you."

He grinned. "We'll think of something."

Going on the information that Clinton had already left for work, he boldly marched into the shed. In front of the stove lay a figure wrapped in a blanket. He approached cautiously and jammed the rifle barrel against the man's head. When there was no movement he cursed and tore away the covering. There was nothing more than logs laid end to end.

He raced out into the yard and examined the snow-field. There were only Clinton's tracks leaving and his own coming.

"Now, where in the hell would I go if I was a stupid damn nigger?"

Amos Mobley was hardly stupid. He knew that with dawn would come a woman's wrath and a man's guilt. Nettie nor Clinton were neither one safe bets for his own safety. He had waited until the falling snow would cover his tracks and departed for the only place in town where he knew he would be safe.

One thing Nettie had said caused Timothy to lift his head and suddenly grin.

"Of course! That would be the only place and I know how to smoke the devil out."

Marvin Carson had been wondering for hours if it had all been worth it. It had taken him only two hours to get to Beacon and eight to get back—one of those hours wasted in convincing the others that they would just have to go on without Amos Mobley. He had pondered about the absent man until the snow became his only worry. Time and time again he had had to stop and let the team rest from their constant fight against the quickly growing drifts. Several times he had been forced to lead them, just to make sure that they were still upon the vanishing road.

Bone-tired and wet to the skin, West Point had never looked better to him. He had considered just sitting before a fire and roasting for the duration of the winter.

Five minutes later the heat of a conflagration was searing his skin to near parchment. It was the casket factory building.

The snow lay two feet deep around the factory and made it difficult for the West Point men to get the pumping rig close to the building. The fire had been noticed too late, and the bucket brigade, formed by Timothy Caruthers, applied their water to the funeral office building and the house to keep them from igniting. But there was no hope for the barnlike factory; the fire roared with inferno intensity because of the vats of pitch, used to make the caskets watertight.

Timothy Caruthers stayed with Marvin until the last ember had been pounded out with the back of a shovel. Timothy was greatly disappointed. Nowhere among the ashes did he find any evidence of human bones, and he had foolishly put himself out of a job.

"I just can't believe this," he said sadly. "How can a fire start in there when we haven't even been working the better part of the week?"

Marvin couldn't answer. Sheriff Addison didn't want to answer. But they both harbored the same horrible thought. Someone was getting desperate in searching for the missing black man.

Arnold Beetle had become one of the most desperate of all. He had been anything but pleased at being awakened at such an hour, but ten minutes after Fremont's arrival he had been grinning broadly.

"So it *is* Jeff Davis's man," he said, "and right here

under our noses. I must admit, Hunter, I've always had a suspicion in the back of my mind that you were less than loyal to the military. This goes a long way to alter that impression, my boy. I'll telegraph Washington as soon as I can arouse an operator. Then, we shall go and talk with this girl as soon as it's light."

Fremont smiled in satisfaction. "The bounty-hunter is also there, Colonel Beetle. Our first concern, sir, if I may be so bold to suggest, is to win Miss Laura to our side."

"By God, she's the one who has done wrong!" Beetle roared. "She has an obligation to give us every scrap of information for our intelligence people."

Fremont slowly shook his head. "I believe, from a personal experience last evening, that she'll do anything to protect the man from capture. If we can just assure her that we are the ones who will protect him . . ."

Beetle's eyes were round in his fat face. His bulbous lips puckered in a whistle of agreement. He was eager to get away from the academy and into the war. He would never become a general training cadets. He would wire his report directly to Edwin Stanton and make sure that the secretary of the war department understood that he was the most logical choice to bring the black man to Washington and interrogate him. He would make his report very strong. There were, however, two factors that he had to consider. First, he had to gain information from Laura; and then he still would have to capture the man.

Having been a frequent dinner guest at Highcliff-on-the-Hudson, he knew that his first barrier would be Lucille. He would not presume to question the girl without the mother's prior approval. He received it with an alacrity that amazed him.

Lucille had first fixed a hard look upon him, scrutinizing and resentful. She considered his request an intrusion into a family matter. Besides, she stood to lose a great deal of money if Mr. Wilkins didn't capture the slave. Then she softened, a more important thought entering her mind. Mr. Wilkins offered only money. Colonel Beetle could offer her the chance to save her good name and reputation. Information gained from Laura would turn the girl into a heroine. Yes, Arnold Beetle was the man to handle the situation.

But Arnold Beetle found the situation hard to handle. He had tried it Fremont's way and was getting nowhere. He dismissed the cadet from Laura's bedroom and his little eyes sparked with fury.

"Now I will have the truth!"

"About what?"

Beetle clenched his teeth. He would handle her as he would a cadet standing for discipline.

"You are in serious trouble," he said sternly. "Very serious trouble that could call for your arrest. This man you were trying to help escape is a wanted man. Do you realize that?"

Laura didn't answer. Her expression became more stubborn. She felt betrayed by Fremont.

"Perhaps you don't," continued the colonel, and in spite of himself his voice became somewhat softer. "You were trying to help him escape because you thought he was some poor slave creature. He is not. He is a manumission black with a very good education and a vast knowledge."

"What is manumission?" she asked innocently.

"It means that he has been freed by his owner."

"Then if he is free, why are you chasing him?"

Now he spoke through lips like iron. "That is a military secret."

"But that's so silly," she said, becoming convinced that Amos was in more danger from this man than from Garth Wilkins. "You must not be speaking of the same man I was with last night. He was a ruffian and didn't even know how to swim. Educated? I seriously doubt it."

"The man was probably acting."

Laura turned and stared at him. How could she convince him? Then all at once she began to laugh. It was at once a wild and weary laugh. He rubbed his eyes with the back of his hand, as though she had suddenly gone crazy.

"Oh, Colonel Beetle, if you could have seen and smelled the man, you wouldn't be questioning my word. There was an aroma of farm about him that was near sickening. The man was hardly capable of putting words together into a logical sentence. I'm sorry if you've been led to believe otherwise."

He seemed about to speak. Then he closed his livid lips and bowed his way from the room. He was being made to look the fool and he would not stand for it. Was it a trick by that Southern-sympathizing young scoundrel? He felt suddenly broken and exhausted. There was no way of calling back the report from Washington. It had been foolishness on his part to send it solely on the basis of the information gained from Fremont. But it all had seemed so logical.

As he went down the stairs he saw Clarence Dahlgren leaving the dining room. He hailed him, on a sudden inspiration.

"Mr. Dahlgren, your daughter is being most uncooperative. I believe you are due to see me this afternoon to discuss the contract on the uniforms being supplied by your son's factory. Let's change that to one o'clock—with your daughter present. Perhaps by then she will have changed her mind. I must say, it certainly is a nice contract." He smiled meaningfully at Clarence and then left the house.

Lucille had heard all. It seemed incredible to her. Laura was not helping the family; she was damaging it even further. She had half a mind to turn Laura right over to Mr. Wilkins and try to gain a reward for the deed.

"Surely he wouldn't cancel Laddie's contract?"

Clarence gazed at her expectantly. Then he turned away. How could he force Laura to do something that would be totally against her good sense and judgment? He stared hopelessly up the stairs.

Now Lucille's impatience rose up so strong in her that her eyes flashed like steel.

"You will march right up there and tell her that I demand to see her at once, Mr. Dahlgren. I've had just about all the trouble I can stand from that girl!"

"I will go up," he said dully, "but only to tell her to pack. I think it best to send her to your sister for awhile."

"Why her?" she said sharply. "It is Ruth Ann and I who need to get away from the scandal she has caused."

"If there be scandal, it is only in evil minds."

She was outraged. He was making it sound as though she were the scandalmonger. Her face flushed scarlet.

"Clarence, the only place that chit of a girl is going is to the academy to bare the truth before Colonel Beetle.

That contract means just too much to Laddie. Do you hear me?"

But apparently he chose not to hear her. He walked up the stairs, with a sudden chilling about his heart. This house would seem empty without Laura. She was the only being who breathed life into it for him. He had tried to be a good father to Laura, to grant the small favors she did ask. He was well aware that the others considered him pitiless and common and a poor provider. It no longer mattered. He felt empty, used up.

6

ON THAT SAME morning, in the fall of 1863, there appeared off Cape Lookout an old trawler, hardly seaworthy in appearance, which flagged for permission to bring a message aboard the Union's *Atlantic*.

While the officers on deck in the *Atlantic* were debating as to whether they should disturb their captain with the request, a young, neatly uniformed officer came springing onto the deck from the trawler.

"I am Ensign Roger Lockwood and I must see Captain Tougcourt at once." With which he went past the startled officers, flung down the hatchway of the wooden three-master, and walked into the captain's quarters without knocking.

"What the hell?" Kramer Tougcourt exploded, straightening up from his chart table.

"Lockwood, sir!" the young officer announced pompously, with a snappy salute. "With a vital message from the secretary."

Tougcourt's steel gray eyebrows closed together like battling insects. "Barnacles on Gideon Welles's butt! Had you lame-brains given me a vital message on the *Nashville* she would not have slipped through with tons of munitions from England."

The ensign blinked. He was only used to the polite protocol of the Navy secretary's office. "I'm not even sure of the message I now carry, sir."

Tougcourt cleared his throat as though he were going to spit on the youth, but instead he extended a weather-beaten hand.

Lockwood knew there were certain formal words he should be uttering at this moment, but decided it would be best to hand over the water-proof pouch silently.

"Damn the bastard!" Captain Tougcourt exploded anew, even as he read the dispatch. "It is more men I need, not to have men taken away. This will be the third time this year. Bah! I'm probably better off without the likes of him." He pivoted toward a desk where an able-bodied seaman sat inscribing in the log. "Boy, fetch me down that worthless Lieutenant DeLong. His shipbuilding father probably wants him home again."

Roger Lockwood stood stunned. He had taken the only vessel available to him out of Norfolk, an overhauled trawler, had been violently seasick because of its corklike sway, and all because of a father's personal request for his son. He was highly indignant, forgetting for the moment that his own father had pulled strings to keep him safe in Washington.

To underscore the fact that he took no personal interest in the messages he carried, he averted his attention to the chart table and tried to look interested.

"Know what you're looking at?" the captain demanded.

"No, sir."

"Thought not," Tougcourt said drily. "At least you should know that you're off the North Carolina coast. That's Beaufort. Most unlikely port for Captain Robert B. Pegram to enter, but damned if he didn't. That pin is his ship, the *Nashville*. Best damn side-wheeler ever built. He's run our blockade with it time and time again. And that pin, son, is for the *Alabama*. It's under the command of Raphael Semmes, the best damn jaunty seaman to put his feet to a deck."

Lockwood frowned. "Excuse me, sir, but I detected almost a note of admiration in your voice for them."

"A note?" he bellowed. "A trumpet chorus! Semmes has personally presided over the destruction of fifty-eight Union vessels and there he sits, along with Pegram and the wiliest fox of them all, Harvey Derrick and his iron-clad *Palmetto State*. This is the sea, Mr. Lockwood, where your enemy is as big as life and you salute him for his feats of valor. Oh, here's your man, Ensign."

Lockwood turned and disappointment immediately clouded his face. This could hardly be the son of Horace DeLong. This man was . . . was a disgrace! His uniform was impossibly filthy, his brown muttonchop whiskers so bushy that they nearly reached his thin nose, and the walrus mustache could have been braided out to a full five inches. Although he was quite tall, he seemed to slump and his face and piercing eyes seemed to have a sullen and resentful look to them. But without betraying his surprise, Lockwood went right into issuing his verbal orders.

"Sir, I am ordered to return you to Mr. Welles, as soon as possible."

"For court-martial, I hope," Tougcourt sneered.

DeLong's head jerked up. Lockwood braced himself for trouble over the insult, but the man was grinning at the captain.

"Did you hear that call?" DeLong said. "They're coming out!"

"Hot bloody damn!" Tougcourt cheered. "To your stations!"

Suddenly the morning silence was broken by a sharp cannon report, and another and another in quick succession mingled with the savage yells of seamen going to battle stations.

"We'd best get to the trawler and leave at once," Lockwood declared before realizing he was talking to thin air. He raced to the companionway and caught just a glimpse of the two of them disappearing through the hatch and onto the deck. He followed, determined to get away with or without the man.

The deck was a madhouse of activity, as were the other eight ships forming the blockade of the port. No one had expected the Rebels to try to run through them for several days yet. But naval battles were not as cumbersomely put

together as land battles. Here were no thousands of troops
who had to be marched up to each other before firing their
first shot. The cannon range aboard ship was such that
one never need even see the enemy's face—only the approach of his ship.

Lockwood ran for the railing. The skipper of the
trawler had smartly shoved off from the *Atlantic* at the
first cannon report. The trawler was a small target; they
would not waste valuable ammunition on it. Fuming,
Lockwood turned to the shore.

A fearful sight met his eyes. Two years in the navy,
and this was his first glimpse of a forming sea battle.

The Rebels appeared to have worked out a master plan;
the Union had not, because each captain fiercely maintained the independence of his own ship.

The *Nashville*, its massive black funnel emitting an
ominous smoke cloud, looked stark without a single sail
upon its twin masts. But Captain Pegram knew exactly
what he was doing. The side-wheel power would allow
him to dart and weave among the Union ships, still fighting to unfurl their sails, while his two comrade ships
fought the battle to allow his escape.

The thunderous cannon of the *Alabama* already had the
decks of three of the Northern blockade ships aflame.
Their look-outs had not been as alert as the men in the
crow's nest of the *Atlantic*. Captain Tougcourt already
had the anchor weighed, the sails falling like massive white
clouds and the massive wooden-hulled ship turning to
give his cannoneers the best shot at the *Nashville*. It was
still out of range, but closing fast.

Someone came along and gave Lockwood a resounding
slap across his youthfully rounded buttocks.

"Get your bloody arse to work, matey!"

Looking around for his attacker, Lockwood saw it was
the very man he was to take off this ship. But was it the
same man? This officer's eyes were alight with excitement,
his face flushed with the expectancy of danger; his manner with the seamen he ordered about was assured, direct
and positive.

For several minutes it was the last thought Roger Lockwood was able to focus upon. He heard an odd whistling

and then a thunderous roar that lifted him off his feet and crashed him almost instantly back down upon the hardwood deck. He smelled smoke and singed hair, without realizing that part of the odor came from himself.

Rough hands lifted him and pulled him away from the gaping deck hole caused by the cannon ball. Just as roughly he was slammed into a gunwale.

"Stay there," Calvert DeLong shouted, "and keep out of the bloody way."

"Behind you! Behind you!" he gasped. "That ugly thing!" Then he fell back unconscious.

"That ugly thing" was the *Palmetto State*, rightly described by Lockwood, who had never before seen any of the ironclad warships that sat low in the water, three cannons jutting from each iron-sheeted side, and appearing like an inverted flat-iron.

Calvert DeLong could no longer afford to spend time looking after the novice. The *Palmetto State* was a death machine. Cannon balls had been known to bounce off its armor plate like rifle shot.

"The funnel," he screamed at the control officer over the cannons. "Get them to fire at her funnel. It's her weakest point to the interior."

The captain of the iron-clad was well aware of that point, as well. This was not the type of battle Captain Derrick would have chosen to fight, but the escape of the *Nashville* was more important than his ship.

"Load the forward battery guns," Derrick ordered, "and turn sharp to port."

"But, Captain Derrick," the helmsman gasped, "that will put us across her prow."

"Exactly," he said coldly. "An experiment to see the ramming power of metal over wood. I want our prow to eat into her hull just as we fire our forward guns."

The young man from Kentucky, who had never seen the ocean until the year before, grew wild-eyed with fright.

"We'll all be killed!"

To no one in particular Derrick said, "Must not we all one day?"

But Kramer Tougcourt was a manner of captain Derrick had never before confronted. Forgotten was the rapidly escaping *Nashville*. Forgotten were Raphaél Semmes's massive guns sinking the other Union blockade ships— many before they'd fired a single round.

Of sole importance was the *Palmetto State*. To avoid the iron-clad's ram and give it full battle he caused the masted ship to toss, to pitch, forcing the sailors to hold onto cannon and deck as the ship turned about in a constant effort to damage the iron-clad before it sank them.

No one stopped, no one cared to stop. Everyone forgot the blisters that were forming on their hands in the desperate fight to save the ship and themselves. But the *Atlantic* was dying. The wooden-hulled ship was going back to the sea, piecemeal: the bulwarks went, the stanchions were blown out, the ventilators smashed, the cabin doors burst in. There was not an area of the ship that a fire of some size did not attack. She was being gutted bit by bit. The Rebel fire power changed the long boats into matchwood. And there was no break in the *Palmetto State*'s attack. It was like an ant darting about a cockroach, worrying it to death so it could pick at its shell. They were the old and new of sea power caught up in a furious duel for primacy.

The sails were blown away and the *Atlantic* became immobile.

The *Palmetto State* could now come in for the final kill.

What day of the week it was, what hour of that day, Calvert DeLong would never be able to recall. All that he was aware of over the howling battle was a horrendous meshing of metal and wood. At first he thought it was just the report of many cannons being fired at once, but this report had sound that grew in intensity. The *Palmetto State* had fired its forward guns right into the gaping hole their ramming had created. The *Atlantic* listed, the ocean poured in, the inner hull became an inferno.

From far off the *Nashville*'s funnel whistle opened for a long, mournful wail.

"What the hell?" Ensign Lockwood gasped, pulling himself up onto the bridge.

"A ritual, dear lad," Captain Tougcourt said through teeth gritted against pain as he took another turn of the leg tourniquet to stem the blood flow. "She's saluting a valiant foe who will never have the opportunity to fight her again."

"You let her escape!" Lockwood screamed. "You played around with that toy ship and let the real prize escape!"

"Shut up!" DeLong bellowed, coming upon the scene. "Because of men like him, we've been able to strangle the Confederacy to death."

"Really now, Mr. Delong, that's giving me much too much credit, I would say. The order to abandon ship has been given. You'd best take the lad and be about your business."

"Get below," Calvert muttered to the ensign. "I'll meet you shortly."

"But how shall we get to the trawler?"

"Swim, if we must," he said with disgust. He turned his full attention to the captain. "Shall I help you down, sir?"

"No, lad, Porter is standing by to help me down." Then his eyes turned compassionate. "Is it another dirty job they have in store for you, lad?"

"I wouldn't know, sir, but I would assume as much."

Tougcourt sighed. "You're a fine man to have aboard when we must go against these sea-going monsters of metal, Mr. DeLong, but your talents are best used else-where. No matter how dirty the assignment, my boy, do it with pride." Then he chuckled. "I was supposed to burn your file upon your departure. Harvey Derrick seems to have done the chore for me."

"Burn my file, sir?" DeLong asked. "For what ever reason, I wonder?"

"For whatever reason Gideon Welles has on his mind, my boy. He's having you drummed out of the service." He chuckled again. "Of course, don't let the old billy-goat know you learned the fact first from me."

Calvert DeLong grinned, pulled himself to attention and smartly saluted. He would sorely miss this old man of the sea and the *Atlantic*, even though his three months aboard had been little more than a calculated lull in his regular work.

But to be put out of the service? The Naval Secretary better have a damn good reason for such a drastic move, he thought, or my father will balk like hell.

* * *

The wail of the Hudson Valley Limited was as mournful as that of a ship setting sail.

Laura Dahlgren had just arrived at the station with her father.

She paused on the platform and gazed with a shiver of astonished awe at the man Sheriff Addison was ushering up into a train car. It was a huge black man, well known to Laura—but dressed in oddly formal clothes. He was unlike anything Laura had seen.

"A butler, he looks like," Clarence Dahlgren said slowly. "The suit is one Marvin keeps on hand for farmers who may not own one for burial."

"This *is* more like a funeral than a going-away."

"If you believe Garth Wilkins, there may be several funerals in West Point unless the man is turned over to him."

"And you *do* believe him?" Laura asked seriously.

"I wish Colonel Beetle to believe it, child. It's the excuse I shall give him for removing you from your home. By the time he storms down to see why I haven't brought you to him, I fully expect Mr. Wilkins to be in frantic rage. That's his bowler hat and cane the black man is sporting."

"But, Papa," she laughed, "that cane is . . ."

He cut her short. "I know about the cane, Laura. I learned its secret while stealing it. It shall serve as a good weapon to protect you in case anything goes amiss."

"Protect me?" A look of deep seriousness swept the fair young face. "It's Amos who needs protecting."

"Your good friends think otherwise, Laura. But in any case, Sheriff Addison is of the opinion that no one will question a young lass under the escort of a family retainer, especially if they're riding in the privacy of a roomette." He chuckled drily. "And the man can sound more British than Harrison Holmes Dewitt."

Laura was in no mood for joviality. "You can't afford the passage of two in a Pullman car, Papa."

Clarence gazed at her with deep tenderness. Several events had lessened the burden on his heart for having to send her away. He had learned that he was not the only one who loved her and would miss her.

"Marvin and Mildred Carson are paying the fare, Laura."

"But he'll need that money to rebuild the factory," she protested. "And Amos shouldn't be going back to the South."

Clarence diverted his eyes. He did not wish his daughter to see the tears that had welled up in them. These good people were doing what they wished to do out of love and respect. The black man, who had been in hiding at Sheriff Addison's, had amazed him the most. The man had flatly refused to allow her to go into New York City unescorted.

The train whistle for departure kept Clarence from having to explain further. He would have enough explaining to do to Lucille as it was. The woman was under the impression that her ranting and raving had won her a battle and that her husband had taken Laura to see Colonel Beetle. Clarence prayed that Theda DeWitt would be understanding of her niece's arrival without a single parcel of luggage. At the thought of her, he sighed, wondering. . . .

It was several hours later when Laura Dahlgren stepped into a totally new and different world. Peekskill to the south and Albany to the north had been the mundane limits of her travel. This had to be fairyland.

She gaped at the rows of awnings above the store fronts that extended all the way up Broadway to Grace Church. But it was the people that kept her staring. They seemed to swarm everywhere, dressed in fabulous variety, and all rushing madly.

"Miss," Amos said on a worried note, "I must take you by the arm or lose you."

Laura didn't mind; it gave her more ease to gawk at the wild stampede. Amos, however, was aware of the raised eyebrows and warning glances. New York was not new to him. He had been here several times with Mr. Jeff before the war. He saw it through informed eyes.

This was the height of the evening rush hour. The people were workers, fighting to get home after their twelve to fourteen hours of daily labor, fighting for one of the seats on the uptown stages and caring nothing about the black man and his young charge.

Amos kept holding Laura back, until she began to wonder why. Then she got her answer—and an education.

No one fought to get onto the next stage; the crowd seemed to part for Amos to steer Laura forward.

Amos mumbled something to the driver, while Laura stared up into a sea of negro faces and saw the sign: Colored Allowed On This Stage.

"Don't go this way, boy," the driver called down, looking disapprovingly at Amos and Laura. "Walk!"

"Which way?"

But the driver wasn't listening. He had a full load to Thirty-fourth and lashed his team forward.

An old woman clinging desperately to the side of the stage took a daring chance by quickly pointing. "Go dattaway, man!"

"Dattaway" took them out of mayhem and into the more tranquil brownstone world of Fifth Avenue. Now Laura was transported. The gas street lamps were flickering to life, the carriages rolled at a leisurely pace, heavily starched nursemaids pushed their charges along in three-wheeled perambulators, hurrying now that the evening air was growing crisp. The clothing here was Parisian in elegance and made the people on Broadway look like slum waifs.

"Amos, are you sure we're on the right street?" Laura asked in disbelief.

"Quite sure, miss." He beamed. "That's the Astor house, where Mr. Jeff stayed when he was a senator. Over there is the Belmont mansion, and all those columns of gray marble across the street are the entrance to Mrs. Pierre Lorillard Ronald's little home."

"Little?" Laura giggled. "It's breathtaking in size."

"No more so than this one."

Laura turned and stared up at the edifice. The windows were tall and rounded at the top, with an inset column to each side. Unlike the other buildings it sat a little back from the street, with a sweep of stairs leading up to a porticoed entry. The windows grew shorter as the stories climbed, becoming dormers jutting out of the garret-topped roof.

"It's just beautiful," she exclaimed.

"Good, because this is the address."

Laura stood stupefied. "I can't believe it. Mama always claims that Aunt Theda is a penny-pinching pauper."

A glittering landau carriage pulled silently to the curb and a liveried footman quickly helped the occupant down.

"Bother! Bother! Bother!" the woman scolded as she bounced across the sidewalk to the stairs. "It's just utterly impossible."

She stopped short and spun back around to the footman. Her black hair was just too glistening dark to be a natural hue and was fastened into hundreds of little finger curls that bobbed and weaved. Her hard visage softened into a smile that crinkled the corners of her puffy eyes and made the button nose curl slightly at the end.

"Give Mrs. Jerome my heartfelt thanks for the carriage ride home, Reeves. You may stop back for her list in the morning."

He bowed grandly. "It was our pleasure, Miss DeWitt. I'm sorry our stop was not more fruitful for you."

Theda DeWitt sighed and spun her dumplinglike body back around, her face returning to stone again. "Bother! Why should I always be plagued? It just isn't fair. Not fair at all."

Laura stepped forward hesitantly.

"Excuse me, ma'am, but I am . . ."

Theda DeWitt stopped her with a wave of her pudgy gloved hand and then brought it flat across her lips as she eyed Laura and then quickly took in Amos's immense frame.

"A godsend," she gasped. "That's what you are. I'm glad someone can do something right in this town, just once. Bother! They said two weeks. Well, come along! I've questions galore for each of you."

Laura opened her mouth to speak again, but Amos waved her to silence. It would be best to straighten the flighty woman out once they were within the mansion and off the street.

Obediently, they followed the woman up the steps to the front door of the mansion. Amos was looking at the littered steps, the dirt on the leaded glasswork of the door, but Laura's mind was on a family matter. Except for being of a similar weight, this woman was nothing like her mother whatsoever. Her head and face were small, the pointed chin and pouting mouth almost too small for the rest of her fleshy features. Although fashionable, the Russian sable coat gave a single dimension to bust, waist and hips.

They went into a foyer with a marble floor, and from nowhere a dour-faced girl appeared to take the silently offered sable, gloves and purse. Laura and Amos were totally ignored. Then Theda hurried toward one of the many doors opening off the circular hallway and the young girl nearly tripped herself to rush there first and throw the door open with a flourish. Theda sniffed as though she could not stand another minute of such clumsy foolishness and they all went in.

The room in which Laura found herself was like no other she had seen in her life. A soft rosy glow spread itself over everything. After a moment, Laura saw the reason. Everything in the room, right down to the highly polished floor, had been created out of light rosewood or pastel rose-hued fabrics or paints.

Amos was properly impressed by the cut and style of the furniture and decor; it bespoke genteel simplicity and elegance. But for the life of him, he could not repress the feeling that the room could stand a good cleaning.

"Now to business," Theda said smugly. "Names first."

Amos, seeing Laura's slight start, thought it time to set matters straight.

"This is Miss Laura Dahlgren and I am Amos Mobley, who has escorted her here."

Theda smiled and nodded at his politeness. "A woman in my position, unfortunately—and undeservedly—has servants stolen away from her after they have been properly trained. Envy, you know. If I find your credentials to my liking, having a black butler might put a stop to that. And one can always use another maid, my dear . . . Dahlgren? I was unaware the name was in such common—"

Laura's blue eyes widened in mirth and she could no longer hold back a broad smile.

Theda put her lorgnette onto the end of her nose.

"Am I being laughed at, girl?"

"No, Aunt Theda," Laura replied. "I'm Laura Dahlgren, your niece. I have a letter for you from my father."

The lorgnette slipped from her fingers. She had counted

on servants and landed only a relative. But when she spoke, her voice still held out a note of hope.

"And him?" she asked.

"That's a long story, Aunt Theda. I hope that father has explained it all in the letter."

Theda scowled. "Bother! Just my luck. Well, let's have the letter. I certainly hope he isn't one of those runaway slaves. Elma Patterson had three of them working for her and some ungrateful crusader took them all away to send back south. I just won't be bothered with all of that folderol. I have enough problems with that brother of yours living under my roof. If one can call his manner of life living."

Laura's face paled at this unexpected blow.

"Laddie is here?"

Theda DeWitt always prided herself on being able to do more than one thing at a time. All the time she had been chattering away she had been breaking the seal and scanning through the tight little scrawled lines.

"For a month," she said absently, her eyes beginning to water. "An impossible child. An embarrassment to our good family . . ."

Her words just seemed to shrivel and die away. Her hand began to shake as she read through the letter once again. It had been a quarter of a century since Clarence Dahlgren had called her "my dear" or asked anything of her. But she did not question the identity of the author. The tight little scrawl was the same as that on a ribbon-wrapped packet of yellowing papers in her cedar chest. Once it had been her hope chest, filled with the promises of many happy tomorrows.

Lucille had taken away her hope and her happiness. At first Theda had not been perplexed at this change of heart in the man she loved; she would just have to win him back. As a youth Clarence had been little more than a great bounding puppy, needing affection and in love with love. Theda knew that Lucille really couldn't be in love with him—or he with her. It was a fancy that would pass. But Lucille reacted with such bitterness, such hatred, such vindictiveness toward Theda that Claudine Schofield De-Witt had to step between her two daughters.

"Neither shall have the man! Lucille, pack your bags! Your father is taking you to your Uncle Theodore in Waverly!" Then she had softened toward Theda. "My dear, your sister is all DeWitt and you are all Schofield. We Schofield women have always worn our hearts on our sleeves. Give this matter a little time. Imogene Schofield, my cousin in London, would dearly love to have you come for a visit."

Theda had been on the high seas when Lucille talked Clarence into eloping. Her mother wisely kept the news from her. Then her heart was broken twice by a single letter from her father; her mother was dead and the news was out about Clarence and Lucille.

Lawrence Dahlgren was a week old upon her return, but she refused to see either the baby or its parents. As the eldest daughter, she spent the next two years of her life being the hostess in her father's home and seeing to a proper marriage for her younger brother. But when Clarence and Lucille came to call, she was mysteriously out.

Then she could no longer avoid them. Her father, Holmes DeWitt, was dead. They had all been forced to sit side by side in Grace Church.

"My dear," Clarence had said, taking her hand, "I am so terribly sorry."

She had felt nothing. The moment had set her free. For the next twenty years she lived in London, Paris, Vienna and Rome—escaping her terrible empty feeling but never really feeling happy.

And now, five years after her return to New York, the old memories were back to haunt her . . . and the same old words.

"My dear," Clarence had written, "I am so terribly sorry to burden you with one of my family troubles . . ."

"Schofield," she said unexpectedly, looking up from the letter and planting her gaze on Laura. "Should have seen it at once. You have that same natural beauty as my mother's cousin, Imogene Schofield. Of course she used her beauty to get on, and became the Duchess of something or other. Your chances for the same wouldn't be so good, living out with your countrified mother."

Without changing expression or taking a breath she turned to Amos. "From what my . . . my brother-in-law tells me," she said, nearly choking to get the words out, "you are not so countrified, but pose a big problem. What's to be done with you?"

"Amos was only escorting me here to New York, Aunt Theda."

"I can read," she said curtly, "but that hardly answers my question. Well, young man?"

"Briefly, ma'am," Amos said slowly, looking around again, "it would appear that you are in need of some expert help. If you wish to examine my qualifications, I'm more than ready to answer your questions."

Laura was not sure she had heard correctly. "Why?" she stammered.

"Why not?" Amos grinned. "Who would ever think to look for me here."

"But . . . but are you sure, Aunt Theda?"

"Piffle! We'll worry about the problems when they arise. As Laddie has seen fit to take over the whole of the garret, you may select any room on the third floor, Amos. Laura, you will take the room next to my own. That will be convenient so that we can immediately start handling your other problem."

"Problem?"

"Clothing, my dear. Your father informed me that you were being sent without any."

Laura flushed. "There was no time. And my father wanted to get me away before my mother could object to my coming here."

"I know," Theda chuckled. "Isn't that delightful?"

Laura frowned. She knew nothing of the past problems between her parents and her aunt, so the comment struck her as quite odd.

"And Amos," Theda chortled, beginning to see all manner of glorious prospects ahead, "we have a million things to do, as well. A tailor to be summoned—I can just see you in a red velvet jacket and white knickers. And the staff to be met—although they aren't up to my standards at the moment. Tonight, as we are just dining *en famille* you may wear the clothes you have on—though they are a bit snug, aren't they? Oh, I wonder if I can get Monsieur Worth to do your uniforms. There's no question but he

will have to do Laura's wardrobe. Aren't we lucky? He's
still here fitting me for my fall and winter wardrobe."

Laura suddenly grew alarmed at the woman's great
plans.

"Aunt Theda, I should warn you from the start that I
was not sent here with any money for a wardrobe."

Theda laughed, ignoring her concern. "If your brother
tries to borrow as much as a *sou* from me, he is flatly refused. When I offer something, without being asked, I
can be most generous."

But in a way she had been asked. Clarence had asked
her to look after his daughter. Because Clarence had asked,
it had filled her with love and pride. She was needed . . .
she was wanted. At last.

Why not, she reasoned in her own determined way.
After all, this could just as well have been *my* daughter
. . . and I certainly do need a butler!

Theda DeWitt's scatter-brained manner was considered
by many in the know to be a carefully calculated facade.

She might delegate authority within her own home—and
end up with a disorganized mess. But her authority within
the social and business world was exercised with knowledge and skill.

If one lived in New York one lived within its society.
War? What war? From the moment the first gun had been
fired on Fort Sumter, New York had quickly adopted European habits and customs. As flighty as she was, Miss Theda
was the expert in that field. No social event was planned
unless she was given an opportunity to scan the proposed
guest list and grant her approval or cross through a name
with a blue pencil. So infamous did her practice become
that those so snubbed created their own little social circle.
To tweak Theda they had all of their names printed in a
little blue book, with her name included but crossed out.
To show that she had a rousing good sense of humor, she
obtained a copy of the book and sent an invitation to a
gala evening to each and every name in the book. Expecting to rub elbows with the real *crème de la crème*, some
even got out of sick beds to see the inside of the DeWitt
mansion. It was a stunning success, except for one minor
matter. The hostess had been crossed out of the blue book,

so could hardly send herself an invitation. She dined out with friends that evening.

But a name and knowledge cannot give a person the power that Theda possessed. Only money can do that, and Theda let very few know her true worth.

Most considered that she was still living on the legacy left by her father. Lucille still believed it, and resented the fact that her own legacy had had to be squandered paying off Clarence's debts—never considering that the bulk of it was in fact spent building Highcliff-on-the-Hudson. Their brother, Harrison Holmes DeWitt, also believed it, and resented the fact that as the only son he had obtained only a third.

Those who did business with her knew differently. Many was the time when she leaned close to a partner at a dinner table, apparently to make idle chatter.

"Why, John Jacob," she might twitter, "that new law is utterly fascinating. Imagine, it just takes five or more individuals now to secure a charter and organize a national bank."

"And fifty thousand dollars, Theda," Astor chuckled.

"But, John Jacob," she would coo, wide-eyed, "that's only ten thousand dollars per person."

As though that had ended the discussion she would turn and chat for a while with the partner on her other hand. Then, just before the ladies were ready to leave the gentlemen to their cigars and brandy, she would plunge.

"I've just been thinking, John Jacob, that banks should be an institution of service to the people—the people in Brooklyn, Staten Island, Queens—places other than just Wall Street. You may put me down to invest in five or ten such, John Jacob."

She might quietly invest in a company which had developed a machine to sew soles onto shoes, and never once think to inform her brother that he was buying those very same machines for his shoe factory in Boston.

She would invest in America, but do all of her own personal buying from Europe.

7

Laura paused in a moment of indecision before the inner stairway to the garret. It was abject weakness not to wish to say hello to her brother, not to jump at the chance to gain his support before Lucille reached him.

Why should she worry? If Laddie tried to do anything against Amos she could counter with the information she had gained from Wilf Jamison.

She turned away. She just couldn't play at life like the rest of her family. She knew that nothing she might say would make an impression on her brother's conceit. No, she would wait and make her hellos to Laddie at the dinner table.

She walked rapidly back to the second floor hall, stopped abruptly, turning to view the closed doors from one end to the other. She had totally forgotten which was to be her room.

"Anyhow, it has to be one of them," she muttered.

She selected one at random, knocked lightly and waited. Her hand was on the knob to turn it when the door was pulled from her grasp.

Betty, the young Irish maid from the downstairs hall, stood smiling graciously and knowingly. Because she had been so dour-faced before, Laura misread her expression, feeling as if she had been surprised snooping. The girl saw Laura's blush and giggled insinuatingly.

"You found Miss Theda's room quick, miss. I ain't found nothing yet—"

"What?" Laura gasped.

"I'm so busy listing this year I haven't had time to look at last year for you."

Again the girl giggled and again Laura flushed over not understanding.

"You come on in, though."

Laura stepped in and stopped. Once again she was within a room that made her gasp. It was as large as her mother's entire salon, but light and airy. A massive four-poster, with Swiss lace canopy, commanded one wall. A single cream-white color was predominant, with a touch of jonquil yellow to contrast. A living room setting was before the white marble fireplace, and an eating ensemble before the towering east windows. Banks of doors and built-in drawers consumed the south wall. Most of the doors stood ajar to reveal racks of clothing, hat shelves, shoe trees and accessory cubbyholes.

In the center of the white and yellow Persian rug was piled an enormous mountain of boxes and tissue paper, while every available chair was smothered in gowns and fabrics.

"It's the same every year," the girl sighed. "That Frenchman starts delivering the new before I have a chance to clear out the old. It's a whopper task, I'm telling you. Nearly three hundred items have to be listed and put in proper order."

"I . . . I don't understand."

She lifted her laughing brown eyes to Laura. Laura could now see that she was quite a pretty girl.

"It's what Miss Theda will require for this year's social events, miss. It's all planned out in advance like a dinner menu. I usually have help, but we usually have a problem keeping them."

"Do let me help you!" Laura cried. "I've never seen

anything like this in my whole life, I'm afraid. My sister would just go pea-green with envy."

Laura took a gown from the back of a chair and thrilled at its touch for just a moment.

"Hold it up to you, although it's a mountain of goods."

Betty's eyes lingered on the beautiful picture Laura made with the flushed face and tangled ringlets of golden hair falling over forehead and cheeks and white rounded throat. The blue silk was infinitely impressive with her dark blue eyes. It suggested to the maid how startling the girl might be in other than her simple gingham dress.

"You'd be lovely in that gown, Miss Laura," she said with earnestness. "Miss Theda will wear it for Mr. Ward MacAllister's dinner party the 24th of November."

Laura gasped. "You know that, already!"

Betty chuckled. "I know that for forty-five gowns for various occasions, along with the cloak, shoes, hat, chemise and accessories that go with each. Normally, I'm just Miss Theda's personal maid and dresser, but of late I'm more in the kitchen than on the second floor. Bless you for bringing along that Amos. He's already got cook in tears."

"Tears? Why?"

"That man knows his beans, Miss Laura, and he's been given full authority already. Mrs. Blaney don't cotton to taking any order, especially from a negro."

"Oh, I hope there isn't any trouble."

When the girl didn't answer for a moment, Laura's dread increased. Just when things were starting to go smoothly for Amos, he didn't need trouble from a cook.

"The only trouble," Betty said slowly, "would be for Mrs. *Blaney*. She'll talk herself right into Miss Theda's disfavor. That you don't do around here. A body don't have to agree with Miss Theda. A body only obeys her orders." She marched smartly to one of the open closet doors. "And my first order was to find you something to wear for dinner. But that's a challenge. She has perfect taste in her dress, *without* Monsieur Worth, and knows how to wear it, too. But honesty will out—she's plump. And you . . ." She gazed a moment admiring Laura's exquisite figure, then giggled. "For you we could make two gowns out of each of her old ones."

"Those hardly look old to me."

"Seeing as how they're last year's wardrobe, they are old to Miss Theda. Now let me see what might be suitable. As you're expecting that handsome brother of yours for dinner I must make you look your best for him, now mustn't I?"

She smiled with such charming audacity Laura had to laugh.

"I suppose you must," she agreed, "even if he is only my brother."

In ten minutes Betty's capable hands did the work of an hour for any other seamstress. She had selected a blue and green tartan dress that had been Theda DeWitt's costume for a single outing in Central Park. Betty took the dress to a handsome piece of furniture near the north window. Laura thought it was some sort of dressing table until Betty removed the cover and sat down at a complicated-looking contraption.

"Whatever is that?"

"A sewing machine, something that Miss Theda invested in and so they gave her one. It's quite an improvement. Watch me work that treadle and see the needle jump."

"My stars! Look at it eat the cloth right through. Why, you should be sewing up all of her wardrobe."

Spinning about, she handed Laura the garment and laughed. "That's why I learned to use the machine. Her clothes always fit her at the first of the season, but not near the last. The designer always puts in extra fabric for me to compensate for the twenty or so pounds she puts on and refuses to acknowledge until summer time."

Laura looked her straight in the eye in silence and slowly asked, "You really like her, don't you?"

Betty's slender boyish figure suddenly straightened and her expression sobered. "She's done right by me and my sister and our family, miss. I'm with her five years, and am free in December."

"Free?"

"Aye. She paid our way from Ireland and we've been working it off since."

"You can't mean it!" Laura cried incredulously.

"What ever is the matter?" Betty asked slowly.

"Everything," was the quick answer. "That's just as much slavery as what we're fighting over, isn't it?"

Betty's eyes twinkled. "Not when you work for a woman like Miss Theda."

"But the whole world isn't made up of people like my aunt. I've come to look upon any form of slavery as inhuman and degrading to the spirit of man."

Betty looked at her curiously. "I'm afraid I'm not very political. I leave that all to my sister Maggie."

Laura blushed. She realized that she had been doing nothing more than aping the words and thoughts of Marvin Carson.

"I'm not very political, either. But I'm dying to try on this dress."

"Then run along next door and do it!"

"But I promised to help you."

"This will take days and days. You'll have plenty of opportunity to help."

"Are you sure?"

Betty smiled up into Laura's face. "Do you doubt it, looking around?"

Laura danced away, her heart filled with amazement and joy.

Betty's eyes twinkled with mischief as she watched her depart. It was going to be quite fun having such a spirit about the house. Then she frowned. She just couldn't fathom how this girl could be a sister to that . . . that . . .

She crossed herself quickly, so she would not have to go to confessional over the thought she had almost let escape.

"Is that your brother?" Amos asked with a quick intake of breath, lifting his head toward the slender figure rapidly coming down the wide marble steps.

Laura looked up with a frown. "How did you recognize him?"

"There is a resemblance to you."

"Do you really think so?"

A low mischievous laugh was her answer as Lawrence Dahlgren lifted a hand in greeting and stood smiling before them.

"Hello, Laura. And this must be Amos, whose praises

Auntie T has been chanting *ad infinitum*. I'll have a gin and bitters before dinner, Amos—and without the ice. Auntie T is trying to teach me to be continental."

There was a touch of irony in the smile Amos cast at the young man as he hurried away, but Laura was too much absorbed in the striking picture Laddie made to notice. Could this actually be her brother? Her sparkling blue eyes took him in from head to foot as though she had never really seen him before in her whole life. He was a strikingly good-looking man, and to her surprise did not at this moment have the self-consciousness and conceit that he wore like outer clothing while at home in West Point. The high forehead, the thick brown hair that curled at the ends and the straight heavy eyebrows suggested at once a man of business and brains. He looked younger than he was—say twenty, though he had just turned twenty-seven. The square jaw was pure DeWitt and nothing like Laura's own. His smile revealed two rows of white, perfect teeth behind the closely clipped mustache. Only about the eyes did Laura think they were similar, and still, his were a darker shade of blue than her own—so dark they were near black in shadow. A dreamer's eyes, her mother had always called them.

"I needn't say that I'm glad to see you, Laura," he began, with a friendly smile. "The last I heard from mother, I fully expected to see Ruth Ann come popping in, however."

"This trip came up a little unexpectedly."

He looked into her eyes with mischievous challenge. "You're not in trouble are you?"

The question caught her off guard and her mind spun foolishly. Then she recovered her poise, realizing that "trouble" would mean only one thing in her brother's mind.

"No, no trouble."

He laughed, and a shadow suddenly swept his face. He prayed that he would not be stuck with her for the whole evening. He had a party to attend. He would have been more than willing to take Ruth Ann along . . . but Laura was still the baby of the family. Even a visit from his mother would have been more acceptable.

"Well," he went on, "your first trip to New York, I believe. Will you be content to resume a normal life back in West Point after visiting here?"

"I've only just arrived and I'm not sure when I shall be returning—"

"Mother didn't give you a time limit?"

"No, you see . . ." She paused and the faintest suggestion of a smile flickered about the corners of her eyes. The rumors rather than the facts, behind her reason for being there would have greatly tickled his fancy, she realized. But for the moment she thought it best not to let him know about either.

Aunt Theda, dressed in a cloud of pink chiffon, came bouncing down the steps and saved her from having to go on.

"Let me see! Let me see what Betty has wrought," she said merrily.

"What do you think of it?" Laura asked, turning left and right and then spinning all the way around.

Theda shook her head in wonder. "It's remarkable! You are divine!"

"Nonsense," Laddie broke in. "It's a most simple costume. Now, Ruth Ann is the real clothes horse of the family."

Laura was crushed. She had thought the dress most becoming and she loved it.

"Don't pay him a bit of notice," Theda chided. "He's like the males of nature, wishing to be the colorful peacocks and leaving us as the drab hens. Well, just wait until he sees you strutting about in your new wardrobe."

"Wardrobe?" he exploded. "Is that your reason for being here?"

"And why else?" Theda answered for her.

Laddie's sensual mouth tightened. "I've been waiting this whole month for money from home for my business. This is utter foolishness. It doesn't sound like my mother."

"Oh," Theda remarked drily, "I've known your mother to do many foolish things."

Laddie was seldom angry, but now he was enraged. He grasped the banister in a tight grip. "How dare they waste money on you like this! They've lost their common sense. Ruth Ann, at least, could snag a rich husband if she were

properly attired. This, without a doubt, is the most outrageous thing I've ever heard of."

He stormed by them and snatched a cloak and hat from
the hall-tree.

Laura stood aghast, but not totally surprised. This was
the brother that she really knew.

Theda, delighted at his anxiety and anger, stood with
a quizzical smile on her lips.

"Laddie," she said softly, "I wish you would learn to be
more original. Those are almost the selfsame words you
used on me last week when I refused you a loan."

He turned, but the venomous quiet of his voice was directed at Laura. "You've forgotten one little thing, sister
dear. I can have a message wired back from mother before
you can purchase a single thread. When I speak, mother
jumps!"

. Then he slammed out the door.

Laura turned in misery to Theda. "I should have told
him the truth, Aunt Theda, to save you this embarrassment."

Theda shrugged. "Who's embarrassed? I heard the same
tone, the same words from your mother for twenty years.
It's pure DeWitt bluster. Besides, what can your mother
answer?"

That's exactly what was worrying Laura. She would be
ordered back to the castle posthaste.

The milk train from Washington possessed but a single
passenger car and at four o'clock in the morning a single
passenger. There was no one in the train station to pay any
attention to the young man, and had there been they would
never have guessed that nearly twenty-four hours before
he had been in a naval battle . . . and in uniform.

Now he sported what was almost a uniform of another
kind—the Bohemian look of New York: stove-pipe hat,
Edwardian pants of so tight a cut as to leave no doubt as
to his gender, coattails that reached to the back of his
knees, a vest of a vivid hue and an ascotless shirt unbut-
toned to expose his hairy chest.

Because of his attire neither address given amazed the
cabbie. He was quite used to taking young men like this
to Charlie Pfaff's cellar restaurant, on the west end of

Broadway, although it had been much livelier before the war. And to be paid to deliver the young man's luggage to a Fifth Avenue address was quite logical. Only rich parents could afford to keep their young men out of the war and let them go about sowing their wild oats.

But Calvert DeLong wasn't going to Pfaff's just for fun and then returning home later. He couldn't stand to face his father with another lie and so was going right to work.

Four hours earlier, he had left the White House with a new sense of pride and purpose. It had amazed him that Gideon Welles, a Northern Democrat, had taken him directly to a man Welles neither trusted nor wished to be re-elected. But this problem transcended party politics. Calvert didn't know whether he had a full grasp of all his mission could entail. It would take time, and he would have to play many different roles to even learn if the rumor was correct.

The rumor had started at Pfaff's, and that's where Calvert would start. He felt very confident of finding a certain young man in attendance.

At the far end of the cellar, beneath the Broadway sidewalk, there was an alcove, a kind of vaulted cave containing a long table and many chairs. The genial Charlie Pfaff had reserved this spot for the Bohemian coterie for a decade now.

In the early morning hours, two young men sat at the table, but at distant ends.

By midnight Laddie Dahlgren had been quite drunk, but now his mind was back to a point of near sobriety. He was bored. New York was dull. Pfaff's was dull. The young man at the other end of the table was duller still. He could vaguely remember the snide comment he had made at some earlier hour, when he was very drunk.

"Sorry, old lump, but this is not my night for boys!"

It had not been his night for girls, either. It had not been his night for anything but to sit and feel sorry for himself. Why hadn't he been born a *true* DeWitt—back during colonial days and the Revolution, when the De-Witts had real money? And why didn't he have a single cent left in his trousers for another drink? Damn, he was growing too sober and could use another drink. He was toying with the idea of playing with the young man's affections to gain a drink out of him when another young man entered the cellar and gaily ordered a drink from the barkeep.

"No one," Laddie mumbled grimly to himself, "should be that jolly at this hour."

As though he was at last being recognized, the table companion perked up. "Did you speak?"

Laddie was just preparing to say that he had, and let it go from there, when the man at the bar turned and Laddie recognized him.

"Not to you," he said rudely. He turned back to the bar and began waving. "Callie, Callie-boy, is it really you? Come, join me!"

Calvert grinned broadly. He slipped into his role as the wealthy and carefree nonconformist as though on cue.

"How is your hand fixed, Laddie?"

Laddie roared. Cal DeLong always put him in a good mood and had a bottomless pocket to buy drinks.

"It's not about a glass or anything else of equal size or interest."

"Gin and bitters, coming up."

"Oh, Callie, you remembered. How remarkable."

"That's not the only remarkable thing about me, as you should remember."

Laddie snickered and his table companion rose in a huff. He glared at Laddie, as though he had been made a fool of, and flounced out. That made Laddie roar all the louder. The poor sap couldn't know that Calvert DeLong was all tease and no action.

Laddie knew that for fact. The DeLong family lived next door to Theda DeWitt and he had first met the young man on that social plateau. It had utterly amazed Laddie to run into him at this social level. Calvert had been his companion on many tours of inspection of every watering hole and dive in the city. His quick wit and brilliant mind were a constant diversion. He was cool and self-possessed and it delighted Laddie to be near him. But he was also a disappointment. Calvert seemed content without lovemaking—with either gender. Laddie could never get him near the flat he had let before he moved into Theda's. He could never get him near any of the parties he attended.

There was never a moment when he could catch the challenge of sex in a word or attitude. The only thing Calvert would do was tease about it. And the only time Calvert would grow gloomy and stop buying drinks was when he and some of his wilder friends would start discussing politics.

That, also, had been how Calvert had planned it. From the first he had watched Laddie with the utmost caution. The first sight of his handsome face at Miss Theda's dinner table had convinced him of Laddie's boundless vanity. And beneath it, he was certain there was a streak of something cruel. He would have liked him instantly but for this. His vanity he could forgive, and his character was a study of which Calvert never tired. Laddie strangely distressed and disturbed him, however, and this kept piquing his curiosity. How could a war hero say and do some of the things that Laddie was constantly saying and doing? But that was one of the things that had brought him back to New York.

"Here's something to wrap your hand around."

Laddie made a face. "Hardly what I had in mind."

Taking a seat, Calvert laughed with glee. "Someday I'll surprise you by putting something different in your hand."

"And it will have a big price attached to it, too, I'll bet."

"What does price have to do with it, when you decide that you've been missing out on a few things in life?"

"Are you being serious?" he asked in surprise.

"Yes. Laddie . . . I . . . I've been . . ."

He took a swig of his drink and hung his head.

"Yes. . . ?" Laddie prompted, his heart beginning to beat with excitement over what he expected him to say.

"They booted me, Laddie. Kicked me right out of the service. They're out to hand the rest of this war to the South on a silver platter and I just don't care. Always did think it was a farce. Now I don't give a damn. I want to enjoy myself. I want to have women. I want to have . . . anything . . . that is fun. You've got the right friends, Laddie. When's the next good party?"

It was not exactly what Laddie had been hoping for, but it was a vast change, and welcome for two reasons. Yes, Laddie did have the right friends and some of them would be more than happy to hear about Calvert's com-

plaints about the navy. But his new sexual interest Laddie
would keep quite to himself for the moment.

"You're in great luck. This weekend, none other than
Mrs. Pierre Lorillard Ronalds is giving a gala costume
ball. I'm sure I can get our names on the list through my
Auntie T."

"I don't know. I was thinking of something—"

"Tut! Tut! That's only the beginning of the evening. I
will personally select those who will party afterward in my
humble abode. Eh?"

"What's to do in the meantime?"

Laddie looked at him quickly with new interest, pressing his hand with a lingering touch.

"How about making the rounds like we used to do?"

"Fine! And it's all on my discharge pay!"

"Then we're on!" he cried with a joyous wave of his
arms.

Calvert sat back, grinning broadly. This had been almost
too easy. He had played on Laddie's vanity like a finely
tuned instrument. The costume party was perfect. It gave
him several days to be his old self with Laddie, teasing
him to tautness. In his twenty-four years no man had ever
touched him, and he was certain that if he lived to be a
hundred no man ever would. But under the pressure of
such desire, Laddie would have no choice but to link
Calvert up with the men he really sought to learn about.

He had thought to use Laddie for one purpose alone—
for making contact with the rapid-fire New York grapevine
system to spread the news about his untimely discharge.

Laddie would be much more useful—if he could keep
him drunk enough.

8

"IMPOSSIBLE," ADRIAN WORTH CRIED, fluttering his hands up to underscore his feelings on the matter.

Theda smiled courteously, but did not reply. Amos studied her through narrowed eyes. She was not winning the man over. Then he studied the Frenchman. His reddish sandy hair lay thickly about his narrow head, and his slate-gray eyes, so dark and penetrating, were at the same time aloof and cold. He wore his intransigent and perdurable attitude like a cloak.

"Nothing is impossible, monsieur," Amos said quietly, in fluent French.

"What is this?" Worth squeaked. "You allow a servant to correct me, and in my own tongue?"

"Amos is quite right, Adrian," she said. "Impossible? Why is a costume gown impossible?"

"Because Adrian Worth says it is impossible!"

"And who are we to question you?" remarked Amos, still in French.

Laura, who had been gloomily staring at the gray day through the windows, turned abruptly and stared at Amos as if seeing him for the first time. The man was utterly amazing. They had not been there a full day and he was already acting as though he had full command—and was speaking French.

"I don't mean to cause trouble," she said. "After all, I may not even be here for the ball."

"Nevertheless," said Amos, in a hard voice, "the wardrobe is something that Miss Theda wants for you, Laura. Just as she wants my uniforms to be designed by the man."

Worth's eyes remained on Amos, indomitable and relentless.

Theda, in her annoyance, wondered if she had made a grave error. The day had already been impossible enough as it was. Her breakfast cooked by Amos, because Mrs. Blarney refused. The scathing telegram from Lucille, sent to her and not Laddie. The ugly little scene with Laddie over his drunken arrival home at the breakfast hour. Perhaps she should bow on the request for the ball gown. After all, if Lucille did go through with her threats, Laura might not be with her by the weekend.

"I don't mean to cause trouble," Laura repeated. "If it is a matter of time, perhaps Betty could make over another gown for me, as she did this one."

Adrian Worth stared with great amazement. Then he burst out laughing, his thin face becoming scarlet with mirth. "That the great Adrian Worth utterly forbids. No one has the right to alter his creations for a body other than the one that they were designed for."

Theda gasped, and appeared shocked and affronted.

"Adrian, don't be absurd," she said. "Once I have approved them and paid for them, then they are mine to do with as I please."

"I will not have them bastardized!" he snapped.

Theda's eyes grew flinty, her mind business-sharp. "All right," she said calmly, "then the matter is settled. Amos, you may tell Betty to start repacking my wardrobe for this season. I have just decided to disapprove the whole lot."

Worth was incredulous. "But you cannot do that, Mlle. DeWitt. I have twenty thousand American dollars invested in that collection."

"Had!" Theda corrected sharply. "No approval, no pay! That has been our agreement for five years—five years in which I have been personally responsible for building your clientele and bringing you yearly from Paris."

Adrian Worth was quite accustomed to having to fight certain stubborn clients over certain gowns or accessories. He knew how to put a sudden stop to her ridiculous behavior.

"As you wish," he said gently, "but I question what you will now wear during the coming social season."

"Adrian Worth originals," said Theda, trying to keep the mirth out of her voice. "In the cellar I have barrel after barrel of five years' accumulation."

He laughed contemptuously. "But they are out of style, my dear woman. What will the world say?"

"What do I care about your world, monsieur? This is New York! Do you really know the people that you dress? I set the styles here by wearing *your* gowns. If I resurrect something that is five years old, then every seamstress in this town will be working her fingers to the bone to tear apart your originals and copy me before the next event."

Above all else, Adrian Worth was a realist; the woman could ruin him.

"You are a tyrant, Theda my dear," he said without malice. "But with the time given me, the costume gown will have to be most simple."

"Forget that for the moment." She paused. A profound silence filled the room. Amos was smiling faintly, and examining the fright that was creeping over Worth's face. Laura, embarrassed and confused, looked at the floor, her lips trembling. Theda was letting a sudden inspiration develop in her mind. She wondered why she had not thought of it that morning when reading Lucille's wire. It was the most perfect way in the world to spite her sister—and endear herself to Clarence.

"And now," she continued, with a knowing smile, "I also wish for you to forget all talk about a basic wardrobe for my niece." Worth nearly fainted; Amos was puzzled and Laura crestfallen. "No, I now desire for her a *full* social wardrobe. I have just determined that I shall make her the *prima* debutante of this season."

Worth looked up now and regarded her with a derisive and mocking look.

"Your idea is charming, to say the least, but that will mean a delay of my return to Paris and cost considerably. Can you afford to make a lady out of a country ruffian?"

Theda's face turned livid. She drew in her little mouth until it was a malignant pout. Had the man not sounded so much like Lucille DeWitt Dahlgren she might have handled the matter more economically. But now she was on a rampage.

"You have a blank check," she said with venomous calm. "Hire all the women you deem necessary. Dress Laura and Amos as you have never dressed anyone before, but don't let me see your face. You suddenly sicken me. Everything will go through Amos—approval and payment."

She was quickly onto her feet and marching away. "Come, Laura. We'll talk to Betty about your ball gown. I've just had a marvelous idea. I didn't live in Europe twenty years for nothing."

"Well," Worth huffed, in the face of Amos's fixed and steadfast silence. "What ever got into her?"

Amos drew a deep breath. "Sometimes," he said, very quietly, "scoundrels push a lady like that just a little too far."

Adrian Worth bowed gravely and profoundly to him, as if he were an equal in station and color and importance. He knew he would not be able to pad his accounts with this man peering over his shoulder. It would be to his advantage to create as he had never created before.

There was great consternation in the Ronalds mansion. On the next evening was to be the gala costume ball, yet shortly after Adrian Worth had delivered Mrs. Ronalds' costume that morning—and dropped a minor bombshell— all decorating had ceased.

Now Mrs. Pierre Lorillard Ronalds was closeted in her bedroom with Leonard Jerome.

The servants were aghast at that; some even considering posting their notices. Among themselves they could snicker about her coming to the attention of a man notorious for his scandalous love affairs; but this meeting was hardly discreet. Jerome had come running at her first wail, and had blatantly left his glittering carriage in front of the mansion door.

"It's all your wife's doing," she moaned. "I saw Theda DeWitt come home in one of her carriages the other day. Your wife is jealous, Jerome, because she is not having the first social event of the season—and that fat cow has played right into her hands."

The tall, dark man blew out his cheeks so rapidly that his enormous walrus mustache stood straight out and quivered.

"Lovey, you're being unreasonable," he said gently, with a sweet smile and patient air. "My wife is planning nothing more than an affair centered around our three daughters."

He was the only person allowed to call her anything other than Mrs. Pierre Lorillard Ronalds. Being the "second" Mrs. Pierre Lorillard Ronalds, it was a strong point with her. Not even her husband was allowed to call her by her given name. New York had been stunned when Pierre Ronalds had chosen this florid, red-cheeked, black-eyed young woman—nearly twenty years his junior—as his second wife.

"Then *you* are being unreasonable," cried Mrs. Ronalds, advancing menacingly upon him. "Damn it, I worked hard to become the belle of last season. I should have the glory of this first affair."

"And who is denying it to you, lovey?"

She glared at him furiously, as if he were an idiot and not a man worth over ten million dollars.

"Let me spell it out one more time, Jerome. It's not only your wife's party, but Theda plans on introducing some niece of hers at *my* ball. And they are not allowing Adrian Worth to do her costume or learn anything about it. They want to take the spotlight away from me at my own expense."

Leonard Jerome sighed. The woman was still such an amateur in putting together a great party—except when it came to a party for two.

"I can't understand your fears. Will your costume not be the hit of the evening, no matter what? Worth has always made the hostess look the focal point of her own occasion."

"You may know Wall Street, Jerome, but you don't know

men like Adrian Worth. I've a sneaking hunch he has sold my costume design as 'Music' to Theda DeWitt."

Jerome chuckled. "Then I would strongly suggest that you slightly alter it without the man knowing."

"To what?" she pouted.

"To anything that will make this girl look like an over-dressed washwoman—although I really doubt that Worth has given Theda the same costume. Or, for that matter, that Theda would risk embarrassing her niece."

"But all of my decor is centered around that costume. Oh, for two cents I'd invite in the riff-raff just to spite Theda DeWitt and her arrogance."

Never at a loss in any situation that demanded gallantry, Jerome suddenly had an inspiration. "Perhaps not riff-raff, lovey, but an expansion of the list that Theda approved, shall we say."

"Impossible! The mansion will only handle the number already invited."

"Then we move it. The second story of my stables is empty and could handle a thousand or so. I'll send over servants to gather up your decoration and you get your people busy on changing the locale and inviting whoever else you wish. It will require a slight change in theme, however."

"Yes," she giggled, striking an attitude of exaggerated inspiration. "And I have it!"

She cuddled onto his lap and whispered in his ear. And he burst into raucous laughter. "Outrageous! But I love it!"

He slipped his hand under her wrapper and began to caress her thigh.

"Now, Jerome," she chided. "Don't we have a lot of work to do?"

"Later . . ."

She rose and started leading him toward her bed.

"Oh," she said, as she slipped out of her wrapper and stood before him nude. "What about the cadets?"

"What cadets?"

"Pierre made arrangements for a hundred from the academy to come down and stand around like wooden soldiers."

"To hell with them! Let's just be thinking about *my* wooden soldier!"

* * *

The next morning the DeWitt household underwent a crisis of its own.

It had been a frantic few days. Adrian Worth had been constantly in and out for measurements, fabric selections and fittings, as well as money. He had twenty women in Brooklyn sewing night and day. Betty had been sewing night and day as well, and was very happy doing the thing she loved the most. To avoid Adrian at all costs, Theda had been spending most of her time with Maybelle Jerome at the new palace Leonard had built his family on the corner of Madison Avenue and Twenty-sixth Street. The debutante ball for his daughters was to celebrate the opening of the palace.

Laura was pulled between fittings for Adrian and Betty, and was nearly exhausted. Laddie took all of the activity in stride. He had not heard from his mother, but was too busy with Calvert DeLong really to worry about it. He had not worried about going to his blanket and uniform factory in days.

Busiest of all was Amos. Everyone was beginning to rely upon him for everything. He was getting very little time to do the one thing he most desired to do—hire more staff. He had just about decided on a mother and daughter for cook and kitchen girl when the front door bell rang again.

"No respect! No respect!" he muttered, having quickly picked up Miss Theda's habit of repeating everything. "Don't these white folk know that servants are supposed to come to the back door?"

He saw the uniform on the man at the door and started.

"I am Cadet Captain Fremont Hunter. Please inform Miss Laura Dahlgren that I am here."

Amos heard the voice, and nothing else. It seemed to fill all the air about him, and he tensed in sudden apprehension. This was the voice of the man who had taken Miss Laura away from Clinton Bell's shed. He had the oddest impulse to pull the man inside and throttle him. Amos composed himself.

"Would you kindly be stepping in, Captain. I'll inform Miss Laura of your presence."

Fremont was impressed. The butler's manner, carriage

and voice were refined. British trained, he thought. As a youth he had been used to negro butlers in black broadcloth suits and string ties, but this man was immaculately turned out in blue serge morning coat, striped vest, gray trousers and spats.

Fremont was also duly impressed with the mansion. He had always considered the Hunters' South Carolina plantation, Hunter Hill, to be graciously beautiful, and the Hunters' Charleston town house was a thing of unequaled elegance. But this residence reeked of boundless wealth and sophistication. It was a far cry from the taste of Lucille Dahlgren and her Highcliff-on-the-Hudson.

Flushing deeply and hastily brushing away one or two thread ends which remained on her bodice, Laura came hurrying into the parlor.

"Laura. How prettily you're dressed," said Fremont, beaming at her affectionately. "And how glad I am to see you again."

"Hello, Fremont," she murmured, almost inaudibly.

"I've just come from the academy. A hundred of us are in town and have been given some free time for sightseeing. Miss DeWitt's address was given me by your mother."

Laura was silent. The beating of her heart did not subside. She had the strangest notion she should be fearing this unexpected visit.

"See here, can't we sit? I've a million things to tell you. It seems years that you've been away."

Laura nodded, indicating the settee for Fremont and placing herself, straight and rigid, on the very edge of a Queen Anne chair.

"Well, first, your mother is a little upset in not having heard from anyone in this household since your arrival."

Laura's color increased with sudden distress. She knew that to be a bald-faced lie, but one that Fremont might not be aware of. She said nothing.

"Your father sure got you away in a hurry. Colonel Beetle was furious. So was that bounty-hunter, Wilkins. Is it true that the nigger got away without anyone seeing him?"

"I don't know," Laura murmured.

"Now what in the devil is wrong with you?" Fremont asked, leaning on the arm of the settee and scrutinizing her closely. "You're usually so full of life and chatter."

"I have things on my mind. I'm right in the middle of a final fitting for tonight's ball gown."

"Would that be Mrs. Ronalds' ball?"

"Why, yes, how did you know?"

"Know?" he chortled. "That's why I'm in town. I have my dress uniform out in the . . . Oh, Lord! I forgot I have a hansom waiting! Laura, may I presume upon your aunt's hospitality to change here before the ball? It's all your mother's fault, anyway. She convinced Colonel Beetle to put me in charge of this little affair. Oh! I'll be right back."

"But I . . ."

It was too late. He was gone and the front door slammed shut. Before she could start sorting out the situation the door slammed again and he was back.

"I left it in the foyer. Your aunt's man-servant can tell me later where I might change. That is, after I've asked her permission."

Laura smiled to herself. That was the first real kernel of information she had gained from him. He didn't suspect Amos.

"Now, back to us. I'm gaining the distinct impression that you are angry with me for some reason."

"Angry!" she exploded, unable to retain her calm any longer. "I *should* be *livid* with rage at you, Fremont Hunter. You had no right, no right in the world, to bring that Colonel Beetle into the matter. You almost got me arrested."

"Oh, that's absurd, Laura. The man is an idiot. I did it all to protect you from that nasty Wilkins man and the even nastier tongue of Nettie Rivers. You did leave yourself open to a bit of scandal there. I can't even get Clint to talk to me, he's so ashamed."

"Oh, no! That was foolish of me to leave all the burden on Clint. I bet Nettie has been just horrible to him."

"I don't think he gave her a chance. He moved the same evening you left town."

Laura looked up. Her face was white and deeply troubled.

"Moved? Where?"

"Rented a room from the Carsons. That's another thing your mother wanted me to—"

Theda DeWitt burst into the room. She stopped and gave Fremont a rapid inspection. She laughed lightly and musically. "A uniform always does bring out the best in a man," she commented in her sweet and trilling voice. "Do I get an introduction, Laura?"

From that moment on Fremont used every ounce of polish and grace to win approval from the woman. He was good, he was very good in acting the perfect gentleman. For the moment, the true mission Lucille had sent him on was forgotten for through Theda he saw a new force that could help him further his own personal mission.

"Now there is a real man," Theda later commented as Betty was putting the final touches on Laura's ball gown. "The type of man you should set your cap for at once."

Laura began to laugh. She could not stop. She fell back on the bed, in uncharacteristic, nearly hysterical mirth. And Theda stared at her, affronted.

This particular use of the stables failed to win the unreserved approval of Maybelle Jerome. But even stables, in the world of Leonard Jerome, were far from common. The stalls were lavishly adorned with black walnut paneling, plate glass and rich carpets. On the second floor the great hall, by the use of thousands of dollars of floral decorations, had been transformed into "Old New York." Because Leonard Jerome was a generous patron of young, beautiful singers, actors, actresses and musicians, he had personally added them to the guest list to retain Mrs. Ronalds' "Music" motif, although it was now the provocative musical era of the previous decade. Everywhere one turned was to be seen the recreation of a Jenny Lind, a Lola Montez, a wide parcel of nearly nude Maria Bonfanti costumes from *The Black Crook*—and the duplication of almost every character out of P.T. Barnum's Museum.

The beginning of the party was unusual in many aspects. No one stood at the stable doors to check or receive invitations. Through the stables and up the wide stairs the superbly costumed guests were flanked by rigidly erect and staring cadets. The only rhyme or reason for their presence was the display of their new dress parade uniforms, designed by Adrian Worth and paid for by Pierre Ronalds for the occasion.

No hostess greeted the guests at the top of the stairs—just two immense fountains, one of which spouted champagne and the other *eau de cologne*. Because the stable stretched for a full block on Twenty-sixth Street, two raised orchestra areas had been built, one at each end. Neither was to let its music carry to the center, where culinary marvels abounded on ten buffet tables.

Mrs. Ronalds sat fuming in an ante-room. She was not about to expose her costume until Theda DeWitt had made an entrance with her bumpkin niece.

Theda was a half a block away in the huge building of red brick faced with marble, made unique by a steep mansard roof, tall windows and double porches of delicate ironwork fronting on Madison Square Park.

"I cannot believe what I've been seeing," Mrs. Jerome wailed. "All of New York must be arriving at the stables—and many so common that they're actually afoot."

"Now, now," Theda soothed, "it will not be a reflection on you."

"I should say it will not be! While that woman is making a monkey of herself and my husband, my maids will be packing. I've already sent word to the dock. Until Leonard comes to his senses, the girls and I shall remain in Paris."

"But the girls' coming-out party," Theda stammered.

"Give the date to someone else. After tonight I would be too ashamed even to admit that they are his daughters."

At the moment Theda thought the woman was totally wrong in what she was doing. Later that night she wouldn't think so, but at that moment her only concern was to get Laura to the ball.

"That's my entrance music," Mrs. Ronalds gasped.

"And past time for you to make that entrance," Leonard Jerome said darkly. "There are already over five hundred guests gathered, lovey—from the Devil right down to three Daniel Websters. The DeWitt carriage is still up at the palace, so to hell with Theda and my wife."

"But shouldn't I stand on protocol and let the debutantes be introduced first?"

"After they see you, lovey, there will be no protocol left to stand on. Go to it!"

It had not been planned, but the Lorenzo Delmonico supper tables had served as a dividing line between those with invitations before the change of venue and those with invitations after the change.

The group approved by Theda DeWitt was gowned and masked and costumed in fantastic creations by Adrian Worth. It would have rivaled the French court of a century before. The Ronalds and Jerome invitees had attended the function dressed in costumes selected to expose as much of their persons as possible; trunk hose and fleshings and ballet dresses predominated. On that side of the social barrier, there was no attempt on the part of the men to assume imposing or elegant disguises; most of them wore only a mask, and some resorted merely to cheap dominos.

As the orchestras combined once again on a piece that sounded like it was right out of Harry Hill's Concert Saloon, liveried servants scurried around to lower the gas jets on the wall sconces and Leonard Jerome stepped from the ante-room.

He was uncostumed and unmasked.

"Ladies and gentlemen," he bellowed. "Your hostess— Music!"

There was a great gasp as Mrs. Ronalds strutted out to the provocative beat of the music. The loudest gasp came from Adrian Worth, outfitted as a silver-suited and silver-haired Beethoven. All she had retained of his creation was from the head up. And for the moment, because that was all they could see, it was all that was causing the gasps and ripple of applause.

In her hair she wore a harp contrived by Adrian in Paris, illuminated by hundreds of tiny gas jets. Then, as she strode further onto the dance floor and the servants began to raise the lights again, a hush began to surround her. From the other side of the food tables giggles began to erupt, then a few cheers, a spattering of applause and finally a roar of approval as more and more caught on to her true motive.

Fully enjoying the sensation she was creating, she

rounded the supper tables and the crowd pulled back so that everyone would get a chance to see the scandalous short dress, lace stockings, and her feet encased in scarlet boots ringed with tiny bells.

No one on that side of the room had to be told that the boots were *de rigueur* for the prostitutes in John Allen's brothel on Water Street.

Her most recently invited guests loved it. Witty, unconventional Mrs. Ronalds was presenting a sardonic verdict on New York society—all artificial glitter at its apex, all conspicuous vulgarity at its base.

Because she was getting the most notice at that end of the stable she remained there and encouraged the orchestra to continue with a concert saloon sound. Having let her have her whim, Leonard signalled the other orchestra leader to return to a more sedate selection, then prepared to retire for a few hours. He loved arranging a gala affair, loathed attending more than the start and finish. But at the top of the stairs he stopped short.

He nearly burst out laughing. Even in Wagnerian horned headdress and simulated chain-mail gown, there was no mistaking the plump, bouncy walk of Theda DeWitt. But his attention stayed on her advance toward the stairs for only a moment.

"Captivating," he murmured and openly stared at the floating vision behind Theda.

The filtering music, rowed cadets, and lavishness of the surroundings were already filling Laura with a quivering sense of awe and excitement. She didn't have to be told she made a fantastic picture; she could feel it.

Her costume was a marvel of French lace and ivory silk, triple bustled and so widely hooped and weighted by twenty tiers of lace that it was near impossible to make it sway. The tiers were alternate powder blue and white, creating a top and bottom musical staff. Delicately sewn onto the powder blue tiers were hundreds of clefs, notes and rest signs, cut from dark blue satin ribbon goods. The bodice was off the shoulder and cut daringly low—too low and too daring, Laura had thought, but she had been overruled by Theda, Betty and Amos.

Her golden hair had been rinsed in bluing-dye and piled into a curled cascade upon her head. Crowning this at a jaunty angle on the front of her head was a blue satin and lace heart, adorned by white musical notes.

The lorgnette mask was ivory silk with pasted-on blue musical staff, clef sign and notes, the whole notes placed to make the eye holes.

"Sorry, sorry, Leonard," Theda puffed, barely making the top of the stairs. "I've been waylaid by Maybelle."

"Oh?" he said, his eyes still on Laura's ascent. "She isn't with you?"

"No, Leonard, and she won't be. She's in a huff and even wants me to cancel the girls' ball."

"Is that so?" he said absently, even as he started to bow.

"Oh, forgive me. This is my niece, Leonard. Miss Laura DeWitt Dahlgren."

He quickly took her free hand and raised it to his lips. Laura lowered the mask on a note of puzzlement, but not over the kiss. She had always considered it quite phoney for her mother to add DeWitt to her name and it sounded even stranger having it added to her own.

"Captivating," Leonard Jerome murmured again, and rose to look into eyes that seemed even bluer because of the costume accessories. His response was heartfelt—he *was* captivated. "My compliments, Miss Dahlgren. You will capture many hearts here tonight—young and old."

"Thank you, sir." She smiled, which brought a genuine radiation to her face.

"Oh, Leonard, where might I find Mrs. Ronalds? I wish to make arrangements to have Laura properly introduced."

"That, my dear Theda, is a chore that I shall personally handle. And what title, Miss Laura, shall we give to this fetching costume?"

Laura laughed lightly. "They called it 'Heart of the Serenade,' sir."

"They?" He cast a dubious glance at Theda, then re-membered. "Oh, yes, I seem to have heard that the in-sufferable Frenchman wasn't allowed even to know about it."

"Word travels fast," Theda chuckled. "My maid, Betty Duggan, sewed it up, and Adrian will be pea-green with envy."

Jerome grinned, but mainly at Laura. This was now

going to be more fun than he had anticipated. He clapped his hands and called down the stairs. "You, Captain! Bring up yourself and four of your cadets. Miss Laura, if you will wait for them over behind that arbor of flowers I will instruct them and then escort your aunt. Do exactly as the officer tells you."

For the first time Theda began to relax. She might not like what Leonard Jerome did with his personal life, but he was a fantastic showman. Besides, Laura would now be brought in on the arm of the strikingly handsome Fremont Hunter, making a couple that would draw the eyes of everyone in the room.

Mrs. Ronalds had found a wit to match her own in Calvert DeLong, and they were chuckling over the audacity Laddie Dahlgren had shown in arriving dressed as a Paris dancing girl when the music stopped in mid-tune.

Puzzled, she reached out and grabbed the servant who was coming away from the orchestra leader, and demanded to know why the music had stopped.

"Mr. Jerome send me, mum. That's all I know."

Just then, Leonard Jerome called for attention.

"This is quite a night, my dear friends. I have just had the honor of escorting in our own Miss Theda DeWitt."

Polite applause came from one side of the stable only.

"I now have a double honor. A new and exciting young designer by the name of Betty Duggan, truly a New Yorker with a name like that, has created a costume called 'Heart of the Serenade.' Wearing this fetching ensemble, in her New York debut, is the equally entrancing Miss Laura DeWitt Dahlgren."

The blare of trumpets and roll of drums stifled Mrs. Ronalds' furious gasp. Then both orchestras took up a slow-tempoed serenade.

One by one, the four cadets came through the flowered arbor, fanning out in a half-step march until they had formed a double honor guard and Fremont was out of the bower and standing to the side, cool and elegantly erect.

The music swelled triumphantly.

Laura's knees were shaking as she came through the bower, paused and extended her arm to the side. Fremont stepped up as close as he dared without stepping on the lace fringe of the wide hoop. Their finger tips barely touched, but he could feel her trembling.

"You all right?" he whispered.

"Scared stiff," she barely got out.

"Just keep the mask to your face and no one will ever know. Laura, you are without a doubt the most beautiful creature in this entire room."

It was an opinion soon shared by many, not least Leonard Jerome. He hardly glanced at Laura's grand promenade and its smoothness. He looked fixedly at the guests—on both sides of the tables—and saw his own triumph in their envious faces. It was strange, then, that he did not see the pouting departure of Adrian Worth, whose thunder had been stolen by a mere seamstress maid. Nor did he see Mrs. Ronalds' frantic attempt to get servants to help her rid her body of the harp and hidden gas-containers so that she could put an end to this show.

His mind was on the future of Laura Dahlgren and not the past of Mrs. Pierre Lorillard Ronalds. As the four cadets went to select the young ladies he had pointed out to them for the beginning of a quartet waltz around Laura and Fremont, his thoughts had crystallized on one matter.

The gleam in his eyes had been shared by every man in the room—and especially two others.

"Theda," Leonard exclaimed, "she is more than just a DeWitt, she is a masterpiece! But this affair as an introduction hardly does her justice. Wouldn't you agree?"

"Well, I . . ."

"Besides the date for my daughters' ball, what other dates are open on the calendar?"

"I'm really not sure. Why?"

"You leave that part to me, dear woman. You select two more dates, and seventy-five to a hundred guests of such immense prestige that—"

"I want to see you," a feminine voice growled behind him, cutting him short.

"Later, Laverne," he said impatiently. "Oh, there's Lorenzo. Excuse me, both of you. I'll be right back."

Laverne Ronalds stood stunned. No one, not even

Leonard Jerome, was allowed to utter that name in public.

"What are you trying to do to me?" she snapped at Theda.

Theda blinked innocently. "Nothing, my dear, that you may not already be doing to yourself."

Mrs. Ronalds' eyes narrowed to slits. She said nothing, but she would not have the limelight taken away from her without a fight.

Because she was considered the hostess, the servants did as she ordered. They knew better than to go to Mr. Jerome for a counter-order when he was busily engrossed in conversation.

By midnight the stable was crowded, the two dancing floors jammed with people, and the liquor from Jerome's private stock flowing freely. As the "riff-raff" grew in numbers, "society" diminished.

Leonard Jerome saw none of it. An hour before midnight he had approached Theda.

"My wife has just sent a servant for me, Theda. Check with Lorenzo Delmonico on what we were discussing."

Theda was momentarily rattled, but he was gone before she could question him. She had been so preoccupied discussing the course this affair was taking that it took her a few moments to recall his words on a future affair and then find the frenzied restaurateur.

"Pigs!" Demonico was nearly in tears. "Look at these pigs as though my food tables were a trough. I'm going to be sick if I see one more of them cramming it into their faces with both hands. And would you believe, Theda dear, that the food that I was going to serve for breakfast is nearly gone as well. I can stomach no more of this vulgarity. May I escort you out of this madness, my dear?"

Theda hesitated. She had been praying for just such an offer for over an hour, but hated to drag Laura away. On the "social" side of the room, Laura had not missed a single dance. Every time Theda had caught sight of her she had been with either Fremont or a costumed partner—the Devil capturing her more often than even Fremont.

The Devil had her at that very moment. Theda waved until she caught Fremont's attention and called him over.

"Dear boy, Mr. Delmonico has kindly offered to see this tired old lady home. I will leave Laura and the carriage in your capable hands."

He opened his mouth to protest and quickly shut it. He had yet to explain to Laura his true reason for being there that evening and time was running short. The special train back to West Point was due to leave with the cadets at one o'clock. He had promised Lucille that he would have Laura on board.

Even as he was nodding his assent, Theda was walking away with Delmonico.

"Now, Lorenzo, what is it that Leonard is trying to get me to put together?"

The Italian slapped his forehead and rolled his big black eyes as though that was an even greater madness than he had just experienced.

"What are people coming to?" he cried. "Jerome has arranged for a competition in dinners between himself, Belmont and Travers. As they are all in honor of your niece, you are to select the guests and I the menu. Simple! Lorenzo says sure, why not? Bah! Each gentleman comes to Lorenzo and each one demands that Lorenzo make his dinner the best of the three. Each says to Lorenzo, 'Charge what you will, but make my dinner the best.' Lorenzo thinks smart. He says, 'The best are Silver, Gold and Diamonds.' But Lorenzo not so smart. Ha! Mr. Belmont is now Silver, Mr. Jerome the Gold and Mr. Travers the Diamond—and each wants novelties to correspond. Please, dear woman, the dates as soon as possible."

Theda nodded, numb to what she had just heard. Even in her wildest dreams she never would have been able to come up with anything to equal such an opportunity for Laura. Already her mind was putting blue pencil lines through names to cut the possible list down to a hundred. Mrs. Pierre Lorillard Ronalds was the first to be scratched.

Horace and Louisa DeLong had been one of the first costumed couples to depart. They had only come in the first place out of a sense of social duty. As none of their friends were yet aware of the disgrace their only son had visited upon them, they did not want their absence to raise questions and start rumors. But once Calvert was spotted on the rowdy side of the room, Horace had to make excuses for his wife. Nor was he lying. Louisa was indeed sick, sick at heart.

Calvert wanted to tear off his mask and run after them. He might be casting his nation's nets with dexterity, but wondered if seeing his parents suffer so was really worth it all. But there was no turning back. That night had so far been most rewarding. New York had become the center of the Copperhead conspiracy. Everyone knew that men like Samuel F. B. Morse and the eminent lawyer, Samuel J. Tilden, were the conspicuous leaders. It was the inconspicuous, unnamed radical leaders that interested Calvert. He felt he had been put in touch with some of them at the ball and didn't want to ruin his chances.

Laddie was drinking far too much. But as drunk as he was becoming, he still made a strikingly attractive female.

"Party! Party! Party!" he bubbled. "I promised you a party after the party, Callie-boy, and it is time!"

"Oh, Laddie, not yet. We're all going to Pfaff's first."

Laddie laughed. "I can't go like this. I presume the only thing I can do is return to that mausoleum on Fifth Avenue and change."

"No need," Calvert said hurriedly. If the discussion went as he thought it would in Pfaff's, he didn't want Dahlgren along. "You go home and I'll bring everyone along to your party. Who else have you asked?"

He waited while Laddie affected to give the matter serious thought. He was not surprised when Laddie sighed resignedly and said with a humorous shrug: "No one yet."

Calvert winked. "What about that cadet Captain. You always did go for a uniform, and I've seen you try to get close to him all evening."

Laddie giggled foolishly. It was a wonderful joke. He could not tell Calvert that he knew Fremont Hunter, had sat across the table from him that night for dinner and had purposely tried to see if Fremont would recognize him under the make-up and dress.

"Well," he drawled, "see if he will dance with me and I'll try to set it up."

Fremont had been desperately trying to catch up with Laura, but the young swain in the devil costume was successfully keeping her occupied on the dance floor.

He quickly accepted the bohemians' offer of the dancing girl just to get out onto the dance floor and effect a change in partners. His second in command was already giving him a hard time about their running out of time to get to the railroad station.

Laddie bit his lip to keep his smile from broadening. He even controlled himself enough so that he was able to dance soberly and press his body close to his partner. Every chance he got he would grind his hip into Fremont's groin and twist about.

You filthy tease, thought Fremont, fixing a wicked expression on his partner's overly painted face. But she returned the look with bland enthusiasm and great innocence.

You unknowing boob, thought Laddie, his expression becoming more girlish each instant.

"Splendid!" cried Fremont, as they came next to Laura and her partner. "Let's change partners!"

He grabbed Laura away so quickly and roughly that she gasped. "Fremont! What do you think you're doing?"

"I've got to talk to you, Laura, and I haven't much time before the train leaves. Your mother wants me to bring you home with me tonight."

"You must be joking. You told me just a while ago that you were to take me back to Aunt Theda's in the carriage."

"We'll still use the carriage, but only to the station."

"No, Fremont!" she cried, trying to break away from him.

He squeezed her hand hard and pulled her so close that the bustles and hoop were forced up and began to press against her back. People behind her began to giggle at the sight of her petticoats and pantalets.

"Fremont!" she shrieked. "Do you know what you're doing? Let me go! Let me go, do you hear!"

People stopped dancing around and stared. But when Fremont tried to drag her away by the arm, a young hellion grasped her other arm and tried to drag her back.

Laura began crying and screaming at both of them. Two more young men came to the aide of their friend and quickly got Laura out of Fremont's grasp and started racing her across the floor.

"Sir," the cadet screamed, racing up to Fremont, "the carriages are filled and ready to leave."

"Then leave!" he bellowed.

"But sir, you'll be counted as absent without leave."

Fremont was frantic. "To hell with that! Can't you see that I still have to get Miss Laura?"

The only thing the cadet could see was that they were all going to be in big trouble with Colonel Beetle if they missed the train. He turned and bolted.

Fremont tried to break through the laughing and cheering throng. He was not aware that while he was talking with the cadet Laura had fallen and the drunken young ruffians were having trouble raising her back to her feet.

Then a wag had a clever thought. They grabbed her by her hands and feet and swung her back and forth and then into the air.

Fremont's curse was drowned out by Laura's scream as she sailed upward.

The crowd rushed forward to catch her as she fell. They rolled her over, enveloping her head in her own skirts, while ripping away handsful of petticoat material as they tossed her high again. In that split second the game caught on with others. All manner of women were being caught and tossed into the air, including a very drunk Mrs. Ronalds.

The more this proceeding outraged the few decent people left, the better it was liked by the majority. The women were now being bundled onto the food tables and fallen upon by the crew of half-drunken ruffians. They were mauled, pulled and exhibited in the worst possible aspects, amid the jeers and laughter of the other drunken wretches upon the floor. What "society" was left fled.

Fremont was pounded and buffeted back from getting to Laura in the crowd's delirium of excitement. Then he lost all sight of her for a moment.

A strong arm had closed around Laura's waist in her last fall and smartly twisted her onto her feet. In a blur, she saw the fiendish papier-mache devil's mask. The arm stayed about her waist and started ushering her toward the fountains and steps. She knew that he was issuing her orders, but the mask slurred and muffled his words. Then, at the top of the steps, he put the slit of the mask-mouth right next to her ear and whispered.

Laura turned and stared at the mask as though it were

really the devil himself who had spoken. She nodded weakly and let him hurriedly escort her down and out to the awaiting carriage.

"Wait!" Fremont called, catching a glimpse of them. But before he could move a strong hand held him back.

"Who are you calling for?"

"Miss Dahlgren. Please, I must catch up with her."

"You mean Laddie Dahlgren's sister?" Laddie simpered, batting the false eyelashes.

"Yes. I was to see her safely home."

"Then you're in luck," cried Laddie. "She's probably on her way to the party that Laddie is having, and you can be of great service by escorting me to the same place."

"But aren't you already escorted, Miss . . . Miss . . ."

"Call me Landa, handsome. That devil you just saw depart *is* my escort . . . or was."

"Why the cad! I'm Fremont Hunter and I'll be happy to help you catch up with him . . . and her."

Laddie allowed his pleasure and enthusiasm to make his mask-like painted face quite mobile and brilliant for a moment. He thrust out his hand with an affectation of generous if restrained delight. Fremont took his hand and held it warmly. They beamed at each other to seal the bargain. Fremont was enraged that her escort could have treated such a beauty in so outlandish a fashion. He had really started to enjoy being with her and was sorry that he would have to so quickly snatch up Laura and get to the train. She would be highly diverting if he only had had time to stay for Laddie's party. He was under the impression, from what Ruth Ann had said, that Laddie's parties were quite out of the ordinary.

Laddie Dahlgren didn't know who was under the devil's costume, nor did he really care. He was just looking forward to the moment he could reveal himself to this pompous ass. Oh, he could hardly wait until he would have an opportunity to tell his mother and sister about this young man they held in such high esteem.

9

THEY WERE NO SOONER settled in the carriage than the mask was whisked off and he bent over and caught her in a warm and lingering kiss.

"Jehosaphat!" she exploded. "What got into you!"

Clinton Bell grinned sheepishly. "It must be the costume."

"Which brings up a couple of good points, Mr. Bell. Why are you here and why didn't you tell me it was you?"

"There was no place private enough to tell you anything. Besides, everything was just so unreal. I've never seen anything like that in my whole life."

"And probably never will again," she said cruelly. "People are expected to have invitations to an affair like that."

"Oh, I had an invitation, all right, but no one ever asked for it."

"And how did you get an invitation?" she scoffed.

"Listen here, Laura Dahlgren," he protested, "I'm the one who is angry with you, so get off your high horse! You'll never know the horrible mess that you left me in with . . ." He started to turn crimson even thinking about Nettie Rivers and couldn't bring himself to utter her name. "Well, I don't even want to discuss it. Besides, it was Marvin who got the invitation for himself, through one of the servants in the Ronalds house, but this morning someone fired a rifle from across the field and caught Marvin in the leg, so I had to come in his place."

"What?"

"Look, Laura, I'm doing the best I know how to tell you everything. I just need more time. Oh, things have gotten horrible at home . . . I can't just start in the middle about all of this hauling around of slaves." He raised his voice to call to the driver. "Sir, could you drive us around some more?"

The driver shrugged indifferently. He had been paid for the rental of his carriage for the whole night and, if need be, he would drive around for the whole night.

Laura was so choked with rage that she could not speak for a moment, and her round and pretty face turned crimson. She motioned for Clint to watch what he was saying in front of the driver.

"I think we'd better find a safer place to talk," she whispered.

Clint smiled sadly. "You're still at the ball, Laura, with your head in the clouds. The driver is black. I saw Amos hire him this afternoon."

"You've been here that long and didn't let me know?"

"Will you be patient! I had to pick up the invitation from the maid that Marvin knew was sympathetic to his cause. He had seen your aunt's name in connection with this party in the paper and thought it a perfect way to contact you without getting you into further trouble. He seems to have a very high opinion of your shrewdness and your ability to understand a situation. He must be daft."

"I'm sorry," she whispered. Then she tried to turn jovial. "I guess it was the fancy dress that made me act like such a prig. I really do owe you an apology for the last time we . . . well . . ."

"I don't want to go into that," he snapped. "And just to begin with I'll tell you that I am not here because I believe in what Marvin wishes of you. I came to see you and to warn you to stay out of trouble. Besides, Mildred worked too hard on the costume to let it go to waste."

"Am I really in so much trouble?"

"The whole Underground Railroad is. Garth Wilkins has brought in twenty more men to comb every lead from here right on up to Albany. I'm not suggesting that the idea originated with your mother, but there are those who are making it sound that way. Doesn't help any that your father won't say a word about where you are."

"But you found out."

"Not from your father. Marvin found out from Sheriff Addison."

"What is it Marvin wishes of me?"

"I don't even want to tell you, Laura," he said gravely.

"What's the matter with you?" she demanded. "What will you tell Marvin? That you didn't see me?"

"All right," he said reluctantly. "He's given me a list of names for you—people here in New York. People he wants you to contact so they won't try to send anyone up for awhile. The people in Peekskill were so scared that they've moved. That's what frightens me, Laura. You never should have kept Amos with you."

"I didn't keep him, Clint. Aunt Theda gave him a job. You, of all people, should see that was the proper thing to do."

"Does she know the whole story?"

"No, why should she?"

"Oh, Laura, haven't you had enough of other people's problems?"

"Amos is not a problem."

"But all these other people will become a big problem if you do as Marvin asks."

"How can I say no?" she cried, and to her horror, she began to sob.

"One way would be to come back to West Point with me on the morning train. I suppose it means nothing to you that I—that I like you and want to protect you from all of this."

"But Clint, you should want to fight this injustice just as much as I do. None of us is free unless we are all free."

He tried to remain disgusted with her, but could not.

"Laura, I want only to fight for your place back home, where you belong. I more than like you. I want you to be my wife, but not under this cloud you've created with your Harriet Beecher Stowe actions."

"What?" she asked, a furious intensity in her voice. "Is that your bargain? Well, for your information this is the second time tonight someone has tried to take me back home."

"I don't need to be told who that other would have been," he said, on a note of hurt pride. "Would you have gone with him if I hadn't revealed myself?"

"No! And I have no intention of going with you either, Clint. You all seem to think that you can pull me this way and that way like a puppet on a string. I'll go home when my father sends for me."

"In this case your father doesn't really know what's right or wrong for you," he insisted. "*I* know. Now, for the last time, shall I tell the driver to take you home so that you can pack and leave with me?"

She stared at him with cold fury. "You can tell him to take me home and leave me."

"I will tell him to take me to the railroad station," he said bitterly.

He didn't have to tell the driver. The man turned that way on his own. He had never heard two white people fight about his people with such fierceness. It saddened him.

Neither spoke until they were at the station.

"I will have the list," Laura said quietly, but with a note of determination in her voice.

He held her eyes with his own strong and unrelenting eyes, and then quickly reached within the costume and extracted the list. Without a word he threw it at her and turned away.

As quickly as he could, the driver urged the team into motion. It seemed forever before he was back on Fifth Avenue, the back of the carriage now as still as death. To his amazement only the dormer windows of the garret were ablaze with light. He jumped down and ran back to offer up his hand.

She took his hand quickly. Hers was like ice and rigid as steel. He helped her down and stood back. Then he did something he would not have dared do with another.

"Miss, you best figure out if ya'all wantta live for yourself or for others."

She turned and stared at him, her face drawn with misery, overcome with the same thought he had just uttered.

"Yes," she said, and slowly turned to go up the stairs.

Amos was more than pleased with Mrs. Courtney and her daughter Ellen. They had fully taken the burden of the kitchen off his shoulders. As they were not live-in servants, he could still enjoy the quiet, private moments just before dawn. Left alone with his thoughts he could fire up the kitchen range, set the kettle to boil and contemplate the day ahead.

Today he was very contented. Recalling Miss Theda's description of the party, the most cherubic and peaceful smile came over his large face. He nodded, pursed his lips and lifted his eyebrows, as if he was carrying on with himself a most delightful and satisfactory conversation. A noise behind him pulled him out of his reverie.

"Well, now, if it isn't the belle of the ball!" he exclaimed, a look of supreme sunniness on his face. Then he started upon meeting Laura's cold blue eyes and impatient look.

"I've been waiting until you got up to talk to you, to help me decide."

She sat down, touched her disordered hair. Her eyes were tired and her voice dull as she recounted the visit from Clinton Bell.

"So you see, Amos," she ended in a tone of gloomy regret, "Clinton is now furious with me and we really must decide what to do about Marvin's list."

Amos stood quietly regarding her. In his opinion, neither Clinton Bell nor Nettie Rivers had call to impose their narrow views upon others. He wished very much that he could voice his candid views of both of them. On the other matter, however, he could indeed speak with frankness.

"I can agree with Bell on one point, Miss Laura. You shouldn't get involved."

"Amos! How can you say that?"

"Look, I know that you are concerned. But up to this point you've been working only with people that you knew and could trust. These will all be strangers and some you may not be able to trust. You agree with me, don't you?"

Laura, more confused than ever, shook her head. "Oh, Amos," she stammered, her color mounting, "we can't just let them walk into a trap."

"They won't, Miss Laura. The news spreads fast in the underground. But that isn't the point. You were listening with your heart and not your head. As I gather from what you said, Marvin wants you to work with these people in order to keep the slaves in New York. Therein lies the danger."

"Amos, how can you turn your back on your own people?"

"I want you to listen carefully, Miss Laura," he said, in a very slow and purposeful manner. "And measure the truth. I am still a wanted man and you can be held responsible for helping me. I wouldn't want to bring that kind of trouble down on Miss Theda's head. She's been too kind to me—to both of us."

"You're only thinking of yourself," Laura said coldly.

Amos opened his mouth and shut it quickly. He wondered how long Fremont Hunter had been standing in the doorway listening to them. But as he looked more closely at the young officer, his attention was arrested by a strange and penetrating gleam in the glassy eyes. Fremont appeared to be in a state of shock. His dress uniform was awry, as though quickly donned.

"I've been waiting for you," he said dully.

Laura spun about on the chair. "Fremont! Didn't you go back with the rest of the cadets?"

"No. I came back here to wait for you and . . ." His voice trailed off. His head ached miserably and his tongue felt dry and swollen.

"Well?" Laura snapped.

"That girl . . . your brother . . ." Again he paused.

"What about them?"

But Fremont refused to answer this. He frowned, remembering that others had begun to arrive in Laddie's wildly decorated rooms, but not Laddie—and not the carriage bearing Laura and the devil. The girl, Landa, had taken over as though she were the hostess. He had at first refused a drink, but as the time passed had finally accepted. He couldn't recall how soon after that he began to feel most strange, as though he had stepped outside of his own body into a soundless void. He saw the faces of the others as though in a distorted mirror, laughing and jeering at him.

"And that's all I remember," he mumbled, as though he had been narrating right along, "until I woke up."

"Fremont, you're not making a lick of sense."

Amos, however, was not deceived. He had heard the party going on over his head until the wee hours of the morning. The back stairs had been a constant clatter of pounding feet and drunken voices. In his opinion, Fremont was being a fox. He did not want Laura to know that he had made a night of it and in a foxlike manner would now twist and shunt the blame onto others.

Fremont frowned in concentration. He had no proof of the matter, but the mere thought of what had happened made him violently ill. He spoke in an abstracted tone, upon a completely different subject.

"You must hurry if we're to make the morning train."

Laura shook her head wearily. "I am not going to go over that ground again with you, Fremont. My mother had no right to insist upon your bringing me back. And you have no right to keep pestering me on the matter. Now, I wish you would just leave and go catch your own train."

"I object to your tone," said Fremont, with injured severity. "Now, more than ever, I agree with your mother. As a gentleman, I cannot leave you in this house of . . . of . . ."

His stomach heaved. The remembered scene pounded upon his brain harder than the headache. Nude bodies all over Laddie's living room, including his own. There had been something heavy pressing on his stomach. He had painfully raised his head and focused his eyes. The masklike face of Landa swam into view. Then his eyes widened. Her hair lay upon the carpet and her body was that of . . .

He continued, with a note of thin irony, "A house of people who are other than what they pretend to be."

Laura took it as a personal affront. She rose, trembling, pulling her wrapper closer about her as though she had felt a sudden chill. "Goodbye, Fremont," she said, her voice emotionless. "Give my regards to those at home."

"You are going with me," Fremont started to protest, but Amos caught him by the arm and restrained him until Laura was out of the kitchen.

"She'll stay," Amos said with an undertone of warning.

The man's a fool, thought Fremont, with hot disgust and rage.

"Unhand me, nigger! You and that old biddy may be deaf and blind, but I'm not. There's a den of vice in the attic, and a parcel of degenerates. Laura is an innocent and shouldn't be exposed to such creatures."

Amos looked at him with simple and dignified despair. "I will bring your charges before Miss Theda the moment she arises, sir. I was under the impression that Miss Laura's brother was just having a wee party. If it was so disgusting, you should have excused yourself."

"I was doped," Fremont insisted.

Amos turned a ribald grimace upon him. "I will convey that charge as well, sir. Or, if you prefer, I shall go and awaken Master Lawrence and let you make the charge directly."

Fremont drew a deep breath and looked at the butler with stern resolution.

"I never want to set eyes upon him again. As your tone implies that my word is in doubt, I shall voice my opinions in a quarter where they will count. Now, hail me a cab, while I change uniforms."

Amos nodded, knitting his thick black brows. The man had backed down too quickly. He had never intended to bring the matter up with Miss Theda, but now resolved it would not hurt matters to approach Laddie. He was not overly fond of the arrogant young pup, but if Fremont meant to make trouble, then Laddie had best be warned.

Laura heard the carriage in the street and raced to the window. She breathed a sigh of relief to see Fremont depart. Then, without conscious volition, her fists clenched and unclenched.

"Selfish!" she mumbled. "Everyone about me is just downright selfish!"

She threw herself down on the bed and pulled the list to her.

"I bet *these* people aren't selfish, even if they are strangers."

She let her eyes drift down the page, as though to turn unfamiliar names and addresses into friends. Mainly, she was looking for the Ronaldses' address. She was curious to learn the name of the maid who had given Clint the invitation. There was only one Fifth Avenue address and it was not the Ronaldses'. It was the DeLongs'.

Laura sat up on a frown, gnawing her under lip savagely. She had heard Theda mention the name Calvert DeLong in the past few days. But concerning what? And could it be the same man? And if so, how would she go about meeting him?

Two names later, she stopped short.

Had the name suddenly taken on form and emerged from the page, she could not have been more astounded, more taken aback, more shaken.

Then all at once she burst into a shout of wild laughter. "Strangers?" she shouted. "Holy Mother! This one can't be considered untrustworthy!"

She pondered a moment and then sprang from the bed. She began to snatch clothing from the closet and hurriedly dress. Already she was formulating an excuse in her mind for this unforeseen little trip.

There was a sudden pregnant silence in the narrow garret hallway. Amos stood as still as a statue. There were streaks of rough red on Laddie's sallow cheekbones that were not rouge.

"Bastard," Laddie said at last. His lean veined hands clenched on the corner of the door that shielded his nude body from Amos's view.

Amos regarded him fixedly. "Perhaps," he said, "but not a man you can trust with such a secret. What you do with your private life is not my concern, Mr. Dahlgren, and perhaps I had no right to speak at all."

Laddie spoke in a thin whisper, leaning his head far around the door.

"My mother won't believe a word the twit says, if that's his intention. And Laura and Auntie T need not learn of his lies either."

Amos nodded carefully. The fox had had more to bark

about than he realized. There was no question that he
would keep the *truth* from Laura and Theda.

"You have my word, sir."

"Excellent!" Laddie gave him a cunning beam. "And
Amos, for being so understanding, you may come back
and visit me any time—when I am *alone*."

Amos had to clear his throat several times before he
could speak, and even then his voice was thick and hoarse.
"What one is sometimes compelled to do in youth, sir, can
be forgone as an adult." He bowed and turned away.

Laddie thrust out his tongue at the man's retreating
back. He loathed himself for having even made the suggestion, but it had been a horrible night. He was furious
with Calvert Delong for not having shown up, and those
who had dropped in had been totally unexpected and
rather boring—Fremont being the biggest bore of all. It
had started as a whim after Fremont had said he would
have a drink, a whim to make Calvert jealous when he did
walk through the door. But he had made the potion a mite
too strong. It had been like skinning a dead snake—and
remained that way. Fremont had shown more arousal on
the dance floor.

No, he would be able to counter any claim that Fremont
made without a tinge of guilt.

He would have many charges to overcome if everything
rumbling about in Fremont's brain at that moment was
brought into the open. Laddie might be Lucille's son, but
Fremont was not about to take the full brunt of her anger
for not having returned with Laura. He began to include
everyone in his plot—including the butler. And he would
have to include Lucille in the plot, too, to safeguard himself against Colonel Beetle's wrath.

Having convinced himself that he had covered all points
adequately, he stepped jauntily as he boarded the train
and looked for a seat. Halfway down the aisle he turned
back to see if there were two empty seats together. He
had no desire to get into conversation.

"What!" he exclaimed. "Is that you, cousin?"

Clinton had seen him enter and had held his silence.
The last thing he wanted was to have Fremont for a traveling companion. He could no nothing more than nod.

There was a vacant seat next to Clinton, and Fremont shrugged and approached. As he sat he saw Clinton's feverish face and dull sunken eyes.

"What's the matter with you?" he demanded. "You look ill."

Clinton pressed the back of his hand against his burning cheek. "I didn't get any sleep last night," he admitted.

Fremont chuckled. "Good God. Don't tell me my staunch little cousin has been in the evil city visiting Water Street."

"Hardly," Clint answered curtly. He drew in a deep breath. His heart was like a fixed knife in his chest. One evil woman in his life had been quite enough. "I was on business."

"Must not have been very successful."

Clinton scowled. "Why do you say that?"

"Well, just look at you. Dressed as though you were just coming from the foundry. Really, don't you have more pride in your personal appearance?"

"I have other clothing here in my bag."

Clinton allowed himself a reflective and melancholy smile. Wouldn't his cousin Fremont be amazed to learn what manner of clothing he had removed in the men's room of the station?

A silence fell between them as the train jerked into motion.

Fremont smiled boyishly. Clinton had not asked him why he had been in town, but he was certainly anxious to tell him.

"Saw a friend of yours last night—and this morning."

"I know no one in New York."

"You do, but you just don't know that she's there."

"Can't think of a soul."

"I thought you were sweet on her," Fremont murmured sarcastically.

Clinton ignored this. "As you know, with my work hours and pay, I can't afford to keep company."

Fremont, delighted at trapping him, chuckled.

"I suppose it really doesn't cost anything if a young lady comes to your quarters in only her chemise."

Clinton regarded him in brooding silence. His face had flushed. Then he glanced away from Fremont's eyes.

"I take it you saw Miss Laura," he muttered. "I was not aware where she went after that day."

"Oh, she's gone a long way since then. She was the belle of a great ball last night. Every man was after her. Especially a real devil in a devil's costume. You'll never get her back to the country now, Clint."

Clinton quickly excused himself to go to the men's room. He did not want Fremont to see the tears that threatened to run over his cheeks.

Fremont smiled secretly. He would have no more competition from Clinton Bell where Laura was concerned. And he was now convinced that once he had fully reported to Lucille, Laura would be bundled home on the afternoon train.

Contented, he stretched to get more comfortable and his feet kicked something. He dropped his eyes and cursed Clint for not putting his carpetbag in the overhead rack. Then he leaned forward and looked a little closer. The straps had not been pulled tight and an odd shade of red showed through the gap. A snoop by nature, he quickly pulled the opening a little farther apart and stared at the beaked nose of the fiendish mask.

A woman across the aisle cleared her throat, as though preparing to call the conductor.

Fremont sat back quickly, turning crimson. To avoid looking at the woman, he turned his head on the seat and closed his eyes.

Now what is this all about? he thought darkly. And how do I trap Clinton into telling me? And how do I use this as one more piece of evidence in my favor?

He kept trying to sort it out as he listened to the clicking of the wheels on the tracks.

A hand gently nudged his shoulder and he straightened, thinking it was Clinton wanting to get by to his seat.

"West Point, son," the conductor said gently. "You had yourself a nice snooze."

Fremont bounded up, nearly knocking the man over. The seat was empty and the carpetbag gone. He ran from the car and onto the platform.

"I don't believe it," he muttered.

Two feet of new snow lay on the wood deck of the raised platform without a single footprint having disturbed it. It was almost as though Clinton had put his costume to a good use.

At the far end of the train the baggageman threw a bundle of papers off into the waiting arms of Sheriff Addison.

Fremont turned in the other direction. He had enough questions on his mind without having to answer any.

10

THE QUESTIONS POPPING into Laura's mind were myriad. She had taken a dirty, dilapidated stage across Williamsburg Bridge and then had to walk south from Brooklyn's Broadway.

There was no one in the street; everyone had been at their work since daybreak. From the skies there filtered down a constant film of soot, from the fires of the blast furnaces at the shipyards and the tightly crammed-in factories.

The street she sought was short and narrow, the dirt-filmed window panes of the building hardly discernible from the walls.

Outside the main door, Laura could see a little huddle of children, ragged urchins stamping cloth-bound feet, their breath steaming from their nostrils. But her attention was not on them, but on the sign above the door.

"Dahlgren Mills?" she muttered.

For a moment she could not blame Laddie for never wanting to come to work. The depressing bleakness of the place was overpowering.

She picked up her skirt and waded through the slush, past the children and up to the door.

"Ain't open," a thin voice informed her before she had a chance to try the latch. "No jobs today."

She rapped anyway, with half-frozen fingers, chiding herself for not thinking about bringing along gloves. The top half of the Dutch door sprang open.

"No jobs," a beefy-faced woman growled.

"I'm Laura Dahlgren," she said quickly, before the woman could slam the door. "May I come in?"

The plump, ugly woman hid her surprise, but quickly opened the rest of the door. It was slammed and bolted shut just as soon as Laura was through.

"If they can't work they steal," she said, as though that explained everything. "As if there was anything worthwhile to steal around here. Well?"

"Oh! I would like, if possible, to see a Miss Maggie Duggan."

She shrugged and led Laura through a dingy hallway and paused at a steep stairway.

"Maggie," she called, "lady named Dahlgren to see yah!" Then, turning to Laura, she said, "Didn't think he had a wife."

Before Laura could correct her, a woman bounded down the stairs. She appeared to be as plump as the beefy woman, but her face was very thin and finely chiseled. From under a head scarf jutted strands of deep red hair.

"He hasn't," she corrected for Laura, sizing her up through the lightest green eyes Laura had ever beheld. "But from what my boasting little sister says, you'd be the sister."

"Yes, I'm Laura."

"I'm Maggie. You look frozen. Come on up to the only fire in the whole damn place. Bertha Butt, get her a blanket. But don't count on getting too much warmth out of it, because it's a Dahlgren blanket. Oh, by the way, her name ain't really Bertha Butt. We all have to wear so many dresses to keep warm that it just makes her look like a lard ass. Well, come on."

Maggie Duggan certainly wasn't anything like her soft-spoken sister. Laura saw failure in her mission already.

Still, she followed her up the steep incline and through a long room that had plate glass along one side. For the first time Laura became aware of a whirring and thumping noise.

"This is the design room, but as we turn out just a basic uniform and blanket, there's no need to design. In here. It's the room I share with your brother as an office—when he decides to show up. As I said, it has the only stove, and I usually have to bring fuel from home. I don't know what the poor fools downstairs are going to do when it really turns winter."

The room was filled with a piercing whistle the moment they entered. Without comment, Maggie took down from the wall a speaking tube and blew into it.

"Maggie here." She put it to her ear to listen, then spoke into it again. "Then change to any color thread on hand. They're only uniforms and they'll fall apart in the first rain or snow anyway. And Lonnie, I don't care if Mr. Dahlgren does say to use the coal only for the steam engines. Send me up a scuttle—I've got his sister in the office."

Laura looked at Maggie Duggan wonderingly. How had this young woman become the foreman of a uniform and blanket mill? She would expect it of a Bertha Butt type, but Maggie Duggan was different.

Maggie saw the look.

"I was here before your brother bought it," she said. "It was a sailcloth factory, hence the ship's speaker. Times change."

"I didn't—" Laura began, but Maggie held up a silencing hand.

"I know. Saw you were puzzled. Started on the looms when I was fifteen. That's late in this business, but a loom is a natural thing to an Irish girl. I was the most experienced person here when your brother bought and changed to . . . Well, let's just say I'd change things, given a free hand."

"How?"

"By hiring back the older, more experienced hands and paying wages accordingly—and paying on time. Can you smell the shipyards from here?"

"Yes."

"That's how I made the payroll the last two weeks. Selling them the cotton remnants from the cutting tables. Oh, here's Bertha Butt."

The woman draped the blanket over her shoulders like a shawl. It was so thin and light Laura could hardly feel it.

"Don't flex your shoulders," Maggie laughed, "or it will shred to pieces."

"This is horrible," Laura gasped. "How can my brother produce such a thing for our fighting men?"

Maggie smiled a slow, quiet smile.

"It's called profit! Child labor, low wages, cheap materials."

"And no fixing up," Bertha put in, "until the whole place is a danger! Why, since summer, three girls have lost fingers and a boy his whole arm."

Laura shuddered. "Then why do you stay?"

"Where's to go?" Maggie explained simply. "We get paid extra as foreman and floor lady. Bertha's got three at home and no husband. Where's she to go?"

"I see," Laura said quietly.

"Well," Maggie said suddenly, "you aren't here to hear about our minor problems. What is it? A message from his lordship? A report on your ball gown? Slumming?"

Laura hung her head. The anger and shame over her brother was bitter as wormwood. She felt guilty having Theda spend so much on her wardrobe when something like this was going on.

"That wasn't fair of me," Maggie said quietly. "You can't take the burden on your own shoulders, honey. You've got enough problems of your own."

"I have no problems."

Maggie shrugged. "I guess you shouldn't have . . . now that you're out of the undertaker business."

The young women exchanged swift looks. Laura was momentarily stunned.

"I'll save you the question mirrored on your face, Laura. It wasn't hard to put a few pieces together after Carson's man asked Patty Cummings for an invitation to last night's ball. Patty ain't smart, but she reports good. So does Betty, without knowing it. A good butler like that just doesn't fall out of an apple tree."

Laura let out a long sigh. She fumbled in her purse.

"I was given a list and some information to pass on."

Magige took the list and scanned it quickly, frowning here and there at a name.

"There were only two names that I recognized. I came to you first, but didn't know what to really say."

"Now," she said, "we're out in the open, aren't we? Bertha is the Finnegan. What was the other name?"

"DeLong. But I only recognized it as Aunt Theda's next-door neighbor."

"Then you don't know him?"

"No."

"Think you could get to meet him?"

"Yes, but why?"

"This list is quite old, Laura. I don't know more than about four or five of these people. The man who got me involved is now in the army, but he used to speak quite highly of this Calvert DeLong. DeLong used to bring the slaves up the coast in his boat, but I somehow got the impression that he was in the navy now."

"That's it!" Laura yelped. "That's why I recall the name. I heard Aunt Theda and Laddie saying that he was home from the navy."

"Good. Then you will try to meet him?"

"Yes." Then she hesitated. "But we can't send anyone more up to Marvin."

She smiled. "We know. But those we can't keep right here in New York City we can send west to Chicago, and north to Canada through Maine. We haven't even begun to think of the possibilities."

Laura was looking at her with wide-eyed admiration. "Why do you do it for them, Maggie?"

Maggie walked over to the window and looked down on the mill.

"That's slavery too, Laura. Children who should be in school, but forced to work so that their families can eat. And Bertha. That's slavery, too. She was forced to come from Ireland with her two infant children to work off her husband's indenture, because he had run away to the west. It will last, as long as the black slavery lasts. Break the back of one form of slavery and maybe you can break the backs of the other forms. Dear Mother of God, give me strength to see all of those days come about."

Laura frowned as she nodded agreement. She just had to make Amos see it as Maggie Duggan saw it.

Bertha was frowning after Laura left.

"You gone soft? You handled her like she was a little princess or something. And what's this about her seeing DeLong?"

"Bertha, don't be a fool," Maggie said in a low voice of warning. "The girl is just as simple as you or I, but she has a few things that we don't have—Theda DeWitt's money and a personal relationship with Amos Mobley. The one problem we've always had with these black people is the lack of a leader. From what Betty says that man can make worms stand up and march."

"And DeLong?"

Maggie laughed lightly and musically. "I just want to find out if everything Rufus King said about the man is true, that's all."

Bertha wasn't fooled, but didn't comment. If that was all Maggie Duggan wanted to find out, she could have found it out on her own. After all, the DeLong Shipyards were right behind them and Maggie was forever selling cotton remnants to Horace DeLong. No, Maggie Duggan had something else afoot, but Bertha knew better than to pry.

Clinton Bell cursed his luck. Of all times to twist his ankle. He had been a fool to jump from the train as it slowed for West Point. Now both he and Marvin Carson would be laid up with a bum leg. Things would have been much different if Laura had returned with him.

Fremont Hunter was also cursing his luck and blaming Laura for it.

"Not home!" he bellowed. "What the devil!"

Kitty smiled pityingly, as one smiles at an unwanted house guest.

"In Albany on business is all I know, Mister Fremont."

"Blasted luck! Well, I could use some breakfast before going back to the academy."

Kitty had no desire to do extra work with Lucille gone, and especially not for Fremont Hunter. She thought it was a disgrace for young men like him to do nothing more than strut about in their fancy uniforms.

"I'm sorry, Mister Fremont, but Miss Ruth Ann ordered no breakfast prepared until nearer noon."

"She's here? Why didn't you say as much? Go fix breakfast and I'll call her to join me."

He could feel his luck changing for the better. He threw his hat onto the hall table and bounded up the stairs.

Kitty turned slowly, a cunning smile on her lips. She was not about to break the first egg until she saw the actual form of Ruth Ann enter the breakfast room. To soothe the wrath of some of the young cadets who had not been selected for the New York trip, Ruth Ann had graciously hosted two dozen of them throughout the evening—and some into the wee hours of the morning. She was quite sure Ruth Ann was going to be in no mood for anything.

When there was no response to his light rap, Fremont barged right in. He started to call her name and then crept to the bed. Always before, the lamp had been out. Now the dawn was turning the blacks and grays of darkness to rosy pinks.

Ruth Ann was stretched out full upon the bed, lovelier than he had ever seen her before. Her cheeks were flushed and rosy, her face masked with a smile of sleeping happiness. She was at that moment totally desirable—slender-limbed, snowy-skinned, golden-downed . . .

He bent down and kissed the inviting coral lips.

Ruth Ann stretched and murmured. "No more now. I want to sleep."

"But I've just arrived."

Ruth Ann struggled to separate dream from reality and forced her eyes open.

"Where did you come from?"

"New York," he grinned.

"Can't be," she said drowsily. "Most everyone took off in a rush when they heard the train come back."

"I missed it. I had some trouble with your brother and sister and an arrogant black butler of your aunt's—"

"You talk too much. Kiss me like that again."

Fremont did so, then nestled next to her ear and whispered. "Now, do you want to hear all about New York and the ball?"

She shrugged, half-turning on the bed, so she could begin playing her hand over the breast of his tunic and popping the brass buttons through the eyelets one at a time.

Fremont didn't mind. He wanted her in the right frame of mind, and needed time to work up his story before he started making accusations. But Ruth Ann's fingers became clumsy and slow as he recounted the stunning success Laura and her gown had made. She laughed mirthlessly over Laura being accosted and thrown in the air. Her hand was motionless when the identity of the mysterious devil was scathingly revealed. Her heart had turned to stone as he began leading up to the events surrounding his return to Theda's house.

But the coldness suddenly gave way to a more urgent consideration. Over his rapidly spoken words she had heard something, but dared not look. She suddenly reached out to the bedside table and picked up a long pair of pointed shears out of the sewing basket. It gleamed in her hand like a savage knife.

"No! No!" she screamed. "How dare you!"

Before Fremont could react to this unexpected happening, she rolled off the other side of the bed and stood shaking the scissors at him.

Lucille screamed on seeing her daughter's nudity, and put her fingers to her gaping mouth.

Her presence was a shock to Ruth Ann, as well as to Fremont. She had expected no more than the snooping Kitty. Now she had to make her act very convincing.

"Beast!" she wailed. "Oh you beastly man!"

Lucille quickly reached Ruth Ann's side, but she made no attempt to take the scissors. She was looking at Fremont to determine his condition of undress. He rose, paralyzed with surprise, and regarded her sheepishly. He saw murder in her eyes, and a thin icy tremor ran down his hot and sweating back.

As for Ruth Ann, she laid the shears calmly on the bed, and waited with a sweet expression of evil.

"It's not what it appears," Fremont stammered.

Lucille laughed with dangerous restraint. She pointed at the bed pillow. Muttering savagely, Ruth Ann snatched up her nightgown, pulled it over her head.

"Mama, I was asleep. I don't know how he got it off."

"It was off when I came in," Fremont protested.

Lucille turned on him ferociously. "Shut up!" she shouted. "Don't try to lie, you snivelling, foul creature. If Mr. Dahlgren had returned with me I'd have you whipped. Thank God the snow stopped us last night and I had sense enough to return this morning."

"It's not what it appears," Fremont repeated.

"Why, you sneaking wretch!" she said. "Do you think me blind? I can see when my daughter is being mauled and raped. If I had a gun I'd shoot you on the spot and no court in the land would convict me."

Fremont burst into laughter. "Raped? Half the cadet corps could claim that against her—myself included."

Ruth Ann paled and swung to her mother. "What a horrible lie!"

"You don't have to tell me that, lovey. I've thought for some little time that he had a twisted mind, and this proves it. Only a sick mind would try such a deplorable thing. What a vile way to repay our past hospitality."

She was talking as though Fremont were not even in the room. It infuriated him. This wasn't fair. It wasn't fair at all. He would not take such abuse. And he would not have his plot foiled in this manner.

"Vile?" he hissed. "Twisted mind? You, who have produced the vilest creature of all from your womb, have no right to make accusations. Nudity shocks you? Picture my own nudity, Mrs. Dahlgren, and the sick mind and head of your son nestled right next to my most private parts. I leave it to your mind to guess the deplorable things he visited upon my body while I was in a drugged state."

Lucille stared at him incredulously. "Well, I'm damned," she said in a hushed voice. "I can't believe you. Why, Fremont, you're sicker than I thought. Have you also a story you wish to make up about me, or Mr. Dahlgren or Kitty?" She paused. "Where is my other daughter?"

"I'll tell you later," Ruth Ann said sullenly. "Just get him out of here, Mama."

She turned to the bed and flung herself upon it, sinking her head deeply in the ruffled pillows and faking a very convincing wail.

Fremont was truly horrified. He was not being believed.

He backed slowly to the door and regarded them with shocked eyes.

"You've got to believe me, Mrs. Dahlgren," he said in a subdued tone. His face puckered as if he was going to cry. "Oh, it was terrible. He made me think he was a girl."

Lucille said nothing. Then all at once she began to smile. Shouting, she reasoned, only brought about more shouting in dealing with the deranged.

"I want you to leave now," she said quietly. "We are all getting upset and overwrought. Later, we will handle this in a much calmer manner."

"Thank you," Fremont stammered, flushing. "I'm sorry I exposed the truth in such an ungentlemanly fashion."

Now that his plot was again returning to its proper course, he felt he could return to the academy and face Colonel Beetle.

After he left, Ruth Ann pushed herself to a sitting position and spoke as though nothing had happened. "Just wait, Mama, until I tell you all he had to say about Laura."

Lucille gazed steadfastly at her. "When did he have time to tell you so much?" she asked quietly.

"Why, he told me all about the ball and the money Aunt Theda is lavishing on Laura's clothes and even Clinton Bell being at the ball."

Lucille stammered with real horror. "Later, Ruth Ann."

She went from the room as fast as she could. Hardly seeing her way, she entered her own bedroom and threw herself on the bed. Then, abruptly, she rose and fled into the bathroom, where she was violently sick.

She now knew the truth. She felt deathly ill at the thoughts that swam in her head. Trembling, she rang for Kitty. What must be done, must be done quickly. Clarence was not there to protect his family, so she would have to be the tigress again.

"Yes, mum?"

"Kitty, the pony cart is still in the drive. Please bundle up warmly and go fetch Colonel Beetle. Wake him, if you must, but I must see the man at once."

Then she stood for many minutes gathering her thoughts. When she was quite sure that she was composed, she marched back to Ruth Ann, gathered her up into her fleshy arms and cooed, "Now, my little darling, tell mother all about it."

She listened for almost an hour, puzzled and frowning on some points, smiling with delight over others.

"Interesting!" she whispered, her watery eyes narrowing. She stood up slowly, and walked toward the window. "Interesting!" she repeated as she looked down upon the return of Kitty with the colonel.

"What are you going to do about Laura?"

"For the moment, nothing."

"That's not fair," Ruth Ann pouted. "Why should she be having all the fun while I'm stuck here?"

"All the fun?" Lucille echoed mockingly. Then she sailed from the room.

"How long?" Lucille asked, her voice faint and abstracted.

Arnold Beetle sat back, folding his hands across his expansive belly until he looked like a pleased Buddha.

"A matter of degree," the colonel murmured deprecatingly. "An investigation. A board of inquiry. Review by myself."

"How long?" she echoed on a quaver, not removing her dilated and shining gaze from Colonel Beetle.

"He's not the only cadet who broke the bed-check rule, Lucille, although he was far later than the others. Normally, with a record like his it would only be a demerit. But your . . . ah . . . information would settle the matter posthaste."

"No!" Lucille gave him a murderous scowl. "The scandal would ruin her forever. How would you like your own daughter branded for life? There must be a way of punishing him without risking her reputation."

"I couldn't agree with your reasoning more," said Beetle in a soothing tone.

Lucille gave an impatient and irritated shrug. "Then what good is any of this? Not that I'm ungrateful for your time; I'd be an uncaring mother if I were. But a slap on the wrist?" Her lip curled with contempt. "He was trusted in this house, as you well know. Trusted even to bring my other daughter back from where her father had her hidden,

a job he botched by allowing her to be taken from the
ball by another. Knowing he had erred badly he proceeded to get drunk and then made a most obscene approach toward my son. The man is twisted. I do believe
that because my Laddie thwarted him he came to take it
out on my dear Ruth Ann."

"Approach?" he questioned, with a twinkle of delight,
and moving his round fat mouth in an expression which
Lucille found as obscene as the conversation.

"What would that have to do with it?" she asked with
increasing impatience.

Colonel Beetle put a plump finger to his temple and
tapped. "The difference between a slap on the wrist and
expulsion from the academy."

"What!" exclaimed Lucille, sitting up straighter.

Colonel Beetle started laughing, turning purple with
his mirth. It would be a marvelous revenge for the way
Fremont had made him look the fool in Washington. It
would go a long way to prove the point he had made to
defend himself: the cadet had to be a Southern sympa-
thizer and spy and had used that occasion to embarrass
the whole academy. He regarded Lucille merrily. "It may
surprise you, my dear, to know that that is an offense that
is held above and before all others. Your son, of course,
would have to come up to give his testimony."

Lucille slowly sat back, a new worry wrinkling her
brow.

"No one will know of it but the board," Colonel Beetle
continued. "I will personally select five very discreet officers, I assure you. And Hunter will not know, Lucille, for
he will be confined to quarters from this day until it is
finalized. I would say three weeks at the most."

Lucille was speechless. She stared at Colonel Beetle
unblinkingly, but with a new cog beginning to slip into
gear in her brain.

"What can Laddie expect for doing this?" she asked
bluntly.

Beetle was no fool. Without the verbal testimony of
Lawrence Dahlgren there was no case against Fremont
Hunter.

"The new Worth uniforms are most becoming," he said,
as though purposely changing the subject, "but a hundred

such uniforms do not cover the backs of eight hundred on parade. I'm sure that your son and I can come to an agreement on the contract when he comes up to the academy."

"Colonel Beetle," she said solemnly, "allow me to thank you for this kind service."

"My pleasure," said Beetle, repressing a glower. He took her hand and kissed it before bowing his way out.

After he had left, Lucille's spirits fell to a depression. She paced back and forth, up and down the room, chewing her lip. She had to get Laddie home secretly to make sure his story against Fremont was airtight. That meant that she could not insist that he bring Laura back with him. No, it would be best to leave Laura with Theda for the moment. Ruth Ann would just have to weep and wail. She didn't want Laura's problems complicating this. She was thankful that Colonel Beetle had not raised the point. It was a shame that Theda was wasting all of that money on the wrong daughter, but that matter could be dealt with later. Ruth Ann and Laura were of roughly the same size and she would just make Laura turn the wardrobe over to her sister. After all, what did Laura need a wardrobe for? For nigger-chasing?

Suddenly she stopped pacing. How would a nothing like Clinton Bell get an invitation to such a ball? From Laura? Impossible! She was aware that he had moved away from Nettie Rivers and into a room . . . Marvin Carsons!

"Oh, Laura, you are such a fool!" she cried angrily. "Why must you do these things that constantly embarrass me? Wasn't it bad enough that you got yourself involved with that—"

She stopped short again.

She went back very carefully over every word Ruth Ann had uttered, chewing a fingernail in deep thoughtfulness.

"Of course," she said at last, "it *must* be the same man. And as much as I would love to see dear Theda caught with a runaway slave on her staff, I'd best keep this from Mr. Wilkins until after Laura is out of that house."

11

"TIME, TIME, my dear," said Theda in a pained voice, pointing a finger at the mantle clock as though capable of making it stop. "It seems to me that I rise on a Monday morning and it is already Friday by the time I'm ready to retire. It is just an impossible schedule this season. Barely three weeks along and it's already a disaster. Spite. That's what it is. That woman is out to form her own society. Well, let her. This rash of masked balls her party brought about will soon grow old and tiresome."

Laura sat very still in the horsehair chair. She had been hemming a dress for what seemed hours, but her thoughts were hardly on the dress and only now and again on her aunt's prattle. Time had indeed seemed to fly, and with little or nothing accomplished. There had not been a single moment to think about Maggie Duggan or Calvert DeLong. Nor had she been a party to the rash of masked balls. Those guest lists had been approved by Mrs. Ronalds and not Theda DeWitt. She had been subjected to teas, dinner parties and musicales, which did not quite match the excitement of her first ball. August Belmont's Silver dinner had been just too august for her simple tastes and she almost dreaded the thought of Leonard Jerome's coming dinner party. As naive as some saw her, she was not fooled by Jerome. She found his secret little advances repulsive.

"Now, that will never do," Theda admonished in a severe tone. "No, no, my girl, you're making the hem most irregular. Oh, I could just kill the man for leaving me in such a lurch. Once again it's the doing of that Laverne Ronalds. But you mark my words, Laura. The worm will come crawling back when it comes time to start my wardrobe for next year."

"You would take him back after the nasty things he said about Betty?"

"What else can I do? There's no one else of his quality."

"I disagree," Laura said quietly. "He flew into a tantrum because someone had bested him, as I see it. And how many of your friends have tried to hire Betty away since then?"

"Only as a dresser, I am sure, Laura. One dress does not a fashion designer make."

"Everyone has to begin somewhere."

For some reason Theda felt a queer embarrassment. "Yes, Adrian wasn't much of anything when I first met him in Paris, that is true. But he did have the artist's eye. One who possesses it need have nothing else—except a rich client."

Laura's brow furrowed as she considered. "Well, Aunt Theda, I know nothing about business, except that if you've got money, you make it work for you. From what I've heard since being here, you invest your money. Mr. Jerome says that you're in all manner of silent partnerships. I think I know what that means, but I'm not quite sure."

"Well, dear, it means that—" She stopped short, suddenly understanding Laura's point. "It means that you are far more far-sighted than this old clunk-head. Why, it's a most exciting idea. Dear, go tell Amos to get out our new carriage and I'll go fetch Betty."

Theda came and bent to touch her cheek to Laura's. "Dear child," she murmured, "you have brought such joy into my barren and fruitless life. Now you have shown me how to bring joy into another life."

She straightened, her eyes twinkling. "We must first go see Mr. Livingston to draw up a proper document. Then a location must be found, machines purchased and talented seamstresses hired. As I have traveled this course with Adrian· Worth, it will not be so difficult the second time around. Betty and I will steal his clients away so fast that he'll be left with little more than his social-climbing friends."

When an idea seemed right to Theda DeWitt it had to be accomplished at once—even if she had to drag all concerned along in a dizzy state of shock.

"No time, no time," Laura heard her aunt call out at the front door. "Check with Laura in the east sitting room."

Laura thought the statement most odd and wondered what it could be about. Everything concerning the house was now placed in Amos's hands. Even Mrs. Courtney and her daughter Ellen never bothered a soul with a kitchen problem.

Laura sat bolt upright in the horsehair chair. She had been prepared to see a maid framed in the doorway, but not a young prince. Yet that was what Calvert DeLong seemed to her. He reminded Laura suddenly of a painting of Henry VIII in his youth, with tightly curled brown hair and bushy sideburns, soft and compassionate eyes, a thin bridge to the nose and the thin straight lips crooked at the corner in a quizzical smile.

"I've not had the pleasure, Miss Dahlgren. I am Calvert DeLong."

Laura got clumsily to her feet.

"Well, Mr. DeLong," she stammered. "It's a pleasure to meet you."

"I hate to intrude, but I'm seeking your brother, Laddie."

He was now into the room where the sunlight from the window spotlighted him. The princely aura was fading. His clothing was of the extreme bohemian look, and a bit on the seedy side. The knees of the tight trousers were beginning to develop a bulge and the black broadcloth coat had not been brushed in ever so long, Laura decided. She turned once more to his undeniably compelling good looks. There was an exotic quality about him, she decided. Not haughty, as she might have expected, but shy—almost timid.

"I'm afraid he's not at home, Mr. DeLong. He left yesterday on an unexpected business trip."

Calvert's slender figure stiffened. It put a touch of truth to the rumor he had heard the night before at Pfaff's. The Copperheads had sent a most unlikely representative to St. Louis to talk John C. Fremont into leading a third party ticket that would gather together all of the radical Republicans. He had thought he was so smart in avoiding Laddie of late, but he was the one, he now thought, who had been duped.

"I'm sorry to have missed him. Will it be a long journey?"

"I'm afraid that I'm not in my brother's confidence, Mr. DeLong."

"That's a great oversight on his part, Miss Dahlgren. Had I a sister such as you, I would surely make her my closest confidante."

Laura laughed lightly. "Then you don't know my brother very well, sir."

"Oh, I would heartily disagree. He is vain, conceited and we quarrel at every opportunity."

"Quarrel?"

"Over politics."

Laura's laugh was genuine. It was a picture of her brother that she just couldn't fathom.

He had meant to be serious and hoped that she would expose whatever she might know of Laddie's political involvement. But she refused the challenge with such amusement that he was piqued.

"I see your point, Miss Dahlgren. Ladies don't concern themselves with things like politics."

It was her turn to be piqued.

"Perhaps that is a shame, sir. If the roles were reversed, would fathers send their daughters and wives off to war?"

Calvert looked at her uncertainly. For the life of him he couldn't make her out. Was this the same beauty who had captured everyone's heart at the ball? He had expected to find a female version of Laddie. Instead he was finding her sweet and appealing, a creature with a mind of her own.

"I'm sorry, it was impolite of me to bring up the subject of politics."

"Why?" she demanded. "Sometimes you men act as though women are incapable of reading, or listening or determining what is going on in the world. Although, I must admit, that here in New York the European and society news does push any mention of the war to the back of the newspaper, and then one gets the impression that we have a nameless president in the White House."

Calvert's amazement was growing. Perhaps he was getting somewhere after all. "Many hope to change that name come next year."

"Then they are fools. They don't want to see this a union, or to have the slaves freed."

"You seem to be an admiring fan of Mr. Lincoln."

He was unaware that Laura was also playing a game, trying to bring the conversation to a point where she could bring up Maggie Duggan's request.

"I agree with him over the slaves," she said, "and that the union of the states should be perpetual."

Calvert was puzzled. An Abolitionist, Copperhead, Democrat or Republican could make the same statement and twist it to fit his own meaning.

"I was speaking of the man himself," he explained.

"I wouldn't know how to answer that, Mr. DeLong. I know him even less than I know you. Men never seem to be the same on the inside as they seem on the outside."

By now he was thoroughly nonplussed. It was as though she was reading his double life like an open book.

"If you say so," he said lamely.

Laura knew she wasn't handling the conversation too successfully. She needed more time to win his confidence.

"I'm sorry that you've missed my brother. But being such a close neighbor can't you dine with us this evening, Mr. DeLong?" she asked, unconsciously bending toward his straight, well-poised figure. His answer, in a sudden surge of anger, amazed her.

"Impossible! I've been blue-pencilled by Miss Theda."

"But I just heard her tell you to come in."

"But did you see her face? I'm a black sheep because I was booted out of the navy and have taken up with the likes of your brother. My parents let me stay at home, but it's like living in a tomb. Your dinner table would be the same." He cursed himself for a fool for coming over that morning at all. He was making life rough enough for his parents. It hurt deeply to have Theda DeWitt look at him in such a hateful fashion; she had always been one of his favorite people. And at any other time he would have jumped at the chance to get to know this fascinating girl better. It was the first time in weeks that he had been able to cast aside the supercilious playboy guise and feel his natural self. But for the moment he couldn't afford to make friends with her.

"Thank you," he continued slowly, "but as I said it will not be possible. I've other friends to meet for the evening."

He turned abruptly and left her.

Laura was puzzled. Now she recalled that it was an argument and not a discussion that Laddie and Theda had been having over the man.

"Booted out?" she mused. "I wonder if Maggie is aware of that; and I wonder why."

The bell shrilled. Because Amos was always on hand to answer she paid it no mind.

It shrilled again and again, insistently.

Remembering that Amos was out with Theda and Betty, she started into the hall when Ellen Courtney came running down the hall from the kitchen.

"I'll get it, mum," she said. Then she walked toward the door as rigidly erect as though she had an ironing board strapped to her back. She was determined not to be a scullery maid all of her life and had been practicing to get rid of her milkmaid's waddle. It so amused Laura that she had to step back into the sitting room to hide her smile.

The smile froze on her face.

"Mornin', little lady. The name's Garth Wilkins. I would be seein' your missus."

"Miss Theda is not at home, sir," Ellen said slowly, trying to sound very formal.

"I was speaking of Miss Dahlgren, my fair beauty. Miss Laura Dahlgren."

Laura pressed back against the wall, her mind spinning. Oh, don't let him in, she thought; please, don't let him in.

Ellen knew that she was no "fair beauty" and resented the man's impertinence when she was trying to be so proper. And her mother had boxed her ears many the time over the point that proper young ladies do not receive gentlemen when they are unattended.

"I'm sorry, sir, but are you expected?"

No, Laura wanted to scream. He'll lie his way in.

"No, my pet. But I'm an old friend of her mother and wanted to pay my respects."

"Most thoughtful of you, sir," Ellen said pleasantly. "As the missus does not receive callers until after tea, kindly leave your card and I'll inform her of your visit."

Good girl! Laura cheered silently.

Wilkins glanced at the girl suspiciously. Too well coached, he thought, letting his eyes roam around the foyer for some clue. Then he launched into the real intent of his project, blurting it out awkwardly, forgetting completely the careful approach he had planned.

"I may not be able to get back," he said thoughtfully. "It would save me a return trip if I could leave a message." He gave a short ribald laugh. "But the content of the message would be best passed on to male ears—say the butler."

Laura nearly fainted. Now he would learn everything.

Ellen pulled herself up haughtily. She was not going to be able to prove to Amos that she was capable if she couldn't even take a simple message.

"Really, sir," she said icily. "I *am* the front hall maid and quite capable of receiving any confidential message worth leaving in this house."

"Call the butler," he demanded darkly.

"Sir, Mr. Finnegan, the patrolman, is at coffee with my mother in the kitchen. He's a man. Shall I call him to take your message?"

Laura heard no reply, just the soft closing of the door. A moment later Ellen was in the doorway.

"Did I do proper, Miss Laura?"

Laura stood there looking at Ellen with dawning respect in her eyes.

"I—I think *most* proper, Ellen. I'll bring it to Amos's attention."

Ellen smiled brightly, curtsied and went happily back to the kitchen.

At once Laura was abject.

"Amos can't come back here," she murmured. "Wilkins knows he's here and mother probably told him. I've got to find them."

She went to the hall tree to get her coat and hat. There was no card on the silver salver, which meant that Wilkins no doubt planned on returning in person. She got into a cloth coat, put her hat firmly down upon her soft golden hair, and ran to let herself out on the carriage-house side of the mansion. She had no wish to run into Garth Wilkins on Fifth Avenue.

It had taken Wilkins's men nearly three weeks to locate Laura. It had been a simple matter that they had made complex. They had been able to locate the Dahlgren Mill, with very interesting results, but had found no address for Lawrence Dahlgren's residence. Even though the army had mysteriously halted their search for Amos, Garth Wilkins had turned adamant. He had been made a fool of and that he would not tolerate.

Nor could he tolerate wasting any more money by having men chase ghosts, or try to frighten Marvin Carson.

That morning, reassigning the men from West Point, he had accidently stumbled onto a most interesting clue.

"Miss Nettie says—" the man had started, but Wilkins cut him short.

"The way you quote that woman you'd think she was your wife."

Lem Gunther grinned. He had become somewhat of a favorite of the boarding house lady and rather hated leaving West Point.

"Well," he drawled, "she's on our side, ain't she? Anyway, she says she can't stomach that Lucille DeWitt Dahlgren and her uppity ways."

DeWitt . . . ? Wilkins mentally kicked himself. The woman had so constantly made a point of bringing up her family's illustrious past that he had simply ignored it after a time. As soon as he had obtained the addresses of her nearest DeWitt relatives, he did not hesitate.

Nor had he come away from Theda's foyer empty-handed. One glance had told him that it was his own cane resting in the hall tree receptacle.

But Laura would not have had to fear running into him.

Stepping along jauntily, he had returned to his office to lay new plans, issue new orders, and prepare to return after tea time.

As Laura had been into the Wall Street district only once before, she got herself almost hopelessly lost. To search out the lawyer, knowing only his last name, was proving even more hopeless.

The stock market was nearing its noontime frantic rush. Call boys were racing from broker to broker, filling the street and not caring or looking to see who they shoved aside. Laura, having been buffeted around quite enough, was ready to give up in despair.

"What's this," boomed a voice in sudden cheeriness, grasping her arm and pulling her out of the fray. "Miss Dahlgren, what are you doing down in this madhouse?"

"Oh, Mr. Jerome, thank you. I was looking for Aunt Theda at Mr. Livingston's office, but got completely turned around."

"Everett Livingston?" he asked with sudden interest. "Is she up to some new little business venture?"

Not knowing the world of business matters, Laura saw no reason to lie. "I believe so, and it's really all your fault."

"My fault," he chuckled.

"Your introduction of my ball gown. Aunt Theda is going to set Betty Duggan up in business because of it."

He threw back his head and roared. "That woman doesn't miss a bet. And I hope the first thing that she designs is your gown for my Golden dinner."

"Oh," Laura gasped, suddenly remembering her mission. "If I don't find Aunt Theda the only place I may be going is to prison." She gasped louder, knowing she had just blundered. "Please, can you direct me to Mr. Livingston's office?"

"I can do better than that, Miss Dahlgren. As it is in the same building as my office, I will escort you."

It was a calculated lie, but he was a gentleman and saw her distress. In street clothes, she seemed more child than woman. But, he thought, she was even more appealing as a helpless and vulnerable child than as a dressed-up woman.

He led her to a dimly lit and musty office. A clerk in

a high starched collar stared in recognition of the infamous Leonard Jerome. A few whispered words from the millionaire sent the clerk scurrying through an office door.

"Don't let the looks of the office deceive you, my dear," Jerome whispered. "He is most successful and astute."

The clerk came forth and nervously motioned for Laura to enter.

"Thank you, Mr. Jerome."

"My pleasure."

In total bewilderment over her arrival, Theda, Betty and Amos sat like wax figures. Laura's heart sank as she stared at them, then at Mr. Livingston's vast rosy countenance.

"I—I wish to speak to my aunt and Amos alone, please."

"Laura, what is it?" Theda gasped.

"P-p-please," she stammered.

"Laura, Mr. Livingston is my attorney. Anything said in front of him is confidential."

Amos was on his feet. The despair in Laura's face told him all he needed to know.

"It's all right, Laura," he said sadly. "I knew it couldn't last forever. Wilkins?"

She nodded, fearful of breaking into tears.

He sighed. "Miss Theda, I think it's time I saw you ladies home and made my farewells."

"What! What is going on?"

Betty patted Theda's hand. "I think I understand, Miss Theda, and Amos is right. Let them explain on the way home."

"Nay, nay," said Mr. Livingston, in the most soothing of voices. "I've handled DeWitt affairs for nearly thirty years. If a problem is afoot, let's keep it within the confines of these walls."

Amos paled. He dropped his eyes to his boots, and his big mouth set itself sullenly. "I'm a runaway slave," he muttered.

"That's not the whole truth," Laura cried. "Mr. Jefferson Davis granted you manumission."

Theda sat blinking and speechless.

"Very good," said Livingston, with sardonic heaviness. "We'll just wire President Davis in Montgomery for verification. Now, if you please, I shall have the full story from the beginning."

Everett Livingston had learned several times in life never to dot an *i* or cross a *t* without the full knowledge of a situation. He wasn't even sure what Miss Theda would wish to do on the matter once she knew the full story, but the fact that she had enough confidence in the black man to bring him in on a business conference told him a great deal.

And as the story unfolded he turned new eyes upon Laura Dahlgren. He could hardly believe that the courageous lass of the tale was the same one ready to burst into tears in his office. After sixty-three years of living, people still amazed him—and he had seen his share of all varieties.

Throughout it all, Theda DeWitt never uttered a sound or looked at anything other than the clenched hands in her lap. Oddly enough, all she could think about was Trientje Schuyler, the matriarch of the American DeWitt clan. Trientje had brought both the wealth and the breeding of her Dutch ancestry to the English DeWitt family. Once Theda had seen an oil painting of the woman that had been taken from the old family manor house in Dutchess County. Before she had tried to compare Laura to the Schofields and not the DeWitts. She had been wrong. The girl was as Dutch as that mite of patroon blood that flowed in her veins.

Now she gazed into space, and her smile took on a curious quality, as if measuring every DeWitt ever born. There had been very few who had risen above the clan's age-old contempt for the "rabble." Laura, it seemed, was one of the few who had the necessary grit and intelligence.

"Well, Everett," she said, as though she had asked him a question and had been waiting for the reply.

He colored, as if embarrassed. "Well, now," he began, "there are certain people I might be able to contact to see him safely into Canada."

"No, no, no," Theda exclaimed. "I do not want to lose him. What can we do to protect him and keep him here?"

"I was afraid you would ask that," said Livingston, trying to smile pleasantly but only succeeding in bringing a strained expression to his face. "As my knowledge is essentially of the business world, I shall have to look into the matter most carefully. Might I suggest that you do return home now and give me a chance to get out and about with gentlemen who have run into this sort of . . . ah . . . situation."

Theda rose slowly, never taking her hard stare from the lawyer. She smiled faintly.

"Don't trouble yourself, Everett. I've just had a thought of my own. Please complete those papers and have them to the house by this evening."

"What do you plan on doing, Miss Theda?" Amos asked nervously as he opened the door for her.

"I don't know, Amos, I don't know. All I do know is that I couldn't sit there and do nothing while he hemmed and hawed."

As they entered the outer office Leonard Jerome stood and saluted with a finger touched to the tip of his beaver hat.

"Miss Theda, good day. I trust that everything is all right."

Theda looked at him sharply. "You have me at a disadvantage, Leonard," she answered ironically. "What shouldn't be all right?"

"Well, I found Miss Dahlgren on the street, quite lost and in great despair. I was so concerned that I stayed about." He looked quickly from face to face but no one would meet his eye except Theda.

"May I see you all to the street?"

"You may at least do that much, Leonard," said Theda, with gentle regret.

There was no sound in the steep wooden stairway other than the dropping of feet, from one step to the next. It sounded like the last march to the gallows, to the ears of Leonard Jerome. Having taken Theda's arm, he could feel her arm trembling violently.

He leaned close. "My dear, if I can be of service, in any way, you need but ask. I gather that Everett couldn't be of help to you."

Theda shook her head, smiling weakly. "It was a little out of his line, I'm afraid."

"I know everyone in New York. Tell me the line you seek and I'll set you in the right direction."

"It's my Amos," she admitted on a near sob.

Jerome waved this sad comment aside with a light gesture of his hand. "No more! The street is full of ears, but I think I fully understand. Ah, here is your carriage." He turned to the following trio, who had only heard them mumbling, and took immediate command.

"Amos, hail that cabbie for the young ladies. They must begin work on Miss Laura's gown for my Golden dinner. I'll see Theda into the carriage. You're going to take us on an errand."

There was a deep silence among them as Amos did as directed and Jerome helped Theda into the carriage.

"Where are we going?" Theda asked as Jerome seated himself opposite her.

Jerome laughed loudly, reaching forward to pat Theda on the hand. He winked. "There is only one man in all of New York who will be able to solve all of your problems in one fell swoop—William Marcy Tweed."

Theda was not startled. She raised her eyebrows with injured innocence. "That's going to be most embarrassing, Leonard. Boss Tweed and his Tammany Hall boys won't feel exactly overjoyed to help Theda DeWitt. I've blue-pencilled that man for years."

"Perhaps," he said, in a meditative voice, "you could consider reinstating him, Theda. The man has everything in this city that he could ask for except the one thing his wife asks constantly of him—an entree into the inner circles of society. If you like, you may use my dinner party as a lever."

Theda nodded. That might be the price paid to the man who ran New York, but she had a horrible feeling as to the price Leonard Jerome might try to exact for his helpfulness. She would have to be extremely careful. She would rather sell her own soul to the devil than let him get his lecherous hands on Laura.

Laura had held her unyielding wrath for several hours, still stunned that Betty could merrily run off to share her good news with her sister while nothing had been resolved concerning Amos.

The day had turned as gray as her mood. The drawing-room window reflected back her ghastly pallor. Tea time had come and gone and she began to fear the worst. She had only one ploy left to save Amos. Reluctantly, she turned from the window and went to pull the bell cord. Ellen came popping forth at once.

"Ellen, if Mr. Wilkins returns before Aunt Theda, you will show him directly in here. If others are with him, they are to stay in the foyer. You may serve tea upon his arrival, and you will stay in the room to pour."

Ellen curtsied and smiled. Her mother would greatly approve of the properness with which Miss Laura intended to handle the visit.

Laura hadn't been thinking of propriety. She just didn't want the arrest being made out on the street and she didn't want to be alone with the man. She even prayed that her aunt might return without Amos. Time seemed to drag.

The drawing-room fire hissed sulkily. Ellen came in once to light the lamps against the early twilight. Laura finally seated herself before the fire and stared somberly at the coals. She sat but a few minutes, sweeping back to the window like a ghost in swirling and rustling hoops. She was just in time to see the arrival of the paddy wagon. For one instant her rounded young breast rose on a quick breath, and then was still and calm again. In full control, she returned to the fire, rested one hand on the mantelpiece, and turned to face the doorway.

Garth Wilkins had prepared as though actually invited back for tea, austere and elegant in a new suit of black broadcloth, moving into the drawing room as though such settings were his daily fare.

He bowed gallantly. His smile brightened, but did not warm.

"Mr. Wilkins," she murmured, "we were told you might not be able to return. Ellen, tea. Please be seated, sir."

He sat down near the fire, carefully lifting his coattails, and then stiffly looked about the room.

"I was looking forward to meeting your aunt."

"Shortly."

"I hope not long. After all, time is money to me."

"You make it sound as if this call is business, sir." There was a hard choking in her throat. She didn't know how much longer she could retain her calm.

"What else would it be but business, Miss Dahlgren?" he asked softly. "That was some little slip you gave us all in West Point, deny it though you will."

She stared at him, incredulous. Then she uttered a short laugh.

"What is there to deny, Mr. Wilkins!" she exclaimed. "When a parent says go, a child obeys. What mystery is there in that?"

He smiled faintly. "Miss Dahlgren, I said you would deny it. Deny it because of certain things about that journey you wish to keep hidden. But Garth Wilkins has eyes that have given him certain facts. As a minor, I can only take you into custody and return you to your parents. So, to save us all time, I'll be having the full truth."

She regarded him, white with anger, but determined to tell him nothing.

"That, sir, is a matter you will have to take up with my aunt."

"Then call her," he demanded harshly, "and produce that black devil. And don't try to deny that he's here. Did you think that I wouldn't recognize my own cane, the one that now rests in the hall? That gave his presence in this house away."

Laura's smile was grimly amused. She knew she was taking a horrible gamble, but she had to try. "Is that your proof, sir? The truth is that I was forced to use that cane because of the beating I took at the hands of your hired thugs. Is that the only manner of man you're capable of getting to do such foul work—men who would rip away a girl's clothing to sate their lust?"

Laura had purposely raised her voice to a malicious tone. Ellen had heard all as she entered. She had caught her breath, nearly dropping the heavy tea tray and then slowly placing it on the table before the settee, as though her strength was gone. She dared not leave Laura alone with such a creature, regardless of the police standing in the foyer. She poured the tea as though she wanted it to come out of the spout a drop at a time.

Wilkins sat fuming, and gazed at the maid with murderous intent. He dared say nothing until she had left the room.

Laura caught her breath. At last she heard the faint sound of the arriving carriage, but now it would be too late. She was shaking visibly.

Wilkins had heard, too. He rose very slowly, and turned to go into the foyer. His face changed strangely. It was almost going to be too easy.

Ellen raced around him to get the door open before the bell pealed. Laura followed him as though in a trance.

Theda DeWitt came through the door and blinked at the two policemen as though the paddy wagon had not given her warning of what to expect. She pressed her clenched hands to her breast and continued to gaze at them. Amos stood in the doorway, his arms laden with parcels, his face as aloof and uncaring as though nothing was amiss.

Then Wilkins spoke, in so low a voice that they all had to lean toward him to catch his words.

"That's the man! Arrest him!"

"Arrest?" Theda cried. "Who are you? What is going on here? What right do you have to be in my home?"

"I shall take your questions one at a time," Wilkins answered grimly. "I am Garth Wilkins, here to apprehend a runaway slave. Anticipating trouble, I obtained an order to bring along the police. I'm in your house quite legally. Take him along, men."

With a gesture clumsy with despair, Theda extended a fleshy hand at the policemen. "You stay put," she said icily. "You are shameful and I will have strong words to say to William Marcy Tweed about you both. This is no military state where you can barge right in and take people away on a whim. Now, I wish to know why my butler is being arrested."

"I have already made that quite—" Wilkins started.

Theda stopped him with a scathing look. "Sir, in my house I expect to be answered by the person I address and not by a total stranger. Well?"

The police sergeant bowed slightly, with surly reticence. What was to have been a routine matter had become complex with the mention of Boss Tweed.

"Well, mum," he said, "Mr. Wilkins here is a bounty-hunter and has orders to pick up one Amos Mobley, a runaway slave."

"And that is what I want done immediately," Wilkins insisted.

"Don't lay a hand on him!" cried Theda. "Now, I will make my protest heard loud and clear. I shudder to think what might have happened if Amos had not been driving me about shopping. Idiots! His name is Amos Schuyler and he is a manumission slave from Jamaica."

Wilkins, unable to contain himself, burst out with a savage laugh. "What a contrived lie! Do you really expect me to believe that nonsense?"

"Lie?" Theda said indignantly. "Sergeant, you will excuse me. Down the hall is my office and the safe in which I keep all my important documents. I will be but a moment and will let you judge the validity of my words."

Wilkins continued to smile in grim satisfaction, as if he had not heard. The old woman might be able to cow the policemen, but the slave was as good as money in his pocket.

Electrified, and as wondering and puzzled as Ellen, Laura could not see how this stall about calling Amos by another name was going to help.

Theda was back almost as soon as she had left—mainly because she had only to take the documents from her purse. She ignored Wilkins and addressed herself to the sergeant. She held out the documents, some looking quite old and others more recent.

"This, Sergeant, is a record from the Schuyler plantation ledger outside of Kingston, showing the birth of a baby named Amos, along with his slave record. Here is my receipt of purchase from the Schuylers, descendents of ancestors of mine; there's also a Jamaican manumission certificate and a receipt for his ship passage from Kingston to New York last month. Now, do you leave quietly, or do I have to take this matter up in the courts?"

The policemen wanted to run away in shame. Wilkins waved his hand mockingly. "You may depart, gentlemen, and my thanks." He turned to Laura, whose full young face was flushed with joy. "But we still have the matter of Miss Dahlgren to settle. It is my duty to return her to her parents, at her mother's request."

"Sergeant," Theda purred, "please wait. I want a witness for what I am about to say, for I never dreamt I'd need documentation on this score as well. My niece, Miss Laura Dahlgren, was put in my charge by my brother-in-law, Clarence Dahlgren, because of certain accusations and threats against her at home. Under the law, he has that right and privilege, no matter how many greedy bounty-hunters my poor sister may hire. If that child ever disappears from this house, I shall immediately swear out a warrant for *this* man's arrest for kidnapping. And now good-day to you all!"

Garth Wilkins uttered a helpless and disgusted exclamation and then marched out in front of the policemen. Ellen, who had been holding the door open with wide-eyed wonderment, softly closed it and turned.

"Mum," she said, her voice quavering, "shall I be serving tea now?"

"Tea?" Theda blinked, as though suddenly coming awake. "I think we all—and I mean *all*—would be much better with a glass of champagne. Amos, your arm. I think my knees are just about ready to buckle."

12

THE GLASS of wine and all the excitement had gone to Laura's head. She had excused herself until dinner time and once upon her bed had fallen almost immediately into a deep sleep. Her dream kept repeating itself. The door bell would ring and she would race to answer it, only to find a brick wall beyond the door. The fourth time that it happened she pulled herself out of the dream and out of the sleep to realize the sound of the bell was real.

The room was dark and cold, with no fire or lamp lit. She sat up. A sleeting snow was pounding against the window pane. As though drugged, she went to open the door so the hall light would give her enough illumination to find the lamps and light them. The hall was as dark as the night outside.

For a moment she thought that she had slept through dinner and that it was now quite late in the night. But at the end of the hall she could see a faint glow filtering up from the foyer. Careful not to bump into the side tables, she stayed in the center of the hall and used the glow as a beacon.

Three of the foyer lamps were lit, but no light shone from any other open door. She had an eerie feeling as she came down the stairs, keeping her back angled into the curve of the wall, her fingers trailing on the wainscote molding. When her feet touched the marble tile, a mumble of voices drew her attention to the right hallway. A shaft of light came from the partially closed dining room door. She tried to recall if they had been expecting guests for dinner that evening. No longer feeling a stranger in the house, she went to the dining room door and entered.

"Oh, Laura!" Theda gasped. "You gave me a start."

Laura looked about in great surprise. The table was still set for dinner, but with no food upon it. Everyone was still in their afternoon attire, except there were three additions huddled about the table.

Plump Mrs. Courtney sat rigid, clutching her daughter's hand. Amos and Theda sat at the head of the table, a bizarre queen and king reigning over the room. To their right was a frightened Betty Duggan and her sister.

It was Maggie Duggan that Laura stared at the longest. Her hair was awry, her dress tattered. A purple discoloration was beginning to encircle her eye and her lower lip was badly swollen.

"What—what is all of this?" Laura stammered.

"We didn't want to disturb your sleep, Miss Laura," Amos said softly, rising and drawing out a chair for her. "There was trouble at the Dahlgren Mills this afternoon."

Laura took the seat. "Trouble? An accident?"

"A well-planned one!" Maggie said savagely. "Twelve bounty-hunter thugs stormed the place and took away six negroes we had hidden in a room behind the boilers. Bastards put Bertha Butt in the hospital with a nasty blow to her head."

"How did they know?"

"Couple of them have been coming around lately, posing as salesmen to see Mr. Dahlgren. Big snoops. Don't matter now. They got what they came for, wrecked some machinery, and scared the hell out of the help. I'm fired, for sure."

"No one is fired," Theda said sternly, "because Laddie is not to hear about this."

"Excuse me for saying so, Miss Theda," Amos said

thoughtfully, "but he's bound to find out. We've all agreed already that they had to be Wilkins's men. He'll keep raiding that place time and time again, looking for my folk, and Mr. Laddie will learn sooner or later."

Theda's violent reaction to this was even more startling to Laura than the strange gathering.

"But that foul man will not find any of your folk there, Amos, or anywhere, if I have a say in the matter. He's as foul as some of the people who owned them in the first place. Batting away at innocent women and children. Bah! Laura, your late arrival is causing us to go over ground already covered. We were discussing what is to be done with the five that got away."

"Aunt Theda?" Laura gasped, casting a wary eye at the cook and maid.

Theda DeWitt laughed richly, reaching out and patting Mrs. Courtney's hand.

"Laura, after our little to-do with Mr. Wilkins, I thought it best for Alice and Ellen to know what was going on. Oh, the house has been a mad one, with the comings and goings. Everett with the papers for Betty's shop, then Betty, then Betty off to fetch back Maggie, then Amos off . . . Well, dear, if this madness was going to surround us I just thought all the servants should know what we're facing. Oh, Calvert, I didn't mean to include you as a servant."

"That's quite all right, Miss Theda."

Laura spun on her seat. The tall young man sat on a chair against the wall, his eyes greatly amused. He winked.

"No more double-talk, Miss Dahlgren."

Laura turned away, her cheeks flaming.

"Maggie thought it best to include Calvert," Theda went on, "although I'm still a little mystified. But that will right itself in due course." She turned to Maggie. "Now, what about the five who are left?"

"For the moment they are safe," Maggie said.

"A moment doesn't last long," said Amos with a cynical half-smile. "Sorry to say, but those bounty-hunters are bloodhounds. They will hound and hound until they've run them to bay. Can you get them away by boat, Mr. DeLong?"

"I'm not in the best of favor with my family at the moment, but I can try to borrow the—"

"No," Theda cut him short. "Maggie, I want you and Betty to bring those people here—and tonight."

"Gladly!" cried Maggie.

"Aunt Theda," Laura said, her breath labored with fear. "Do you know what you are about?"

For the first time in years Theda DeWitt was thinking of people other than herself, and the experience was giving her a glimpse of the alien world, a world peopled by the likes of Garth Wilkins. It both sickened her and made her more determined.

"I know very well what I am doing," she remarked soothingly. "The servant quarters above the carriage house are vacant and it cannot be seen from the street. A most safe harbor in this storm."

Wishing to further the good favor she had gained, Ellen rose abruptly. "I could see to the lamps, the fires and a bit of tidying up, if you wish, mum."

"And if they're like the rest of us," her mother chimed in, "they're probably without supper. Shall I be adding a bit to the stew pot, Miss DeWitt?"

Theda beamed her approval, but turned to the butler for his agreement. "Amos?"

"Very well," he replied in a dull voice. "That has merit for tonight, at least."

"Oh, far beyond that, Amos," Theda exclaimed, as though the matter were a simple one. "When one wishes to hide a thing, the best place is in plain sight. We shall do with them as we did with you. I see no problem at all in placing them with my friends as servants. Lord knows this war has brought about a servant shortage. With Betty being lost to us, we can use at least three maids, can't we, Amos?"

"I gather so," he muttered, unaware that a most curious expression had crossed his face. She was getting him involved, whether he liked it or not. "But we've got to learn a mite about them first."

"I agree," said Maggie. "They are never more than faces to us that we pass on to the next station in the Underground. And their clothing makes them stand out just like a Mick straight off the boat from Ireland."

"If some of them can sew," Betty volunteered, "I can help them to make uniforms."

"Doesn't take a body long to learn kitchen chores after spending a day with me," Alice Courtney boasted.

"If Mr. Amos agrees," Ellen chimed in, seeing the whole thing as a wonderful opportunity to gain front-hall maid status, "I could help training the maids in their cleaning and polishing chores."

"Wait! Wait! Wait!" Amos chided, sounding like Miss Theda with his triple warning. "We are only speaking of five people, and their gender hasn't even been mentioned. You make it sound like an ongoing process."

"Why not?" cried Theda enthusiastically. "While Mr. Wilkins is trying to find out how they're escaping north, we'll be hiding them right under his nose in the city."

"I think," Maggie said, on a note of caution, "that should we decide on this course, we should keep it very strictly to ourselves. We do have to protect Miss DeWitt."

"Thank you, my dear, but I have no fears or qualms."

"There is another point," Amos warned. "It will cost money to feed, reclothe and train them. You all better consider that."

As one they looked at Theda. She was about to be overly generous and offer to foot the bill, when Betty cleared her throat.

"This may sound silly, but couldn't we raise the money?"

Maggie let out a boisterous laugh. "We just agreed to keep it quiet and now you want to advertise the fact by soliciting funds?"

"I didn't mean it that way, Maggie. What I had in mind, we could say we were going to raise money for the war effort, and in a way it would be."

"What *was* it you had in mind, Betty?" Theda prodded, her interest pricked.

Betty blushed. "I may be speaking out of turn, mum, but I bet there are hundreds of women in the city who would pay something to get their hands on any of the garments you got stored away from past years."

Theda blinked as the idea settled on her mind and then she began to smile. She chuckled. "My dear girl, they won't just pay 'something.' They will pay whatever price the auctioneer can raise the bidding to. Excellent! Excellent! Excellent! We'll make it a gala affair and tie it in with the opening of your shop. Oh, I haven't been so excited in years!"

As the discussion continued, Calvert DeLong quietly took the corner seat at the table next to Laura.

"We seem to be the silent members in the room. I fully expected you to be in the very midst of the planning."

Laura's face remained sullen for a moment or two, then involuntarily it lightened into an embarrassed look of pride and affection.

"Oh, I'm a little stunned, I suppose. I hardly expected my aunt to involve herself in this way. It's usually just little people who look out for other little people." She paused, suddenly remembering what Maggie had said about the man's past help with the slaves.

He grinned. "For one very important reason, I intend to jump into their game with both feet."

"What reason is that, Mr. DeLong?"

"So that I can stand in the long line of men in New York who wish to know you better."

She laughed reluctantly. "There is no line, Mr. DeLong."

"Splendid! All the better chance for me."

Laura stared at the man, wondering how in the world he could be a friend of her brother. They seemed to have so little in common, except for a vaguely similar taste in attire.

"And Laura, you may pitch in as well," Theda said, breaking in on her thoughts. Laura wasn't sure what the comment implied and directed her attention to the other end of the table again. All were on their feet and disappearing in various directions. "And you will stay to supper, of course, Calvert. Now, let's get cracking before the girls return with the others. Laura, please assist Mrs. Courtney in the kitchen."

They rose and Calvert whispered quickly, "I'll stay, if you promise that I may sit next to you."

Blushing, Laura scurried out through the pantry. She found that she suddenly wanted to know more about this strange man.

Calvert DeLong waited until all the ladies had departed

the dining room. He had purposely remained quiet during the discussion, his attention focused on two people—Laura, for personal reasons, and Amos for professional reasons. When Amos had come to fetch him, he had been most curious. As he had sat listening, as a fact here and there had been dropped, he had begun silently to kick himself and curse Laddie. Amos had never been mentioned by Laddie and Calvert had stupidly given the man no more thought than he would any other servant. Now, he studied Amos with keen interest.

"I trust," said Calvert with austere delicacy, "that serving in the North is not too different from serving in the South?"

Amos, still trying to fathom the man, found nothing offensive in the inquisitiveness which the master class feels is its right with regard to the servant class. He answered with simplicity.

"Every boss has his particularities, Mr. DeLong."

"Even when one of them has been elevated to the position of the presidency?"

Neither saw that just then Laura had propped open the swinging door from the pantry, so that she could turn back to gather up a tray of condiments for the table.

Amos's short laugh stopped her.

"I don't even know this Mr. Lincoln, sir."

"I was speaking of Mr. Jefferson Davis."

Amos pondered, gazed bemusedly down at the plate he had just set, and studied his own darkly shimmering image.

"Were you now, sir? And what would make you think I had served that gentleman?"

"At the present moment, Amos, neither of us is what we are supposed to be. Let me tell you a little tale that I have learned, but don't ask me where I have learned it. A certain servant was sent out of the South, for reasons known only to the servant and his master. Now, there are certain men in Washington who fear that servant, just as there were men in the South who feared him. But the Washington men fear him the more, because they think he is here to work with certain groups to gain support for the South and help bring about a revolt in the North. Because the man mysteriously disappeared, they began to believe it all the more. But it's funny. These certain groups are indeed plotting all manner of plots to make the war and the election go as they wish it to go—but nowhere has this man popped up among them. They seem as curious about his disappearance as do the government men. Both sides are being very quiet about him at the moment."

"Interesting tale, sir, I am sure." Amos turned to gather up silverware from the sideboard.

"I can't help but wonder why he keeps both sides guessing," said Calvert, baiting his hook. "Three sides, if you consider that he may not have been able yet to get information back to a certain president and his generals."

The light entirely left Amos's face, but it remained serene. He continued, as if Calvert had not spoken. "And more interesting if one knows how to read, sir. Seems to me that all presidents want to be generals and all generals want to become presidents—North or South. Servants? They are bodies, sir, with no eyes, ears, mouths or memories."

"No doubt you're quite right," Calvert said admonishingly, "but how can a servant work to support a system that would keep his own people in slavery?"

Amos did not answer. His smile was bemused and confident. Calvert's tale had told him much, but nothing about Calvert DeLong and his interest in the matter.

Laura came through the open door and slammed the tray down on the table. Her face was distraught and angry, and her blue eyes, as they flashed at Calvert, full of warning.

"I couldn't help overhearing you in the pantry," she said thinly, "and I think it's time you took your rude questions and went home, Mr. DeLong."

"Now, Miss Laura," Amos soothed, "I took no offense."

"None of it is his business," she declared.

Calvert resented the intrusion. He had been leading up to a point whereby he could be candid with the man, and was not about to let her ruin this great piece of luck.

"It's more my business than you realize," he said icily. "If that man is about to sell out the future of this country to some radical force, then I am under orders to stop him, even if it means his death. You don't see the implications of all this, Amos? You are a quietly hunted man. Fortunately, Wilkins doesn't know all the facts; he's just a greedy bounty-hunter. There is a threat implicit in your presence North, no matter what reasons you may have been given. I can always deny what I am about to say, but think upon the fact that I have given up my integrity, family honor and love just to keep my country from becoming the vassal of some foul and treacherous group of men who think themselves right and all others wrong. And if you are the man they are waiting for to help bring that about, then I cannot allow you to hide behind Miss Theda's petticoats!"

He was overcome with his own rare passion. He sat down, holding stiffly to the arms of the chair, never once taking his burning gaze from Amos.

Laura stood transfixed, having seen still another aspect of this strange man.

Amos sat down also. He seemed very thoughtful. Then he quietly closed his hands together on the table top.

"You picture me quite falsely, sir," he said firmly. "So, it would seem, have others. All that I came here with was Mr. Jeff's blessing for a long and fruitful life. He's a loving and compassionate man. It's true that I know much about him, but I am not his agent or the agent of any other man. Nor, sir, am I about to lie to any man."

"That I can believe," Calvert said softly. "I am sorry if I sounded harsh, Amos."

"It would seem to be your job, sir, though I don't envy the manner of soldiering you must be doing."

Calvert's smile was both dark and sad. "I was Navy, Amos."

"Odd lot, then, that you find yourself in, sir."

Calvert stirred in his seat. He forgot that Laura was even there. He felt such a strong compulsion to trust this man, to place his faith in him. If he could just win Amos's confidence, the man could still be a great asset to him.

"Would you agree with me, Amos, that the South can't survive more than another year without massive imports from Britain, France and Spain?"

Amos nodded.

"One of my concerns is to protect the supply of new ships which the Navy will require to blockade the South." He added, very softly, "The report I have suggests that

Mr. Davis has ordered the destruction of the DeLong Shipyard, even if the men doing the deed must blow themselves up with the debris."

Amos suddenly came to life with feverish passion. "That
cannot be, sir!" he cried. "Mr. Jeff would never order such
a thing! Even when General Lee was close enough to fire
upon Washington City, Mr. Jeff wouldn't allow it. He reminded everyone of the hate that still remains for the
British for setting it aflame in 1812. No, any man who says
that of Mr. Jeff is a liar, and I will gladly say so to his
face."

Calvert smiled again, and shrugged fatalistically. "It is
still a fact that such a plan is being considered, no matter
who gets the blame for being the originator. There are
over two thousand men and boys who could lose their
lives in such an accident, Amos."

Laura gasped. She could endure no more. "Why do you
tell us these things, Mr. DeLong? I don't understand."

He rose and looked fixedly at Laura, knowing that he
would have to hurt her badly in order to gain support
from Amos.

"Perhaps you will understand better, Miss Dahlgren, if
I disclose that your brother is a part of the radical group
that is considering this plot."

"Then you must be too," she insisted.

"I certainly pray that it appears that way. I can learn
nothing without gaining their confidence and getting into
the inner circle. I must appear to be as selfish and self-
centered as Laddie—and as free-living. I strongly urge that
the operation you're considering be kept from Laddie's
eyes and ears. He has a reputation, within the group, of
being most loyal where the reward is the greatest."

To his great surprise she did not become angry with
him, but turned to Amos with a worried frown.

"Amos, how are we going to keep him from learning?"

Amos looked at Calvert rather than her, a bemused
twinkle dawning in his dark eyes. He couldn't help but
like this young man. Just as Mr. Jeff might have done,
Calvert DeLong put all his cards face up on the table and
then sat back to watch the others turn theirs up one at a
time.

"Well," he drawled, "seems we have to trade something to keep that from happening."

"I don't understand."

"No, but Mr. Calvert does."

The two men locked eyes. Yes, they understood each other quite well now. In the back of Amos's mind he had seen Calvert as being much like Laddie, just as Calvert had seen Amos as something other than what he was. They could now start quite fresh.

"And as he does," Amos went on, "we might just call on him to keep Mr. Lawrence occupied from time to time. In exchange, we might pass on information that comes our way."

It was now Calvert's turn to be a little confused. "How do you propose to gain information that might be useful to me?"

Amos chuckled. "Mr. Calvert, you've never been a servant. Mrs. Abernathy tells me that you threw tantrums and wet the bed until you were close on to fifteen."

"My God!" Calvert gasped, blushing crimson.

"So, if you need to know anything about the folk that Mr. Lawrence associates with, you just tell me which ones you're curious about."

You're all right, Amos, Calvert thought with pride. Too bad for Laddie that you're on my side. Yes, it's too bad for Laddie. . . .

13

THEY DID NOT have to worry about Laddie Dahlgren for a week—a frantic week. Theda DeWitt acted as though she could single-handedly find employment for every man, woman and child who had ever been brought from the shores of Africa. She was encouraged in that belief when her clothing auction raised over thirty-seven thousand dollars on the same day that a most unusual "overground" railroad train arrived in New York.

The three boxcars of the military train were packed to the point of suffocation with over three hundred blacks. They had been sent north from Chattanooga by the Federals, who were trying to gain a foothold at Chickamauga and had hoped to divert the Rebels to recapturing the slaves. The tactic had failed. The engineer and fireman had been given no specific location to off-load, and seized the opportunity for a free ride home to New York. They left the train on a siding, blithely went to their homes, and didn't give another thought to the passengers.

The blacks labored until they had broken the chains holding the boxcar doors secure. What they wanted was very simple. After three days in the boxcars, they wanted food to save them from starvation. They came out of the cars in a swarm and started across the railroad yard.

From practically the first day of the war, radical groups had constantly kept the rumor alive that Commodore Vanderbilt was going to bring north great masses of cheap black railroad labor to replace the Irish and Italians. The railyard workers who first saw the stream of blacks thought the day was coming about and the rumor spread like wildfire.

By the time the blacks were across the multiple tracks and approaching the roundhouse and station, a hundred burly men had gathered to make sure that they went no further.

The blacks, who had been boarded by military men, thought these were more of the same. Without fear they went right to them. At first there was no noise, no outcry, no panic, until a hundred railroad spikes and crowbars cracked against black skulls. Then the panic came so swiftly that the railroad men could not corral them. The blacks fled shrieking in all directions, and behind them came the railroad men, swinging whatever they could find as a weapon in deadly earnest.

As they fanned out from the station, pedestrians were quick to grasp the situation and take up the chase. They were equipped with only their arms and fists, but they swung at anything that looked darker than they. As the mayhem spread, local black men and women in the street going about their business were beaten with the rest.

Amos, returning from Betty's new shop and the auction, unknowingly pulled the carriage into a street that was fast filling with the advancing mob.

Terror-stricken, the blacks swarmed to either side of the carriage. Amos had to rein in the horses to keep the people from falling under the hoofs.

"Oh! Oh! Oh!" Theda began to wail, fluttering her fan. Then a gray-haired old woman started to fall by the carriage and Theda reached out and hauled her over the carriage door with a single tug.

"Go!" she screamed at Amos, but the chasing mob was upon them. Liveried coachman or no, they would pull him from his perch. Amos slashed left and right with the carriage whip, using his other hand to rein the horses back even farther to rear and slash with their hoofs. Then he gave them their head to dash ahead, praying the blacks would scatter before the carriage overtook them.

"Aboard! Aboard!" Theda kept screaming at them as they passed. A few of the more agile men were able to jump and grab hold of the carriage and pull themselves up.

Turning left and right and then left again, Amos was able to outdistance the shouting mob. He slowed and was amazed to learn they had picked up eight additional passengers.

Theda glowered at the terrified faces of the black men. "I will give an address but once. Then I want you to go back to your people and spread that address. Send them there or don't show up yourselves."

"Miss Theda, do you think—" Amos started.

"Think?" she bellowed. "I think this is *war*, Amos. I think this is bloody and savage and I don't give *a damn*! Let the whole city know what I'm doing!"

She struggled to regain her usual innocent composure. The tears were thick in her eyes and she had to swallow several times before she could go on. After a moment she spoke again, tonelessly. "We have much to think about, Amos. People to house and feed. Mrs. Courtney might be angry if we don't give her proper warning." Theda turned to one of the women. "How many are you and where are you from?"

Huddled in the corner of the seat, the frail black woman could hardly understand her quick patter. If it had not been for Amos's presence she might have refused to answer the finely dressed woman.

"Best part of three hundred," she said so low that her voice seemed to come from a great distance. "By train from Tennessee."

Theda blinked and looked at Amos.

"Oh, Miss Theda," he moaned, "you've invited yourself a parcel of trouble. Three hundred! Are you forgetting that tonight is Mr. Jerome's dinner and that Mr. Lawrence wired that he was returning this evening?"

"I haven't forgotten," she whispered, not taking her eyes off the fearful woman. The frail muscles of her neck stood out and trembled. "Those events are suddenly not very important."

All afternoon, November 24, 1863, citizens charged anyone who was black and shabbily dressed, dragging them off to Garth Wilkins to gain a reward. He was ill-prepared for such an onslaught. The police did not want them and the hospitals were filled to overflowing. Wilkins asked for help from the district military commander, but the man had no knowledge of the people or their fantastic story of being sent by the military. Washington wired him back that they could get no information out of Chattanooga because it had been under siege for days. Nor would they put any bounty price upon the slaves without knowing the full facts. Wilkins was advised to feed them and await further instructions. He was not about to take money from his own pocket to feed anyone—let alone the number that filled his office, crammed the stairs, and overflowed his living quarters.

"I'm going to dinner, Lem," he snapped.

"What about them?"

"For all I care, feed them to the fish."

The statement was made to a mind that took everything literally. It was impossible ever to gain a true count of the number who were anchored and slipped beneath the waters of the East River. Only 37 slaves ever arrived at the Fifth Avenue address of Theda DeWitt. That cauldron of humanity fast becoming known as Harlem had silently absorbed many of the train riders. Liberal and conservative newspapers alike saw fit to regard the entire incident as unnewsworthy.

Irony was also playing its game. One of the Federal soldiers who had put the slaves aboard the train had been called Dahlgren—Lawrence DeWitt Dahlgren.

Because of his previous experience, Wilf Jamison was re-enlisted as Infantry Corporal Lawrence Dahlgren and sent to join the sixty thousand-man Union force under General Rosecrans. The move had been accomplished so swiftly that he had yet to receive his bonus money.

Major General William S. Rosecrans had already out-flanked Chattanooga and forced the evacuation of the Confederate troops by the time of Wilf's arrival. Hardly given time to catch his breath, Wilf was marched out to the southeast. Rosecrans had Braxton Bragg's Rebels on the run into the deep South and would follow.

It was only a few miles, but this was the mountainous country of northwest Georgia. They could hear the Chickamauga Creek as it wound through the dark woodland, but Rosecrans was so set on crushing Bragg with his superior force that he was constantly overtaking his advance scouts. They were unaware that Bragg was just across the creek.

It was quick, bloody work the next day for the Southerners to turn and engage the enemy at Reed's Bridge. With the cunning of a tiger General Bragg allowed that column to advance and probe, so that the many winding curves of the Chickamauga would mask his real intent. At five separate points downstream the Rebel columns forded and converged unseen northwest along the State Road until they joined forces with the advancing Bragg column.

The battle lines were quickly formed and a steady fusillade from the Confederates began to pick off the Federals with deadly accuracy. At times every man in the advance line was down. New men were rushed to take their places and they fell in turn.

The signal was given to the artillery and a hundred and seven great guns suddenly began to sweep the doomed Union line. Rosecrans steadily pulled his men back. His forces were being whittled down to the same size as Bragg's. Throughout the day it was an infantry battle of retreat and regroup.

Wilf snatched but a few hours sleep that night before his regiment was up and forming a new line from the Kelly Farm down to the Widow Glenn's house.

With the first report of gunfire on that second day Wilf had been very much amused at an old woman who had been driven from her home by the Northern marauders. She had taken refuge in her hayloft throughout the night and now hung perilously out the loft door. Her wrinkled old face beamed with joy at the sight of the grey battle lines and her eyes flashed with the gleam of triumph as though given the right to conduct the battle.

"Give it to them damned Yankees, boys! Over here's a parcel of 'em! To the right, you blind rascals! Push 'em back! Push 'em out of my house."

With help they pushed them farther than that. Rosecrans was not aware that General Longstreet had arrived
at midnight with reinforcements for Bragg. Hardly had
the battle commenced when Longstreet's attack force was
able to strike a gap through the Union line and split the
army in two.

In near panic, Rosecrans fled back toward Chattanooga,
leaving General George H. Thomas to fight his own battle
on the right.

Although they fought tenaciously throughout the day,
Wilf was never able to understand how they survived.
Steadily, stoically, the men in blue stood with "Pap"
Thomas and met the flaming torrent from three directions.
But as the day waned, so did the battle. And for no
reason known to man Bragg allowed the broken and tat-
tered Federals to quit the field and follow Rosecrans to
Chattanooga.

That had been the month before. A month in which
Washington refrained from letting the country know that
Rosecrans had lost sixteen thousand men and was dug in
at Chattanooga. Nor did they deign to let it be known
that Bragg had Chattanooga under siege.

Forces were on the way to break the siege, but it was
taking time. Even though his own men were hungry and
deserting, Bragg tightened the siege, controlling almost all
the traffic into the city from positions on commanding
heights and in valleys south and west.

The real starvation was taking place within the city.
The bombardment was constant. Houses crumpled like
eggshells and fires blazed night and day.

To break a line in the siege a desperate gamble was
tried. Three hundred blacks were put within boxcars and
the engineer told to roll out of town. Rosecrans felt confident that the Rebs would not let that many slaves escape
and would follow in pursuit.

It didn't work. Rosecrans cursed his men individually
and the whole army collectively, and consigned them to
the lowest depth of the deepest hell.

General Thomas's men had stopped calling him "Pap"
and were now calling him the "Rock of Chickamauga."
He knew that he had to act on his own and without authority from General Rosecrans.

"They're out there to help us," he told his officers, "because we can hear the skirmishes. But we've got to help them by letting them know our situation. Who could get through the Reb lines for us?"

Captain Homer Pearson mused a moment. "I've got a corporal that might be able to pull it off. He was already thin as a rail before the food gave out and he's got a gimpy leg. Dressed right, he might just be able to limp through their lines as one of their own fleeing this pesthole." He paused. "Name's Dahlgren and he's a damn good soldier."

For two days the armies of General Hooker and General Sherman had been pouring into the area to join under the combined command of U.S. Grant. They had been pushing Bragg's men off the cliffs of Lookout Mountain. The fateful morning of November 24, 1863 dawned in heavy fog. Its grey mantle shrouded the town, clung wet and heavy to the ground in the silent valley before the crescent-shaped mountain and veiled the face of its heights.

Under the cover of this fog the long waves of blue spread over the mountain and took their places in battle line. The grey men in lower reaches and valley crouched in their ditches and behind stone walls, gripped their guns and waited for the foe to walk into the trap Bragg had set.

No one paid the least bit of attention to the crippled man who passed among them begging for a crust of bread or a handful of corn. As he passed in and out of the fog banks his line of direction was not heeded.

Unseen, Wilf slowly rose above the misty curtain and the sun burst about him. The fog in the valley lay like the smooth ground of a vast snow field, and back of it rose the silent mountain, tier on tier like the seats of a mighty amphitheatre. But the men crouching on the mountain were not spectators; they would be the actors in that day's tragedy.

Generals gave way to a mere corporal to direct the battle, for Wilf had recorded in his memory the position of the enemy in what would be termed the "Battle above the Clouds."

The precision of Wilf's memory sent batteries of artillery rattling and bounding into new positions. Infantrymen crawled about the tiers like an ant-swarm under attack. Officers were given new commands.

The long roll beat from a thousand drums, the call of the buglers rang over the fog-shrouded valley—and then came the strange, solemn stillness as God holds His breath and averts His eyes, not wishing to see what manner of men He has given the earth.

The Rebels braced for the attack but the flame and fire and minié balls that rained down on them came not from the expected direction but from the heights of the mountain. The grey lines were mowed down in swaths as. though Jove himself were directing the cannoneers from the fog banks in the sky.

Again and again came those awful volleys of musketry and artillery crossfiring on the confused lines. The men staggered and recovered, reformed and moved to new positions over the dead bodies of their comrades, but it seemed as if the Federals had eyes that could see through the fog. The fire would be just as great at the new position as the old.

Wilf Jamison was the all-seeing eye. He was everywhere at once, describing the terrain below and the positions Bragg's men would most logically take.

A ripple of admiration ran along the crouching lines for the accuracy and detail of his directions. Filtering up through the clouds was a sound that made all believe that the gates of hell had been opened wide and the demons set loose to rant their agony.

As the Rebel lines fell back, staggering, bleeding, cut to pieces, Bragg ordered fresh brigades to throw down their knapsacks, fix their bayonets and charge through their own melting ranks into the fusillade—to fall back in their turn.

Now, although none were aware of it at that moment, came the turning of the tide.

With a mighty shout the blue lines swept down the mountain, took the ditches at bayonets' point, and captured two hundred grey prisoners. But only for a moment. From the supporting line rang the Rebel yell and they were hurled back, shattered and themselves cut to pieces.

"Who ordered that stupid charge?" Wilf shrieked. "Idiots! The enemy is now over there!"

The curved lines on the hill followed his pointed finger and raked the charging Rebels with their murderous cross-fire.

"Now, down!" he ordered.

The men followed Wilf's lead and fell flat on their stomachs as a battery of artillery blazed from the hillcrest. They could hear the shrill swish of the big shots pass no more than two feet over their heads.

The colonel, irate at having his command abrogated by a corporal, had stayed on his horse. His first lieutenant felt he must do the same. A cannon shot fell short and severed the lieutenant's arm, glanced off and killed the colonel. As though to underscore the fact that it was his last battle, the lieutenant unbuckled and dropped his revolver and cartridge belt.

It was an odd moment of *déjà vu* for Wilf. He had been here before but had no time to think on it. He picked up the lieutenant's equipment, took his colonel's place and led the charge.

Men were falling on the right and left but Wilf Jamison loaded and fired with steady, dogged nerve.

The blue billowed in force off the mountain now and the greys fell back in confusion. The din was incessant and overpowering. The color-bearer of Bragg's regiment, confused by conflicting orders, paused and asked for instructions. Braxton Bragg, mistaking his words, ordered a hasty full retreat.

Shrouded by the fog that the sun was only beginning to burn away, the shattered Confederates slowly fell back down the bloody valley, stumbling over their dead and wounded. The dim smoke-bound area was a slaughter pen. Where the siege lines of grey had waited with flashing bayonets and ready guns at eight o'clock, the dead lay in mangled heaps, and the wounded huddled among them awaiting capture. The siege of Chattanooga was over. The Yankees stood at the gate to the deep South. The Confederacy's fortunes were dying.

A stout bearded man had watched the drama with flashing eyes. Beside him stood his officers, reluctantly dutiful. They did not like the bourbon on his breath, or the cigar held firmly between his yellowed teeth. They were well aware that he was there under direct orders from Lincoln and that rankled even more. To a man, they thought that General McClellan should have given the order, and not a civilian. Many had even prayed that the battle would go badly.

Now he turned to them, and in a flat voice that expressed his regard for them as a lot, he said, "Who is that man again who brought us the information and led that last charge?"

"A soldier, sir, sent up by George Thomas."

Grant took the cigar from his mouth as though it had become distasteful. He eyed them each, and his dark eyes glittered with his pain and anger at having been overlooked for so long in this war.

"I have eyes to see and ears to hear those facts," he said, in a restrained voice. "I want a name."

"Dahlgren, sir. Corporal Lawrence Dahlgren."

He nodded. After a moment he spoke again, tonelessly:

"It is now *Major* Lawrence Dahlgren and he will remain in command of the regiment that he so successfully led."

A colonel muttered, "But that is ridiculous, sir. Perhaps you meant to say sergeant."

Grant coldly fixed his eyes on the man.

"Had we more men like him instead of men like you leading the war, our military cemeteries might be only half-full. You, personally, go and get me the tunic and insignia off any fallen major. That man will be on my staff, at the rank I designate, and I'll shout his name for the whole country to hear and praise. I like him. He's every bit as resolute, as businesslike, and, by damn, as brilliant as I am!"

14

THERE WAS A LONG silence in Laura's room, while Laura stood stunned before the full-length looking glass, the reflected image behind her one she had least expected to see that evening.

"Betty is not a servant, Ruth Ann," she said at last, her voice hushed and infuriated. "She is a dress designer and we don't have time for her to go away at the moment."

"I don't care if she's the Queen of Prussia," Ruth Ann said contemptuously. "I told her to get out of the room."

"Ruth Ann," Laura muttered, "you have acquired Mama's habit of being rude to people you consider your inferiors. Might I remind you that you are in Aunt Theda's house, not Mama's."

Ruth Ann stared at her grimly. She was not used to having Laura speak back to her, but knew that much of what she had said was true. She boldly took a seat on the side of the four-poster bed and glared angrily at Laura.

"All right," she said finally, "let her continue. It's a waste of time, though. Mama has sent orders by Laddie that you're to be returned home tonight. I am to take your place and you are to leave your wardrobe here."

A month before, Laura would have lashed out at her without thinking. She looked at her sister's calm and haughtily contemptuous face. It was so small, so pale, imbued with such a delicate English regality. The lines of the mouth were selfish; the fine nostrils seemed always to have just smelled something foul. Laura decided upon a course of action she had never taken with Ruth Ann before—she ignored her.

"I don't think we need another rose on the gown, Betty. Let's add that last one to the two you've set aside for the wristlet. What do you think, Ruth Ann?"

Ruth Ann shrugged, her face impassive. But Laura could see a glow in her eye of real envy.

The gown was a masterpiece in golden velvet. Because it was a dinner party, Betty had decided to forgo hoops. The bodice was simply cut with three-quarter-length straight sleeves. A garland of velvet rose buds, whose leaves and stems had been fashioned out of gold braid, swept off the right shoulder, under her breast and down to encircle the waist. The main skirt was cut straight, without a single pleat or tuck, giving her an angular tallness. The overskirt, of a lighter gold velvet, was only a gathering and draping of the material over the three descending bustles. The remaining rose buds would be attached to her left wrist by trailing velvet ribbons. Her hair had been parted in the middle, brushed flat, and braided about her head with intertwining golden cords.

"Thank you, Betty. You'd best go see to Aunt Theda now."

"That probably won't be necessary," Ruth Ann said. "She's probably still in conference with Laddie."

"You have much to learn, Ruth Ann. Others conform to her schedule, not she to theirs."

Betty hurried out, carrying a large number of unfinished Worth dresses.

"Don't let her take those. I want to look at them."

"Oh, hush!" Laura said fretfully. "They're unfinished gowns."

"Good! Then Monsieur Worth won't have any trouble redoing them for me."

Laura was silent for a moment. Her eyes did not leave

her sister, though their sternness increased. "Aunt Theda doesn't use him anymore," she said flatly.

"Then she'll just have to get him back. It is Mama's orders that he is to do my wardrobe."

There was no shame or hesitation in her voice. She looked at Laura steadfastly. Laura felt her uncompromising hardness, as though Lucille were there to support her. She regarded Ruth Ann incredulously. She had forgotten how relentless, how ruthless, her sister could be.

Almost inaudibly, she said, "And is Mama willing to pay his prices? A social wardrobe runs about twenty thousand dollars."

"Mama says that Auntie T is obliged to pay for it."

"Obliged?" Laura exclaimed, hardly believing what she had heard. "Tell me, Ruth Ann, what brought Mama to such a strange conclusion?"

"Why is it strange?" she asked, her tone as measured as always. "As long as it is DeWitt money it is also Mama's and mine."

She spoke with no emotion at all, as if she and Lucille were the only two who mattered, as if the rest of the world was populated with superfluous creatures.

The strangest emotions swept over Laura. She could not fathom them. She could only gaze at this creature, with her haughty and beautiful face, her inflexible rosy mouth, her blank and unreadable eyes.

There was a polite rap at the door and the new upstairs maid entered.

"Excuse, miss. Miss Theda has ordered the brougham brought 'round and Mr. Calvert has arrived."

"Thank you, Sue-Ellen. Tell Calvert I'll be right down."

"Calvert who?" Ruth Ann demanded. "And where in the hell do you think you're going?"

Laura shot her a reproving look. She suddenly realized she could treat Ruth Ann as a stranger.

"He is Calvert DeLong, of the DeLong shipping family. Most handsome and charming. He will be my table partner this evening for Mr. Jerome's dinner at Delmonico's. And I'm sorry to leave you, Ruth Ann, but in New York one just doesn't squeeze in last-minute guests."

For a moment Ruth Ann stood confused and shaken.

She had expected Lucille's word to be accepted as law
the moment she arrived. She was still determined to see
that it was. She slithered off the bed, smiling with a cold
cruelty that paled and molded the lines of her mouth.

"All that will have to be changed," she said. "Mama's
wishes come first. So, little sister, I would suggest you
take off the gown so that I might dress to take your place
at the dinner and with your escort."

"No," Laura said firmly, though her heart plunged. "I
will speak with Aunt Theda and Laddie."

They looked for a long time in each other's eyes. Then
Ruth Ann's smile became triumphant. Wordlessly, she
turned and went in search of Laddie. He would straighten
this little baggage out.

Laddie stood tensely in the drawing room, unable to
sort out his feverish thoughts. It was a shock that Calvert
was there for Laura and Theda—and not to see him, a
further shock to see Calvert so elegantly attired and
groomed. Although Calvert had made his meeting with
Laura sound very casual, Laddie could not help but feel
a pang of jealousy. Was his little sister trying to steal
Callie away from him?

And Laura had been the central theme of his feverish
thoughts even before he entered the drawing room. His
"conference" with Theda had turned into a tongue-lashing.
The woman was disregarding Lucille's edict as though it
had never been issued. Nor did Laddie have room to fight
her on the point. He was desperate for her help. Colonel
Beetle had made good on his word for his secret testimony
against Fremont. But the uniform contract was only a
piece of paper unless he could produce the finished product. There had been a horrible family exchange over the
capital he required to modernize the mill's ancient machinery, with his father pleading abject poverty and his
mother insisting that Theda DeWitt be ordered to advance
the money or stand in line of Lucille's wrath.

That comment, however, had made Theda laugh with
glee. She had already made known to Laddie her feelings
about the gall of Ruth Ann's arrival. Ruth Ann's attitude
was repugnant to her. The girl would be allowed a "short
visit" and that would be that.

But she had looked at Laddie's financial needs with pure businesslike logic. Maggie Duggan, whose name she did not mention aloud, she could trust to run the mill in a manner that would provide her with a return on her investment. But she wanted something far different from Laddie before she would approve such a sizable loan.

Laddie had no recourse but to agree to her terms, although he felt as though he had sold both himself and his mother to the devil.

"Laddie, do you know what that brat is intending—" Ruth Ann stopped short, catching sight of Calvert DeLong. Good God! she thought. Handsome and charming? Why, he's a Greek god come down to mingle with the masses. Look at that figure!

"Oh, Ruth Ann, let me introduce a good friend of mine, Calvert DeLong. Calvert, my sister, Ruth Ann."

Calvert came gracefully forward, bowed and touched her hand to his lips. "My pleasure, Miss Dahlgren. I was unaware that Laddie was blessed with two charming and beautiful sisters."

"Two?" she smiled. "Mr. DeLong, you are indeed a gentleman, but you need not lie to Laddie and me about that ugly duckling."

"I scarcely regard Laura as being ugly," said Calvert, flushing with indignation. "She has courage, refinement and elegance. My words were not a lie, Miss Dahlgren."

Ruth Ann was not offended. She laughed comfortably. She honestly believed that he was just being kind toward Laura. No one in his right mind could compare the two of them. She favored Calvert with a suggestive smile. "Forgive me if I must speak about her in front of you, but this is urgently important. Laddie, Laura isn't making the first move toward getting ready to leave. She believes that she's going to some dinner this evening."

"What is this?" said Calvert, with fresh indignation. "I know it isn't my place to remark on this, but Laura is the guest of honor tonight."

"That's utterly preposterous," Ruth Ann said flatly. "Who would wish to honor her?"

Laddie laughed uncomfortably. "His name is Leonard Jerome, Ruth Ann, and I think we had best let things stand as they are, for tonight."

"I will not," she protested. "If she goes, then I insist upon going also."

"Insist! Insist! Insist!" Theda exclaimed, bouncing into the drawing room in her new gown of golden silk. "One does not *insist* upon *anything* when one has arrived as an unannounced guest. For *that* oversight you can thank your thoughtless mother and brother. Laddie, Mrs. Courtney will lay out a supper for you and your sister. Good evening, Calvert. My, don't we look handsome tonight!"

Ruth Ann, for all her obtuseness, finally began to understand her situation. She said in a more subdued voice, "I'm sorry if I sounded insolent, Auntie T. It's just that it is my first night in New York and I thought it would be much different, what with Laura supposed to be going home, and all."

Theda glared at Laddie. He shrugged, as though he had been helpless to get a word in edgewise with his sister.

"I will be candid," Theda said severely, "and to the point. Laddie and I have discussed the situation thoroughly and I have made it clear that Laura will return upstate only when I am ready to send her in that direction."

"But, Auntie T, mother said—"

"I have never formed the peculiar habit of taking orders from your mother, young lady," she said icily. "And further—I loathe that rude and flippant name. Both you and your brother may address me as Miss Theda, Miss DeWitt, or Aunt Theda. I leave the choice to you. Now, where is . . . ah, here she comes. Oh, Laura, I just knew that golden sable was exactly right for that costume. I'm so pleased I remembered it, before someone snatched it up at the auction. Isn't she just stunning?"

Laddie was greatly impressed. Theda's words of praise had brought a high flush to Laura's countenance that radiated her beauty and brought a misty sparkle to her blue eyes. She was every inch a lady, a thing he could not in truth say of Ruth Ann, for all her handsomeness. His bargain over Laura with Theda now seemed far too cheap. To keep such grace and beauty in New York, he had been remiss for not asking triple the fifteen thousand dollars.

His appraisal of Laura was shared by Calvert, but breeding will out. Calvert could not help feeling that Theda had been unnecessarily severe with Ruth Ann. Although she did have the earmarks of a very spoiled young woman, her pouting face was softening him.

"Excuse me for intruding, Miss Theda, but it it would be acceptable to you and Mr. Jerome, I will gladly sit out the dinner in the bar so that Miss Dahlgren could occupy my seat at the table."

Ruth Ann instantly glowed like the sun on a calm sea. Impulsively, she grasped Theda and hugged her with generous abandon. "Aunt Theda!" she burst out, "is that possible? No one could be sweeter than Mr. Calvert to make such a gentlemanly offer! My poor heart is just aflutter with excitement!"

Swinging instantly from delight to despair, she said mournfully, "But it cannot be. Just look at me. I look like a country girl ready to do the milking."

"Nonsense," Theda chided, wishing to get to the party even if she did have to drag an extra body along. "That dress is most fetching. Besides, I believe you would be nearly twenty-four now, and beyond the point where you ought to look like a debutante. Well! Well! Well! Let's be on our way. Sorry to leave you alone, Laddie."

"Quite all right," he beamed. "I've many things to do this evening. Will I be seeing you later, Callie?"

Calvert winked. "You can count on it."

Laddie Dahlgren's world was suddenly rosy again. He would meet Calvert later at Pfaff's. He had so much to catch up on in that world. And he had to think about the world of tomorrow. Once he had Theda's money in hand he could really put the mill into . . . but he was getting so threadbare. Perhaps he could divert some of the money for a few necessary personal purchases.

The majority of the guests had already arrived, a bevy of ladies elaborately dressed and begemmed—although careful to forgo diamonds, as they were to be the theme of the third dinner—and elegant gentlemen in gleaming evening dress. Leonard Jerome beamed sunnily as he greeted them. Everything was golden, down to the last detail. The horseshoe table was covered in golden cloth and napkins, and the dinner service and ware were of solid gold. The hundred chairs had been covered in golden velvet, and even the candles and floral arrangements were dyed to match the theme.

The banquet was held in Delmonico's large ballroom, which was almost filled by the huge table. The guests were to sit only on the outside perimeter of the table. Jerome had transformed the center of the horseshoe into an undulating fall landscape of golden aspens and mum gardens, in the center of which there was a thirty-foot lake, where four superb swans, brought from Prospect Park, swam in an enclosure formed by a delicate network of golden wire. Above the sheet of water were suspended little golden cages containing rare songbirds that filled the room with music.

Their music, however, was largely ignored as two conversations were fervently pursued. The first, the news that President Lincoln had promoted the disreputable U.S. Grant to the rank of lieutenant general and given him command of the army. The second, the startling addition of a one hundred-and-first guest. This unheard-of break with the plan nearly caused Lorenzo Delmonico a heart attack; just to begin with, he would have to place an unmatched chair and service at the end of the table. Exactly one hundred of every specialty item had been laboriously prepared, molded, jelled and decorated. The odd man out would just have to be content to dine off the regular menu.

Ruth Ann Dahlgren was out to take the spotlight from Laura at all costs. She smiled regally at the guests, and her curtsy was controlled and graceful. She acknowledged every introduction with lofty dignity, her head tilted. She was being pure English and pure DeWitt. Her show of breeding antagonized the ladies and charmed the men, though it also intimidated them. Her nearly plebeian attire surprisingly threw the ladies in all their finery quite into the shade, giving them an almost vulgar look.

Mr. and Mrs. William Marcy Tweed arrived, an ebullient and quite cherubic couple. They came forward to bow, blushing, affable, radiating their pleasure at being included in such company. Boss Tweed could not hide his Cockney-like New York accent and Ruth Ann answered him in her cultivated and courteous tones, which brought the first involuntary smile to all but one in the group. Theda DeWitt came bouncing forth and escorted the couple away to the refreshment bar. To her it was a devil of a predicament. Even her short acquaintanceship with this niece assured her that here was a girl full of all the violent impulses and voracious self-interest of a new Lucille. There was no predicting what she might do to embarrass the Tweeds and no way to bring her quietly to bay. But she would keep the Tweeds away from Ruth Ann. Boss Tweed was now very important to Theda DeWitt. She wanted him to enjoy this evening as none he had ever before enjoyed.

"Calvert!" Ruth Ann suddenly chirped. "You've been ignoring me. I didn't know I was going to have to stand in this stuffy reception line. Take me away before I have to shake another of these fish-liver hands."

Leonard Jerome's indignation temporarily choked him. His iron fingers reached out and tightened on Laura's arm. Laura, who had been smiling mechanically all evening, now frowned. But she kept her voice under control.

"I apologize for her, Mr. Jerome. My mother has filled her head since her birth with the most grandiose idea of herself. She's been told, for example, that only a titled marriage will be good enough for her."

His face cracked in an ironic smile. "I hope your mother gets her wish, Laura. Only someone just as insufferable could stand her. Would you mind if I altered the seating arrangement slightly?"

"Why should I? It's your party."

"Yes, and I plan to reclaim it right now."

His change required very little of Lorenzo's waiters, liveried in gold silk knee britches, fluted shirts and velvet weskits, and brought a bemused smile to Lorenzo's fleshy pink face.

Upon being informed of Mr. Jerome's wishes, Calvert was a trifle upset, but kept his face calm. Ruth Ann beamed with cunning triumph. She had stolen Laura's table partner away without even trying. Now she would go to work on stealing him away for good. She knew she had already made herself the hit of the party with her proper grammar, perfect gestures and elegant aloofness. Once she was properly outfitted she would make them all appear to be even more gauche and awkward than they already seemed to her.

"Gentlemen, seat your ladies!" Lorenzo called, in announcing dinner.

Theda was delighted with the change. It put her between the Tweeds and gave Laura her seat next to Leonard Jerome. It also delighted her that it put Ruth Ann and Calvert at the very bottom of one leg of the horseshoe.

Jerome helped Laura into her seat and remained standing.

"Ladies, your napkins, if you please."

The room erupted into squeals of utter delight. Hidden within each of the ladies' napkins was a handsome bracelet of solid gold, with a delicate filigree overlay. For years afterward it would be a symbol, when worn, that the lady had been one of the chosen; just as epicures for years would recall that the menu had included an *aspic de canvasback*, a salad of string beans with truffles, and a truffled ice cream—one of the great Lorenzo's novelties which sounded rather odd but turned out to be delicious.

Ruth Ann sat stunned into silence. Her napkin was empty.

"I presume," Calvert said, highly embarrassed, "that you must be in my original seat, Miss Dahlgren." He felt his own ordinary Delmonico napkin to be sure a mistake had not been made. But no mistake had been made; Rudolph Tiffany had hand-crafted only the fifty originals and then burned his sketch.

Ruth Ann looked down at the head table and the standing figure of Leonard Jerome. Their eyes locked and she saw his craftiness. Wild anger suffused her. She flew from her chair on what sounded dangerously like a sob. But she was smiling wickedly to herself.

"Oh, darling!" she gushed, coming up behind Laura. "Isn't that absolutely divine? Let me see! Let me see!"

Laura surrendered the bracelet, and saw Ruth Ann's face. She was literally yellow with envy.

"Oh, Laura," she said in loud delight, slipping the bracelet onto her wrist. "You are already wearing those tacky roses, so I'll just keep this on for the evening. Gold never was your color anyway, darling. Just look how that dress makes you look as pale as death. Oh, I must get back to Calvert. He is so witty and urbane, so charming."

"Well, I'll be . . ." Jerome gasped and sat down. His face was filled with astonishment. He had meant to put her in her place, and he was not used to being topped.

"It's Christmas all over," Laura muttered unthinkingly.

"I beg your pardon?"

Laura blushed. "I'm sorry, I was just remembering our childhood Christmases. No matter what we got, if Ruth Ann liked my present better, she always found a way to get her hands on it—for good."

Jerome felt as if his chest were contracting painfully about his heart. The sight of Ruth Ann vamping Calvert DeLong and showing off the bracelet as though she were the only one in the room to have received one gave him a feeling of great discomfiture.

"I pity her," he said suddenly. "A moth that flies too close to the flame gets its wings singed."

Laura didn't fully understand the comment, but followed his gaze. She had seen Ruth Ann like this before. All dignity was being forgotten; she was bringing out all her female wiles in a sort of mating quest. She was not uneasy that Ruth Ann would embarrass her so much as that she would embarrass Calvert. Laura had come to regard him highly as a friend, and knew her sister to be an unreliable and unpredictable creature.

It was folly, she told herself, even to be thinking on the matter. Calvert meant nothing to her, except as a friend. He probably found Ruth Ann just as appealing as the cadets always did. Still, she couldn't help but feel uncomfortable and barely tasted the food placed before her.

Never had Theda DeWitt been so relieved to see an evening come to an end. The Tweeds had eaten as though it would be the last meal they would see for a month, and Ruth Ann had purposely turned her back on everyone else and paid her undivided attention to Calvert DeLong.

Amos had stayed up to let them in, and was thankful that Calvert had escorted them back. He had only to nod his head to inform Calvert that he wished him to stay a moment.

"I wish to see you in my room," Theda muttered, touching Ruth Ann on the arm.

Ruth Ann started violently. She turned and stared at the glowering face, slowly becoming aware that this was not a woman like her mother who could be easily fooled. She struck off the hand, thrusting Theda away from her so ferociously that the plump woman lost her balance and thumped her head against the doorframe.

"Oh, damn you, damn you all!" Ruth Ann cried out, her voice broken by theatrical sobs. "You made me look the fool on purpose by not allowing me to dress properly! No one paid the least attention to me, except for Calvert. And . . . and this . . . was the biggest insult of all."

She snatched off the bracelet, throwing it down on the marble tile, and fled up the stairs.

Amos was already gathering Theda to her feet. She was dazed by the blow to the back of her head.

"I will see her to her room," he muttered. "Coffee is laid out in the drawing room."

There was no confusion in Laura's mind. She had seen both her mother and sister pull this stunt far too many times, twisting the facts in a screaming tirade to suit their own needs.

Calvert was confused. He stooped down and picked up the broken bracelet, the filigree having popped loose from the solid base.

"I'm sorry," he said, as though he had been responsible. He placed the bracelet in Laura's hand.

"That's Ruth Ann," she said dully. "She has a passion for breaking things she cannot have as her own." She sighed. "You will learn that, as soon as she tires of you or someone more interesting comes along."

"Whoa! Who said I had any interest in her?"

"I know my sister," she said, slowly starting to walk to the drawing room door. "She has a certain knack for making people take an interest in her. Even Leonard Jerome did it tonight, by saying that he pitied her. That's interest, of a sort."

She took off the sable and draped it over a chair, going straight to the fire to warm herself.

"I wouldn't say that what I feel is pity," he said with a

laugh. "I'm afraid I'm rather a shy person when it comes to women, Laura. Need I tell you that she made my lack of knowledge on that subject quite obvious?"

"I realize you got stuck with an impossible situation."

"I did it to myself by trying to be gallant. Still, she scares me in a different way. She is not stupid. Is she aware, in any way, of your involvement with the slaves in West Point?"

It was a thought that had not crossed Laura's mind until he raised the point. Now she did wonder how much Ruth Ann knew, other than what she might have guessed the night she had come for her at Clint's with Fremont. He quickly grasped the portent of her face.

"Well, I can see that she might. As long as she's here, I think it's wise to keep them away from here."

"Why?" she insisted, turning to face him. "Why is she any more of a danger than my brother?"

He laughed again. "I can control your brother, to a certain degree. But I can't control her, of that I am sure."

"It isn't fair."

"What is fair in this world, Laura? Look at Amos. Did you know that his people were slaves even before they came to this country? And even before they were brought to Jamaica? His people were Ashanti—a tribe born to slavery. Oh, not the type we have in the South, but similar. They were born chattel to their king, and lived their entire lives within his service. The king, or the *muzkal* elders, also used them for human barter, trading them to the British, French and Portuguese for cattle, wheat, or a bolt of foreign cloth."

"Would Amos have been a *muz . . . muzkal?*" She stumbled over the strange word.

"Perhaps. But he can't look backward. Not anymore than your sister should," he added, "with her foolish notion that the DeWitts will regain their titled status."

On that point she could laugh. "You certainly did learn a lot from her—and from Amos, it would seem."

"He's a most interesting man—and she is an interesting woman, in a curious way. Did you ever stop to consider that she's also a slave? A slave to your mother? At twenty-four, she's still unwed. Some would say that was a sure sign of remaining an old maid for the rest of her life—just because your mother holds out for a titled marriage for her."

Laura laughed lightly. "See, she did capture your interest!"

"But not for marriage. I have my own thoughts on that subject."

"You deserve a very special girl," Laura said, with genuine emotion.

He looked down at her as she stood beside him, and he thought: and you are more than special enough for me.

The blue eyes fixed so urgently upon him saw his thought. She turned aside her head, and he saw her profile, delicate and beautiful.

"Calvert," she whispered. The frail muscles of her white throat stood out above her golden collar and trembled.

"Laura," he said. Involuntarily, his hand reached out and seized hers.

She struggled to regain a semblance of their old relationship. It would be wrong of her not to speak her true feelings. A current came through his fingers that she didn't understand. She swallowed.

"Please," she said tonelessly, "I can't lie to you, but . . ."

She could not look at him. Her eyes were fixed on the carpet. But she felt the grip on her hand loosen, fall away.

His voice seemed to come from a great distance. "Is there someone else . . . back home?"

"I—I think so. He's the only one that . . . *I've* ever kissed . . . but . . ."

He looked at the turmoil in her face. She was unsure what she should be feeling at that moment, but he was sure of his own feelings. He was sure that he could never love another but her, sure that no other woman would affect him in this way. It was total misery when he was not near her. He could not spend a waking moment, or a dreaming night, without her face and name a constant part of his thoughts. But his shyness toward women had held him speechless, until that moment. And the moment might never come again.

He caught her in his arms and pressed his mouth hard upon hers. Laura was momentarily startled. For a second she was reminded of Fremont Hunter rather than of

Clinton Bell. Then of neither of them. She was against a broad, muscular chest, through which she could feel a tremor. It touched and stirred her. She melted against him. He felt the tumultuous beating of her heart against his chest. A wild rapture swept over him. He pressed her body to him with his hands, and her firm flesh softened and yielded under them.

They were aware of nothing but their turbulent coming together, satisfying their desperate hunger.

Then he felt a power rise in her, impassive, immovable.

"No," she said, with firmness and calmness.

"Did you think of him again?" he said, his heart plunging.

"It has nothing to do with Clint Bell. I cannot deny that I find you attractive . . . Oh, I don't know the words to say. I don't know what I'm really feeling, Calvert. Please, let me just say goodnight for now."

He was too much the gentleman to press her. He had time to let her heart soften toward him. He still had a duty to perform and a war to fight. But at that moment neither one of them seemed very important—nor did Laddie Dahlgren. He just wished to go home and savor again and again the memory of her kiss.

Laddie heard the sharp knock, sounding clearly through the garret. "I'm coming, Callie," he called. Oh, yes, tonight at last, I'll have you alone.

He threw open the door—and stood there, his emotions crumbling. In the dull glow of the hall lamp, Ruth Ann stood flushed and eager.

"Laddie," she whispered. "May I come in?"

"Come in," he said gently. "But I'm due to go out soon. I—I'm to meet Calvert."

"Impossible! He's downstairs mooning over our simpering little sister. That seems to be the only subject the man cares to discuss."

He followed her mutely into his small parlor, unable to imagine what Calvert and Laura would have in common. Laddie had always thought she was so dull.

"Sit down," he said. "Would you like some wine?"

"No—yes! God knows I need some. Even though I was the hit of the dinner party, it was just utterly ghastly. I came to New York to live, Laddie, not to be bored to death. And what was this double-talk between you and the old crow over Laura?"

"There are good reasons why I had to change my decision, Ruth Ann."

"Oh, God!" she breathed. "Don't say that she's going to stay. That will just ruin everything for me."

"Don't be alarmed, Ruth Ann," he said slowly. "We just have to work things in a little different way, and I think Mama will agree with me. I've written her quite a lengthy letter on the subject this evening."

"I don't understand, Laddie. Put it a bit more simply, won't you?"

"It is really very simple, my pet. Laura stays so that I can obtain a loan for the business from Auntie T."

She scrambled clumsily to her feet.

"That's fine for you," she said stoutly, "and fine for Laura. But where in the hell does that leave me? I'll tell you! With nothing! Laura will keep the wardrobe and where will I get one?"

"Don't be a ninny, Ruth Ann!" he growled. "You'll get everything you deserve—but you have to work for it."

"Work?" she scoffed. "I've never worked a day in my life."

He smiled wickedly. "This type of work will be right up your alley. Once we get the money from Auntie T, then we can subtly go to work on getting her to send Laura away on her own. It shouldn't be hard for you to clip the dear little angel's wings. After all, you've been quite successful on that score for years."

She stood there looking at him, her eyes widening and darkening in her fine face.

"You started off all wrong," he went on hurriedly. "Granted. But no damage done if you were such a success at the party tonight. You've got to remember that Auntie T and Mother cannot be handled in the same manner. You and I both know that Mother is a very poor manager of money *and* of people's lives. That's not the case with Auntie T. For all her fluffiness, she's quite shrewd. Do you understand?"

She looked at Laddie as though she had suddenly become Lucille and he just another Clarence—a foolish man who talked foolish prattle. Nothing mattered other than gaining the things her mother had promised. Nothing counted, other than the fact that she would get rid of Laura her way, and not Laddie's. For the first time in her life she put on a false face for her brother.

"I understand," she whispered, "but it's going to be dull as hell around here for me."

"Dull!" he exclaimed. "It doesn't have to be. Have you any money with you?"

"Mama gave me some to buy a few things I might want."

"Good! Then we'll begin by buying you a good time. Oh, don't worry, I'll have scads of Auntie T's money tomorrow to pay you back. But tonight we're going where there is fun and life and . . . and men, my pet."

"But it's so late . . ."

"Late? My dear, you are about to learn that New York is just now waking up for the night. Come, I'll show you how to sneak out of this tomb without arousing the dead souls who inhabit it."

15

LAURA FOUND her fierce resolution to return Calvert to the status of friend a difficult one to keep. Because they all agreed that Ruth Ann was a danger, the Underground work was curtailed. Days began to slip into weeks in which Calvert hardly called at all. The first few weeks were not so hard. They were busy getting Betty fully established in her shop, attending various functions—including the diamond dinner—and preparing for Christmas.

Using the ruse that Lucille had authorized the payment, Laddie was able to get Betty to start on Ruth Ann's wardrobe. It took every cunning ploy he could devise to convince Ruth Ann that they had no other choice. She was like a sleeping volcano, spitting occasional clouds of smoke, but with no lava flow as yet. Her tantrums, when they came, were cleverly directed at Laura and not Theda DeWitt. And in each case Laura came out looking the fool in Theda's eyes.

Theda allowed the "short stay" to elongate itself because Betty was still not experienced enough to turn out a wardrobe as quickly as Worth might have; and she counted the days until Christmas, knowing full well that her sister would demand that her children be home for the holidays. Oddly enough, it never crossed her mind that it would also mean the departure of Laura. Also, Theda was content on another score. Ruth Ann seemed disinclined to attend any of the major social functions, being content to spend her evenings with her brother. That was also a relief to Theda. A stay-at-home Laddie meant that he was applying himself to the business and putting her money to sound use. She no longer minded his entertaining friends in his quarters, because Ruth Ann was there to act as a calming influence, and even Amos had told her that the parties were now more subdued.

Yes, a few more days and she would be rid of the lot.

Ruth Ann was constantly more chagrined at the conceit which had led her to imagine her conquest of Calvert would be easy. He was with them at Pfaff's or Delaney's or the concert dance halls almost nightly. But in such places the talk was always politics, politics, politics. And never once would he return with them to Laddie's quarters for the intimate little parties that she was beginning to enjoy so much. She began to look on Calvert as a cold lover, even though she strongly desired him. But Laddie had other friends who did come to the parties. Strong, manly, masterful friends. Crazy, daring, fun-seeking people. Laddie ruled his guests as though it was his God-given right. Whatever he suggested they went along with— because he was paying the bill—and Ruth Ann joined in enthusiastically.

On the first day of Christmas week, Ruth Ann came into Laddie's bedroom, her face gray with misery. Laddie took one look at her and jumped nude from his bed.

"Don't tell me Betty is pressing for money!" he roared. "We aren't caught, are we?"

"No," she whispered. "She's only half finished. It isn't that."

"Then what in thunderation is it?"

"It's Mama," she sobbed, opening her hand to reveal a crumpled telegram. "She wants us home tomorrow night at the latest. Oh, I don't want to go. You know how dull her Christmas parties are."

"Is that all?" he growled, parading around shamelessly as though he were fully clothed. "Well, that's a simple matter to handle. We shall just take a few selected people home with us. Mama has always loved my friends before."

"She wants us to bring along Miss Priss," Ruth Ann said grimly.

"That," Laddie said, "could put a damper on things." He thought a moment. "Unless you could somehow convince Laura to stay here."

Ruth Ann grinned. "You could say that it's as good as done."

A million ideas ran through her brain on how best to bring it about as she went in search of her sister. She found that no one had seen Laura, until she learned from Amos that Laura had an unexpected visitor in the breakfast room. She immediately concluded it would be Calvert DeLong, but it was not his voice filtering out of the room. She stood to one side of the door and listened.

"You could say that the whole thing was dishonest," Clinton Bell said sadly. "Who would ever have thought that your mother and Nettie Rivers would ever join forces on anything? As Marvin's letter there tells you, he and Mildred just couldn't take any more of the harrassment. He had to sell dirt-cheap or go broke. He'll send you their address when they decide where to settle. I still can't figure out how your mother got me fired from the foundry, but she did. The only way I can figure out that she knew I was here for that costume ball is that Fremont must have found out somehow. But his plight is even worse than mine. The rumor is that your mother and brother got him kicked out—"

"Wait a minute!" Laura cut him short. "I just saw someone on the street who will be willing to help, I know."

"Who? Help with what?"

"With finding you a new job," she replied. "You've all but accused me of being responsible for getting you into this mess. Now, let me go talk with Calvert DeLong and see what suggestions he might have."

Laura came out of the breakfast room and down the hall so fast that she didn't even see Ruth Ann.

Ruth Ann pressed even harder into the wall, her mind

suddenly fearful of what Clinton might be about to reveal concerning Fremont Hunter. In no way did she want Laura learning any aspect of that situation.

She heard a chair scrape and footsteps. She did not want to confront Clinton Bell, and so she hurriedly slipped along the wall and into the drawing room. From the window there she could spy on Laura and Calvert.

Her first sighting turned her smug. Calvert was doing all the listening, his face a grim mask. She waited for Laura to be turned down flat.

"Look, Calvert, I know I don't have this right. But I do somehow feel responsible for getting Clinton involved. Please, all I ask is that you take him to the shipyard. He's a good foundry man and can get the job on his own."

Calvert's face at that moment was a study in misery. He had had to fight the devil himself to stay away from her, and now she was asking a favor for the very man who stood between them. It was difficult for him to imagine what life had been like before she came into it. He was unable to eat, to sleep, to do his work effectively. The only solace he got in seeing Ruth Ann and Laddie was that they served as proof that Laura was real and not just a figment of his imagination. How could he refuse her anything, even if it meant that Clinton Bell would be closer at hand?

"Send him out," he said sourly.

On an impulse she went up on her tiptoes and kissed his cheek.

"Thank you, Calvert. You're a dear, sweet friend."

Damn, he thought; I would rather be a scoundrel.

Ruth Ann could not hear their words but could guess at them. Her mind was torn between considering Calvert an idiot or praising him for getting Clint away before he could tell Laura about Fremont. She heard Laura come back for Clint and then take him to the street, and it only slowly dawned on her that Laura was certainly going to learn sooner or later.

Worse luck, she thought, leaving the drawing room. Now the safest bet would be to take her back to West Point. But she would give Laddie the honor of breaking the news to Laura.

"Amos, my brother would like to see Laura when she's finished with her company. And by the way, I have no fresh towels in my room."

"Sorry, miss. I'll fetch some down from the extra linen closet in Mr. Lawrence's hallway."

"That's all right, Amos. I have to go up to his rooms anyway. Send her right along."

Ruth Ann wanted to warn Laddie about Clinton Bell. She just couldn't believe how stupid her mother could be at times. Nettie Rivers? She could hardly believe that her mother would stoop so low as to be in league with the woman—unless Nettie had found out more than she should have.

"The world would be a lot safer place without women like that around," she said to herself, as she stepped into the long, narrow linen closet.

"Damn, you can't see a thing in here! I'll have to get a lamp from Laddie."

She was about to step back through the partially open closet door when she heard running feet upon the stairs. She shoved the door violently open with her shoulder and instantly braced against it. The crashing thud jolted her. There was no outcry or scream; only the deathly sound of limp flesh rolling back down the steep incline.

Ruth Ann calmly stepped into the hall, closed the closet door and stared down at the silent heap on the third floor landing.

Laddie's door came flying open. "What was that?"

She moved to block his view. "What was what? Oh, the noise. Just me running up the stairs. Laura is busy, so I'll talk with her later. In the meantime, what say you and I have a nice tall glass of wine and plan the parties we shall have at home? Just think, we won't have Fremont around to bore us this year."

It is remarkable that some men, like Calvert DeLong, must work feverishly to penetrate the inner workings of an organization, and other men, like Fremont Hunter, can fall into the center without a bead of sweat expended.

Fremont Hunter was in the offices of Fernando Wood when the former mayor entered the foyer from his sanctum.

"Mayor Wood! Mayor Wood, please sir, a moment of your time. I'm Fremont Hunter, and I've been waiting every day for two weeks to see you, sir."

The supercilious secretary who had been denying Fremont an appointment was quick to step forward. "Now look here, Hunter," he warned, "I'm telling you for the last time that there will be no loitering in this office. And I will not be putting you down in the appointment book until you state your business."

"It is only that I wish Mayor Wood to learn why I am no longer a cadet at West Point. Please, Mayor Wood, you may recall my father. Jethro Hunter, of Charleston, South Carolina."

If Fernando Wood was momentarily taken aback by the expression of desperation on Fremont's face, he did not betray this. He, himself, had assumed a not dissimilar aspect since being turned from office, although his was tempered by a mournful hopelessness.

He held out his hand, and said in a rich trembling voice, "I am no longer mayor, my boy, but your father I fondly recall. How would he be?"

"I am really not sure, sir. News from South Carolina is hard come by. The last I heard he had remarried, a widow named Ida Vaughan. But he's heard nothing from my brother Jared in some time, and is concerned that he may have been wounded or captured."

Mr. Wood's countenance revealed his sorrow at the news. He shook his head a little and sighed.

"What a pity that friends and family have to be so tragically separated . . . Lovely plantation home! Lovely! I have fond memories of it and of your gracious mother, Miss Mary, before her unfortunate death. I am about to meet my brother, Benjamin, for lunch. He, too, has fond memories of your parents. Will you please join us, Fremont?"

The secretary stiffened. "Your Honor may be forgetting that Mr. Benjamin is bringing along Representative Vallandigham."

"I am forgetting nothing, Throckton. Come, my boy, you look like you've had one deuce of a time of late."

Fernando Wood cautiously listened to the whole tale as they strolled in the biting December air to his favorite

restaurant. There, in a private room which was reserved
for Wood daily, Fremont was introduced to Benjamin
Wood, a representative in Congress from New York, and
Representative Clement L. Vallandigham of Ohio, and
asked to repeat his story again from the very first.

Never have three men shown such compassion over
such a tale of woe; never were three pairs of ears so intent
upon listening; never were three mouths pulled into such
righteous anger and indignation, and never did three heads
shake so convincingly. Fremont could see all this in spite
of his wretchedness. His fury and hatred had been like
a dull sickness for so long that not even the excellent food
would stop the burning in his stomach.

Fernando Wood lifted his head and gazed at Fremont
so steadfastly, with such affection, such simple grief and
shock, that Fremont's voice dwindled into silence.

"My dear boy," Mr. Wood sadly began, "my heart is
your heart, because I too have political enemies—as do
Benjamin and Clement. We are all brothers in that respect. As brothers, we are obligated to bind up each
other's wounds. You are to be commended for staying out
of this bloody and costly travesty of a war to pursue your
studies. But that has now been ignobly taken from you.
What now?"

Fremont uttered a throaty cry, and looked about him
with a frenzied aspect, as though searching for a weapon
to grasp.

"I wish to clear my name, sir, but I've been thwarted by
Colonel Beetle. I—I was not one to make close friends at
the academy, sir, so I cannot hope for help from the other
cadets. The evil rumors that have been spread are flagrant
lies. If I could just get around Colonel Beetle and have my
case heard by a higher authority in Washington . . ."

Vallandigham, tall, handsome and humorless, rose from
his chair and went to the sideboard for a cigar.

"Simple matter," he said tonelessly, "which I shall personally see to. Benjamin?"

The younger version of the pink-faced, rotund Fernando
had sat making intricate patterns in the white tablecloth
with the blunt edge of his knife.

"Mr. Hunter," he said slowly, as though he were carefully selecting each word, "now that you are no longer

bound by the military code and the war powers given to
the President to suppress opposition to the military effort,
might we hear your views on this conflict?"

Fremont cautiously laid his hands in his lap, shaking
his head dolefully while gathering his thoughts on the
matter. Then he straightened with resolve and regarded
them soberly.

"You won't condemn me, gentlemen, if I must give
credit for some of these ideas to my father. Nearly four
years of military supervision have made me tend to forget
the underlying cause of it all. It is my father's contention,
and my own, that the industrial East had for years ex-
ploited the farming regions of the South and West and
that their instrument of control was federal power to take
away our states' rights. He has always been convinced
that the war was mercenary in intent."

"Well said," Vallandigham muttered. "I am wholly devoted to agrarian ideals and interests. What else is Ohio
but farms and farmers and more farms?"

Benjamin Wood had begun to fray the tablecloth. "And
do you have reason to feel, Mr. Hunter, beyond the rumors
that you have alluded to, that this Dahlgren family had
other motives to go against you in such a fashion?"

"That ungenerous thought has been on my mind, sir. I
have been as close to them as if they were a second family
to me. It is common knowledge that Mr. Dahlgren is constantly in hot water over his contracts with the academy,
and that the son's mill here in New York turns out most
inferior uniforms and blankets for the army. Why would
they strike at me when that is a laughing matter all over
West Point?"

"But this is not West Point," Benjamin scoffed. "They
are not known to me as a part of that vast army of traitors
who disguise themselves as patriots and plunder *our*
treasury. A million dollars a day, sir! A million dollars a
day Lincoln and his cohorts are wasting on this war
when men such as myself have time and again given him
a simple way to end it: make an armistice and withdraw
the armies from the field. But he will not listen. That
imperial despot, with all his vast armies has failed, *failed*,
failed!"

As quickly as his voice had grown shrill, it now dropped to a dangerous whisper.

"Are there other family members who might have military contracts or connections?"

"They—they're related to the DeWitts," he stammered. "There's a boot factory in Boston owned by Mrs. Dahlgren's brother; her sister is Miss Theda DeWitt of New York."

"Now *there* is a jolly little bit of news," Fernando said in a grave and sonorous voice. "Lady Bountiful has skeletons in her closet. Well, Benjamin, I think that as long as Mr. Hunter is temporarily without position, we might discreetly avail ourselves of his talents."

"He might be full of jolly little news items for the *Daily News*," Vallandigham said smugly.

"But that's the Copperhead newspaper!" Fremont gasped.

"It's the newspaper of the Peace Democrats, my boy," Fernando Wood said, rising to lay his hand with strong affection on Fremont's shoulder. "A voice out of the wilderness to keep reminding Mr. Lincoln that the holy trinity is not a quartet."

He paused, then lowered his voice so that it had an insinuating quality about it. He bent over Fremont and whispered:

"You now join a very select handful of people who are aware that Benjamin owns the *Daily News*, and that Clement and I are in any way involved. There are legions, son, who might join the over thirteen thousand that the monster usurper has already thrown into prison—although imprisoning them does no more than make him a further laughingstock. We, however, have chosen to stay in the shadows to do the real work of uncovering the truth. I can smell revenge on you like burning brimstone. That's no good at all, my lad. Your revenge has to come from a secret power base if you mean to fully unmask them."

Fremont lifted his head very slowly. He looked from one man to the other, the question in his eyes becoming a growing resolution. The trio nodded with grim satisfaction.

"That's what I'm after, gentlemen—and unmasking the

truth. I have information on each of them—and on Colonel Beetle—that had never before seemed important. But there is one family member who must be protected from all of this."

"I take it it is a lady—a young lady?" Fernando grinned.

"Yes. She is not like the rest of them at all. I intend to make her my wife."

"Then her protection is entirely in your hands, my boy. You have all the information and we do not. You can count on us to be gentlemen in that regard."

Fremont gazed at the fat hand extended to him and grinned. "I will keep her safe." Then he frowned. "I hate to begin by asking a favor, but do you have contacts who can get information out of the South . . . from home?"

"You can be sure of that, my lad!" exclaimed Fernando, his hand still extended to seal the bargain.

Fremont grasped it in exultation, and shook it frenziedly. "Thank you! Thank you all! Do you know, even though I still wish to clear my name, I haven't felt this good in nearly four years! It's like being back with home folk who understand you."

Fernando Wood reached up and laid his other hand on Fremont's tall shoulder. He knew that Fremont's views were similar to his brother's and Representative Vallandigham's. They hadn't felt so confident in nearly four years. They had just been handed a gift on a silver platter. This scandal would be the opening wedge to keep Lincoln from gaining re-nomination. With this gambit they could play both sides of the fence without wincing. It was a bombshell! They could throw all of their other plans right out the window. This time next year they would be dictating who would be taking the oath of office under the nearly completed capital dome. The bronze goddess of Freedom crowning the tiered dome would ensure that the freedom of the blacks did not mean the enslavement of the whites.

16

W HEN THEDA SAW the tray and the demure chamber-
maid, her brows drew together quickly. Laura had
never missed personally bringing her luncheon tray
unless she was out shopping, although it seemed there
were now enough black servants in the house for Theda to
be served by a new one each day. Theda sat up abruptly,
glanced at the clock on the mantel, and saw that it was
just after one. She could hardly believe it. Why had she
not been awakened an hour before? She found something
very disturbing in the whole situation.

"Alice, isn't it? Is Miss Laura out shopping?"

Seeing the girl's puzzled expression, she instinctively
braced herself without knowing why.

"No, Miss DeWitt. Amos said she was called up to see
her brother and sister after the telegram came. She ain't
been down since. Mrs. Courtney finally told me to serve
your lunch."

Ah, thought Theda, the Christmas homecoming message
has finally arrived. Then a new realization came to her.
Never had it dawned on her that she would not have
Laura with her at Christmas.

She sent for Amos, who left her chamber feeling both alarmed and annoyed. Headhouseman or no, there were some things Miss Theda expected of him that a colored man just couldn't do—and one of them was to tell a white man and woman what to do.

A few minutes later, however, he felt no hesitation.

"You!" he bellowed. "You, up there! Come help me. It's your sister! She's fallen down the stairs!"

He had already scooped her up into his huge arms before the door cracked open. Ruth Ann smiled down at him, her eyes glazed.

"What _are_ you bellowing about?" she cooed.

"It's Miss Laura. She must have fallen down the stairs. I'll take her to her room."

"I'll tell my brother," she said, as casually as though he had just called them for lunch.

She closed the door and tiptoed back into the parlor, spilling wine from her glass onto her bare breasts. The room was heavy with a pale blue smoke.

"Laura fell down," she said matter-of-factly as she sat back down on the carpet next to her brother.

Laddie shrugged, without taking his head away from the incense bowl in which the hashish was smoldering.

Even if he had felt an impulse to go to Laura's aid, his mind at once drifted back to the conversation he and Ruth Ann were having before Amos had called out.

Then he realized he would have to change the subject. He was not about to lie to Ruth Ann about her attractiveness. He did not have to hallucinate to know that even at twenty-four her breasts already sagged, her uncorseted belly looked as though she was pregnant and she was undeniably bowlegged. Still, he wondered how she was in bed. The thought titillated him.

"Shall we try?" he said, as if he had already put the thought into words.

"She's only fallen down the stairs. Join me for another little glass of wine to toast the Christmas that lies ahead—without little sister underfoot."

Laddie snickered. "You know I think we should invite Darren Sumner. I think he likes you—and I know he likes me. We might just find ourselves all in bed at the same time."

"Oh, no," she giggled, "I'll not be having Mama walk in on a scene like that. It was bad enough when she came in on Fremont and me."

"You actually went to bed with that bounder?"

"Laddie! How can you ask such a question after what you did to him?"

He turned to her, flushing.

"Ruth Ann," he said in a changed voice, "I hope you believe that I never touched him."

Her giggles now turned to near hysteria.

It instantly had a sobering effect on him. He was fuming in his sudden haste to be out of this house, where all laughter and contentment seemed somehow to be at his expense.

"Get up," he snapped, "and go get packed. We have plenty of time to catch the late afternoon train."

Ruth Ann blinked. "But what about the people we were going to invite along?"

"I've decided not," he said petulantly. "Besides, Mama always supplies plenty of cadets—for both of us."

Dr. MacKenzie pressed Theda's hand with significance. He regarded his contemporary with real affection. She was one of the few patients who called him only in an emergency.

"Could you tell me one thing? Is there an object on which she could have bashed her head? The lump that seems to be causing the concussion is on the forehead, dangerously near the temple. But the broken leg—and the bruises to the back—would suggest a backward fall down the stairs."

Theda slowly shook her head, never once taking her eyes from the pale, almost lifeless form on the bed.

Amos clenched his teeth a moment. Then he said, "There is only a linen closet door at the top of those stairs, doctor. Could it have been left open?"

"I'm sure she would have seen that, Amos," MacKenzie answered. "Now, why don't you retire, Miss Theda?"

"No," she protested. "I will not leave this room until I know that my Laura is awake and will be well!"

"Miss Theda," Dr. MacKenzie said soothingly, "the

break is compound. Setting it is not going to be a pretty sight. Fortunately, she will feel no pain."

Theda looked at him with fixed eyes, their brilliance intense. A long tremor ran over her. Then, with infinite dignity, she rose, walked composedly to the bed and lifted Laura's skirt to look at the broken leg.

"I've seen much worse, Harold. You forget, my friend, I am not one of your fainting Park Avenue prima donnas. Amos, fetch three of the maids. Pick them for strength, Amos, and not for intelligence."

"Might I not be of assistance, Miss Theda?"

"Amos!" she blushed. "Are you forgetting that we shall be dealing with Miss Laura's uncovered limb? No! No! No! You stay downstairs and run the house."

Harold MacKenzie had to turn away to hide his smile.

Tears moistened Amos's eyelids as he turned and left. Some days he didn't understand white folk and some days he did; but Miss Theda he understood all of the time. She had just paid him the highest of compliments: servants might be allowed to look upon most anything, but gentlemen were expected to stay within certain bounds of decorum.

All of the staff were huddled in the foyer. Amos had hardly uttered his request when four of the maids rushed up the stairs with remarkable swiftness. He dared not call one of them back for failing to count. Miss Theda wasn't likely to object to their eagerness to help.

"How is she, Mr. Amos?" Mrs. Courtney asked.

"Not good, Mrs. Courtney," he answered. He could always share the truth with her.

She studied him closely, her gaze sorrowful yet keen.

"We must keep the faith, Mr. Amos."

He could not resist extending his hand to her, and she took it with dignity. Now her lip trembled, and her eyes filled with tears.

"And the expression of faith for you, Mrs. Courtney, shall be the immediate preparation of all her favorite dishes for tonight's supper."

"I'll be doing just that thing, Mr. Amos," said Mrs. Courtney through tremulous lips. "Girls, come, Mr. Amos has just given us reason to keep busy."

Ellen Courtney started to follow and stopped abruptly.

Footsteps, slow and halting, were coming down the stairway. Amos motioned for her to stay in place. It was too soon for the leg to have been set. They both feared that it would be Dr. MacKenzie bearing the worst of news.

Amos watched the curving stairway. He felt uncertain and awkward, and wondered if he should run up to be with Miss Theda. Now two figures appeared around the sweeping bend of the stairway. Laddie Dahlgren was elaborately suited, sporting a travel cape of such volume that it trailed on the steps behind him like the heavy train of a gown. He descended like an actor making his opening act entrance. Behind him, Ruth Ann struggled with three pieces of luggage, her face a study.

"Ellen," he said softly, "please help Miss Dahlgren."

Stepping onto the foyer floor, Laddie raised a hand dramatically.

"The carriage, Amos. We've a train to catch."

Amos bowed. "It's at the curb, sir. Harry has just returned with Dr. MacKenzie."

Laddie didn't comment but went directly to the door and impatiently waited for Amos to come and open it for him.

Amos was thinking very rapidly. He opened the door and turned back to await Ellen and Ruth Ann.

"Have a nice holiday, Miss Dahlgren," he said softly, and then innocently added, "Oh, by the way, did you find ample towels in the linen closet?"

A wave of darkness ran over Ruth Ann's face. Her eyes gleamed with sudden savagery. She opened her mouth and then clamped it tightly shut, striding out the door.

Amos stood silent until Ellen had returned to the house. He could hardly endure the emotions that were surging through him. He now knew the answer to Dr. MacKenzie's question. He would have to store it away for the moment, but if Laura did not survive he would bare it to the world.

Mrs. Courtney's dinner went uneaten, as did the next. The second floor of the mansion remained hushed but the main floor became like Broadway at rush hour. The servant news network spread the word rapidly. Leonard Jerome arrived daily with a dozen fresh roses, and no one questioned where he might have acquired them at such a season. Food poured into the house in such abundance that Harry was kept busy carting it to Maggie Duggan to distribute to the mill workers' families.

Maggie, Betty and Bertha Butt came nightly and sat in the parlor sipping tea. Clinton Bell also came. He was now a foundry man at the shipyard—although Calvert's father had been reluctant to take on anyone recommended by his son—and he came directly from work and sat without exchanging a word with the other young man in the room.

Calvert had no desire to speak with Clinton, or with anyone. He would mumble his greetings to the women and then go sit in the furthest corner and stare off into space.

His mind was a jumble of thoughts. His primary mission was to keep vigil for Laura, but the atmosphere of the room seemed to help him sort out many puzzles in his professional life. Things were happening fast—too fast. What had been was no more, and there were only rumors as to what was pending. Every time he thought he had his finger on the pulse of a rumor, the beat would stop or change rhythm. Gideon Welles was screaming for him to make an appearance in Washington, but even if it meant a real dismissal from the service, he was not about to leave and give Clinton Bell the advantage of being present during Laura's days of recovery—if there were to be days of recovery.

No one wished to dwell on the other possibility, but each day Harold MacKenzie's face grew a little more haggard, seamed and filled with despair. The girl was in a very deep state of sleep and there was nothing that he could do but visit three times a day, berate Miss Theda for not taking better care of herself, and wait.

Everyone waited.

The Christmas tree remained bundled in a corner of the foyer, for no one had any desire to break out the gay decorations. Society matrons cancelled or greatly reduced the arrangements for Christmas Eve and Christmas day affairs that would have included Theda and Laura. They came by scores to leave their calling cards on the silver salver; Amos and Ellen were forced to work the front door in shifts. Boss Tweed personally delivered a "get-well" wreath; unfortunately, to many it looked more funereal than cheering.

As though Theda's home had become an open house, a wide variety of people gathered in the parlor on Christmas Eve to gain comfort from each other.

More to keep them occupied than to celebrate, Mrs. Courtney supplied large bowls of hot spiced cider and heaping plates of frosted sugar cookies.

"Might as well have had a party," Amos mumbled, "the number of times I've been to this door tonight."

He drew it open, blinked, and tears swelled into his eyes.

"My prayer has been answered," he said, beaming. "Come in, Mr. Dahlgren, and let me take your things."

Clarence Dahlgren hesitated, measuring Amos from head to foot. Then recognition cracked a small smile on his worried face.

"You seem to have come up a bit since your bowler hat and cane days, Amos."

"Thanks to Miss Laura for bringing me here."

The mention of her name brought a desperate look back to Mr. Dahlgren's eyes.

"Laura? My child?" he asked brokenly, now clutching Amos's arm.

"The same. But she's becoming less a worry to me than Miss Theda. Mr. Dahlgren, that woman won't let anyone stay in that room but herself. She won't eat or sleep or listen to common sense. I'm almost out of my mind over the two of them."

"Take me to them . . . Amos? It was Amos Mobley, wasn't it?"

"*Was* is about right, Mr. Dahlgren. Miss Theda has had it changed to Amos Schuyler."

Clarence was about to comment when he caught sight of the people in the parlor.

"Who are they?" he asked.

"Friends of Miss Laura and Miss Theda. Been here almost every day and every night since the . . . accident."

"Just like the lass," Clarence sighed. "Always did have the knack of making a friend of every creature she ran across. My, isn't that Clinton Bell?"

"Yes, sir. Miss Laura got him a job here in the town the same day as the . . . accident."

"Amos," Clarence said, frowning, "you seem to hesitate each time you say that word. Is something amiss here that I haven't been told?"

"Come along upstairs, sir. Mind you, I'm not pointing a finger, but I've got to get this misery off my heart."

To Amos's utter amazement, Clarence Dahlgren listened to Amos's suspicions without comment, without even any indication of surprise. That Ruth Ann might have been party to the "accident" did not seem in the least unlikely to him. All manner of excuses for Laura's absence had been given to him until that very noon, when Lucille had finally admitted that Laura had suffered a "slight accident." Demanding further information, Laddie had revealed that it had been a "minor fall down a flight of stairs." Ruth Ann, as usual, had remained aloof.

It sickened Clarence that they could blithely leave this house without asking a single question about their sister's condition. It suggested guilt to Clarence, as surely as it had to Amos. But it was easier for Clarence to believe it than for Amos. There was very little that would now startle him about his older children.

"For the moment, Amos," he said dully, "it shall remain our secret."

Thereafter, he determined, matters would be quite different in his family. He smiled a little as he opened the door to Laura's room.

Theda was sitting near the bed, in the shadow. In the large plush chair, her figure seemed dwarfed, but she sat straight and calm. She turned her pale face to Clarence when he entered, but in the dimness of the room she thought it was Dr. MacKenzie. She locked her eyes back on Laura's waxen face.

He drew near and studied her silently. He saw the hollowness of her blue eyes, the sag of her multiple chins, the wrinkled white brow, the tremor of her hands on the dove-gray silk lap. But she appeared to him as a young woman, as always.

"My dear," he began, speaking gently, "it is Clarence."

Her white lips parted; her eyes flashed. She had to turn away to blink back the sudden tears.

"How kind of you to come. It is my duty to inform you that Laura has met with a most unfortunate accident." Her voice was low and neutral, but it shook uncontrollably.

His eyes filled with adoring light. She was being very proper—a true lady.

Tenderly, he put his hand on her shoulder.

"Everything will be all right, my dear. Our Laura will be fine; I know it."

She grasped his hand and pressed it to her neck, to her cheek, to her eyes. Sobbing now, she turned his hand over and buried her lips in the palm. He stroked her hair with his other hand, the mysterious sorrow in his heart making his touch gentle and loving.

"How good! How good! How good of you to come!" she sobbed, pressing her lips again and again to his palm, to each finger of his hand, wetting them all with her tears.

"It is you who are good, Theda. It is I who should be thanking you for looking after her."

Then she drew away a little, taking both of his hands. "But Clarence, it is Christmas Eve. You have the rest of your family to consider."

He stood for a moment in embarrassed silence. "They don't consider me," he mumbled. "They won't even miss me, as a matter of fact. Lucille will have the house filled with young people for Ruth Ann and Laddie."

At the sound of their names, Theda turned abruptly to Clarence. The hurt showed clearly on her features, and her mouth set in a brutal grimace.

"I shall never forgive them for leaving as they did," she muttered.

"Amos told me, my dear. We needn't go into that. Amos has also given me Dr. MacKenzie's latest report. Time, my dear. We must give nature time to take its course."

He drew a chair up beside her. A quiet sparkle slowly appeared in her exhausted eyes.

"Dear, dear, dear Amos. I don't know what I would have done without him."

"But Schuyler?" he said, and he suddenly laughed, loudly and foolishly. "How ever did you come up with that?"

She took his hand again and smiled sheepishly. "Trientje Schuyler was on my mind that day, because Laura so reminds me of her portrait. The reasons behind the name change are complex enough for a long dinner conversation, Clarence, so I will answer simply. Somewhere in my clouded memory I recalled an old tale about one of Trientje's great-grandchildren—through her son Schuyler DeWitt, if I'm not mistaken—establishing a plantation in Jamaica, so I fastened on that. I must also be honest and say that it crossed my mind what Lucille's face would look like when she learns that there is a black Schuyler in the family."

"It would no doubt kill her," he said, his voice amused and affectionate. "By God, Theda, you're still a whipper-snapper, aren't you? Now I know where Laura gets her spunk. She's got some Schofield in her too, I think, from your mother."

"I had thought of that . . ." she said musingly. Then she smiled broadly at the thought.

"I'm glad that she's with you, my dear," he said. With a wry smile he added: "You're the only one who would stand a chance of turning her into a lady. I'll tell you, Theda, her involvement in this slave business was beginning to unnerve me. Thank God, there'll be no more of that."

"Then ask her about the slaves she keeps in the carriage house and basement." The soft voice came from the bed.

They looked at each other in alarm and then turned to the bed. Laura was weakly wetting her lips, but her eyes were still closed.

"Laura?" Clarence gasped.

The tired eyelids fluttered, the in-drawing of breath dilated the pale skin of her nostrils. She was still not fully aware that she had been listening to their conversation and had responded. They saw the weary eyes open and look at Clarence with slow recognition.

"Papa," she whispered.

"Yes, yes, yes, my sweet. It is your father," Theda said tenderly. She took Laura's small hands and pressed them in hers. Warmth and life were returning to them. Theda had to bite her lip to control her emotions.

"Rest, my child, rest," Clarence said, his voice breaking.

"I always rest well on Christmas Eve, Papa," she said, her voice thin and exhausted.

"How did you know it was Christmas Eve?"

Her voice, low and hoarse, came falteringly, feebly.

"It's the only time you come to say goodnight anymore."

Clarence had to turn away, tears of shame and hurt flowing hotly down his cheeks.

Dr. MacKenzie slipped silently into the room and came at once to the bed. He gently lifted Theda's hand away and took Laura's wrist. Then he bent over to listen to her breathing and feel of the pulse again.

When he rose, his face was excited, for all its dignity. "Thank God. He's the only doctor who could have saved her," he whispered. "Amos told me that you were here, Mr. Dahlgren, and I ask you now to do me the favor of escorting Miss Theda away so that I might be spared an assistant during my examination. I'll be down shortly, but I think it's safe to inform the others that she's now conscious."

Theda did not protest. She had struck a bargain with God that she would not leave the room until Laura was awake. As Clarence helped her to her feet her heart was full of thanksgiving. She allowed Clarence to guide her out of the room. When they reached the top of the stairway she stopped. A smile, surprised, delighted and very soft, parted her lips.

"She'll be awake for the morning."

Clarence looked at her, puzzled. "I should certainly hope so."

"Then we shall have Christmas after all, Clarence. I don't know what preparations have been made, but anything remaining to be done must be taken care of before Amos brings her down in the morning."

He tightened his grip on her arm.

"Theda, my dear, something has been on my mind since I first sent Laura to you. Tonight has made my decision on the matter. May I give you your Christmas present right now?"

She had never heard such a tone from him, or such words. He was being more manly and assertive than she had ever known him to be. She could not take her eyes from him.

"I wish, with all my heart, my dear, to give you my daughter, for forevermore. No natural mother could have given her the love and devotion that you have shown her."

Theda listened, her eyes fixed on his face. Wonder and delight coursed into her expression and brightened her color. Then, she went on tiptoe and kissed his cheek. She started to speak, but he silenced her with shake of his head.

"No, no words," he cautioned. "It would spoil the gift of giving. Now, we were about to prepare for Christmas."

It was the most joyous tree- and house-decorating party that any could recall. Amos and Leonard Jerome set up the tree as amicably as though they were old comrades. Mrs. August Belmont sat and gaily chatted with Bertha Butt as they unwrapped the boxed ornaments from their tissue paper. Clinton Bell and Maggie Duggan, who had secretly been eyeing each other across the room for several evenings, accidentally touched finger tips—more than once —as she passed the ornaments up the ladder to him.

The roses came back to Mrs. Courtney's plump cheeks and she replaced the cider with brandy-laced eggnog and the cookie plates with vast trays of sandwiches. Ellen and the maids decked the halls with boughs of holly, their voices beautifully blending in carol after carol. Betty Duggan got out needle and thread to repair the costumes for the small china figures of Mary and Joseph and the kings and shepherds for the crèche.

Clarence Dahlgren was like a boy, directing Clinton and Maggie in each and every ornament placed on the tree, then blushing with pride when given the honor of climbing up and crowning the masterpiece with the hand-blown glass star that had been on Theda's first Christmas tree.

Calvert DeLong whispered to Amos, warmly shaking his hand before he made a hasty departure. Amos fully understood. *The lad carries a heavy burden*, Amos thought. *Even on a night like this he must be alone.*

Their carols filtered outside, where a light snow was falling. Calvert looked up and the flakes wet his face along with his tears. His love for Laura was never stronger than at that moment, but he could not stay to see her in the morning. He had also made a solemn promise to God.

Stepping down to the street, a caped young man tilted his stove-pipe hat and cheerily called, "A Merry Christmas to you. Sounds like a happy party."

It was just the note that Calvert needed to lift his spirits. "A most happy celebration, my friend. A young lady of the house was very ill and is tonight on the road to health. A very Merry Christmas to you too."

Calvert went whistling down the street. The man had looked vaguely familiar to him, but he was too distracted by elation to dwell on him. Laura was going to be all right, and if the signs he saw tonight were any indication, Maggie Duggan had her cap set for Clinton Bell—and vice versa. . . .

Fremont Hunter stood for a moment longer in front of the mansion, listening to the voices give heartfelt warmth to the strains of "Silent Night." Tears of thanksgiving welled into his eyes also.

As a houseguest of Fernando Wood, he had overheard the servants' gossip about the sick young lady at the DeWitt mansion. He had walked this street nightly, wondering and worrying, sorely tempted to go up and ring the bell, but fearful of the manner of welcome he might receive.

But his tears mixed both joy and sorrow. Fernando Wood had been as good as his word in obtaining news from Hunter Hill, but the news had not been good.

Now his hatred for the Dahlgrens was even more bitter, if not wholly rational. As if they had personally fired the gun that had killed his older brother Jared, he determined that he would not rest until he had ruined them. Then he would come back to this house and take Laura away from it all. . . .

"*Silent night . . . holy night . . . all is calm . . . all is bright*," Theda sang softly, kneeling over the manger scene beneath the tree. All was in place but the babe in swaddling cloths that she gently held. "*Round yon virgin mother and child . . .*"

She placed the delicately painted china doll in the crib and smiled down at the cloth-draped image of the Holy Mother.

"Yes," she murmured, "tonight we each have a new child."

17

THE TALL FORM bowed and gestured Calvert DeLong and Gideon Welles into the room. Calvert was amazed at how rapidly the man was aging. Then a wonderful smile transfigured the homely face as he motioned the two men to seats.

"Gideon, as a good Democrat, you may choose to either stay or leave. I wouldn't want you accused of being a spy for their all-but-nominated candidate."

"This issue cuts a little deeper than election politics, Mr. President," Welles said uneasily.

The President realized, as no other man could, the profound truth of that statement. He sat behind his desk, his face returning to a grey mask, his eyes sorrowful.

"You are doubtless aware, Mr. DeLong," the President began, "that there is a great clamor again for the return of McClellan. A week ago I sent for General McClellan and offered to withdraw from the race in his favor and make his election a certainty." He paused and drew a deep breath. "Of course, using the information you obtained from your . . . ah . . . secret source, DeLong, I asked for his denial that the coterie of groups behind him were in touch with the Davis government in Richmond. He thought I was coupling his name with the word *treason* and flatly informed me he'd beat my britches off without my withdrawal. Still want to stay, Gideon?"

"You had to phrase it as you did."

"Granted," the persuasive voice went on, "and that's why I can't give him back his command. He's so stiff-necked he refuses to believe that they're out to use him. Which brings us to your reports, Gideon."

Welles cleared his throat and opened a thick folder. "Your latest reports have been most accurate, Calvert. They fit in with what we are learning from a typesetter at the *Daily News*. Let me give you just a brief summary."

When he was finished, Calvert sat stunned. The President shook his head doggedly. "Can they make all these charges against this group stick?"

"I know some members of each of these families, Mr. President. I'm sure that some of the charges will apply, but not all."

"Good. Then let's beat them to the gun. You have the power, Gideon, to start investigations into each of these matters. If we strike first, then there won't be so much thunder in their accusations against the administration."

"I've already looked into one matter that is bound to arise, Mr. President. This Colonel Dahlgren in Grant's command couldn't possibly be the same man we first suspected."

Calvert threw up both hands with a gesture at his own stupidity. "Excuse me, please, but it never seemed important before. Lawrence Dahlgren has been living off the honors won by a man his mother hired to serve in his place. If the man's real name is Wilf Jamison, then it simply means that Jamison went back into the service."

"And what will we do in that event?" Welles asked.

The President's sombre eyes smiled as he slowly said, "Everyone stormed at me not to make such an unusual battlefield commission. But Grant was adamant, and has even advanced Dahlgren to lieutenant colonel. He wanted the man under his own command and refused to have it any other way. If Jamison won that much respect from his general, then let's let the man have his own name back.

I doubt he'll want the Dahlgren name after the *Daily News* gets finished with it."

"I shall see to it, Mr. President, and I'll start the other investigations at once. Now, there is this matter Vallandigham has raised over this cadet. You know how the army gets riled over the navy having the only investigative arm. Colonel Beetle informs us it was for the good of the service; however, if one looks more closely it is an odd little honey-pot with some most amazing names popping up. First, Lawrence Dahlgren was the secret witness against the dismissal of Cadet Fremont Hunter, and now Hunter's name pops up in the typesetter's report as the one informing on the Dahlgrens and DeWitts. Personal feud, or chickens coming home to roost?"

Calvert sat stunned again. Now he knew exactly who the man on the street had been last night. He felt the fool for having been right on top of all this and not seeing a bit of it.

"What were the charges against Hunter?"

Welles read off the official version, claiming that Hunter had attempted to seduce Ruth Ann and Laddie Dahlgren.

Calvert couldn't help but laugh. "Excuse me, sir, but if the truth be known just the opposite probably took place."

"So I have gathered from your reports on this Laddie Dahlgren," Welles said drily. "But that's no reason for you not to worm your way into a similar relationship with Fremont Hunter."

"But, sir, I was supposed—"

"I am well aware of your desires, DeLong, and I can sympathize. As can the President. But you are sitting in the catbird seat, my boy. We have no knowledge of where Hunter is at the moment, except that he must have some pretty powerful friends among the Copperheads to get Vallandigham to go to bat for him. He could very well lead us right to the real leaders and financial backers. Mr. President, I would like to let Representative Vallandigham know the results of our investigation and imply that it is being submitted to you for final review on the matter."

"Why imply? I still think he is the snake in the grass who hisses at Miss Liberty. Let's give him room to choke on his own venom. You know, that reminds me of a little story—"

Welles quickly rose and motioned Calvert up. He knew what the wily politician was up to.

"We shouldn't take any more of your time, Mr. President."

The two men bowed their way out and then Calvert turned to stare at the secretary.

"What was that all about?"

"As a young man the President was once bitten by a snake and nearly died. Lately, his own death seems to constantly come into the conversation. That's another reason you've got to go back, Calvert. We've learned from the typesetter that the *Daily News* keeps a black-bordered front page always in readiness. I fear they plan to embarrass him with these headline scandals to cover up their real plot. There are only six months until the convention. He is a Republican married to a Southern woman. I am a Democrat. But he is the President of all the people. The nation needs this man. I can, I must and I will protect him at all costs. Six months, my boy, six months."

Calvert knew the task would be greater than Welles realized. He was now personally involved with some of these people.

It was Christmas day, but the holiday spirit had just left him.

Vallandigham was elated. He did not mind in the least using the man he intended to crush. He even began to hope that the President would exonerate Fremont—thus putting the young radical squarely in his debt.

Surprisingly, the news did not please Fremont.

"It's happening too fast, Fernando. Naturally, I want to go to Laura with a clean slate, but *after* I've finished striking back at her family. We must start the articles at once."

"But it is Christmas week, Fremont. People don't read during Christmas week."

"Do the guns stop firing or the blood stop flowing just because it is Christmas week?"

"All right! All right! But only one article until after the New Year and one we can attack from a different angle later if the circulation is down this week."

* * *

Snow came down in blizzard gusts out of Canada on December 27, 1863.

"War hero a fraud!" the newsboys thundered on the New York streets. Evening and morning papers reprinted the charge up and down the coast, with editorials asking how it could be.

The thunder was answered by a lightning bolt from Washington, not only concurring with the charges first made by the *Daily News* but putting the matter to rights by crediting the real hero.

So careful had Welles surveyed the case that Edwin Stanton declared to the press:

"This is foul infamy. Wealthy parents thwart the draft on behalf of their legions of spoiled sons and arrogantly send their servants off to face the bullets in their place. But fate is laughing today with double irony. The man the army has known as Lawrence Dahlgren was wounded and released, while the real Lawrence Dahlgren claimed the honors—and now has been revealed as a fraud. The true hero, healed and persistent in his devotion to duty, honor and country, re-enlisted, again under the name of Lawrence Dahlgren. Here is the irony, gentlemen. Had the real Lawrence Dahlgren had the wit to keep a lower profile, he might now be claiming the distinction of being the key to General Grant's victory at Chattanooga and the distinction of being named a colonel of his own regiment because of his military expertise. But those honors belong to one man alone. We wish to thank the *Daily News* for bringing this matter to the attention of the war department and the nation. We intend to right this wrong by having all the records and facts changed to reflect the hero's true identity: Colonel Wilf Jamison."

Laddie considered the whole fuss amusing, while Lucille actually considered suing Wilf for breech of contract. Kitty was dumbfounded over Wilf's rise in the world, when all the time she had thought he was out west. She asked for her money back so that she could go to him. Lucille claimed no knowledge of the money and fired the girl on the spot. Clarence remained above the battle.

Clarence would have his own battles to fight over the next three months as charges and counter-charges were leveled against the Dahlgren Mills, the Dahlgren Purveyor Company and the DeWitt Leather Company. The scandal was so often repeated that the Dahlgren name seemed to be on every tongue. But the anchor would not stay around the ankle of Abraham Lincoln.

"Who in the hell is she?" the portly man demanded as Theda escorted him into the drawing room.

"She's my daughter Laura," she said, grinning at her brother.

"Don't be ridiculous," Harrison Holmes DeWitt snapped.

"And stop acting like you've eaten persimmons for breakfast, Harrison. Laura has been put in my charge by Clarence Dahlgren. Take a seat!"

He now suspiciously eyed the pale girl lying on the settee, her legs covered by a quilt. Harrison had a girth so expansive that he was scarcely able to squeeze into his chair. Once wedged into it, he ballooned out like a cartoon caricature of the glutted tycoon he was.

"Character assassination," he muttered, still looking at Laura. "Our names, Theda, are being linked with Lucille just because an accident of birth happened to make her our sister."

"Now who's being ridiculous, Harrison?"

He turned his head as though it were on a pivot. The eyes in his round face were small, looking smaller still for his great, rubicund cheeks.

"Then are you guilty as they charge, Theda? Are you the secret backer of your nephew, a profiteer and all but a traitor for producing inferior blankets and uniforms? Well, I for one am innocent of the charges being leveled against my boots."

"As I am sure Clarence is innocent of the charges against him."

"Theda!" he gasped. "Are you then admitting guilt on your part and Lawrence's?"

"The investigation, Harrison, will prove that I have only recently put money into the mill, and that was to improve the machinery and the quality of its goods. I was just about to depart for a meeting with . . . proper authorities on the subject."

"Then you must protect my good name as well, Theda!"

Theda shook her head sadly. Harrison had no God but

Mammon; he worshipped nothing but wealth and power. She could not remember the last time she had heard from him. She was aware that he had children, but they were nameless creatures to her. If they were anything like Lucille's two eldest, she didn't want to know their names, either. None of them, except Laura, really understood her.

"I intend," she said slowly, "to try to protect everyone—because they are family."

"I should certainly hope that you would. After all, as a spinster, what other obligation do you have but to protect the DeWitt name?"

Theda shook her head gravely. "Harrison," she whispered, "I am going to rise from this chair and go for my wrap. By the time I return to the front door of this house I wish for you to be gone. I don't give a damn for the DeWitt name. You and Lucille seemed to hold it in front of you like some protective shield. Well, Harrison, behind that shield are poisonous people. It sickens me to have to go to their defense—but I do so for the innocent people involved and not the guilty. Goodbye, Harrison. I hope we never have the onerous duty of meeting again."

Laura could have cheered. In his anger, the man rose and the chair rose right with him. Theda had already left the room before he extracted himself and he nearly collided with Amos in the doorway. Amos side-stepped and totally ignored the man.

"There's a woman in the foyer," he said, almost apologetically, "who is most distraught. All she will give is the name Kitty, and she demands to see you."

Laura sat up and then winced at the pain in her leg. "Send her in, Amos."

But Kitty was already in the doorway, her face haggard and her color not improved any by the outlandish purple outfit she wore.

"Come in," Laura cried. "Come in! Oh, Kitty, I'm so glad to see you!"

Kitty brushed by Amos and came into the elegant room, her eyes taking in everything.

"You live here, Miss Laura?" she gasped.

Laura laughed. "Yes, with my Aunt Theda. Oh, Kitty, isn't that exciting news about Wilf?"

"No," Kitty said sadly, "it ain't, really. I've been looking for him in Washington ever since your maw gave me the sack. Ain't a polite person in that whole rotten town. They just send you from one place to the next and then on to another place."

"Then you didn't find Wilf?"

"Does it sound it?"

"Don't worry, Kitty. I have a friend who can locate him quickly."

"I hope so," Kitty said fervently. "God knows, I hope so! I ain't got nobody but him. Your maw stole my money and sacked me with back pay owing."

"Sit down, Kitty," Laura said, disgust against her mother rising anew. "Amos, could we get Kitty some tea and a bite to eat? And Amos—"

He nodded and held up his hand. The last part did not need to be asked. He knew Laura was getting well quite rapidly when she could get that "here is a stray puppy" look on her face.

"I'll see to it, Miss Laura," he said, grinning. "And don't forget that you have to interview today for a personal maid."

"Oh, I had totally forgotten," Laura declared dramatically. Then she giggled. "Oh, Kitty, you're an answer to my prayers. You see, I fell and broke my leg and need a strong, healthy person to look out after me. You'd be just perfect and we already know each other."

"Me!" she cried. "Me work in this mansion! Glory saints!" Then she sobered, and eyed Amos. "Is the pay regular and on time here?"

"Indeed it is!"

She quickly turned her face aside for fear her teardrops would spot the fine dress she had stolen from Lucille out of revenge.

"Something told me to come see you, Miss Laura. Something just told me."

"But how did you know where to come?"

Kitty blinked back her tears and giggled.

"Now, Miss Laura, I ain't as stupid as I pretended in front of your maw. Wasn't I always running telegrams down to the railroad station to send to this address for Mr. Laddie? Kitty Jamison has a brain."

"Jamison?" Laura said. "Are you and Wilf married?"

"Same as," she proudly boasted, patting her belly. "This is his little bundle that will come popping out come late summer."

She was such a large girl that it was impossible to tell that she was three months along. Laura and Amos stared at each other incredulously.

"Well," Laura sighed, "I guess I better get my friend *very* busy at finding Wilf."

"Who is this friend?"

"Only a neighbor."

The same question had just been put to Theda DeWitt.

"Now, William, I don't go around asking about your sources of information, do I? Let's just say that I have it on very good authority that the man in question is not only seen frequently with Fernando and Benjamin Wood, but is their houseguest."

William Marcy Tweed sat back and picked a spot of dried egg off his vest.

"And why would that be of interest to me, Theda?"

She gave him a coy look. "Now, William, it is no secret in this town that you helped George Opdyke replace Fernando as mayor, even though he is a Republican. What would you call him? A powerless figurehead so that you can still control the Common Council?"

Boss Tweed blushed. "That's beside the point, my good woman. You must realize that I am no less bitterly opposed to this war than Wood and his Copperhead friends. I even attended many of Tilden's early meetings."

"True! True! True!" she said lightly, then let her voice drop. "But has it ever occurred to you that the South will not go along with their quixotic programs? That *your* New York has gained the dubious title of being the center of the Copperhead conspiracy? That the government has an even greater power of arrest than it did during the draft riots?"

He suddenly sat forward and rested his arms on the edge of the desk. He lowered his massive head to stare straight at her, his great tawny beard covering his crossed arms.

"I don't think you're telling me all you know, Theda DeWitt."

Theda sat back as though insulted. "William Marcy, how dare you imply such a thing!" Then she grinned. She had his undivided attention.

"Think back to 1861, William. Fernando proposed that this city secede from the United States and join the South. The Common Council adopted the project with wild enthusiasm. Where would that put us today? Right under martial law as a conquered foe. Now think of 1864, William. An election year. The Radical Republicans, as you are probably well aware, are planning on running John Fremont—but it is the Peace Democrats who are behind that in order to split the vote. As the Democratic boss of this city, you'll have to make your own choice between him and McClellan for the regular party. But if Fernando Wood has the power base he now claims, can you stop him from becoming mayor again as the Peace Democrats' candidate?"

He went suddenly ashen. "Good God, woman, are you privy to information that shows that is what he intends?"

Theda DeWitt had no idea what Fernando Wood might or might not intend, but it was a very plausible assumption that Calvert DeLong had cooked up for her to drop as a bombshell. To keep from having to lie outright, she sat very silent, looking solemn.

Tweed was rattled. He had the power to over-rule the Common Council and Mayor Opdyke, but did he really have control over the radical voting masses in the streets?

"If he should win," he said darkly, "he would tear the city apart."

"I agree."

"Damn him!" he rumbled. "The time to stop him is before he can get started. I'll start giving this thing thought immediately. Thank you, Theda. Now, what else can I do for you?"

"It seems to me, William, that this mess my nephew has gotten himself entangled in casts a very bad light on this city—in front of the whole nation. They're making it sound as though we were all profiteers and swindlers. Wouldn't you be wise, William, to conduct your own investigation before the Federals do? You do have the power under certain regulations, as I understand it. My nephew is still out of town, so I give you full authority to go into the mill and expose whatever needs exposing—as long as you give me a chance to hear your report first. You might even tweak Fernando's nose by capturing a few headlines for yourself."

He sat back and looked at her admiringly. "You know, Theda, I really should run you for mayor."

"Why, William, you flatter me. You know all I'm good for is organizing social affairs. This city is really like a vast army to run."

That thought stayed with Tweed long after she had left. For two decades he had been steadily climbing upward to become the illustrious tribune of the people—a vast army of over eight hundred thousand. He was the "general" over rather ill-defined political districts, which were large and cumbersome and given attention only at election time.

"An organized social affair," he mused. "Very easy for her to see to the needs of a hundred guests . . . A ward!" he chuckled, recalling his Scottish heritage wherein a county was divided by a hundred, each hundredth being a ward.

"Ward," he repeated. "One to see after the needs of a hundred . . . and if their needs are seen to properly, one to see that those hundred vote accordingly, out of appreciation. I think, Theda, you have given me something more than just an opportunity to tweak Fernando's nose. You've given me the boot to kick him in the ass."

Washington was also giving a boot to the nation that day—three boots, in fact: the DeWitt knee-high cavalry boot, the ankle-high infantry boot and the officer's jodphur. They were dirty, mud-caked, scratched and well worn. Well they should be, for they had been in constant service since 1861.

Next to them reposed three similar boots, from a factory in Representative Vallandigham's Ohio district. They were just as scratched, and had gaping holes right through their soles. They had been in service for exactly one month—and Vallandigham owned a part of the company, though this was not generally known.

The Quartermaster Corps announced to the reporters that Representative Benjamin Wood of New York had been named to head the congressional investigation committee to look into the supply scandals.

January had slipped away from Fremont Hunter with more backward than forward motion. The Wood brothers were beginning to doubt his every accusation. Every charge they printed, Washington responded to with a more sensational counter-charge. Thomas Nast, in *Harper's*, drew a caricature of Jefferson Davis whispering into a printing press labeled *Daily News*. Horace Greeley screamed in his editorials: "Has the *Daily News* turned Republican? For they are helping the 'Springfield Ape' march right into a second nomination. For shame!"

Then, in the first week of February, Fremont allowed himself to smile for the first time in weeks. The army could not refute the charges against the Dahlgren Purveyor Company of West Point. Edwin Stanton refused to comment on the subject.

"Gentlemen," he snapped, "I have a war to fight with the South, not with the *Daily News*."

Stanton smiled as he turned away. The quick removal of Colonel Arnold Beetle from the academy—and the reason behind it—would have made far more scandalous headlines than the mere cancellation of the contracts with Clarence Dahlgren.

The *Daily News* overlooked that point in their eagerness to headline their "victory" and re-hash the story in such a way as to make it sound as though the purveyor company had been solely supplying the entire war effort.

"Why, Calvert?" Laura wailed. "Why couldn't you save Papa?"

"Laura, if Miss Theda understands, why can't you? No one could save him. I couldn't believe the investigator's reports on his books. They were a shambles, and he couldn't begin to explain how he could sell the same item at three different times at three different prices. Nor did it help that the books are chock full of payments to the Dahlgren Mills with no repayments. On the surface the books make him out to be a wealthy man and a pauper all at the same time. Is it any wonder the people are asking where he has hidden his illegal profits?"

"That is mean!" Laura wept. "Why didn't they investigate my mother? Everyone in West Point knows that *that* is where all of Papa's money goes to! Oh, get out of here! I hate you! I hate you!"

"Now, Miss Laura," Kitty soothed, "how can you say that about the man who found my Wilf for me?"

"That's not the same," she cried. "He ruined my papa when he could have saved him."

Calvert knew it was no good trying to reason with her, especially at that time. Laura's leg was refusing to heal properly, and she was in a state of constant pain. No matter what Mrs. Courtney would fix for her, she had no appetite and grew thinner and thinner. The least thing could make her break into tears, and this had been no little thing.

He wished with all of his heart that it could have been different, but Clarence and Lucille had begun to dig their own graves years before and it had finally reached the six-foot level.

He wanted to be the one to hold her, comfort her and soothe her pain, but that couldn't be. He left her crying against Kitty's broad breast.

He knew that the next few weeks would be even harder on her. Things were coming to a rapid head. With Laddie out of town he had been able to cultivate Fremont as a drinking partner at Pfaff's. Fremont's fierce hatred was becoming a frightening thing, almost as if he were becoming deranged, and Calvert wanted the whole affair over and done with before it could produce bloodshed.

He let himself out of the house without hearing the voices coming from the drawing room.

"What a disaster!" Theda repeated for about the twelfth time. "It was the one thing that I was counting upon." Sadly, she looked once again at the report that Tweed had sent her by messenger that morning, a report that had prompted her to send at once for Maggie Duggan. "I have already sent a note of apology to Mr. Tweed. Laddie cheating me out of so much money doesn't hurt as much as the liar I nearly made of myself over the whole affair." Then she laughed drily. "The term *profiteer* is well applied to him, Maggie. A mere three thousand invested into the business, and the remaining twelve thousand vanished to lord knows where."

"I'm so terribly sorry," Maggie murmured, as though she were the guilty party. "He kept telling me that was but a down payment for me to make on the parts and repairs needed."

"Oh, hush!" Theda said fretfully. "I've lost more money than that on a bad day in the stock market. At least that was my own foolishness, without any help from others. William Marcy will have no choice, Maggie, but to release that report to the press. Tomorrow is going to be a bleak day. Well, I've survived bleaker ones. It's going to be up to us, my girl. Here is a letter to the manager of the bank in Brooklyn in which I have an interest and an account. He's to open an account in your name. If you have to hire people for day and night work, Maggie, do it, because I want that mill in tip-top shape immediately. I can see no reason to put all those good people out of work because of this scandal and I am not about to be made out to be a liar. Now, get along with you. The sooner you get to the bank, the sooner you can get on with this."

A light snow was beginning to fall as Ellen let her out the front door. Maggie raised her tattered old umbrella and then stopped. The letter Theda had given her was just a folded piece of stationery and she had to peek.

"Holy Mother of the Blessed Jesus!" she gasped, her face instantly contorted into a shocked expression. "As much as that in the name of Maggie Duggan! Saints alive, I'll be murdered and robbed for sure!"

As though the letter were already cash money she tucked it securely down the front of her dress and cautiously went down to the street. She imagined that she saw figures lurking in every shadow. There was no one in sight—no policemen, no passersby. Then she saw a hansom cab.

She raised her umbrella to summon it. Though she knew it to be a great extravagance, she reasoned that a person who was soon to have $30,000 deposited to her name should travel safely. Then she almost fainted when a voice from behind stopped her.

"Maggie!" it called. "Oh, Maggie—wait a bit, won't you?"

Maggie lowered her umbrella and turned.

"Why, Clinton Bell!" she said in surprise. She hadn't seen him since Christmas Eve.

"I thought it was you," he said. "How is Miss Laura faring?"

"Poorly. I didn't even get to see her today."

"Oh . . . Then I suppose I shouldn't disturb her."

Maggie started to explain why she hadn't seen Laura, then changed her mind. She should have been scolding him for not visiting Laura anyway, but he was more important as a safe escort.

"I was hailing that cabby, there. Would you like a ride back to Brooklyn?"

"Living mighty high there, aren't you, Maggie Duggan?"

"Get on with you! You know that I'm not doing it for myself, but on business for Miss Theda." She locked her hand through his arm. "But I'm not against walking, if that's your mind, Clint Bell."

"If it's all the way to Brooklyn . . ."

Maggie was already raising the umbrella to the cabby again.

"The bank first," Maggie said, once they were settled in the cab, "because that's the most important thing in my life right now. Then it's home to meet my folks and have a bite of supper. If you're planning on asking to keep company with me, Clint Bell, you must meet the family."

Clinton sat very still, staring at her incredulously. Up to that moment he had had no intention of asking to keep company with her. But now it sounded like a very fine idea to him. A very fine idea.

Fremont Hunter saw their meeting and departure and puzzled on it. He had not been aware that his cousin was in town or that Clint even knew Maggie Duggan. He tucked the information into the back of his mind and looked up at the mansion with a wry grin. Tomorrow he would bring Laddie Dahlgren tumbling down. He had already checked off Lucille; now it was Laddie's turn.

The Tweed report in the *Times* caught the *Daily News* off guard. They had primed themselves to report the Wood Committee's findings, which were to be released at noon.

"This is preposterous!" Fremont stormed, banging the *Times* down on Fernando Wood's breakfast plate. "What gives Tweed the right to have this investigated?"

Wood's jaw dropped.

"And the conclusions," Fremont ranted on, "are totally unbelievable. Damnation! Antiquated sailcloth machinery and ill-trained help, my ass! They don't even mention Laddie Dahlgren's name once. The management! The management! The management has recently invested a sizable sum of money . . . The management is well aware of their problems . . . The management's profits are being applied to reworking the machinery . . . Crap!"

Fernando miserably nodded his head.

"We'll wait for my brother's report—"

"Like hell!" Fremont roared. "Let's start tearing this report apart!"

"No, Fremont," Fernando said. "That's what Bill Tweed wants me to do. Suddenly your personal vendetta seems very minor. I will wait to hear from Benjamin—and so will you."

Fremont nodded his agreement, but under the surface he was seething.

His frustrations increased when the ticker-tape announced the committee findings would not be released that day. . . .

President Lincoln also had served in the House of Representatives and was adept at cloakroom politics. It greatly amused him to be getting help from the Democrat William Marcy Tweed.

". . . it takes all manner of mules to pull the load, Harry, but I think we need a little bit of braking."

Representative Harry Tighe of Illinois agreed. The Tweed report was in serious conflict with what he had heard as the Minority Chairman of the committee. The matter had to be reopened to protect the integrity of Congress.

When Tighe had left, Lincoln looked at Gideon Welles for some time before he spoke.

"Someday soon," he said quietly, "I want to ask Pontius Pilate if this is how he felt when he wanted to wash his hands of that whole matter. It is sad."

"It is sad," Welles echoed, "but we are dealing more

with a Judas than a Jesus. Vallandigham must be stopped.
I have the papers here for you to sign."

"It isn't inappropriate, Gideon, to repeat another phrase
from that long ago era. 'What must be done, let it be
done quickly.' I'll sign."

"He will be arrested, Mr. President, as soon as he makes
his first gross error."

The gross error did not come quickly enough for some,
but too quickly for others.

Harry Tighe was able to tie the committee into knots
and let the weeks slip away. The *Daily News* kept screaming about the case; screaming so long and so loud that
people got tired of listening.

Then, in mid-March, four travelers came to New York:
two from the north, who took a cab directly to a mansion
on Fifth Avenue; two from the southeast, who took a
cab to the *Daily News* office, but got off a block before
their destination.

By an odd twist of fate it was Fremont Hunter who
watched the return of Ruth Ann and Laddie Dahlgren,
and a forewarned Calvert DeLong who tracked Benjamin
Wood and Clement Vallandigham to the newspaper. And
each did a very strange thing. Fremont hurried into the
carriage passage, trying the side and back doors to the
mansion, but found them all locked. But a basement window was cracked and he let himself down into the dark,
dank pit.

Calvert had climbed to the roof of the newspaper's
building and went to a skylight that he had long ago
jimmied for just such an event. He slipped down into the
loft and crept over to an area that would be right above
the office. He had tested it before and knew he would
be able to hear everything quite adequately.

To Vallandigham and Benjamin Wood's intense surprise
and annoyance, Fremont was not with Fernando.

"We have come to the conclusion, brother," Benjamin
told him with grim satisfaction, "that Fremont Hunter is
the traitor in our midst."

"How can you be sure?" Fernando demanded.

"Don't be an idiot," Vallandigham said drily. "The
President has reversed the findings against him, but won't

release the papers to me. Why? Because the time is not yet ripe to declare the innocence of a man they knew to be innocent all along. Look at the record! Everything he gave us has come back to smack us in the face—and quickly, too quickly. He must be eliminated to protect the cause."

Much good that'll do, Calvert thought grimly.

"I—I don't know," Fernando stammered.

"Well I *do* know," Benjamin growled. "He is a double agent, and he knows who we are, Fernando. But without him around, we can deny everything."

"But—"

"No buts! Clement, start taking any files we need to save, especially the ones with the code names of the people who will be involved in the assassination. Fernando, in the center of the floor pile anything that might connect you or me with this newspaper or this building. Tomorrow the editors can claim that Hunter was responsible for the theft. Of course, he won't be around to refute their claim."

"Who—" Fernando broke off and gulped.

"Clement has friends who will see to that, don't worry. When you finish with those papers go find Hunter. Send him to see Clement at the Frederick house up Broadway, but make it after ten."

Calvert slowly pulled back and crept to the skylight. Ten o'clock didn't give him much time to forewarn the area commander, but the arrest of Vallandigham had to take place before he had a chance to have Fremont killed. Even though this was as much a part of the war as a battlefield, he didn't hesitate in his desire to protect Fremont's life. War was one thing, murder another.

Fremont's frustrations were increasing. He was unable to hear anything from the basement, and to creep upstairs would have meant having his presence detected. But one discovery did intrigue him. In one of the large basement rooms he found several cots and beds, lamps, a table and chairs and a pile of tattered clothing. It did not take much effort to figure out who might have worn such attire. But his mind was so blinded in regard to Laura that he automatically assumed that this Underground station was entirely the work of Amos and Miss Theda. Now he had something really damaging to use against the older woman. He let himself out of the basement, fixing the door so he could regain access, and hurried back to the Wood house to reveal his find.

Had he been able to hear the conversation upstairs in Theda's home, it would have piqued his interest.

"Gal! Gal! Gal! Your return is an utter amazement!"

"Why?" Laddie blinked foolishly. "I do live upstairs, you know."

"*Lived*, in the past tense," she growled. "Do you think I would allow you back into this house after the way you treated your sister?"

He and Ruth Ann had already been through this argument with their father and he was fully primed for it. "If her condition was so serious, Amos would have stopped us from going to the station that day. Everyone acts as though we were somehow responsible."

"Possibly, Lawrence, because of the manner in which you handle your other responsibilities. I hardly consider the amount you put into the mill adequate."

He sighed with relief. "Tweed's investigators must have overlooked that or I wouldn't be back now."

"Damn your insolence! The man was trying to protect me from being called a liar and I have now had to protect him. But don't think you can get your greedy little hands on that money. It will all go into the mill to try and save that uniform contract."

"I was not aware that I had accepted you as a silent partner."

She slowly shook her head.

"I wasn't thinking of you when I did it. But I can assure you that I am going to take a careful look at the books until I am fully repaid."

"Sorry," he said icily, "but Mama insists that I pay her back first. This mess has made things rather rough for her."

"And you are of course broke," she said bitterly. "I wired your father that I would assist him, but he turned me down. I will not turn a hand for your mother, or for you, or for your sister. I believe Ruth Ann's bill from Betty Duggan is sizable. You might wire your sister and tell her to get a job."

"You tell her," he snapped. "She's upstairs unpacking."

Theda's round face was suddenly contorted. "I will not have her in my house!"

"Then I shall move her in with me," he said sharply. "As you have put money into the mill, I shall expect to start drawing a salary, and you may deduct my rent from it. Mother always said you were a vindictive creature, but I find your attitude inexplicable. You're being terribly rude to Ruth Ann, for reasons I cannot understand. Well, we shall keep from underneath your feet."

He marched from the room, an expression of quiet triumph glowing on his face. It had been a much easier homecoming than he had anticipated. It was an amazement to him too that all of that money had gone so quickly. But she had saved his neck, as well as her own. He couldn't help but wonder how much more money she had invested and how he could get his hands on it. He would have to play the industrious millkeeper for a while to learn all.

He could well understand her rudeness toward Ruth Ann, if they were both thinking on the same subject. During one of Ruth Ann's drunken bouts over the holiday—of which there had been many—she had claimed credit for Laura's accident. He would have to be careful to keep his sisters and his aunt apart.

On the way to Ruth Ann's room he turned another matter over in his mind. His father had no right to turn down aid from Theda, he thought angrily. Hadn't his father made them all suffer enough because of his stupid business failure? His mother had made it clear to him that his own problems with the mill would never have come about if his father had not been so inept in his handling of the contracts with the academy. He hoped that he had convinced his mother that divorce was her only answer.

A month. Lucille had asked Laddie to bring Ruth Ann back to New York for a month. She claimed she needed the time to be alone with Clarence to thwart him in his plan to sell all their assets.

Yes, he just had to find out how to get his hands on this newly invested money. His mother needed it to save her servantless house. . . .

After he had left, Theda sat turning several matters over in her mind. Then she rang for Amos.

"They're back," she said.

"I know," he said grimly. "Ellen told me."

"I really had no choice about Laddie. I had no legal authority to take away his business; I have to keep him around to run it. Ruth Ann is another matter. She is not welcome in any part of this house other than Laddie's rooms. Do I make myself clear?"

"You most certainly do," he said calmly.

Theda's eyes as she looked up at him were cool and remote. "You never told me about the linen closet door being open that day, Amos. Laura tells me she ran into it. I'm not saying you knew it was open, but perhaps you suspected. We can no longer suspect, Amos, but only *ex*pect. She is not to be left alone until I figure out how to get rid of those two."

"Amen," he said. "Amen to that."

Fremont whispered bitterly to himself as he took the stage line up Broadway. Fernando Wood had been unusually curt. Fremont was of course elated that Vallandigham had news on the review of his case, but all of these other matters had to come first. But perhaps this was a lucky break. He might be able to get a more reasonable hearing from Vallandigham than he had been getting from Fernando of late.

Damn it all! he thought morosely. There's no understanding the stupidity of some of these radicals! I wonder . . .

But just what it was he wondered he would never recall afterward, for six uniformed riders came clattering by the stage just as he was about to get off. They wheeled to a stop right in front of the house that was his destination.

He pulled back into the shadows and stared at them. A horrible dread began to overcome him. Five more minutes and he would have been inside the house that the officer and men had just stormed into without knocking.

He was able to move among the trees surrounding the house until he was quite close to the action.

An enclosed carriage, driven by an army sergeant, careened down the street. By the time the carriage had been brought to a stop in front of the house, Fremont was aware of movement across the street. As his eyes became adjusted to the darkness he made out several men and horses in an apple orchard. Now he was really confused as to what was going on.

The soldiers hauled a screaming and protesting Vallandigham from the house in his long-john underwear. The officer was stuffing papers he had found in Vallandigham's bedroom into a saddlebag.

It was not the plot they had been paid to carry out, but the men in the orchard were quick to action, and not quiet. Before they had broken from the trees the soldiers were alerted and ready to return the first shot that was fired. And when the first shot came, Fremont foolishly thought he could rush forward and save the congressman while the others were fighting.

Vallandigham saw him just before he was stuffed into the carriage and tried to make his message known to the assassins who had been hired to kill Fremont.

"Traitor! Traitor! There he is!"

Confusion reigned. Fremont was already diving back into the trees. This was no time to try and convince Vallandigham that he had not brought the Federals; nor was it any time to try more heroics. He kept running, deeper into the trees and toward the south. He could hear screaming and shooting and hoof beats. He couldn't tell if they were coming or going and he dared not look back.

If he had, he might have seen a gunman jump to the driver's perch, fire point blank into the face of the sergeant, and urge the carriage team into a full gallop. The officer with the saddlebag clutched it as though it were laden with gold, took to his horse and rode in the opposite direction, leaving his five soldiers to do battle until their outnumbered ranks perished on the dusty ground of upper Broadway.

This unrecorded battle of the civil strife would give the Union all the evidence it would need to name Clement Vallandigham the leader of the opposition Copperheads, especially with the discovery of a coded message concerning an assassination attempt against the President; but it would deprive them of the real prize. The quick thinking of the radical gunman would allow Vallandigham's carriage to travel far into the night and to make a successful escape into Canada the next day.

Amazingly, none of the papers that Vallandigham had taken with him mentioned the brothers Wood, and the whole office and record section of the *Daily News* was burned out before Boss Tweed's "Big Six" fire brigade effectively saved the rest of the building.

It was near midnight by the time Fremont had double-tracked several times and made it back to Wood's residence. The street was under heavy military patrol. Fremont was not aware that Calvert had ordered them out in an effort to save his life.

Calvert anticipated that Fremont would come to Pfaff's for help or advice, but to his chagrin it was Ruth Ann and Laddie who came waltzing in gaily after midnight. He was forced to put on a long face and commiserate over the troubles they had suffered. He had a cover story prepared in case Fremont did now come in.

But Fremont had gone to the least expected place of all. At that moment he trusted the people within the Copperhead movement just about as much as he trusted the Federal soldiers.

To his way of thinking, the Vallandigham and Wood group had been more harmful to his cause than helpful. He was farther behind than he had been three months before. The thought of it nearly sent him into a frenzy of rage as he let himself back into the basement of the DeWitt mansion.

Alone. He would just have to handle it alone, and from a place where no one would ever expect to look for him.

18

LAURA LOOKED ACROSS the table at the serious face of her aunt. Theda was frowning, her treble chin resting on one hand, the other hand trembling over the stiff pages of a book.

Laura rose and went to the sideboard for another cup of breakfast coffee. She tended to favor the broken leg, but the past month had put color back into her cheeks and weight onto her bones.

"Would you like more coffee?"

Theda waved her silent answer.

"What are you reading?"

Again the silent signal that she did not want to be disturbed.

It was beginning to get on Laura's nerves. The whole house was becoming so funereal and weird. She could understand her brother and sister avoiding her, which didn't upset her at all, but these long, moody silences that everyone seemed to be falling into were becoming depressing. And when she asked a question, people jumped as though frightened and then never gave her a straight answer.

No one would explain why for nearly a month the maids had been quietly quitting, one after the other. Theda would not explain why for nearly a month she had been declining social invitation after social invitation. No one would explain why for nearly a month Mrs. Courtney's food had been declining in quality or why she moped about like a convict on death row.

The only people the atmosphere didn't seem to be affecting were those hardly ever in the house during the night time hours—Ruth Ann and Laddie, who never seemed to rise before sundown or to retire before sunup.

Maggie's excuse for her infrequent visits was that Laddie had shown up at work only once since his return, and she was stuck with the entire revamping of the mill. Laddie's one visit to the mill had told him all he needed to know. Maggie tightly controlled the purse strings extended by Theda; Maggie had things on the mend, and Maggie didn't need him around until it was time to go collect a pay check.

Clinton didn't come around because he was too busy with Maggie Duggan and just too embarrassed to admit it.

Calvert didn't come around because he was frantically trying to piece out the identities of the code-named people in the assassination plot, and constantly keeping his eye out for Fremont. He began to fear that Benjamin Wood's plan to have him eliminated had been successfully carried out.

Benjamin and Fernando Wood thought quite differently. The arrest of Vallandigham, and a secret message from him in Canada, had convinced them that Fremont was the traitor, and as long as he was alive they would live in mortal fear. Fernando never left his house and Benjamin hired a body-guard to be with him at all times in Washington.

Amos came in and set breakfast plates in front of Laura and Theda.

"Are you now a maid?" Laura asked, a little rudely.

"Ellen is doing the shopping," he said, his eyes avoiding hers.

"Ellen is doing the shopping?" she mocked. "Why is the front hall maid doing the butler's normal shopping, while he serves breakfast to a woman who, until a couple of weeks ago, never stirred herself from bed until nearly noon. What in the *world* is going on around here?"

Theda did not look up from her book.

"We're having a bit of a staff problem, miss," Amos said lamely. "Miss Theda doesn't wish me to leave the house until it is all straightened out."

Laura slammed her fork down on the table. "I don't mean to be rude, but donkey-feathers! Aunt Theda, what is it that you're reading?"

She looked up at Amos and shrugged. "Laura, it is not what I am reading, but what I am looking up. I'm trying to find a suitable date to sell this house."

"Suitable? Have you been going to that fortune teller again?"

"Not really, dear. She's been coming here and she's not a fortune teller. She is a medium."

"It's all the same thing. They're all fakers, just out for your money. What excuse has she given you for the need to sell this house?"

Theda's hand went nervously to her throat and played with a beaded necklace as her eyes sought Amos for help. "Well, dear . . . it would seem that . . . that we have a ghost . . . a most *malicious* ghost in the house."

Laura would have laughed instantly, but as Theda had stammered out the unbelievable statement her nervous fingers had pulled more than just a beaded necklace over the collar of her dress. It was an old world crucifix—a kind of ikon—and she unconsciously held it in her hand as though to ward off the creature of which she spoke.

But Laura's common sense returned quickly. "How much did she charge you for this ghost story?"

"That part is not important, Miss Laura," Amos said sadly, "not anymore. I didn't believe it either at first. I just thought it was more noise from their wild parties upstairs. Even the . . . ah . . . nude ghost standing by your bed I just took as one of their depraved friends who had wandered downstairs. But no more."

Laura sat back. "No more?" Her tone was biting.

"I told you we should have told her, Miss Theda. I told you she should have been in on that funny business when that old gal made the ghost speak."

"Hush," Theda scolded. "That's quite enough."

"I don't think so," Laura said quietly. "So, she held a seance and made the ghost speak. I'm ashamed of you both. That old trick is even known up in West Point. They pretend to go into a trance and have the ability to throw their voices without moving their lips. I bet she even recommended a real estate agent, didn't she?"

Amazingly, Amos took a seat at the table and folded his hands in front of him. He held them tightly because they were shaking.

"Miss Laura, the woman did faint, but not until after the ghost let out a most blood-chilling laugh and talked with her. That poor woman *was* a faker up till then. She rose from her chair, clutched at her throat, exulted over the fact that she had actually broken through to the other world and then collapsed. After it was over it took us an hour to bring her around."

"Could she have had an accomplice?"

"Possibly, but that wouldn't account for the voice knowing some of the things it knew. It is frightening."

Laura said nothing. She knew them both to be very reasonable people. She could feel herself shrinking to pigmy size under the thought that this was all a posibility.

"What shall we do?" she said at last.

Theda closed the book. "We go about our lives as best we can, and try to avoid it. It can grow most angry. Laura, do you feel up to going out to dinner and the theater? This was to be the night we were to see Edwin Booth in *Hamlet*."

"Of course," she said cheerfully, although she really didn't feel up to it. "That's exactly what you need—a night out."

It could not have pleased Fremont Hunter more. As much as he enjoyed his sadistic little game of playing ghost and spying, this night he wished Laura far away from the trouble he was about to brew. Everyone had failed him, but himself. But in a single evening he would make up for it all.

After the first few nights in the basement, he had accused himself of cowardice and ventured forth for food.

His nerves were raw during this first venture. But the next time it did not take so long to gather up food. He carefully began to acquaint himself with the whole house by night, finding nooks and crannies that were excellent listening posts. He was gathering a world of information—and of material things. Theda had a habit of leaving money lying around her room, and he did have a need for money. That the maids would be accused of theft and blamed for the missing food didn't matter to him. It had even delighted him after the maids were the ones who first suggested the ghost theory. Then he did start playing the ghost role to frighten as many of them away as possible. The fewer of them around the better, so that he could get to the garret each night before the return of the two party-goers and their friends.

Despite the danger, he would hide in the closet and spy on the wild gatherings. At first it made him sick with disgust, convincing him that Laddie had used his body as he was now able to see him using others. And he was utterly appalled that Ruth Ann could have lied against him when he saw the things she performed during these revels.

If there was a touch of madness already in him, his outrage over the scenes he witnessed in the garret helped to increase it. He let his beard grow scraggy, selected a wardrobe from the slaves' discarded clothing and ventured out into the streets. In this disguise, he made cautious trips to several of his old radical haunts. He was delighted that he went unnoticed by those who had only casually known him, but he was cagey enough not to get too close to those with whom he had been more intimate.

Slowly and carefully, over that month he cultivated a new battery of drinking cohorts. Because he had money (Theda's), a depth of knowledge and a keen sense of their inner feelings, they took the wild-eyed young man to be much more than he seemed, a person of whom one didn't ask too many questions. Because he paid well for information, he received truthful information. When he wished to meet a person, it was soon arranged.

It was warm under the buffalo robe in the carriage. The driver managed the well-trained four with expert ease. The city was left far behind when the driver pulled at the reins and the horses drew to a stop. Looking out of the window to see what was amiss, the passenger gasped.

"You're not the driver I hired!"

"No," Fremont chuckled. "I'm the one who paid him well to take his place."

"But why?"

"Come up and ride with me, sir. We have much in common to discuss."

Their meetings thereafter were less dramatic and more highly successful. They were smart enough to avoid the use of either's name, although Fremont was well aware of the man's reputation.

"I think it is extremely important for you to return to Washington with me on the fourteenth," the man said. "I want you to meet my friends there, and I think they will agree that you are the proper man to take our plan on south. I must go to the theater first, but we'll be able to leave on the late train. Will you do it?"

Fremont smiled to himself. The man had fallen into his trap beautifully. He had all his other plans set and had only been waiting for a date.

Now he had a date. Now all he had to do was prepare himself and put all his plans in motion. They were quite intricate, but they had to be when one was scheming to ruin so many people in a single night.

"Oh, Edwin!" Theda cried, pushing people aside to make it through the greenroom to the actor. "A delight, delight, delight."

"Theda, my dear, dear friend!" Edwin Booth took her by the shoulders and planted a resounding kiss on each cheek. "I'm so pleased to see you."

"I do wish, however," she pouted theatrically, "that the play might have been a little lighter fare. It is not pleasant to sit through a story about a ghost when you have a speaking spectre right in your own home."

"Theda, do be serious," he chuckled.

"I'm being quite serious, Edwin."

He looked at her in amazement, then up at the door where two men were entering. "Oh, this is just breathtaking news. And here are two I must share it with immediately. Theda DeWitt was just telling me that she has an actual ghost in her house. We must have her counsel with the actor playing the ghost of Hamlet's father. Oh, I'm forgetting my manners. Theda, you remember my father and brother, of course."

"Of course. Gentlemen, I know you have not had the pleasure of meeting my niece, Miss Laura Dahlgren. Laura, the Booth family—Junius Brutus and his sons, Edwin Thomas and John Wilkes."

Laura smiled, curtsied and congratulated Edwin on his performance.

John Wilkes Booth stood looking at Laura. She's so beautiful, he thought; what a stunning Ophelia she would make!

"Edwin," Theda exclaimed happily, "I've just had a marvelous idea. Why don't you all join us for an after-theater bite?"

"That would be delightful, my dear, but we'll have to excuse John from the party. He's off shortly to catch the late train for Washington."

Gazing at Laura, John Wilkes Booth was contemplating changing his travel plans for the evening when an agitated Amos came pushing though the crowd and whispered to Theda.

"Say that again, Amos."

"Some man came to the house," he repeated, his voice low but not too low for Laura to overhear. "He was looking for Mr. Laddie or yourself. He says there's to be big trouble at the mill tonight. Those two from upstairs had already gone out for the evening."

"Edwin," Theda said curtly, breaking in on his conversation with another admirer, "we'll have to make supper another evening. I'll send you a note. Come, Laura, we'll drop you off at home."

"No," she said firmly. "I'm going with you."

Theda didn't want to take time to argue, and so she hurried away with Laura and Amos following.

John Wilkes Booth suddenly made the connection in his mind between mention of the mill and the girl's last name. He was well aware that the mill was one of the targets for the radicals that night. But why, he thought, in his whole damn life had all the beautiful women been on the wrong side? He had yet to see a female radical who could stir his interest in the least. He shrugged. Perhaps it was best that he was going to Washington. He and the girl would end up having very little in common.

Even from the bridge they could see the fire. Amos yelled at Harry to give the team their head. The towering flames were so brilliant that they illuminated the dry-docked keels in the shipyard, revealing smaller fires springing up here and there as flying embers landed on the heavily pitched hulls. Looking down from the bridge they could see an army of antlike figures trying to catch each small fire as it burst up and keep the roaring inferno that had once been the mill from spreading in their direction.

Before they could get off the bridge the carriage was jolted as the mill's boiler exploded, sending a shaft of scalding steam five hundred feet into the air.

Laura remembered the streets leading to the mill as always being black as night, but they were now basked in a ghastly orange hue.

There was another explosion, then another, as neighboring factories began to be consumed. The carriage shook with the rumbling ground and Harry was afraid to take the horses any closer. It was impossible to go on anyway. The street was jamming up with people running from the sea of flame, some with their clothing already partly burned away.

Amos bounded from the carriage and lurched forward. "Turn it around, Harry. Some of these people will need to be taken to a hospital." He pushed his way through the wailing people, seeing enough scattered bodies for a battlefield. The mill was beyond all hope.

The surge of people was thinning when Clinton Bell came up, panting, followed by a group of men from the shipyard.

He looked at a huddled little group of children that Maggie was trying to calm and lead to safety. Maggie looked strange and terrible: all the hair had been burned off her head, and her eyes were wild with the effort to keep herself composed enough to comfort the children.

"Get her out of here," he said quietly to Amos. "This started with a bunch of little explosions. Horace DeLong thinks they were trying for the shipyard. We're going to dynamite to create a fire-break."

A man ran up with a wooden box. Amos watched wonderingly as the other men grabbed up long gray sticks from the box and ran left and right. Then he saw that Maggie had joined them.

"No," she said hoarsely. "No, Clint, there are people still in there!"

Clint looked at her, his red face silent and still. He shook his head, then nodded for the men to go ahead. No one could still be alive in that inferno.

"Come," he said, and nodded for Amos to bring the children.

Maggie collapsed against Clint, her silent grief choking her throat.

It was still an unbelievable nightmare. She and Bertha Butt had had a hundred women and children working that night, cleaning gears and parts with kerosene and wire brushes. At first she had thought that it was a foolish accident, someone lighting a match amid the heavy kerosene fumes. But the explosions had continued, one after the other rocking the building.

As she ran down the steep office stairs she had seen the masked man too late. He threw the flaming bottle at her head before she could duck. The flames were igniting her hair even as the bottle broke open on her skull. She fell down the remaining steps, instinctively pulling her skirt up over her head and smothering the flames. Almost at once she was on her feet and charging down the passage to the mill floor, but she was cuffed aside so that the attackers could make their escape.

They had been well trained and organized, each assigned a window or exit door to fire-bomb and prevent escape. Their next bombs were then directed at the looms —which were saturated with kerosene, although the bombers had no way of knowing this. Instantly, the whole work floor flashed into a quavering sheet of flame. Six of the twelve attackers were caught by their own destructive deed.

Thirteen. That was all Maggie had been able to save out of a hundred workers. Thirteen . . .

She was almost unconscious when they got her into the carriage, but a sudden thought revived her at once.

"Bertha!" she croaked. "Bertha Butt is still in there!"

Clinton cradled her in his arms, rocking and soothing her like a baby. "It's all right, my darling. Everything is going to be all right. You'll see."

"He's right, Maggie," Theda added. "Why, in no time at all, we'll have the mill rebuilt, better than it ever was."

"Don't build it back for her," Clinton objected, "because she won't be here. It's enough that she's been beaten up and now almost killed over this damn place. Mr. DeLong knew this was coming, ever since the newspaper trouble. He's offered some of us the chance to go work in the rolling mill he just bought in Pittsburgh. I'm going to take him up on his offer, Maggie, and get you out of this hellhole city of New York."

"My, my," Theda whispered to Laura, "that sounded almost like a marriage proposal, didn't it?"

"I believe that it was," Laura said clearly, surprised at the strength of her own voice. She looked at Clinton Bell and hardly knew him. It seemed a thousand years since they had shared his lunch on the village green. He had been so shy and boyish. Now he was being so self-confident and manly—and so utterly unaware that Laura was even in the carriage.

"I think that they are well suited for each other," Theda declared after they had dropped them off at the hospital, where Clinton had insisted that they go home and let him handle things. "I'm really quite happy for both of them."

Amos was as quiet as Laura. For him as well it seemed far too many years had elapsed since Laura had first taken him to Clinton's quarters in Nettie Rivers's shed. He didn't quite know what manner of man would be best suited for Miss Laura, but he had known since that night that it wasn't Clinton Bell.

The policeman on the beat stopped the carriage a block from the mansion.

"Evening, Amos, ladies."

"Evening," Amos said. "Rather late for you, isn't it?"

The officer looked embarrassed. "We were warned to expect trouble tonight, but nothing like this. I think it would be best if you keep the ladies from the house for awhile, Amos."

"And why?" Theda insisted.

The big Irishman hung his head. "They're arresting your nephew and some of his friends, Miss DeWitt."

"Oh, damn!" she groaned. "This night will be the death of me. Amos, you will let us off at the house and then go at once for Mr. Tweed. Officer, you will come with us."

He obeyed, but he hated to have her see any of the scene that he had witnessed. The screaming, the fighting, the yelling . . . and that had only been the five scantily clad "ladies of the night" who had been carted off in the first paddy wagon. The arresting officers were giving the "gentlemen" a moment longer to reclothe themselves for the ride to jail. The policemen were also giving their own minds a moment to regain a sense of reality. They had burst in on a scene out of Sodom and Gomorrah. Not even the veterans on the squad could recall having viewed anything as depraved as this.

The curious were beginning to come from the neighboring houses and dot the sidewalk. One man was not curious, but simply rode on by, thinking the paddy wagons were there for quite another reason. Tired and smoke-sooted, Horace DeLong crawled from his carriage to enter his house. His mind was such at that moment that he could easily believe that the radical-leaning Lawrence Dahlgren could have fired his own business. Then, glancing at the DeWitt mansion as he climbed the steps to his brownstone, he stopped short. He did not know the first two men the police were hauling down to the paddy wagon, but the sight of the third figure broke his heart. That his son could do this to the family was unforgivable. He entered his house, vowing to never utter Calvert DeLong's name again.

Laura and Theda tried to get to Calvert, but a pushing, demanding throng of reporters cut them off. Theda climbed the stairs as though storming a castle. Two officers were carrying a most reluctant Laddie through the door.

He grinned foolishly, his mind overpowered by hashish and wine. "You're too late for the party, Auntie T. The brassy blond has already burst from the cake."

"Oh," she wailed, "take him away! All of you get out of my house!"

"We'll take him away," she was informed, "but it will be a while before we can leave. Still got two men to bring down and then we'll have to start a search of the whole house for more."

Theda's mind boggled. She didn't dare have them search the basement and carriage house!

"Laura, to your room!" she barked. "You! Take me to whoever is in charge of this madcap little scene!"

A pair of gleeful eyes looked down on the scene from the second floor. Everything was working out just as Fremont had planned it . . . and even better.

Once he had the radicals all prepared to attack the mill, he had come back to give Amos the fake message, chuckling that the black butler did not even recognize him.

Then, knowing the habits of the garret occupants, he entered the basement and immediately went up to the top floor. Using Laddie's toilet articles, he took a leisurely bath, shaved off the beard and mustache, and selected one of Laddie's more conservative suits to wear.

Satisfied with himself, he went down to Theda's bedroom to watch the street and wait. As though they were following a time schedule dictated by Fremont, Kitty, Ellen and Mrs. Courtney came in the back entrance from their evening out, went immediately to their third floor rooms and retired.

No more than five minutes later a fleet of hansom cabs began to pull up at the mansion. Fremont scanned each male face and then began to grin. Ruth Ann Dahlgren had insisted that this would be the night that she would get Calvert DeLong to come back and party with them—and she had done it.

Fremont was ecstatic. Now it was a waiting game. In his mind's eye he could almost see the young girl he had hired running into the police station to scream about the gentlemen who had lured her to a party and then tried to do nasty things to her. The reporters had been forewarned that there would be a sensational break in the Dahlgren case just before midnight.

Ah, yes, Fremont chuckled to himself, everything was

perfect. Laddie would have some explaining to do about the mill, to say nothing of the party. Fremont would have loved to have been around to see how Ruth Ann tried to lie her way out of this mess, and the arrest of Calvert DeLong was frosting on the cake.

Now, he had to await but two more events: the pandemonium that would break out when the police found that the socially prominent Theda DeWitt was running an Underground way station, and then his final triumph.

This he had planned down to the most exact detail. He took the heavy cloak from the chair and went to Theda's bedroom door to listen. Almost at once he heard the footsteps and silently slipped into the hall. The gas lamps were as low as he had been able to make them. Laura was going down the hall at almost a run, her hoops nearly banging each side of the wall as they swayed. As silent as a cat, he bounded and caught her in just a few great strides. Before she could scream or turn, the cloak was over her head and a rabbit punch was delivered to the back of her neck. She instantly went limp and was scooped up over his shoulder. He turned and fleetly made his way to the back stairs, down into the kitchen and out the back door. He paused for a moment to make sure no one was in the drive. Then he darted around behind the carriage house and dumped his bundle into an awaiting pony cart.

He had won! He had ruined all who had tried to ruin him, and had made off with the grand prize. In ten minutes' time he would have Laura aboard the train and would keep her unconscious as long as possible—and by dawn, thanks to the help he would receive from John Wilkes Booth, he would be taking his future bride home to South Carolina.

There was no one to see the pony cart go down the alley. They were all too busy in front of the house or within. . . .

Theda stood her ground in the foyer, refusing to let the policemen start their search and keeping them frozen in place until Amos returned with William Marcy Tweed.

"Lady," the officer growled, "there's nothing you can do about those who have already been arrested. The reporters came here for a scoop and they got it. Not even

Boss Tweed is going to be able to change those facts around, so why don't you let me send the rest of the paddy wagons to the station house?"

Theda nodded her agreement. She thought that Ruth Ann and Laddie were getting their just desserts.

A frantic hand pulled at her sleeve. "But, Aunt Theda," Laura whispered, "they've also taken Calvert."

"That is his problem for getting caught with them," she snapped. "Now, do as I told you and get to your room!"

Amos's arrival with Boss Tweed caused a commotion in the foyer. Every detail had to be rehashed for the burly man, who had been so rushed by Amos that he'd had only the time to pull on a pair of trousers and a dressing robe. It caused a delay in the departure of the paddy wagon and Laura slipped unseen back to the street. The officers and spectators were far more interested in trying to see or hear what was going on through the open front door, so she was not even challenged as she climbed up onto the back step of the wagon and peered in through the grated door.

Laddie was spread-eagled on the floor, unconscious.

"Calvert," Laura whispered. She started as he sat forward and his face instantly filled the grate.

"Laura," he hissed, "get away from here. You don't want to get involved."

"Then why are you?"

He shook his head. "A damn stupid accident. I only agreed to help Ruth Ann get Laddie back here because he was so drunk. Then she asked some of their other friends too. They helped her take him into his bedroom to get him ready for bed and the next thing I knew she and Laddie both came waltzing out without their clothing. Their suggestions disgusted me and I started to leave. Ruth Ann chased after me, pleading and begging, and on the second floor tried to drag me into your room. That's when we heard the arrival of the police. I told Ruth Ann to put on some of your clothes and hide. I went back up to warn Laddie, but by then it was too late for me to get away."

"I will go tell them the truth about you!"

"No, it will do no good. This whole thing has the earmarks of being a set-up. Look at all the reporters. They're not here just by chance. I'll just have to ride out this storm on my own. Now, get away before they think you had something to do with it."

Laura reluctantly obeyed and arrived back in the foyer just in time to hear Boss Tweed make a similar declaration.

"They'll just have to ride out the night in jail, Theda. Those reporters are sitting out there like vultures. I can't risk it, Theda. You know I've been trying to clean up the scandal and loose-living ways that Fernando Wood allowed to run rampant during his administration. This whole raid smells fishy to me, just like someone wanted it to blow up in my face. Let the newspapers have their headlines in the morning. By afternoon I will have it heard by a friendly judge—if there isn't too much dirty linen involved."

Theda clamped her lips shut. Along with the story about the mill fire, any manner of dirty linen was about to be aired. The next few days were not going to be very pleasant.

She was so preoccupied with these thoughts that she paid no attention when Laura finally made her way up the stairs.

Laura had not seen Ruth Ann since her return. Through Kitty, however, she had heard most of the household gossip about her sister. That Ruth Ann and Laddie were making fools of themselves did not really amaze her. But she was deeply angry that Ruth Ann had tried to pull Calvert down to her level. She had never really had it out with Ruth Ann, and the time seemed ripe.

Ruth Ann was not in her room and Laura was not about to go up those stairs to Laddie's quarters ever again. Ruth Ann could just wait until morning, and Laddie and his disgusting friends had only a mite of pride and reputation to lose—if indeed they had any pride. Calvert, however, had much to lose. She stood puzzling over the matter, wondering what she could do to help him.

Still unsure she was making the right decision, she followed nearly the same escape path Fremont Hunter had made—with the wrong girl bundled in his cloak—but in the alley she turned right and marched up to the back door of the DeLong mansion.

The bathrobe-clad maid, aroused by the excitement next door, let Laura in quickly on the assumption she was going to gain the gossip all the faster. The maid's puzzlement grew as the solemn Horace DeLong agreed to see Laura at once and then soundly closed them off in his private study. Through that oaken door the poor girl could hear nothing.

"I wish to speak frankly, Mr. DeLong. But I need to be assured that what I say shall not leave this room." Laura's voice was strong, only a slight tremor revealing her doubt that she had chosen the right course.

A crease appeared between Mr. DeLong's brows. "You need not speak at all," he replied coldly. "I arrived home just in time to see my ungrateful son in the hands of the police. I do not wish to hear any of the details."

"But you *are* going to hear the details, all of them," she said hotly, "because your son was falsely arrested. Your son is not what you think him to be, sir. He is good and honest and decent. What he is doing, he is doing under orders."

The crease deepened between Mr. DeLong's brows at this extraordinary news. But as an aristocratic egotist, he had heard the confession wrong. "Under orders from the wrong people. Are you aware, young lady, that the radicals he now associates with, including your worthless brother, caused death and destruction this night? The death count will surely go over a hundred innocent souls."

"I was there tonight," said Laura, her voice falling to a low whisper, "and Calvert would have been the first to stop it had he known. That's why he pretends to be a friend to my brother and the others. Those are the orders of which I spoke. It tears his heart out that he isn't able to be truthful with you, but I think the time has come for you to know what he's really doing. And you must get him out of jail before someone else stumbles onto the truth about him."

"Miss Dahlgren, you aren't by chance making sport of me?" he asked, his voice quiet and disdainful. He made a slight motion as if to rise. "How would you know such a thing of him, when his mother and father do not?"

Laura eyed him so forcefully that he sank back into his seat. When she spoke, her voice was low and measured. She exposed all that she knew.

Mr. DeLong was silent through her account. He was

crushed that he had held his son in such low regard, that he had never suspected the truth. His thin white nostrils dilated, and his glacial blue eyes widened. A faint hope began to dawn in him. His old heart was trembling.

"I have friends at the precinct house," he said in a constrained tone. "I will go now to have a talk with them and with my son."

Dazed, he rose and left the study without further comment. He passed the maid in the hall as though sightless and went right out into the night without hat or cloak.

Laura uttered a faint sigh and allowed herself a moment of relief. Then she bolted to her feet on another urgent mission. She had to get home and reveal Calvert's words to Theda before Ruth Ann had twisted everything in her own favor.

She, too, rushed sightlessly by the maid and down the hall toward the back door.

The Irish girl quickly crossed herself. Whatever was going on, she figured she could use a bit of protection from above.

John Wilkes Booth had obtained adjoining compartments on the night train to Washington. It was quite a revelation to see Fremont Hunter without his disguise, and a surprise to see the strange cloak-wrapped baggage he had carried aboard and dropped in the next compartment. That there was a female wrapped within the cloak was an even greater revelation.

"A bit of a surprise, Hunter. Did she not wish to come?"

"A mere faint over all the excitement, I assure you, Booth."

"Excitement? Would this be an elopement?"

He leaned toward Fremont, his darkly handsome face alert for such daring, though inwardly he was cursing the unknown girl who might prove to be a temporary obstacle.

"Elopement," Fremont repeated slowly, as though savouring the word in all its meaning. His expression lightened. He grinned pleasantly. "You can call it that, Mr. Booth, for my part."

So! thought Booth, the lady is not here of her own choosing. That did not sit well with him at all. He had to learn more of the matter quickly. But John Wilkes Booth always studied a play carefully before assuming a role. He took a flask and glasses from a travel case.

"We will drink to the good fortune of yourself and Miss . . . Miss . . ."

"Dahlgren. Miss Laura Dahlgren."

Booth paused and stared before taking a sip of his whisky. He composed himself and raised his glass in a toast. He swirled the contents about in the glass, took a neat swig, and shook his head seriously.

"Hunter, I had occasion to meet the young lady tonight with Miss Theda DeWitt. You aren't getting us into a ticklish situation, are you?"

Fremont's expression darkened into complete somberness. "No," he answered. "I've decided to keep her unconscious until I get her over into Virginia. You said you would have transportation for me to Richmond."

Booth went on hurriedly, as if he wished to change the subject. "Transportation, yes! Any manner you might desire. What I have in mind is important to certain people in Richmond. You spoke of marriage. I assume then that you wish to delay such a ceremony until you are among your own people. Am I correct?"

"It hardly matters, but it is a thought. I really just wish to get on the road as soon as possible."

Booth was silent a moment. He wet his thin pink lips and scrutinized Fremont with unusual intensity. Was there a conscience in this cold creature? Or was he going to overpower the girl out of his own desires? He could not overcome the strong suspicion that the girl knew nothing of Hunter's marriage plan.

Fanatic or no, Booth was first and foremost a gentleman. He would hear the lady's side of the tale before he came to a final conclusion.

"Another?" he said grandly, taking Fremont's glass. He turned his back slightly to mask the movement of his hand groping in the bag. He quickly dumped a sleeping potion into the glass and then added the whisky, waiting until the potion dissolved before he turned.

"Here we go!" His face became even more genial. He chattered on, about nothing in particular. He had been anticipating the yawn.

"I say, you have had a most exhausting day of it, and face another tomorrow. Drop down the upper berth here on my side, so as not to disturb the young lady. I hardly ever sleep on this run, as it is."

Fremont hardly got the pullman bunk down and climbed up on it before he was sound asleep.

John Wilkes Booth sat and sipped at his bourbon, slowly and thoughtfully. At the first moan from the other compartment, he jumped to his feet, positively radiating his delight. He could play the gallant knight without Fremont even being aware.

The cloak was pushed back and Ruth Ann sat up in a daze. Booth stared. Dahlgren? Ah, to be sure there was a resemblance, but this was not the Ophelia he had been anticipating. He cautiously pulled the compartment door closed behind him.

"Who are you?" Ruth Ann demanded. "What has happened to me and why am I here?"

Booth assumed an expression of acute concern. "Now calm yourself, my dear. I—I'm . . . a doctor. How do you feel?"

"Feel? Like hell! Are you the bastard who threw the cloak over my head and then bashed me? Hey! This is a train!"

"On that point you are most correct, Miss Dahlgren." He looked at her earnestly. "On the other points you are in error."

"In error, perhaps, but it tells me nothing. Who are you and where are you taking me?"

"I've told you I'm a doctor, and I am taking you to safety."

Ruth Ann eyed him. It was all so confusing, but he was really quite an unusually handsome man.

"Well, you seem to know my name, but I wonder what you consider safe for me." She smiled, as if giving him an opening to be less than a gentleman.

"Would home be safe for you?"

"Yours or mine?"

Booth betrayed no offense. He wondered how Hunter had made such an error. This was certainly not anything like the girl he had met in the theater. But that also raised a most interesting point in his mind. Hunter was still not aware he had made the error, and Booth no longer felt like playing the knight. This girl was loose, far too loose for him. He liked to be the gentleman and not to have some sex-starved female deny him that role. He thought Hunter deserved his stupid blunder, in more ways than one.

He leaned toward her and spoke in a soft and confidential voice, letting his hand take her wrist in a professional manner.

"We will consider that question later. You've been through a very trying experience and I want you to rest during the journey. Your pulse is far too rapid. I'm going to fix you a light potion to make you relax. Don't worry, I'll stay with you until you're resting comfortably. I just want you to put everything that happened tonight out of your mind."

"You know what happened?"

"Everything."

Ruth Ann's face became inscrutable, but a knowing interest grew in her eyes. Someone, for some purpose, had gotten her away from the police and sure arrest. She was not unhappy that they had put her in the care of this Adonis. Why ask questions? Just let come what may.

Booth sat on the edge of the pullman seat, lowering his affable voice to a soothing whisper to get her to drink and become relaxed. His hands comforted her and gave her false hope of where next they might travel. Because he had tripled the potion given to Fremont, her mind sailed away into sleep before she was even aware it was happening.

With two sleeping babies on his hands, he went in search of the conductor and paid the additional fare for the two compartments to the terminus in Maryland. There he had a doctor friend who would provide transportation for the duo on south. If possible, he would keep Fremont from learning the true nature of his cargo until they were well away from him. Fremont was not worthy of being included in his glorious plans. From top to bottom he would change the government overnight. A new thought on how to bring it about came to him and he searched his pocket for writing material. All he had was a small playbill from his brother's performance of the night before.

"This will do for now. A year from this night, dear brother, the night before the Ides of April, you may be begging for this little playbill back as an historical memento. Nor will your little brother be on his way to Maryland, as he is now. He will have long since been hailed as the savior of the nation—if he can just keep away from bumbling idiots like these two."

He looked at Ruth Ann's unconscious face with contempt and raised his whisky glass in mock salute.

"My dear, dear miss, you've had the noble pleasure of John Wilkes Booth's company. I wish you God's speed with your Mr. Fremont Hunter. Aye, I've a feeling you are well matched!"

The conductor, well paid to keep the secret of this elopement under wraps, never once questioned the fact that the bride was lifted from the train like a package bundled in a heavy cloak, or that the bridegroom was completely benumbed. This was war, and marriages of this type had to be kept most secret.

Booth stood alone for a long moment, staring at the disappearing wagon. His gray eyes were like steel. He had not had to call upon his doctor friend. He had found a wagon for hire right in the station. When the black driver had refused to go south, he had bought the rig outright.

"Don't say I didn't give you your bride," he murmured. He chuckled to himself. Life was so simple, if one just took matters into one's own hands.

A hand mightier than any one man's seemed to have come down on the land south of Fremont's debarkation point of Silver Springs. At first, in the April dawn, it seemed as though spring was about to burst forth with more splendor than ever. Then, as the road led through Manassas and southeast to Richmond, dread portents rose everywhere. Once across the Potomac, Virginia was a dead battleground, a sepulchre of armies that would never rise again. The land, as though it would never see another spring, lay torn and bleeding.

He was not challenged as the wagon rolled down roads with the Union hosts camped on either side, strengthened and reorganized now as they prepared for a concerted thrust into the Deep South's vitals. One thing held them back, but did not daunt Fremont from urging the mules forward. They were waiting for the April sun to dry the winter's mud.

A few miles ahead, across the Rapidan, Lee's army was welcoming the spring of 1864; they had been brought up to their normal strength of sixty-two thousand again.

But neither Fremont Hunter nor his passenger were aware of this. Fremont was hardly aware that his passenger had been awake for some time and was staring out at the greatest scene of desolation ever presented to her eyes.

At that point, Ruth Ann was still unsure which of the recent events had been nightmare and which reality. But this, without question, had to be part of the nightmare. The belief was heightened in her mind by the sight of the skeleton frame of a once gracious plantation manor. No graveyard had ever looked more bleak.

"Take me back," she gasped. "Oh, take me back away from this horror!"

Fremont turned and his eyes widened. "Oh, good God, no! Ruth Ann? Jesus! It can't be! It was Laura I took out of the hallway!"

Ruth Ann instantly understood all. She burst into laughter that stopped only when she coughed and choked.

"Forget that simpleton. Where is that doctor on the train? Where in the hell are we? And what in thunderation is . . ."

She gasped and gazed up at a dozen leering faces on horseback.

"Are you lost?" the squad leader, his voice louder than necessary because he had gone slightly deaf in a battle near that very spot the year before.

"Thank you, no, we aren't," Fremont answered innocently. "We've only a short way to go."

Ruth Ann would have challenged his statement with intense satisfaction if an officer had not come riding up with strident orders for them to take cover in the plantation house.

Ruth Ann had listened to his instructions with absorbed attention, her expression becoming more and more inscrutable as she realized Fremont did not recognize the man.

But a bitter smile played about her mouth as she came to realize that Wilf Jamison did not recognize her either. She was unaware what rank his insignia indicated, but the other soldiers' deference suggested that he had a voice of authority. She regarded Fremont with a glitter in her eyes.

"I think we'd best do it. Look!" she said, her tone suddenly awed.

Fremont followed her gaze and stared in wonderment. Lee was allowing Grant's forces to cross the Rapidan unopposed and penetrate the tangled wilds of the wilderness. The vast numbers froze his brain, and a glance at Ruth Ann brought the unpleasant reminder that he was with a young lady who could start screaming kidnap.

As it turned out, however, the generals—Lee and Grant—would keep her from screaming anything, at least for several days.

The battle was almost immediate. The Southerners knew that in those dense woods the effectiveness of the Yankees' superior numbers would be vastly reduced. They didn't falter. They looked to one man. He bowed his tired head and no body of men ever born to woman ever marched to a surer death with deeper love of a leader than those ragged lines of Rebels, unaware that they were facing the fiercest, bloodiest struggle that man would ever be able to record in the annals of military history.

The plantation house gave no shelter from the oppressively hot days and humid nights, and no protection from the din and flare of battle. The burned-out skeleton proved useful to only one person.

Forgetting that he had Ruth Ann in tow, Fremont scaled the rock chimney for a bird's-eye view of both armies. His excitement was like that of a child who has often heard of a thing, but was viewing it for the first time.

All of that first day he had sat in his perch as though he were directing the war.

"What? That is pure lunacy!" he cried as Lee suddenly threw half of his army on Grant's advancing men with savage energy. "Is this all there is? Has the man no backup?"

Fremont was not aware that General Longstreet was

making a forced march from Gordonsville. He hardly breathed through the hours of that day and far into the night as the fierce conflict raged.

When he came down he felt he had to relive everything he had seen for Ruth Ann's benefit.

"I, for one, thought to see nothing but failure in such daring. It seemed near impossible that the march was finally slowed, and by the time darkness started to fall the Confederates had pushed the blue lines back, captured four guns and a number of prisoners."

Ruth Ann didn't comment. Only the night sounds of nature broke the pall of ominous silence hanging over the countryside.

"I'm hungry, Fremont," she said at last. "What are we going to do for food and a place to sleep?"

He waved her to silence, as if such matters were trivial. His mind was already contemplating what the next day would bring.

It looked as though the plantation had been picked bare on several different occasions. Only a smooth surface on the ground suggested that a barn had once stood on the spot. The toolshed was toolless, and only two of its walls still stood. The fields were greening up, but only with wild grass. Ruth Ann even took a stick and poked among the ashes and half-burned and fallen rafter timbers, but with no luck. She cursed Fremont Hunter and then herself for not speaking up and making herself known to Wilf Jamison. She bet that he had food in his belly.

"How far would you say it was to those campfires?"

Fremont shrugged. "A half mile or so. Why?"

"If we aren't going to be able to leave here until after the battle, the least they could do is give us some food. It won't take you long in the wagon."

Fremont's face expressed complete incredulity and disdain. "Going or coming, one side or the other would take shots at me. We'll just wait until the morning . . . after Grant has surrendered."

Ruth Ann burst into wild laughter, and spun away to continue her search. She didn't fear walking across the fields—not if it meant something to eat. She stepped up onto a grass-covered mound to better judge the distance to the campfires and was astounded when the ground gave way and she sank in up to her knees.

On her surprised cry, Fremont came running. He pulled her free and started to enlarge the hole with his hands.

"What is it?"

"A root cellar, if I'm not mistaken. They probably covered over the entry door to keep everything from being stolen."

Because the covering earth had begun to rot away the door, it didn't take much time to gain entrance to the small, dank chamber. It was no treasure trove.

"Here are some candle stubs, Fremont. Quick, before your match goes out. What are those?"

"Pickling vats. Don't you know anything?"

She ignored him and pushed up the lid on the earthen crock.

"You're right! Pickles. Phew! Smell that dill. Hey, I bet we could trade these for other things to eat."

"It won't be necessary. Tomorrow we'll head on south and find plenty of food."

"*South?* I want to go home!"

Fremont stared at her in affront. "I've got to go to *my* home first, Ruth Ann. I don't have time to turn back, so you'll just have to tag along. Now, tonight you have a choice of dill pickles or sauerkraut for dinner. The battle won't take more than an hour in the morning, and then you can have all the food that you desire."

Fremont actually believed that he would be in his chimney perch for only an hour the next morning. Because Ruth Ann had the only cloak between them, he had left the root cellar at daybreak in order to get warm. He was amazed to see that the Federals were already preparing to attack Lee's entire line with terrific force. His certainty that the battle would be quick began to falter as he saw Lee's dangerous position before Grant's legions.

"No!" he cried. "Protect your right wing!"

Unfortunately, the Confederates could not hear his command and the right wing was soon being crushed and rolled back in disorder.

Then, in his excitement, he nearly lost his balance. Ruth Ann was just emerging from the root cellar and he shouted down: "Help is coming! Help is coming!"

She didn't have the slightest idea what he meant and shrugged indifferently. Her stomach was sour from eating too many dill pickles and that was all that concerned her.

Longstreet had reached the field and was throwing his men into the breach on the right wing. Fremont whooped and yelled as though he were a part of the battle. Then his mouth fell open in amazement.

"I know what he's doing. We studied this at the academy. He's repeating the same brilliant maneuver Jackson made at Chancellorsville."

Fremont's memory was quite correct. Longstreet was sent around Hancock's left to turn and assail his flank. The movement was a complete success. Hancock's line was smashed and driven back a mile to his second defenses.

General Wadsworth at the head of his division was mortally wounded and fell into the hands of the onsweeping Confederates.

"We've got them! We've got them!" Fremont chortled. "The Feds are falling back to the river in confusion. Oh, no! Good God, no!"

Tears welled in Fremont's eyes as a group of Confederate officers was caught in a volley from their own men. Longstreet fell, dangerously wounded, and General Jenkins, who was with him, was instantly killed.

His game began to lack spice. Fremont slowly lowered himself from the chimney. "Impossible," he muttered. "Longstreet has fallen in exactly the same way and almost in the same spot where Jackson fell."

He sat on the ground with his back against the stone wall and brooded. Noon and afternoon and evening came and he didn't stir. He didn't see Colonel Wilf Jamison charge and break through the Confederate lines, capturing twelve hundred prisoners and then being driven back with a loss of a thousand of his own men. Near sunset, he didn't see General John B. Gordon break through Sedgwick's Union lines, rolling back their right flank and capturing six hundred prisoners and two brigadier generals.

Nor did he see that Ruth Ann had vanished.

Grant had lost 17,666 in two days. Any other general would have retreated across the Rapidan to reorganize his bleeding lines.

"General, we have a small problem."

Grant, chewing on his cigar, waved his right arm with a quick movement and gave a harsh laugh.

"We have many small problems, Jamison. Thank God we have no major ones."

Wilf cleared his throat. "Sir, this is Miss Ruth Ann Dahlgren. She has pickles to trade for food."

The stolid fighter spun and burst into even harsher laughter.

"Don't tell me that she's related to . . . that's impossible! What in the hell is she doing here . . . with *pickles*?"

Wilf tried to explain the best that he could, but it was still all very unbelievable in his mind.

Grant was silent for a long moment. His hard eyes, so used to finding duplicity and cunning in every quarter, tried to read Ruth Ann's open countenance. But he could read nothing there but hunger and fear. He waved an aide over and directed him to take Ruth Ann to the quartermaster's wagon. Then he turned to Jamison.

"What do you make of it?"

"I'm not sure," said Wilf, with a faint smile. "She always was a spoiled one, and he always struck me as a rounder."

"I don't believe for a moment that they were on a visit —*or* that she now wants an escort back because the war scares her. Hell, I don't think anything scares her. Take her back and see what you can learn from that Hunter. Don't make it too obvious, but take a guard back with you for overnight. I don't want her Southern gentleman slipping away to let them know that we're digging in."

"I have just the man for the job, sir. Shall I have him report back in the morning or stay with them?"

Grant shook his head sadly. "We'll need him back. We'll need every man we can muster. I propose to fight it out on this line if it takes all summer."

Ruth Ann descended the earthen steps slowly. Once in the square and musty chamber, so cool and dank, she lit a new candle and paced about a few moments, chewing her fingernail in deep thoughtfulness. Then she went back up into the evening gloom, and assumed an expression of unbelieving horror. She had been aware since spotting the

absence of the horse from the wagon that Fremont had
left without her. She was delighted, but had to put on a
different face for Wilf Jamison.

"Gosh, Miss Ruth Ann," he said, "I'm terribly sorry. A
man who would pull such a stunt should be horse-whipped.
But don't you worry. I'll leave Ned Fraser to guard you
during the night."

"I don't want a guard, Wilf. I want to be taken home."

"I'll discuss the matter with the general, miss."

"Discuss!" she said angrily. "What is there to discuss,
Wilf? Your obligation as a Dahlgren servant is to me, and
not to any general. Now, go find a carriage to take me back
to New York."

Jamison smiled to himself. Just before bringing her back,
Grant had made him a brigadier general on the field. Ruth
Ann had witnessed the necessarily brief ceremony, but she
regarded him as though he were still the gardener at
Highcliff-on-the-Hudson. He had all but forgotten that she
was so selfish, self-righteous and haughty. Nothing, he reminded himself, would shake that stony young lady, nothing except money—and in this desolate place between the
wilderness and Spottsylvania, money was both useless and
scarce.

"That would be nice," he said, avoiding a direct answer. "I'd sure like to visit New York and see Miss Kitty."

"And you should." Ruth Ann grew coy. "I hate to be the
one to tell you this, Wilf, but Kitty has been keeping company with a policeman and . . . well . . . it's not very
nice to say, but she's carrying his child."

"No!" he said in mock surprise. "That is ghastly. I
really should go and do something about it . . . But then
Kitty and I are now married and that is my child. Goodnight, Miss Dahlgren."

Ruth Ann was not used to being treated in such a
manner by a lowly servant. She fumed and pouted, but
there was no one to see her performance. Wilf had gone
back to the camp and the guard kept his distance.

Nor did Wilf come to take her away the next day. As
though a gentleman's agreement had been reached, both
armies spent the day adjusting lines and constructing
breastworks. With nothing better to do, Ruth Ann climbed
into Fremont's perch and watched the Rebel forces dig

huge ditches and then bring heavy logs to fasten on top of the banks. In front of these, abatis were made by felling the trees and cutting their limbs in such a way that the sharp spikes projected toward the breasts of the advancing foe.

Ned Fraser came back to guard her after sundown. He had been ordered to bring a gunny-sack full of provisions. She snatched it away as though it were her due and disappeared down into the root cellar. He didn't quite know what to make of this woman. He was just a simple farm boy from Illinois, and farm women were never like this.

Within the hour a light spring rain began to fall. It was but the advance clouds of a hurricane that was brewing out in the Atlantic, a hundred miles southeast of Cape Hatteras. By midnight it was lashing with gale force winds.

Ned, feeling sodden and aching in every muscle, pushed himself back against the wall of the burned-out plantation. He looked about him at the chill gloom of the sheeting rain. He shivered again. He poked at the fire, his movements sluggish, and it hissed back at him. A single rosy streamer of light glowed up out of the root cellar.

Even over the wind he heard the faintest of mournful cries and went to glance down the earthen steps. His face wrinkled with involuntary disgust. She was at least dry, and possibly even warm. Then the sound came again and he crept down to peer into the chamber. It was gaily lit with every candle Ruth Ann had found.

She was lying on the ground, clutching the cloak about her, her face buried in a pillow made of rolled-up petticoats. Her hoops stood in a corner like a beehive, the crushed mauve satin gown heaped at its base.

"Did you cry out?" he asked hesitantly.

Ruth Ann pushed herself upright, not looking at him, wiping her tears away with the backs of her hands in a childishly innocent gesture. He stared at her quivering bare breasts. Except for seeing a single breast exposed to nurse a child, he had never before seen such a sight in his seventeen years.

"I'm frightened and cold," she stammered. But even with such a declaration she allowed the cloak to fall away and reveal her full nudity.

His eyes widened and his throat went dry. "Powerful storm," he said raspingly, "and very wet."

Ruth Ann blinked coyly. "Warm me!"

To his ears it was an order and not a request. He went to her quickly, sat down on the floor and pulled her roughly into his arms.

"Ugh! You're wet! Get those things off!"

Without rising, he fumbled to do as directed. Out of the corner of her eyes Ruth Ann watched every movement, her sensual interest rising with each moment. Young he was, but beneath the bulky, oversized uniform, the years of working behind a plow were evident in his muscular build. Because he was naive enough to think that all she desired was to be warmed, there was no hint of arousal. But Ruth Ann knew how to change that. Her intention had been to induce him into taking her away, with or without the approval of Wilf Jamison. But the night was too stormy to leave at once. She fell toward him, pulling him roughly into her arms. Her head fell on his shoulder, her hands smoothing down over his hairless chest and back. She sobbed aloud with convincing poignance, all the while clutching him with desperate and clinging arms and hands. Then he became aware of the position of her one hand and he could not control his emotions.

"Oh, miss, I've . . . I've . . ." He gasped in alarm. Nevertheless, he kissed her urgently, unable to deny his awakening passion.

With the darkness under the driving rain, Grant grew daring and ordered four divisions to creep through the mud and into position within a few hundred yards of the Confederate breastworks.

No attack was expected until dawn, still some three to four hours away. Lee's lines were spread out in the shape of an enormous V. The pointed angle of the formation was its key strength, and Grant intended to capture that part of Lee's forces.

Without a shot, the solid, silent lines of Federals rushed this angle and leaped into the entrenchments before the astounded Rebels could fully awaken and know what had happened.

So swift was the blow, so daring, so overwhelming in force, that three thousand men surrendered without a struggle. Then the silent crawl began to the second series of Rebel trenches a half mile beyond. These were the breastworks Ruth Ann had seen being constructed from Fremont's perch. They were hardly important to her at that moment.

She had unwittingly unleashed a dormant tiger. Once introduced to the sensations within his own body, Ned was insatiable. As Laddie's student, she was now transformed into Ned's teacher, and her pupil was more apt than she had ever been.

The Confederates speedily realized their dangerous situation. They rose from the second trench and poured out a volley of musketry of such terrific power that hundreds dropped in seconds.

"To horse! To *horse!* To *horse!*"

General John B. Gordon didn't even give some of his cavalrymen a chance to dress before he was leading them in a desperate charge to drive the invaders back. The Rebel yell was just as effective in long-johns and saber as in full uniform. Then General Gordon grew daring, splitting his force so that half circled back, as though in retreat, and then made a wide arc that brought them thundering through the plantation grounds.

Horse after horse clattered over the root cellar, dirt and clumped soil cascading down until Ruth Ann and Ned were nearly blanketed in a fine earthen blanket.

"Stop! Stop!" she screamed.

Ned chuckled. "Which? What we're doing or the horses?"

For the first time she could remember, Ruth Ann was afraid; this was something she could not control. "Both," she wailed.

"No use stopping the one, just because I can't do anything about the other. It would be suicide to go up there."

"Please," she begged, "get me away from here. I'll do anything! I'll pay anything! You can tell by my dress that I have money. Lots of money in New York. Take me there and I will make you a very rich man!"

Ned nestled down on her and held her close. "Hush,

now! We're going to be all right. No one knows that we're here. Ole Reb will run out of horses in a minute." He paused. He had no way of judging the monetary value of a piece of dress material. He had never had much money in his pocket. "Do you mean it?"

"Mean what?" she snapped.

"About . . . paying me to get you away."

She started to snap at him again when a quarter of the earthen roof gave way and nearly smothered them.

"Yes, yes, yes!" she shrieked. "Anything to get out of here!"

"Don't worry," he said, with rich enthusiasm. "I'm not about to let anything happen to you."

He might have thought differently if he could have seen the progression of the battle at that moment.

They were right under the range of fire. Gordon's men kept charging and driving the Federal hosts back until at last they stood against the entrenchments they had captured. Every general who could gain his wits was pouring in reinforcements from both sides and the fighting was coming to a point of indescribable horror in its mad desperation. Legions of men in dusty blue and in filthy grey fought face to face and hand to hand. Muskets were fired at point-blank range and blew heads off. The bodies fell into piles four and five deep, blue and grey uniforms now tinged a common blood red. Almost as soon as the trenches could be cleared of bodies to make room for the living, the living were also dead.

In the center of this mass of desperation, Wilf Jamison and his company were cut off and pushed back to the plantation. To his horror, his men began to throw down their weapons and tried to surrender.

"No!" he bellowed, levelling his drawn revolver at his own men. "Attack."

Seeing this, the Rebels shouted, "Shoot their officers!"

In a moment every officer under Wilf began to drop and only his prior knowledge of the area saved him. He ducked the volley and crawled through the bodies to the entrance of the root cellar. It was blocked by two officers, one in blue and one in grey, both riddled with bullet holes and choking each other to death to escape being captured.

He tossed them out of his way and crashed through the door.

Without realizing just who it was, Ned Fraser rolled off Ruth Ann and grabbed up his bayonet-spiked rifle. With a sudden plunge, he ran his supposed opponent through. With a shudder, Wilf Jamison looked on the man's nudity and tears welled into his eyes. Thirty-six thousand of the man's comrades would die in this battle without gaining an inch for their effort, and this man had sought nothing but his own personal pleasure. He stared at Ned Fraser's face, memorizing it so that he would remember it all the way to the gates of hell.

And Ned Fraser stared back, watching him die. In the musty cold of the chamber, his grey eyes glittered with a malevolent thought. Even before he had fully thought it out, he was starting to remove Wilf's uniform.

"What are you doing?" Ruth Ann gasped. "Isn't it bad enough that you killed him?"

"Shut up and get dressed!" It was as though the killing had given him a new personality. He would never be a boy again. "You want out of here and the best way is if you're under the escort of an officer."

"You?" She hesitated elaborately. Then, with an air of determined courage she scoffed, "They'll be after us the minute they find him dead."

"Not if I put him in my uniform. They don't look at faces when they've had a battle like this. It didn't bother you that I killed him, did it?"

". . . I think I'll get dressed now," was the only reply.

Ned Fraser smiled to himself. The woman was as cold as the ice on an Illinois pond. He liked that in a woman. And he liked what this woman had to say about money. He had lost all faith in the Union cause and longed for the rolling cornfields of his homeland. Good land was beginning to cost a fair bundle of money. Ruth Ann Dahlgren meant nothing more to him than acres and acres of rich, black soil.

Ned Fraser meant nothing to her at all.

For perhaps the first time, the course of the war was beginning to mean a great deal to Fremont Hunter. He had always loved Richmond when he had visited it as a

youth. It had never been just a city of buildings to him.
His father had made him see it as a place where his ancestors had walked. Now it was a city that reflected the
glory of the South, even though the spring social season
was just in bloom. They cheered when they heard that
Lee had won the battle of the "Bloody Angle" against
Grant five days earlier. While waiting to see President
Davis, Fremont was invited to countless "victory" parties,
each one a heartbreaker with its down-at-the-heels look,
the gentility making light of its shabbiness and chattering
with anxiety's forced gaiety.

Jefferson Davis gloomily considered the Booth proposal
for a moment, then, after a sad glance at Fremont, shook
his head.

"I have always regretted, Mr. Hunter, that God allowed the first assassination attempt to be made in this
world. I will not be a party to one that would be even
more infamous. Oh, that would be a great mistake . . . and
far, far too late. Today Lee has given us a clear victory,
though a defensive one. He will never win another in the
field."

"That is treason, sir!"

"It is honesty," Davis said, taking no offense. "He cannot replace his losses. He can only hold . . . and never
again attack."

"But sir," Fremont protested, "are you forgetting the
position the Union will find itself in this summer? The
three years of volunteer service are over. The whole army
will fall apart when those thousands go home. A strike at
Mr. Lincoln would send even countless more home in
terror."

"No!" Davis cried, repulsed at the very thought. "Go
home to Charleston, my boy. Go home and forget you ever
heard of this man Booth!"

Fremont rose and bowed. He felt, at that moment, that
both sides of the Mason-Dixon line could stand a new president. Nor would he go directly to the family townhouse
in Charleston. It was spring. They would all be moving out
to Hunter Hill for the summer. His father always came to
oversee the plantation during the summer months. He
would discuss the whole matter with his father. His father
always knew what was best in any given situation.

19

SPRING PASSED UNEVENTFULLY enough. The rain continued and the land was renewed, but God's eternal sign of faith was not noticed by many. The cost of living escalated almost daily in the South. When men heard stories of how the people of Georgia were starving, they found it hard to believe. They were not aware of Sherman's "second army," dedicated to stripping the land to prevent the Rebel armies from getting enough to eat. The South would fight on—or starve.

Amazingly, the further the war drew along, the more the North expressed misgivings. Almost as soon as the jonquils were out of the ground, society deserted New York for Newport. They were sick and tired of that winter of war and scandals.

The first to depart was a highly overwrought Theda DeWitt. Tweed had made good on his promise to have the case heard before a favorable judge in his private chambers, but the disappearance of Ruth Ann overshadowed all else.

It was a total mystery to everyone—especially the police.

It was no mystery to Lucille Dahlgren; it was all her sister's fault for not taking better care of her daughter. She arrived in New York like a red whirlwind and flatly announced that she would remain until Ruth Ann was found.

For once Theda didn't object. Within the hour she was ready to depart for her home in Newport with Kitty and Amos. Laura was to follow with the rest of the staff when Lucille had had her fill of being subjected to Laddie's real life style.

He immediately became sly, however, both about his life style and Ruth Ann.

"How should I know anything about her? I do wish I knew where she went to, though."

To his great relief, his mother remained calm, even over the true facts about the fire and his lack of insurance to cover anything.

"Theda's fault," Lucille insisted. "You will simply have to sue her for not properly covering her investment and your business. You'll have it back on its feet in no time."

When he didn't answer, she knew she had won, as usual. Then she turned her attention to Ruth Ann. In her heart she felt that her daughter had just run away from all the scandal Theda had brought about and was quite safe.

Laddie wasn't so sure. In fact, he was terrified. He had checked with all of his friends, but she was nowhere to be found. It was a total puzzlement to him. He became impatient and restless.

Many things were a puzzlement to Laura—Ruth Ann being the least of them.

Calvert was gone the morning after being released from jail. Horace DeLong had told her. He was feeling pretty grand about it; his son had been restored to him, even though he had to keep it quiet. With Calvert out of reach, maybe the scandal would just go away.

That was Laura's main puzzlement; everyone seemed to be going away from her.

"For Maggie's sake, it's best that we leave, Laura. The quicker I get her away from the horror of the fire, the better."

Laura gradually became convinced that Clinton Bell fully intended to have Maggie Duggan as his bride. She stored away in her heart any sadness she might have had on the subject.

Because she had not been in on the discussion, it then came as a great shock that Theda was sending Betty to Europe for a summer of fashion training.

The house became ghostlike, even though the "ghost" had now departed.

At the end of the week the letter came from Clarence Dahlgren. Laura might never have known about it if she had not overheard her mother and Laddie.

"Don't cry, Mama. You've always got me to look out for you."

Lucille looked crushed.

"Ohio? Who would ever want to live in Ohio?"

See her grimace over the thought, he laughed. "You need not even consider it . . . if you divorce him."

Lucille gave a miserable nod.

"But it is very important that you return home at once and leave me to find Ruth Ann," Laddie added.

"Why?" she said, suddenly petulant.

He thought it might be just as well to give her a little plain sense. "Father may be a half-wit, but he knows he'll have to sell the house and everything in West Point to start up again."

"Over my dead body!" she declared.

By an odd twist of fate Ruth Ann arrived back an hour after Lucille's departure.

Ruth Ann introduced Ned Fraser to Laura as if the introduction were explanation enough of her disappearance. She was glib and gay in pawning him off as a real officer, and offered no other details about the time she had been away.

Alone with Laddie, however, she was frank and terrified.

"Fremont Hunter?" he asked in a harsh voice.

Ruth Ann's lip began to quiver. "He might have been the lesser of two evils, Laddie. We've got to get money for this ape."

"Money? For him? You're crazy!" He was exasperated and confused. "Don't talk blasted nonsense to me."

Ruth Ann began to blubber. Having seduced Ned Fraser was one thing. Becoming the constant tool for his newfound lust was quite another.

"I don't want him touching me ever again," she wailed. "I don't want to die."

"You won't die from just doing *that!*"

He was repelled by her abject expression as she looked up at him, her face contorted as she snuffled back her tears.

"He killed Wilf Jamison and took his uniform. He'll kill me if I don't get him money. Get rid of him, Laddie!"

Without another word, Laddie turned and stamped out. He had his own war to wage, and it was not with Ned Fraser. As though Laura were responsible because Ruth Ann had been kidnapped in her place, he told her of Fraser's demands, ranting at her in the telling.

"What do you expect me to do?" Laura asked, her anger thinly held in check.

"It's quite simple, my pet." He took her by the hand and stamped heavily into Theda's office. He pointed at the safe. "Now, don't lie to me, little sister, because I once heard her tell you to get money for Mrs. Courtney. If you're the one who gives me this little loan, Auntie T will say nothing about it. I think a thousand will buy the man off."

Laura's confusion increased. She was afraid that Theda would consider her a thief. In her heart she had the unavoidable conviction that Laddie wasn't telling her the whole truth. To her relief there was no more than that amount in the safe.

"Now, stay here while I get rid of him."

It was a request she could gladly obey.

He put on a most gracious smile for Ned Fraser, telling him of his deep thankfulness for getting his sister safely home.

"You find us, however, at a most unfortunate time. My aunt is out of the city and her coffer is low. I wish your reward could be far greater, but five hundred is all I'm able to scrape together at the moment."

Ned's big face flushed with anger and he stared at Laddie as if his eyes would burst out of their sockets. "I don't think you understand, bud. She owes me for the use of my body as well as for the trip. Gimme that and then tell me when I can get more."

Laddie swallowed. "I—I would have to consult with my aunt . . . in Newport."

Ned looked around. He had never been in a house like this in his life, and he was in no hurry to leave.

"Then you best get moving. I want double this amount."

It would have been so easy for Laddie to have left for a short time and returned to give the man the rest of the money. But he was like his mother in that he considered the other half of the money now to be his own, and not to be thrown away on this blackmailer.

"It will take me a few hours to get to Newport and back. I'll have Ellen prepare a room for you and some food."

Ned Fraser suspected nothing. The man was being quite kind and gentlemanly. After Laddie had left, Ned waited to be taken to his room. He made himself at home in the meantime and helped himself to a glass from the sherry decanter, but it was not to his liking. He walked to the parlor door and peered out into the foyer. The place was still as a tomb.

He gazed up the stairway, wondering where above Ruth Ann might be found. Where might anyone be found? The place was just too damn big for his simple tastes. Then he thought of the other sister. What was her name? He couldn't recall, but could well remember the lustful feeling that had overcome him when they had been introduced. Then a wild notion came over him.

"Where in the hell is everyone?" he bellowed.

His voice echoed up though the empty house and then back down to him. He began to laugh. As the echo of his laugh returned he went off into peals of screaming laughter, one after the other, drowning all other sound.

He did not see Laura peer around the door of the office, where she had been sittting. She was white-faced and trembling, but not because of this man. She had never stolen anything before and the guilt was unbearable.

Now she did begin to believe the things Laddie had said about the man and she wondered why her brother didn't come and stop his lunatic raving.

Ned turned and saw her. His mouth curled into a leer and then it froze into a grimace. The house quieted as the echo of his laughter faded. Then he spun and stormed out of the house and into the street.

There was a fierce warning shout, a sickening thud

coupled with a blood-chilling scream, a rending of leather brake-shoe against iron wagon wheel and the instant din of voices being raised.

Rooted to the spot, Laura watched a man in blue uniform rush down the hall and turned to see Mrs. Courtney in the kitchen door. Both listened to the diminishing sound of Officer Callingham's footsteps out of the house to the street. It was a full minute after they had died away before either woman spoke.

"He was having a spot of coffee with me when we heard the shout," Mrs. Courtney explained in a hushed voice.

For a moment Laura could think of nothing to say. There was no sound at all but the rapid beating of her heart. Then she lifted her chin.

"Have Ellen find my brother, please."

"Why, they left," Mrs. Courtney said, watching her. "Came down the back stairs to the kitchen and he said he was taking Miss Ruth Ann right home to West Point."

"Was Dennis Callingham with you at that time?"

"Came in the door just as they were rushing out. Why?"

Suddenly Laura started shuddering, disbelief and nausea washing over her. They were going to leave her with the man—without warning or protection. Now she could believe nothing they had said against Fremont Hunter. Now she even questioned what they had said against this man.

The ashen face of the burly policeman kept her from questioning anymore.

"I'm hardly believing it. That was the big war hero, Colonel Wilf Jamison, who just got run down. What would he be screamin' his head off in this house for?"

Laura's eyes were dull. Suddenly she put her hand on Mrs. Courtney's arm to still her words.

"His wife works here," Laura said, "but is away with Miss Theda. He—he must not have known."

Mrs. Courtney didn't understand, but complied with Laura's story. This house had had its fill of turmoil of late, and she was loyal enough to go along with the mistress's word.

"Dennis, be the good lad and see that the remains are taken over to McVicker. We'll see to the arrangements. I wish to see Miss Laura to bed now."

He raised a finger to the brim of his helmet and

frowned. "As you wish, but these were found on him. His papers and a goodly sum of money. Would you be seeing to it, for the next of kin, Miss Laura?"

She nodded. She didn't need to count to know that it was only half of the greenbacks she had given Laddie. Tears came into her eyes and rolled down over her face. Not tears for the man who lay beneath the wagon in the street. Laddie had hold her the truth about this man after all, and she was overwhelmed with horror at what that meant. Her tears were for the real Wilf Jamison, for Kitty and the child that would never know its father.

It wasn't fair, she mourned, for people like her brother and sister to be able to sail through life insensitive to all but their own narrow needs and leaving nothing but destruction and death in their wake.

Her body and mind felt torn and sore and exhausted. Had all of these people been like this before the war, or was this the way the war worked upon the soul—making it greedy and self-indulgent? She wanted to find somebody, any friendly person, who could prove that such things as love and respect and honor still existed in that era of desolation. She feared that no such person still existed.

As May came, the residents of Atlanta became increasingly aware that the Sherman siege was gradually closing in. There were few volunteers to be found to defend the city, and those were mostly men over sixty and boys under thirteen.

The South's great plantations were no less desolate than the cities. Fremont could recall the days when over three hundred slaves had plowed the rolling hills, planted the tobacco, tilled the cornfields, white-washed the twelve-columned house, cooked and sewn and cleaned and laughed and danced and lived. He had been able to find only ten men willing to spend all their time in the fields. There had been thirty at first, but they drifted away as they came to learn that Jethro and Ida Hunter didn't have much cash. They knew that Miss Ida would have willingly found a way of taking care of them, but her two stepsons were too well remembered from their wild, arrogant youth. And though Jared had been killed in the war, the memory of his cruelty lived on. Fremont had to see to the planting of the corn himself. When he was out with Joe-John and Big Adam, he found himself uneasy after the first two days, when he saw that they were not going to do any more work than he could do.

"He ain' nothin' but another Mister Jared," Joe-John would say disgustedly. "Don' see how Mister Jethro could have sired such boys. Mean. See how he chops those weeds like they had names . . ."

Fremont was not as bad in the fields as they made him out to be. There were odd times when he felt a lazy contentment creeping over him. But the war was coming; of that there was no mistake. The thought finally made him restless.

"Is it a girl?"

He turned at the sound of the familiar voice and laughed.

"I suppose that it is, to a degree. I'm not exactly loved by her family, however."

Miss Ida handed him the water bucket and looked over the land. The sky was like a great blue banner over the world. Under it, mile upon mile, ridge upon ridge, were the land and people she had known since she was a girl.

For the first time since he had been home he really looked at his stepmother, the greying of the hair, the crow's feet about the eyes—and the eyes themselves. Even when they smiled there was a hollow core in their depth that could never again be filled.

He had known Ida Vaughan Hunter all his life. Her first husband, Alexander Vaughan, had brought her to a neighboring plantation, and there she had borne him a son, Nelson Vaughan, who was now off fighting in the war. In the space of a few years she had lost her father and her husband, though to natural causes rather than to the war. In a sense, she had now also lost her new husband. Whatever happiness she had felt in marrying Jethro Hunter could not have lasted long, for with the devastation of the South and the death of his older son, Jethro had seemed to shrink within himself, becoming virtually a hermit. He seemed almost unaware of Fremont's return to the plantation, and in a rare moment of sensitivity Fremont wondered how much more his father's withdrawal must affect Miss Ida than it did him. The war had taken too much from her.

Fremont seemed to understand. "Perhaps after the war—" he started, but Ida interrupted him.

"There won't be much left after the war. And there's nothing much for you to wait around for."

"Don't talk foolishness, Miss Ida. Once they get Mr. Lincoln out of the way, things will go our way again."

"That would be a very sad day," she said in a constrained voice. "I can't say this to your father, Fremont, but I pray for Mr. Lincoln and his reelection. He'd be compassionate and look upon us as people of this land rather than as enemies. I'm obliged, Fremont, for the work you're doing on the land. I'd be more obliged if you'd be thinking now more of your own future—and of your young lady."

Fremont shivered, and looked back up the slope towards the house of his youth. He had had so many plans for it on his return. But without proper help he just never seemed to make any progress.

"It wouldn't be fair for me to leave right in the middle of summer."

"It wouldn't be fair for you to stay. I've some money set aside—good pre-war money. Use your education for something more than standing behind a hoe. Do this for your father . . . and for yourself."

Theda DeWitt was once again able to beam like the rising sun. She would not hear of anyone but Laura helping her plan the interior of the new mansion in New York. They both needed the work to close out memories of the past months. The silence from Highcliff-on-the-Hudson was golden—although the silence from Clarence Dahlgren in Ohio bothered them.

For the time being they were staying at Theda's home in Newport. As though the old mansion had been sullied in some way, it was sold lock, stock, and barrel.

Laura and Theda made frequent trips to New York, where Amos and Mrs. Courtney were overseeing each aspect of the new mansion's construction. Laura felt the new residence was vastly too large. Theda, however, was obviously proud that she could boast of all the latest

"modern improvements": central heating, luxurious indi-
vidual bathrooms equipped with toilets, and an intricate
system of bells and speaking tubes connecting every room
with the service quarters.

Laura found in her work relief from despair. The only
comfort was that Theda had felt her actions quite proper
over the money.

"Did you expect your brother to act any differently?
We're well rid of them, Laura. Well, well, *well* rid of
them! What do you think of this mauve fabric for the
chairs in the music salon?"

As the mansion started to be furnished, it became
necessary to go back to New York to consult with Amos
and Mrs. Courtney. To Ellen's delight, she was left behind to look after Kitty and pawn herself off in Laura's
clothing as one of the resort belles. . . .

When Amos brought in the card to Theda, a worried
frown creased his sombre face.

"With the *Times?* Most surprising, Amos. Keep Laura
from knowing this for awhile and show Mr. Hunter in."

Fremont bowed with courtly deference over her pudgy
hand and his voice was touched with deep feeling.

"I want to thank you, Miss DeWitt, for seeing me
privately. I've just returned from a visit to my home in
South Carolina. I hold the counsel of my stepmother
quite dear and at her wise suggestion returned north via
Washington. I was most happy to learn that I've been
cleared of all charges that were lodged against me, but
don't intend to return to the military. I have now seen
war and wish no further part of it."

"To be sure," she said coolly.

He blushed. "I'm afraid you're thinking of the despic-
able way I left Miss Ruth Ann with the Yankee troops."

"I try to think of her as little as possible," she said
truthfully.

"I want the truth to be known, however. Miss Ida says
that I must."

He spoke with the eager wistfulness of a boy. It was
only too plain to Theda that he had indeed suffered at
the hands of her family. Still, she was cautious.

"I've obtained a position on the *Times*," he went on.
"They are quite interested in having me do a series of

articles on how the war is affecting people like my family. It is again my stepmother who put the idea into my head. She is convinced that Mr. Lincoln must stay in office to end the war and save the South."

A smile touched Theda's eyes with tender sympathy. "She does sound wise. I wish you luck."

"Thank you, Miss DeWitt, I shall try to prove worthy of my stepmother's faith. I also wish to prove to you . . . and Miss Laura, that I am not completely the scoundrel that her mother, brother and sister made me out to be."

"That could take near a lifetime," she laughed.

"I've a lifetime to devote to it." He paused and looked straight into her deep blue eyes. "And a lifetime to devote to Miss Laura. That's why I tried to kidnap her . . . to take her away from that family of hers."

"You would have been taking her away from me, as well."

"I had never thought of that," he said apologetically. "I was being most selfish and vain."

Theda laughed again. No woman could laugh with more genuine hearty enjoyment over a man making an honest confession.

"All men are vain. But few are honest about their vanity. I am also vain and honest, Mr. Fremont Hunter. I still don't know if I like you . . . but my opinion may have been colored by seeing you only through the eyes of others. Frankly, I know I don't like you considering yourself the proper man for my Laura . . . but that could be because I've developed a protective, motherly instinct toward her. But I feel that any man has the right to make his confession to the ears that should properly hear it. We are dining tonight at Delmonico's. Shall we say seven?"

He stood to bow and his voice trembled. "You've given me a new lease on life, Miss DeWitt."

Out on the street, he paused and looked at the new neighborhood. His big jaws came together with firm precision and his eyes glinted. It was going to be just like a great master battle plan—slow and carefully plotted.

He began to sing a chapel hymn from the academy:

Mine eyes have seen the glory of the coming of the Lord,

He is trampling out the vintage
where the grapes of Wrath are stored . . .

He stopped and laughed to himself. Yes, he would continue to quietly tramp on the Dahlgrens' grapes, leaving only the most tender for himself. He would make Theda DeWitt love him, so that he could love Laura. But the President of the United States . . . on that score he still was not sure.

20

FREMONT DEVOTED HIMSELF to Theda in many different ways, letting Laura's opinion of him change in her own good time.

"You must look at it from a personal point of view, Miss DeWitt. The war debt stands at the appalling total of two thousand millions of dollars and its daily cost runs four millions. Paper money is depreciating and as you just said, the premium on gold has made the green-back note worth less than fifty cents in real money."

"I fully understand, Fremont. But what am I to do?"

"Don't get caught if the nation goes bankrupt. Have your banks refuse any further loans on government bonds at any rate."

"An excellent idea, Fremont."

Excellent for Fremont, but not for the government.

He sadly reported to them on his attendance of the National Convention of Radical Republicans in Cleveland as a reporter for the *Times*, and on the nomination of John C. Fremont for the presidency.

"Their platform is one of vengeance against the Rebels and their annihilation when conquered. It's exactly what my stepmother feared the most. They're demanding the confiscation of all property, the overthrow of government right down to the local level and the division of the states into conquered provinces."

Theda sighed. "And it was to be a war to end slavery."

Nightly, over dinner or a quiet chat in the parlor, he became their inside source on the political battles being waged. Laura listened out of respect, Theda with growing interest. The mischief he was doing was incalculable; he persisted in telling them only what he wished for them to know and they accepted it because of his position on the newspaper.

Even though Lincoln's nomination became a mere formality, he kept from them the fact that plans were being laid to force the President to withdraw from his own ticket in the midst of his campaign.

Nor did he choose to inform them that the Democratic Party was now the militant united force of the Copperhead leaders, who had cleverly pushed the Radical Republicans into taking John Fremont so they could put General McClellan into the White House.

With his new position in the newspaper world, Fremont once again became the darling of Fernando Wood. All was forgiven, because Fremont could now circulate in the highest social circles under the sponsorship of Theda DeWitt.

"I certainly wish that women had the voice to vote!" Theda declared hotly one night.

Fremont had a sudden inspiration. "Women do have the voice, Miss DeWitt, if not the vote. During your teas, you and Laura could talk to the other women. I will supply you with the information that the women can take home to share with their voting husbands over the dinner table."

It was an idea that Theda took to at once. As soon as she was involved with making plans for her teas, he put his own personal plan into operation.

"Look, Laura," he said, "I know what you think of me from the past. But I'm not the same person I was then. All I ask is that I be given a chance to prove that to you."

Laura shook her golden head. "I don't know, Fremont," she said. "I just don't know."

"Look, let's just start by being friends. I'm forever being given tickets for the theater and social functions. I hate going alone . . . I've no friends here my own age, and dining alone is a bore. I know that Miss DeWitt would agree with me that young people have to be together once in awhile. Can we have it that way?"

"Yes, Fremont, I think we can have it that way."

He did not push too fast. First, it was an outing in Central Park, where friends of Theda waved from their carriages. At the theater they met Leonard Jerome, with a new beauty on his arm. Laura's cheeks flushed scarlet when Jerome made no bones about who was squiring the more beautiful lady. But Jerome's love for Laura had been a fleeting passion; one of many.

Fremont loved to hear the merry note of her laughter at a comedy, see her eyes glint with happiness at the ballet, chuckle at the faces she made in trying new and exotic food.

And the best thing he did not plan; it came about quite naturally.

"Oh, Fremont," she cried, taking his hand, "let's do that again, soon. I never knew Spanish music could be so exciting."

She didn't release his hand and he swallowed hard. Before the moment could escape, he bent down and kissed her—ever so lightly, his lips brushing hers as though they were cotton candy and would melt with a mere breath. Then he stepped back.

"I'm sorry," he said. He suddenly realized that she still held his hand. "Let's do that again, too. And soon," he said softly.

Her face was aglow, her eyes tear-brimmed. She stepped forward and pillowed her face against his chest.

"Yes," she whispered, "oh, yes, Fremont. You have changed."

"It was all for you," Fremont said, his voice quavering. "I love you so dearly, Laura. I would change a million times over, just for your love."

"I'm glad," Laura wept. "Oh, Fremont, I'm so glad. You've made me laugh again, and it's a good feeling."

"And I want to keep you laughing until you have grey in your hair and I sit with the gout. Hunter Hill needs the sound of children. You'll love my stepmother. She already loves you from what I've told her."

"You've already told her about me? What did you tell her?"

"The truth," he said, chuckling. "That you had a face like a possum, all squinty with a pushed-in nose; that you walked like a darky coming in from the field and only bathed when you felt like it."

"Oh," she giggled, "you haven't changed a bit, Fremont Hunter. You're still a nasty little boy who loves to play pranks—but . . ." She turned and raced across the parquet floor of the foyer.

"But what?" he called expectantly.

She paused on the first step of the grand, curving staircase and looked back on a shrug. She blew him a kiss. "That might give you a clue."

"Say it . . ." he murmured.

"Perhaps tomorrow," she whispered, and tossed her skirt behind her coquettishly as she ascended the steps.

Fremont watched her until she turned under the thirty-foot-high stain-glassed window and disappeared in the curve of the stairs. He drew out a kerchief and mopped his brow.

"That," he said, "was well done, my good chap. She is as good as yours."

Laura sank down on the top step and stared back down at the window. It was bright with colors and life and gaiety—but she knew its artificiality. Behind the thick pieces of colored glass and lead molding was a chamber which housed hundreds of gas-jets. She felt the same. At that moment she felt aglow with color and life and gaiety. But behind the facade. . . . She had not been able to get the words out of her mouth because she just wasn't sure. She had never had so much fun as she'd had of late, or enjoyed a person more. They were so comfortable with each other—could talk on any subject for hours—could enjoy the same plays and foods and simple little things.

But love? She knew her problem, and it had nothing to do with Fremont or herself. She knew nothing about marriage and it frightened her. She had only two examples to go by and they weren't much help. If she had to pattern the rest of her life after the marriage of her mother and father she would just as soon stay as old-maidish as Theda. And the more she thought about Marvin and Mildred Carson, the more she realized she had never seen a single expression of love pass between them; respect and concern, yes, but never love.

"Perhaps that's the way it's supposed to be," she mused. "No ringing bells and shooting stars, just this. Well, maybe tomorrow I'll get the words out of my mouth."

"It's incredible! It's just utterly unthinkable," Fremont exclaimed, "but they say that the reveille of Early's drums could be heard from the White House window this morning."

Fernando Wood was overjoyed at the news. "Brilliant! Utterly brilliant, my boy. That false dispatch put through your paper was a stroke of pure genius. What a surprise! They thought that Jubal Early's army was in Carolina while it was sweeping up the Shenandoah Valley. Imagine, parts of Maryland and Pennsylvania already in his hands and bearing down on Washington!"

"Don't cheer too loudly. They've sent for Grant."

Wood grinned. "And I have sent for you. Isn't it time the ladies had some real information to chew on? I've made you some notes."

"I don't know if today would be a good day. Miss Theda has invited the wife of the French *chargé d' affaires*."

"Dear boy, there is very little that is not know to the Knights of the Golden Circle. As the lady has just arrived from Paris, I am most interested in everything that she says." He grinned again. "And what a marvelous opportunity for you to say the things we wish the ladies to hear."

Fremont purposely arrived late, saying he could stay only long enough to give her certain information to pass along. Theda would have none of it. She wanted to show him off as her political expert.

Denise Dubois was more than happy to take center stage and to flirt with the handsome young man.

"I see not why this is such a great surprise. My emperor has been aware of it for some time. He waits only for Lee to take Washington and then he shall recognize the Confederacy. Do you not agree, *mon cher*?"

Fremont politely shook his head. "I think everyone is missing the real master stroke that Lee has achieved with Early's raid. That's what the emperor should be looking at, and not just whether Lee gets into Washington. The man has cleared the Shenandoah Valley with the raid. This has always been Lee's granary. He has now allowed the farmers to reap their crops and give him grain for the whole winter."

"But he will need more than just food to drag this war out all winter," Mrs. DePoole protested.

"My dear woman, he has shown the world that his army is still so terrible a weapon that it can hold the great Grant at bay, drive his enemy from the Valley, invade two Northern states, burn our cities and destroy our railroads, and throw shells into Washington. England will now sell more cruisers to him to sweep the seas of our commerce. And France? Well, all of these mistakes will surely be laid at Mr. Lincoln's feet."

"If he loses Washington, can he still be elected?" Denise asked, unable to resist pursuing any political news that she might bear to her husband.

Fremont could have kissed her. She had opened the door for him to walk right in.

"He may lose more than Washington before the election. If the western states, including his own Illinois, don't get a different nominee before the election, then they're going to establish their own Western Confederacy."

"Is he such a weak leader that he would allow such a thing?" Denise exclaimed.

Fremont smiled to himself. "I would not presume to answer as to what he might do, madame. From experience I can say that he is closing his eyes to the fact that the leader of the Copperheads, Clement Vallandigham, is running for governor of Ohio from his exile in Canada."

He had given them many things to take home and reveal at the dinner table.

A wave of incredulous despair swept over some of the women. They were there to help with the reelection of the president, but everything they heard made it sound as though he was not helping himself very much.

* * *

Laura threw off her depression over the discussion and took Fremont away from the ladies.

"Did you see her face?" she giggled.

"Whose face?" he answered, trying to appear innocent.

"You know very well, Fremont Hunter. The old French peahen wanted to tuck you in her pocket and take you home."

"Aha! Do I detect a faint note of jealousy?"

"Absolutely."

"Then you are all mine now?"

"All yours."

He took her in his arms and held her in silence. Everything was surely going his way that day. He could feel her trembling with deep emotion.

"There is nothing to be nervous about now, dearest," he said reassuringly. "Come, we'll tell the good news of our betrothal to the ladies."

"Let's wait until we can tell Aunt Theda alone," she pleaded.

"But why?"

She hesitated and glanced at him uneasily. She still couldn't bring any words of love to her lips.

"I think we owe that to Aunt Theda, her being my guardian and all."

"Anything you desire, my little pet. We'll tell her tonight. Now, give me a quick kiss so I can get back to work."

After the kiss they stood in awkward silence. He studied her flushed face for a moment, wondering if he should coax her into speaking endearing words. But he remained silent, and instead drew his watch from his pocket and looked at it.

"I'll plan on taking the two of you to dinner," he said quickly. "We'll make it a celebration."

There would be no celebration or dinner out that evening. Amos met Fremont coolly at the door to inform him that the ladies were in the drawing room with a guest, and that he was expected to join them.

A flash of rage came from the depths of Fremont Hunter's eyes at the first sight of the guest. He moved forward a step and his hand trembled in a desperate desire to deny a handshake to Clarence Dahlgren. This man would ruin everything for him.

He stopped with a shock of surprise as Clarence turned his haggard eyes to the door and nodded what could have been taken for a greeting.

"Here's Fremont now."

Theda wordlessly waved him on into a seat and Laura nodded without a smile. Fremont began to fear the worst. Laura had no doubt jumped the gun in telling her father, and the marriage was going to be denied.

But the change in Clarence Dahlgren bespoke something far more worrisome. Anxiety and suffering had etched his face into a wrinkled mask. The drooping eyelids were swollen and dark bags hung beneath them. The man's hair was now totally white. For a moment Fremont was held in a spell by the sight of this walking corpse.

"Ruth Ann has run away from home," Theda informed him in a quiet voice.

"Oh . . . For what reason?"

"Because I was a stern father, for a change," Clarence said, a far-away tone in his voice. "Even though she is of age I insisted that she move to Ohio with the rest of the family. Laddie helped her get away."

"Then he is with her?" Fremont had to stifle a groan.

Clarence shook his head sadly. "Would that he were. He is being his mother's strength and fighting every move I make to salvage something of this family."

"Don't worry, Papa," Laura soothed. "Ruth Ann is probably already in New York and just doesn't know this new address. We'll find her."

"What are you saying?" Fremont flared. "Have you forgotten all of the things that she's done to you? Or to me or—"

"Forgotten?" Laura whispered as he broke off. "No, I haven't forgotten, Fremont. Nor has Aunt Theda. But I can't forget, either, that she is my sister."

He looked at her with glittering eyes. "I too had a brother, Laura," he began slowly. "He was vain and selfish and mean, and thought only of himself—just like Ruth Ann. I was angry when I learned he had been killed in the war, but I think it was anger against the Yankees.

Deep inside, I believe I was glad he was dead. That's how you should feel about Ruth Ann—that she is dead."

Clarence lifted himself suddenly and recovered his self-control. "No. That cannot be," he answered bitterly. "I am well aware, now, of what my daughter and son have been about. I know and see things as they are! But I am told that you were granted forgiveness. Would you deny it to others?"

"It is not the same," he cried. "I came back to ask for forgiveness. But Ruth Ann has run away rather than admit her folly."

Theda lifted her hand in a commanding gesture. "Enough! My own feelings are very mixed on this subject. But we can't just close our eyes to the fact that she has run away, Fremont."

"I can—and I will!" He turned fiercely on Laura. "And you will also if you expect to become my wife."

He knew at once that he had made an error. Clarence looked with startled horror at Theda and then Laura. Laura went white. Theda lifted her hand to her heart and slowly sat to the very back of her chair.

"Fremont!" Laura sobbed. "I—I—can't make such a choice."

He bowed without a word and stepped quickly from the room. His silent curses were for himself and no other. He had handled the matter very, very badly. He would just have to wait until he could reason with Laura—alone.

The opportunity didn't present itself for a week.

When she saw him on the street, she let out a glad cry for Harry to stop the carriage, and Fremont came to take her hand.

"I was a fool!" he said fiercely. "I love you, Laura, and didn't want the ghost of Ruth Ann between us. Is she found?"

"No," she said weakly. "Papa has given himself until tomorrow, and then he's going to give up all hope that she is here in New York."

"And you?"

She sat there in the sunlight, paler than he had ever seen her before—and even more beautiful.

She nodded. It had been a miserable week. She had not realized how accustomed she had become to seeing

Fremont. Her father had been polite, but inquisitive as to their relationship. She had not been able to answer him fully, except to state that she did have a fondness for Fremont. Now, she realized how terribly much she had missed him, and she thought the hurt in her heart was love. Wildly, she pulled his hand into the shelter of her chin.

Fremont sighed in triumph. He had been very wise to stay away for the week, and he would continue to keep his distance until Clarence Dahlgren had departed.

"I'm going to be quite busy until the day after tomorrow, Laura. Let's see . . . that would be the third. Might we set that as a dinner engagement?"

Laura quickly agreed. She wanted life to return to normal as soon as possible. She hated to admit it, but she was getting desperately tired of hearing her father bemoan his fate night after night. He had lived in misery with Lucille for so long that it had become a way of life; divorce, it seemed, was unthinkable.

Then she turned her mind to the errand she was upon. She had been with her father when Betty Duggan had returned from Europe and she eagerly looked forward to seeing her again.

Her eagerness vanished a moment after entering the shop.

"I wasn't quite sure what to do, Miss Laura. She looks like the wrath if God and demanded the rest of the dresses I had done for her that had never been picked up. I'm sorry, but I gave them to her. I was expecting the Jerome girls in for a fitting and . . . well . . ."

"I understand, Betty. Did she give you any indication where she might be staying?"

Betty blushed. "No, but she reeked of the Tenderloin."

"The what?"

"That's what they call the . . . well . . . the area where no decent Irish girl would be seen on the streets unless she had fallen from grace. Oh, here's Margaret with the mauve slipcovers. I hope Miss Theda likes them."

Laura went over and over in her mind what she should do about the information gained from Betty. If Ruth Ann had been able to find Betty's shop, she could easily have asked for the address of the new mansion. For the moment she decided to keep the information to herself. She felt guilty at the thought that revealing the information would only cause a delay in her father's departure, but there it was. She then considered sending a note to Fremont to seek his advice, but she pushed that thought aside as well. She would just have to think the thing out alone for a while longer.

The note would have gone unanswered by Fremont. Throughout that night and the next day he was closeted with Fernando Wood and a group of men who were radical strategists . . . and traitors. They would leave nothing to chance. They had the state legislatures of Indiana, Ohio and Illinois in their grasp. They would have a majority in each to pass an ordinance of secession and strike the Union in the back. A million propaganda leaflets were printed and ready to be distributed.

They had created so deep a depression, so black an outlook on the election, so powerful a campaign to convince people that the election was already the Democratic Mc-Clellan's for the asking, that the Copperheads had been able to convince the National Republican Executive Committee to meet with them to plan a way to avert an even greater civil war.

Because the Republican Committee looked upon a disaster at the polls as the greatest of all evils, they rushed to the president and demanded that he withdraw. Cut to the quick, he agreed to consider the humiliating proposition and give them an answer within two days. They wished for peace at any price, and were now assured in their minds that they were going to win the election before the first ballot was even cast. Still, they kept a vigil at their telegraph key for the signal from Washington, as did Wood and his group.

"Damn that wily fox," Fernando ranted. "How many more times can he adjourn them without giving an answer?"

He started to storm away from the table when the key began to click.

"What is it? What is it? Read it out as you take it down!"

The operator signalled back that he was ready to receive.

The Copperhead group gathered about, barely able to breathe in their excitement.

"Washington, D.C., September 3rd, 1864. Abraham Lincoln, the President of the United States, has just announced the following message . . ." the operator recited a word at a time.

"The Nation is ours!" Wood shouted.

Tears welled into Fremont's eyes. "They've done it! Now we can demand he name a caretaker government!"

". . . the following message," the operator repeated, more loudly this time, "from Atlanta, Georgia . . ."

"*What?*"

". . . from General W. T. Sherman. Quote: Atlanta is ours and fairly won. Unquote. The President has expressed to General Sherman the applause and thanks of the Nation. Stand by for further details."

They needed no further details. They had gambled and lost. Silently, they filed from the room, some wishing never to meet again.

"No!" Fremont vowed to himself, "I shall not give up!"

If the news out of Atlanta dispelled the North's despondency like mist evaporating in the morning sun, then General Philip Henry Sheridan became the sun itself.

He caught General Jubal Early prowling in the Shenandoah and rode his army down to destruction. The fertile mountain-sheltered valley that had served as Lee's breadbasket was devastated; a crow would have had to carry provisions if it had flown across the Shenandoah.

The next morning the Radical Republicans awoke to find themselves without a candidate. John C. Fremont had withdrawn.

"McClellan should do the same," Theda insisted, and prepared to give her reasons. Neither Fremont nor Laura appeared to have heard her.

"I do declare, the country starts getting the best news it has had in four years and you two do nothing but mope."

"I'm sorry, Miss DeWitt, it's just that it is both good and bad news. Sherman is making a military garrison out of Atlanta, and with the course the war is now taking I've been able to get little news of my family."

"I'm sorry, Fremont. I had forgotten about that . . .

But I thought Sherman claimed he was going to start marching to the sea."

Fremont scoffed. "His claim is that he'll make a hundred-mile-wide swath to the sea and then turn north from Savannah. I've about decided to go and get my parents out of his path. What do you think, Laura? Wouldn't it be nice to have them here for the wedding?"

"What? Oh, I'm sorry, what did you say?"

"Laura," Theda scolded, "are you feeling all right? You seem so distant."

Laura painted a smile on her face. "I'm just a little tired. I search and search and just can't seem to find the right pieces of furniture. I wanted everything to be right for the social season and . . . the wedding."

"I see," Theda said on a hurt note. "You both have alluded to the event, but I have yet to hear of a date or plans."

Laura and Fremont looked at each other foolishly. Their moods had not really been compatible during the month of September. He acted as though Lincoln had pulled a great swindle, and Laura just wasn't reacting to anything. She was too tired to think. Ever since being in Betty Duggan's shop she had felt guilty and had been spending her afternoons walking the streets of the Tenderloin on the chance of running into Ruth Ann.

The look that passed between them worried Theda. She still didn't quite approve of this marriage and thought it was high time she quietly took matters into her own hands.

"As I thought," she said, "no plans whatsoever. Laura, hand me my planning book. Let me see, October is upon us and there will be too, too many parties, and then the election and all. June is traditional, but you would probably scream about waiting so long. Still, we can't have it too soon; people *do* begin to count on their fingers and make nasty innuendoes if the engagement is too short. Six months is about right. That would be March. Ugh! Mrs. Ronalds is worming her way back in and I wouldn't want it to be in the same month as her ball. April it will have to be. Oh, how perfect. For the whole week before April the fifteenth there is nothing. That gives time for showers, bachelor parties, rehearsal suppers, everything."

She waited for some sort of protest or reaction and

smiled to herself when none was forthcoming. The wedding was not so sure a thing in her mind any longer, and the seven months' breathing space was a blessing.

Then she flipped her calendar back to the present and gasped. "Oh, heavens! We have a tea scheduled for every day right up to the election. We won't be able to do much about the wedding until after that."

The election was upon them before they knew it—and with stunning results. McClellan, who could have had the election by default but a few months before, carried only three states and twenty-one votes in the electoral college. Even though McClellan received roughly two million votes, everyone claimed to be part of the two million five hundred thousand who had voted for Lincoln.

Suddenly, Abraham Lincoln didn't seem to have an enemy in the world. It brought a quiet smile to his face. He was too humble to hold resentments in his heart, and honest enough to pity them for being such small men.

21

NEW YORK became a fairyland for Christmas. The devil-may-care Yankees marching through Georgia wanted to give the nation Savannah as a present—and they did.

The muffled drums of doom now beat more insistently for the South.

Fremont spent his Christmas at Hunter Hill, and most of the month of January, 1865, as well. His mind could not absorb the simple truth that his father could perish before the cause was lost, but so it was. Jethro Hunter died from a sudden and devastating attack of pneumonia.

His father was gone; this he could not change. His brain was busy. On his return, he spent a week in Washington, bringing back to life an old plan. The South was not yet finished.

Laura flew to the shop the moment the word came from Betty Duggan. She sood back, almost gasping at the sight of Ruth Ann. Her sister was thin and pale, her cheeks hollow, and there were great dark circles around her eyes.

"Had a couple of rough ones over the holidays," Ruth

Ann declared, as though it explained everything. "Damn near killed me, too. But that's not why I wanted you here. I have a proposition for you, Laura—if you'll listen."

"I'll listen," Laura said sullenly, "providing it's clean." She knew from her days searching the Tenderloin that most of its female denizens became prostitutes. Judging by Ruth Ann's costume and her slatternly manner, there was little doubt that she had also taken that course. Nor was there any possibility that she had reformed in other ways.

"In my opinion it is clean. Look, Laura, I need some new clothes to get out of the rut that I'm in—and I can pay you back later. Trouble is, I can't make much more than food money the way I've become."

Laura looked at her wonderingly. "Why? Why have you let yourself become like this, Ruth Ann?"

"Look, I don't want any lectures. I like men. I've always liked men. I just don't like the same man for very long. They get boring and tedious."

"But you wanted something so different—" Laura began.

"Don't go into that song and dance, Laura. Mother wanted that different life for me . . . for her own sake. I could have married a hundred times over, only they weren't good enough for mother. So let's forget it!" She began to cough violently.

"Ruth Ann! You're sick! Come back with me to Aunt Theda's."

Ruth Ann laughed roughly. "That's a laugh. That old biddy would faint if you brought a streetwalker home. And don't worry about the cough. It just comes from drinking cheap booze. Well?"

"I want to help, Ruth Ann, but you know I don't have any money of my own."

Ruth Ann's eyes narrowed into slits. "Don't give me that! You can get anything you want out of Aunt Theda because you're all she has in the world. Haven't you stopped to consider that you'll inherit everything that she has?"

Laura was appalled. "No, I have not considered that and I never shall. It's horrible to think of such a thing."

"Really?" Ruth Ann snapped. "Well, I think differently. What are a few dresses when measured against all of her money?"

"Let me take you home," Laura pleaded. "This isn't any kind of life for you. It's crazy. There are still plenty of men who would want you for a wife."

Ruth Ann's hands flew up suddenly and covered her ears. "Stop your stupid prattle!" she cried. "I won't listen to it. I should have known that you wouldn't help me!"

"I will help you, Ruth Ann, to get hold of yourself."

"Then go straight to hell!" she cried fiercely, and ran out the back door of Betty's shop.

"Wait! Ruth Ann, wait!"

Laura raced into the alley, looking left and then right. The tiny, frail body was just disappearing onto the main street. By the time Laura made it to the corner, Ruth Ann was dashing in a diagonal through traffic to the opposite sidewalk. Pushing against the flow of pedestrians, Laura tried to make it to the crosswalk and still keep an eye on her sister.

"It's hopeless," she muttered, jostled by throngs that eyed her with curiosity. Young ladies arrived and departed by carriage in that shopping district; they didn't run along as though about ready to be pinched for shoplifting.

It was some moments before she became aware of a voice urgently calling her name. She turned about, confused. A young naval officer was leaning out toward her from the seat of his buggy, which was red and black and obviously quite new.

A young buck passing by overheard and thought that here was a demimondaine known to the officer. "I'll better his price for a saucy number like you."

Laura started. Her face turned to scarlet. She quickened her stride, her heart beating furiously. The young man skillfully guided his horse through the press of the other carriages and rode along the curbing. He called out again, much to the amusement of the other pedestrians, but another voice was also calling.

"Laura, will you stop! Come, get into the buggy."

The sound of the voice made her stop and turn. She looked up into the face of Calvert DeLong—but not the Calvert DeLong that she remembered. His face was devoid of the muttonchops and walrus mustache, burned to a deep tan by sun and sea. His eyes sparkled and through the broad grin shown perfect white teeth.

"I found out from Miss Theda that you were at Betty's, but then I saw you running along the street. Come and get in."

"I can't," she said, hoarsely. "I've—I've got to find Ruth Ann."

"Oh? I was given to believe that she . . ." His voice trailed off at the anguish that came into her face. "You've seen her?"

She nodded, then was suddenly quiet, and very pale. He put out his hand to help her into the buggy. She became aware of the stares and curiosity she was exciting and quickly climbed in beside him, flipping the veil from the back of her hat over to cover her face. It made Calvert chuckle to himself. The webbing of the thin veil had given an added allure to her delicate beauty—and furthered suspicion that she was of the demimonde.

"Want to tell me about it?" he said gently, guiding the buggy back into the traffic.

She nodded. She had been able to share much with him in the past and she needed a sounding board. But when she glanced furtively at his profile, she saw that it was not stern and harsh as before, with deep worry lines at the eyes and mouth. He seemed much younger than she remembered, surer and stronger, and his face was animated from a deep inner happiness. This was a kind face, a tolerant one, one with candor and honesty.

She looked away and knew it would have been easier to have told the old Calvert DeLong, but she had to tell someone. Even as she talked she tried to fasten her attention on the streets and crowds they were passing, but all of the faces seemed the same and none of them Ruth Ann's. Nonetheless, her heart began to beat more calmly, and her depresssion lightened. It had been nine months since she had been able to feel this relaxed with another human being.

"You little fool. You've been going into the Tenderloin looking for her?" he asked, in a curt but polite tone.

"Only in the daytime."

"You little fool," he repeated, with more softness. "It's no wonder you didn't find her, Laura. They didn't get their title 'ladies of the night' by going out in the noonday sun. It isn't going to do much good to ride through the

Tenderloin streets now. At night, when they're out on the prowl for customers, would be the best time to spot her. From what you've said the search can be confined to the cheapest dives in the area."

Laura was at first indignant at his words. "It's hard enough for me to take their insults during the day. I don't know how I could go back there at night." She shivered.

He pulled the buffalo robe over her knees and tucked it about her. She felt the touch of his hands and she was pervaded by an intoxicating thrill. Had they never touched before? Oddly, she could not recall. She looked at him timidly, but still could not recall. His longest kiss was a shadowed memory. He caught her look, tried to remain stern, and then could not help his smile.

"I wasn't about to ask you to go in search of her at night, Laura. I don't even know if *I* want to go down in that rat's warren for her . . . but because of my love for you I will do it."

She stared at him incredulously. A soft rose flooded his face over the slip he had made. She opened her mouth to tell him about Fremont, but he quickly reached for her hand under the robe and squeezed it warmly.

"Don't say anything," he said, in a changed tone. "I've had a lot of time to think about this while I've been at sea. I couldn't say anything before because of Clint Bell."

"How did you know that?" she murmured, her disbelief growing even more.

"Know?" he asked lightly, his eye traveling over her face and throat and breast. "You both made it rather obvious, but your hurt over his interest in Maggie is no longer in your eyes. I knew I didn't stand a chance, even though I loved you from the first. No, I don't want to know what you feel. I'll give you all the time in the world to think about it. Right now I am famished, and I know a wonderful little place down in the Battery for fish and chips. Oh, Laura, I've got so much to tell you about these past months. I've only a week home while the admiral's ship is being refitted at Dad's shipyard, so I'll need every available minute that you have during this week. Miss Theda has already taken care of tonight by inviting me to dinner."

"What?" she asked. Fremont was coming to dinner. What was Theda thinking of?

"Don't worry," he laughed, "I know all about Fremont Hunter."

"You know?" she cried angrily. "What manner of game are you and Aunt Theda playing?"

She stared at him with cold fury, and he was delighted at the blaze of her eye.

"Of course. Why shouldn't I know? I still think he lives in some crazy dream world, even though Miss Theda says that he has mellowed. Even though he might still have an idiot's devotion to a cause that's all but dead, I will be a perfect gentleman at dinner and never utter a single thing that I know about him. And I really don't care what he might say about me, because you already know all there is to know. Now, here is our luncheon spot."

She averted her face and looked out over the wharf at the sea, without really seeing it. She had wanted to ask what he knew about Fremont, yet she really didn't want to know. Fremont had been so quiet and strange since the death of his father, as though a part of him had died with the man. In little ways he had become cruel and vindictive. He frequently went to Washington on business and came back fuming that the president was making plans for the South even though the war was not over. Perhaps it would be nice to have the sane quiet voice of Calvert DeLong around. She knew that it would please Theda . . . and Amos. And Laura?

As he helped her down from the buggy the touch of his hand again sent a thrilling tingle through her body. He held her eyes with his own strong gaze.

"And over lunch you must also tell me everything that you have been doing. I couldn't get a thing out of Miss Theda."

Yes, she thought, over lunch I can just let it come slipping out. She cursed herself for not being able to tell Fremont Hunter that she loved him—even though she fully intended to marry him. How could she tell Calvert that she was going to love, honor and obey Fremont, when she couldn't even tell Fremont that she loved him?

Without warning, she burst into tears. She turned and

pushed her face against the blue wool of Calvert's chest. She clutched him with shaking hands.

"Take me home, Calvert," she cried. "Take me home . . . and on the way I must tell you something. I can't stand to sit here and lie to you. . . ."

"Don't be foolish, Fremont. Calvert is nothing more than a good friend."

Fremont uttered a vulgar word of disgust. He cleared his throat loudly, laced his fingers together behind his back and paced in front of the living room fireplace.

"Your choice in friends has always been most odd, my dear Laura. Are you forgetting the acquaintanceship he had with your brother and sister? Most questionable!"

Laura blushed deeply, knowing she couldn't reveal the facts behind that relationship.

"I'm not forgetting, Fremont, but I don't see the point."

"The point?" he scoffed. "The point is that the man is very strange. One moment a true Copperhead and the next back within the Navy. Without evidence, I hate to call any man a spy and traitor, but he certainly raises doubts. I'm glad that he made his dinner stay so short."

"Did he have any other choice?" she stammered, her color rising. "You weren't very polite."

"Was there a reason to be?" Fremont retorted. "You are too naive and unseeing, Laura. The man sat mooning at you like some lovesick cat. Disgusting. I am positive that Miss DeWitt had the good sense to inform him of our pending marriage, but when I brought up the subject his surprise was too theatrical. I do not like the man and forbid you to see him further."

"I doubt that I shall," Laura said coldly.

Calvert had taken her announcement like a true gentleman. She had even been amazed when he had kept the dinner invitation. That had confused her even more. She did not want to lose his friendship, but now felt uncomfortable in his presence.

"That's exactly as I wish it, Laura. Now, I must go to Washington tomorrow for a few days. If I should learn that he's come sniffing about, I shall not like it in the least."

"I ask you to remember, Fremont," said Laura, her voice carrying a warning note, "that I am still somewhat of a guest in this house. Shall I keep to my room if Aunt Theda should invite Mr. DeLong into *her* home?"

"Yes, that would be the proper thing for you to do," Fremont replied grimly.

He was afraid of Calvert, but not because of Laura. He had never considered that she could be interested in any other man but himself. He had conditioned Theda's mind to look upon him with a certain respect, or so he thought. He could not afford to have her start questioning him now that his present plan was ready for fulfillment. He could still change the election around, even after the fact. With one night's work the whole of the administration would have to be replaced. As he thought on it, his eyes became malevolent. Laura thought the look was meant for her.

"As you wish," she said, with grim contempt. "Now, please excuse me if I retire."

"Well, come give me a goodnight kiss—I won't see you for about a week."

"Please, Fremont," she pleaded, "I fear I'm coming down with a cold and wouldn't wish you to take it on your trip with you."

"Very sensible, my dear. Run along and I'll let myself out after I've finished my brandy. I leave early in the morning so I shan't even stay until Miss DeWitt returns from the theater."

Fremont saw her depart with darkening impatience. His funds were running short and his newspaper salary hardly supported his life style. Because his early investigation had revealed Miss DeWitt's fortune, he knew the day would come when he and Laura would be quite well-to-do. It had not been discussed, but he assumed that he and Laura would live with the old biddy after the wedding, and he also assumed that her wedding gift would have to be quite handsome.

But immediate funds were his present concern. One did not conspire to eliminate the President, Vice-President and the entire Cabinet without having to hire accomplices. At first he had had no trouble in raising contributions for such a cause, but he had foolishly used vast sums of the fund for his personal expenses. If the Washington group did not pull off the plot this week, he was going to be in serious trouble. It had to be accomplished before Lincoln was sworn in at his second inaugural.

Theda DeWitt's efforts as a matchmaker had failed. Calvert did not return during the week and Laura found a million different reasons for not leaving the mansion. It was not that Theda disliked Fremont so much, rather that she liked Calvert so much more. But in matters of the heart she knew it was best to let the pot boil for awhile, without stirring it too much.

Then she was given reason to wonder if she shouldn't have been stirring all along.

"Miss Laura! Miss Laura, please wake up!"

Laura came awake with a start and sat up. The room was pitch black except for a halo of light from the lamp that a bathrobed Amos held high at the door. It made his face look like a mask of pure hate.

"What is it, Amos?"

"Miss Theda wants you, quickly, please! It's your sister!"

"Thank God!" she gasped and clambered from the bed. A few minutes later she was not thanking Him so gladly.

Ruth Ann's gasps for breath could be heard even before she entered the guest room. The pungent aroma of camphor filled her nostrils as she stared about the room. It was obvious that Ruth Ann had been there for some time. Dr. MacKenzie stood by the bed, holding a wrist that was more yellow than flesh-toned. Ellen stood pouring steaming water from a kettle into a basin, while Theda fanned the camphor fumes over the head of the bed.

Harry was keeping the fireplace roaring hot. Then, as he turned, she realized that it wasn't Harry. It was a most unusual-looking Calvert DeLong. His face sported a five-or six-day growth of beard and his clothing was right out of the Bowery.

He drew a deep breath, and looked at her with stern resolution.

"She wasn't easy to find."

His words made Laura confused and guilty. It was obvious that he had spent all of his time looking for Ruth Ann, while she had done nothing.

"Thank you for looking for her, Calvert."

"You may not be thanking me," he said gravely. "She's suffering from congestion of the lungs. Dr. MacKenzie is concerned about her."

Laura knitted her brows together and stared at the bed with gloomy anxiety. This waxen figure was not her sister, but a rag doll that had been left out in the weather for too long. She started to say something, then bit her lip.

"It was a very loving thing that you did," she finally whispered.

She paled at the look on his face. It was dulled with bewilderment and pain.

"I'm not sure it was love," he said, speaking in a monotone. "All I have really done is burden you and Miss Theda with a desperately ill young woman. For doing that, I now hate myself."

Laura started to protest.

"Laura, come quick!"

She knew she did not want to turn toward the bed. The sound of Theda's faint weeping was sad and urgent. She closed her eyes. She wanted to remember Ruth Ann from when they were children. No image would come, but neither was there any feeling of hate. There was just a moment of disbelief and nothingness.

22

THERE WAS a new love in Theda DeWitt's life—Wilfred
Alan Jamison, Kitty's plump-faced cheery infant. It
seemed impossible that anything could increase
Theda's joy over the event. But it was a letter from Clarence Dahlgren, of all people, that had exactly that effect.

Theda was in the drawing room when Amos brought
the letter in to her. Seeing her frown of concern when she
recognized the handwriting as Clarence's, Amos tactfully
withdrew, saying that he would be in the kitchen if she
needed him.

Theda settled herself more deeply into her chair and
hurriedly opened the envelope, astonished to draw out a
letter of some ten pages. Her expression was by turns surprised, anguished and touched as she quickly scanned
through the letter. Once finished, she read it again more
slowly.

In the letter, Clarence revealed the astounding fact that
he and Lucille had not one son but two. And Theda understood at long last why she had lost Clarence. It was
because of Lucille's pregnancy, Theda learned, that she
had been able to "win" Clarence from Theda once and for

all. But once the marriage was accomplished, Lucille had become hysterical at the thought that her baby's birth would be construed—and rightly—as the reason for her hasty marriage. Further, she had reasoned that because the baby had been conceived out of wedlock it was illegitimate—which was an insupportable blot on the aristocratic DeWitt name.

Clarence, never the strongest willed of men for all his good intentions, had been given no choice. He and Lucille had departed on a lengthy honeymoon—which had hardly been a honeymoon, with all of his bride's hysterics and tantrums—so that no one would know she was pregnant. He had reluctantly agreed to arrange for the child's adoption before they returned and settled into married life in West Point.

There the matter might have ended, if Clarence hadn't secretly kept track of the child's welfare. When the boy was old enough to go to work, Clarence had hired him. And Lucille had never once suspected that the new gardener, Wilf Jamison, was her firstborn son—as aristocratic as she, by nature if not by name.

It had nearly killed Clarence when Lucille had insisted that Wilf go off to war in Laddie's place, but his protests had been overruled by Lucille's unyielding determination. The best he had been able to do for his unacknowledged son was to send him off with extra money in his pocket. Clarence's pride had been supreme, if secret, when Wilf was named a hero. His grief had been equally strong when Wilf was reported dead.

"So there, dear Theda, you have the whole story at last," Clarence wrote. "I tell you this now because of my concern for my grandson, and because of all that I owe you. I pray you will accept what I am about to say in the spirit of a gift in return for all that I once wanted to give you and didn't, rather than as an onerous duty. It would ease my heart greatly if you would do all in your power to look after Wilfred Alan Jamison. I rather doubt that Kitty, who has come to love you, would object to anything you might be able to do for the boy's present and future welfare.

"Perhaps, by my own cowardice, I have given up the right to ask anything of you or to do anything on my grandson's behalf. But it is the nearest I can come to putting things to rights. I have allowed my life and my children's to go so amiss through Lucille's whims and grasping nature that it seems better to pass whatever was best of myself to others for safekeeping. I did that when I asked you to take care of my Laura, and I do it again now, in so far as I can, with my grandson. This will be our secret, Theda . . ."

Theda still sat with the letter in her hands, her eyes moist and her heart full, when Laura entered the room an hour later.

Seeing Theda's strange expression, Laura exclaimed, "Whatever is wrong, Aunt Theda?"

Theda started and hastily sat straighter, thrusting the letter into the folds of her skirt. "Nothing," she said, her manner abstracted. "For once, dear, nothing at all."

Laura studied her face, curious over the serenity that had settled on her features, smoothing the lines away. But she knew better than to question her aunt.

They sat in silence for some time, Laura bent over her embroidery and unaware that Theda had finally begun to regard her with a speculative look. When her aunt spoke, it was as if her previous thoughts also had been voiced.

"It would cause a delay, but wouldn't it be nice, Laura?"

Laura looked up in surprise. "What is that, Aunt Theda?"

"Little Wilf being able to walk along and carry your train."

"Oh, you!" Laura laughed. "The child is only seven months old. That would be more than just a little delay."

Theda sighed. "Hardly seems possible that the wedding is tomorrow."

"I know," Laura said, her voice as low as prayer. "There are so many things that hardly seem possible."

Theda didn't comment. She felt her eyes fill with moisture. They each, to a degree, had lost a sister. Lucille was no longer the fiery, formidable power she had been. The news of Ruth Ann's death had strangely stilled her. Looking like a mountain of black taffeta, she had sat through the funeral with her eyes closed. Laddie wept uncontrollably, but she paid him no mind. They seemed such a piti-fully small group in Theda's vast music room. Just family, pushing their discord aside for the moment.

Lucille had opened her dull eyes, her expression hopeless and drained, and looked at Theda.

"I understand that you are to marry, Theda. I wish you and Clarence well. Of course, I am destined to marry a count or duke or prince."

Theda had watched her sadly. Lucille wasn't aware of where she was or why she was there. Her mind was locked somewhere in the past when the times had been happy for her; and that's where she would remain forever. She would not even be aware that she would be living in quarters behind a general store in Ohio with Clarence. And she would never know that she had a grandson—a fact which Clarence had only learned that day and which he now shared with no one other than Theda.

The funeral had been held the same day as one of Fremont's frequent out-of-town trips, thus sparing them an ugly confrontation between Laddie and Fremont. Although Laddie was aghast that Laura would even consider such a union, he was intrigued to see if it would ever come about.

Then Laura shocked him and healed over his wounds by calling him back to New York five days before the wedding.

"Papa doesn't think he should bring Mama back for the wedding, Laddie. It's not that I don't want them, but he feels that she wouldn't know that she was even here. I have Aunt Theda, of course, but . . ." She eyed him narrowly. "Let's be honest, Laddie; I've never needed you for anything in life and you've never needed me. Perhaps we don't need each other now, either. But . . . I've talked this over with Aunt Theda and she fully agrees. Laddie, will you stay and give me away?"

He couldn't believe it. "Are you sure, Laura? You know the feelings that exist between Fremont and me."

"I'm quite aware of them. That's why I want you here rather than Papa."

He frowned. "Are you trying to tell me that you aren't sure about this marriage?"

"Laddie, is any woman ever really sure about it at this stage of the game? I'm frightened to hell, and that's about all I know."

"Do you love him?"

"First, Laddie, tell me—what is love? There's been a dearth of it in our family because we have never been able to be more than what Mama wanted us to be. Perhaps we could all blame the war—but would that be fair? Oh, the war has changed us, to be sure. That's what I keep saying about Fremont. He wanted his stepmother out of the area before Sherman marched up through the Carolinas, but she refused to leave with him. I can understand his moods over that. I can understand his moods over his hero, Lee, surrendering the other day."

"Moods, moods," Laddie replied impatiently. "We all suffer from various moods, Laura. I know I'm a fine one to speak. I've been less than a brother and never a friend to you or Fremont. But when it comes to love, I do know you to be a young woman not given to—to—"

"To sexual adventurism before marriage," Laura finished for him. "Therein lies my greatest problem, Laddie. Fremont took Aunt Theda and me to Washington for the inauguration. He came to my room the night before . . . it was quite late and I was in a foul mood. Calvert DeLong had left invitations at the Willard for us to attend a reception, but Fremont never returned to escort Aunt Theda and me. His excuse, as it always seems to be these days, is that business kept him tied up and he just forgot. To make a long story short, he made . . . advances—as a way of making up."

"And you gave in?"

Laura's face became gray and pinched, and she avoided his eyes. "I—I found that I just couldn't do it, Laddie. It was as though Ruth Ann was suddenly in the room standing between us and laughing her head off. I knew I could do nothing then but wait until after the wedding."

"What was his reaction?"

"Relief," she said, frankly. "Anyway, that was what it seemed to me at the time. He calmly returned to the boarding house he normally stays at in Washington, and with his duties as a reporter, we didn't see him until late the next afternoon when we were ready to board the train back to New York. He was again in one of his dark moods and I assumed that I was at fault because of the night before. Laddie," she added pleadingly, "I have no experience in matters such as that and really don't know how to conduct myself. What . . . what do you advise?"

"Patience." He paused and smiled. The past year had aged him, had made his handsome face haggard, had turned his eyes to steadfast grimness. There was no salt left to his life. Without his mother and Ruth Ann, he was a hollow shell. Then he assumed a sober look, and shook his head. "I'm the worst person in the world to be giving you advice, Laura, but the obligation is not on the lady's part. Once you have wed, it is the husband's duty to lead you gently down that path. You may laugh, but I think I'm one of the few people in the world who can honestly say that sex has nothing to do with love. But true love has a great deal to do with sex. If you wish, although I do not look forward to it, I will speak to Fremont on your behalf."

A good opportunity never presented itself. Some even began to wonder if Fremont would show up for his own wedding.

He slammed his bag down next to the front door of the Surratt Boarding House and stormed angrily back to the kitchen.

"Mary," he glowered, "I refuse to wait another minute for Booth. My funds are exhausted and at this very moment I should be attending the rehearsal for my own wedding. At least I can still get there in time for the rehearsal supper."

"When will you return?" the stout woman asked, her voice hesitant as she turned from the stove.

"Who knows?" Fremont answered wearily. "But at the moment, I hope never. I am sick and tired of the stalls and excuses. This has been all planned out five times, and then he has to change things. This is not one of his theatrical productions, although the money invested certainly makes it seem as much. I need time now to worm my way into Theda DeWitt's treasury."

"I ain't got much more time to give," Lewis Paine growled. "I'm wantin' to get on back south and home. I been listed long enough as a dead Confederate. Let me just go ahead on my own so you can list Seward as a dead Yankee."

George Atzerodt's expression was closed and sour, the jowls tight and knotty in the dim kitchen light, his fingers tapping the top of the table. "Nope! Gotta be done all the same time or it won't work. Go about your personal business, Fremont. We'll just wait till John and Davie Herold come up with the right time and place. I can spare a few more dollars from my carriage business for the food Mary is puttin' out."

"Food ain't my worry," she said sullenly. "I just can't help but to feel the same as Fremont. We've wasted our chances. What good is it all going to do now?"

No one spoke for a long time. Every eye was fixed on Fremont. He sighed and shrugged. "I leave it to the late arriving Mr. Booth. But if the past is any hint as to what he might do, he'll find one way or another to change the plan. Besides, he's only working on a rumor that Mr. Lincoln will attend the theater tonight."

"Put it from your mind," said Mary Surratt, coming to pat his hand. "You have yourself a lovely wedding and some happiness."

"It is not for happiness that I'm marrying," he said composedly. "I am marrying for money and not for love."

It was not difficult for Laddie Dahlgren to sense that truth during the supper at Delmonico's. Fremont slyly put on a front with Laddie, as though he feared him. Laddie observed this with both curiosity and satisfaction, which mounted as the evening wore on. Fremont had every right to lash out at him, but instead he was remaining quiet and composed.

Behind the cool exterior, Fremont was infuriated with himself. He could not stand the thought of the next day. He could not stomach the evil he saw in Laddie's eyes, the I-don't-want-this-to-be-happening expression painted on Theda's face or the quiet fear on Laura's. Electricity crackled in the room. Then, very slowly, very cruelly, Fremont began to smile, an evil smile that narrowed his eyes.

"Laddie," he said softly, "you erred in turning your

back on the Copperhead movement. When the true glory of their work becomes known, you'll be sitting quite on the outside."

"Their work? Fremont, you're living in the past. They're as dead as last year's Christmas goose."

Fremont tried not to smile. He shrugged. "You never could see beyond the nose on your face. Someday you'll see that I have been instrumental in—"

At that moment, Lorenzo Delmonico came bounding into the private dining room. His eyes were wide and blinking, his hands nervously hushing everyone to silence. He rapped a water goblet so fiercely with a spoon that it shattered. Then huge tears began to cascade down his cheeks.

"Sorry," he moaned. "Most sorry, my dear friends. The President has just been shot in Ford's Theater. No more celebration, please."

"Impossible!" Fremont said hoarsely. Someone had gotten to Lincoln before his group. The mere thought infuriated him. "I must get to the *Times*. I must learn what's happened."

He raced from the room without another word to anyone.

"My God," Laddie whispered to himself. Now the meaning behind Fremont's words was vivid and terrible. It was madness. During the war he might have supported an assassination attempt. But now? It was stupid and unthinkable. Then the most unthinkable thought of all came to him.

Oh, you slimy scoundrel, he thought. If you are involved in this, Fremont Hunter, I will fight to my death to keep you from marrying my sister and involving her.

He looked from his sister to his aunt. Theda had the aspect of death itself. Her lids half dropped over her eyes. Her mouth had fallen open a little as if she was unconscious. She sat as straight and still as before the announcement, but her hands now lay on her black silk knees, palms up, in an attitude of prostration.

Laddie whispered in Laura's ear, helped her to her feet and turned to offer his arm to Theda.

"Auntie T," he said soothingly, "come, let me take the two of you home. That's the place for all of us at this dark moment. We can send Amos back to the newspaper office for the details."

Theda DeWitt turned in her chair and stared up at her nephew. They looked at each other in a long silence, both faintly smiling, and understanding.

"I'm glad that you stayed, Lawrence. There are times in life when even an old bear like me needs a male arm to lean upon, and a voice in family council. We may have to make different arrangements about tomorrow, don't you think?"

It was hard for Laddie to restrain the impulse to shout out in fury: "Damn it, let's just cancel it forever!"

Laura, as if strangling, placed her trembling hand to her throat.

"Yes, Laddie, take us home quickly. If he is dead, I don't even want to think about tomorrow."

Even if Fremont had felt an impulse to return at once to his bride-to-be, he would have been delayed by the rumors and half-truths circulating through that strange night.

He was one of the few men alive who could sort through the maze and really determine what was rumor and what was truth. His expression turned miserable. Hour by hour it became more and more apparent that Herold, Atzerodt and Paine had horribly bungled their assignments and the egotistical Booth had reserved the President for himself.

Folly! Stupid folly, he thought, for the President still lived and Booth was a fugitive from justice. The vain, foolish dreamer had ruined it all.

His disgust at the handling of the conspiracy rose in strength as the night progressed. He saw himself as a prisoner because of the others' stupidity, even if they said nothing to implicate him. And he could not be certain that they would not implicate him. Oddly enough, he had never considered failure and had made no escape plans of his own.

He must be careful, he warned himself. He would keep giving Amos reports to take back to Theda and Laura, with hints that he might be called upon to go at once to Washington should the president live. If that were the case, he would not hesitate in going to get a quick loan from Theda, with the excuse that it was impossible to get money from the newspaper at such an hour.

Morning came as gray and bleak as the mood of the nation. Throughout the night the crowd in front of the *Times* building had grown until it packed the square and two converging streets. It was awesome in its silence. Thousands of eyes were glued to the third floor windows of the newsroom, where white cardboard had been placed to signify that the president still lived.

Amos pulled out his pocketwatch and frowned. It was just a little over a quarter past seven and he didn't like the idea of leaving the carriage and horses unguarded, but the streets were impossible to move through with the carriage. The crowds in the streets were not saying anything, but their looks were fierce. Then their faces changed, becoming overwhelmed with grief as the black cloth replaced the white cardboard. Their soft sobbing was as one. Strangers grasped hands and held on to give strength to each other. A man raced from the *Times* door and stood on the steps shouting. His words were at first so hysterical that no one could make them out. Then Amos recognized him and strained to hear what he was saying. Like a stone dropped with a pond, the meaning of his words spread a shocked silence through the crowds.

Fremont raised his arms; his eyes flashed. The crowd was his, he was controlling it. This was his moment, his triumph, his moment upon the stage of life.

"Yes, yes!" He reared his head back and roared out his words. "It is true! The bloody, butcher tyrant is dead! Dead! Let us proclaim Robert E. Lee as our new president! Oh, what a glorious morning!"

Fremont lifted his head proudly and started into the crowd, expecting to be hailed as a hero.

The first big fist came from nowhere, with devastating effect. Fremont roared like an angry bull; but the strongest man in the world is helpless against a crowd shattered by grief, armed with revenge.

Amos saw him go down and fall in the street, while the men nearest proceeded to work upon his inert form with their boots. Fremont did not cry out and the crowd was now more silent than ever. Amos tried to work his way to Fremont, but the current of the crowd was now against him.

Julian Livingston pushed the young reporter away from the window and demanded, "A riot? Hardly. What then?"

"Our reporter, Hunter, sir. Yelling like a madman, as though happy about the assassination."

"Probably was," Livingston said drily. "Everything he ever wrote had a Southern slant to it. Humph! Was to be married today, I believe. Well, Jacobs, get down to the street and see if there's a story in it for us. Can't remember whom he meant to marry."

John Jacobs had sense enough to stop by the society desk to check that out before going out on the street. The name of the girl made him whistle to himself. He smelled a new chapter in the old Dahlgren scandal.

Stepping into Times Square, he stopped in amazement. It was as empty and silent as a tomb—no crowd, nobody, no one except a lone policeman casually tapping his billy-club into an open palm and staring indifferently into space.

"Hey, officer," he called, "what happened?"

He stared at Jacobs with a look of open-mouthed wonder. "Have you not heard, lad? The President has been killed."

"Damn, I'm Jacobs of the *Times* and I know that," he said importantly. "I'm talking about the man who was screaming and was set upon by the crowd."

The Irishman pursed his large lips. "No riot here, lad! A black came and took a gentleman away in a carriage, as I recall."

"To which hospital?"

The officer shrugged. His hazel eyes traveled from Jacobs' eager face to the broken stovepipe hat that lay in the gutter. John Jacobs did not get the meaning and it took him two hours of checking at hospitals before he located Fremont Hunter in the morgue.

He drew from his pocket the slip of paper he had received at the society desk and checked the address.

"Well," he mused, "if she hasn't heard about her fiancé by now, it's no skin off my nose if I have to break it to her."

* * *

Amos had made sure that the news was broken in a gentle manner to Laura. Returning from the morgue, he had stopped at the DeLong mansion to plead for help from Calvert. Even deep in his own grief over the death of Lincoln, a man he had valued both as a friend and as a president, Calvert could not shirk the duty of protecting Laura from the agony, the shame and ruin that Fremont had caused her. . . .

Her mouth moved, but she was silent. The eyes fixed so steadfastly on her in genuine worry, in humble grief, were those of Lawrence Dahlgren.

"Laura, there is something I must tell you. It is my duty to tell it to you." His voice was low and neutral, but there was a tremor in it. "Last night Fremont gave me a clue that something like this might happen. After Lorenzo announced it I should have known. I should have stayed with Fremont and stopped this from happening."

"Too late," she said weakly, "far, far too late by then, Laddie. If anyone should be blamed it is I. I should have listened more carefully in Washington, rather than worry about my own failings as a woman. That was part of his ranting, which I found tiresome." She lifted her hand in a helpless gesture. "Oh, all of the resentments against him would be washed away, he thought, after his great accomplishment. It is strange that the immensity of this tragedy is that had I been a woman truly in love I would have been interested in what his great accomplishment was to be. I made the error, one engulfed in—"

"Stop it!" Theda chided. "Blame, blame, blame! No one is blameless. At one time or another in the past few years we have all played a part in fermenting the hatred that placed the gun in John Wilkes Booth's hand. Blame? No, the time is for compassion for the innocent. Poor, poor Edwin. How that sensitive heart must be suffering over this act by his brother."

Laura could not control herself any longer. She cried out in a thin, wild tone, "I can't keep silent! I must tell you! I didn't love him! I didn't."

Calvert held back, although desperate for her to call out for his comfort. Laddie reached out and took her hand and held it strongly. Her face was alive with hysteria, with a desperate bleakness. He got her to her feet and motioned

Ellen and Kitty forward to help. She was sobbing now, her head bowed.

Calvert's strongest impulse was to run and take her in his arms and comfort her. He restrained himself, watching the two women lead her away.

Theda continued as if Laura had not cried out or been taken from the room.

"Nor can we forget that Ida Vaughan Hunter is an innocent victim as well. We must look to that responsibility, too. The waste of it all. This war has devastated her whole family. Lawrence, we should make quiet arrangements to have him shipped home to Hunter Hill. He never fitted here. Let us return him to the only place where he was happy. The war is over. The two last soldiers have fallen. How terrible that one of them had to be such a towering oak."

Amos stepped into the room and cleared his throat.

"Excuse me, Miss Theda, but it's a Mr. John Jacobs from the *Times* at the door. Claims to be a reporter friend of Mr. Fremont and wishes to see Miss Laura. What shall I tell him?"

Theda looked momentarily confused and looked to Laddie. "I would say, Lawrence," she whispered, "that she does not wish to be disturbed."

Laddie pretended not to have heard her. "Calvert, I'm the first to admit I'm no good in matters like this. Could you be of help?"

Calvert looked at Theda, who had such unendurable pain and sorrow on her ruined face, and at Laddie, who was looking at him with imploring eyes, and he could not refuse.

The naval uniform did not deter Jacobs in the least. "Who are you?" he demanded rudely.

"Captain Calvert DeLong," Cal answered calmly. "Amos has already given me your name and paper, sir, but not the nature of your business."

"To see Miss Dahlgren," Jacobs began, glancing uneasily around Calvert to see if she was coming. "And to learn if she has heard about Fremont—Mr. Hunter, that is."

Calvert inclined his head the barest fraction of an inch and pursed his lips. "Yes," he said, "she's heard."

"Well," Jacobs went on, his voice hardening, "seeing

that it's pretty widely known that they were to be married today, I thought I might get some explanation of why . . ."

Calvert held up his hand. "This is a house of grief, Mr. Jacob. Doubly a house of grief, if you will. I see no story here for you."

A wave of dark color ran over Jacobs' face. His eyes gleamed with sudden savagery. "Listen! That scoundrel that swine was ranting with joy in the street over the assassination. I want to know why."

Calvert smiled to himself. If Jacobs thought he would rise to so clumsy a bait, he could be managed easily.

"As Miss Dahlgren was not there at the time, sir, how could she be of assistance to you? How could anyone but Mr. Hunter be of service to you?"

Jacobs felt Calvert's quiet contempt, but was undaunted.

"A good point, Captain," he said slowly, trying to think of a way to trap this man into a disclosure. "Have you known Mr. Hunter long? And if so, I was wondering—"

Calvert studied him coolly. "Who I am and what I'm doing here? Not that it really matters, but I am a friend who came up from Washington for the wedding."

"Then your visit is not official? I understand that Secretary of War Stanton has ordered agents of his department to start an immediate investigation."

"It is not official," said Calvert, smiling to himself. "However, let me give you a solid piece of advice. If every man who had made a comment against Mr. Lincoln or might have cheered today were to be arrested in connection with this horrible deed, then our jails would be full to bursting. I work for Gideon Welles and worked directly for the President, so I know whereof I speak."

"Still," Jacobs snarled, "Hunter got killed for what he said."

"I do not know what he said or how he said it, sir. But during the draft riots in this city I saw firsthand how the least little word or deed can turn a civilized man into a savage animal. I suggest, sir, that would be the case today. You, I believe, have worked with Mr. Hunter. You should then be aware that he lost a brother and a father to the war. Perhaps his statements were little more than the release of his pent-up grief. Now his ill-advised words have created even more grief. Again, there is no story here, sir, and on that I speak with an official voice."

Jacobs stood very still, watching him with calculating eyes. The man was intelligent, far too intelligent for him and his limited experience in getting at the root of a story. But he dared not admit defeat to Julian Livingston, so he would stall.

"You made a good point, Captain. I did work with Fremont Hunter, but can't say that I really knew the man. I'll talk with some of the people at the *Times* first and give Miss Dahlgren a chance to get over her grief."

"You do that, Mr. Jacobs," he said quietly. "But don't bother to call again. I believe the family plans to take Miss Dahlgren away for a spell."

Oddly enough, it was exactly what Theda and Laddie had been discussing. It was spring in Europe. It would not smell of death and destruction and war. It would be a healing place.

"I think it's a marvelous idea," Calvert said, his voice tender. "I shall miss you, Laura. I'll soon be back to work for my father. Will—will you kiss me good-bye . . . for friendship's sake?"

Laura surged forward and buried herself in his arms.

"Oh, Calvert, what would I ever do without you? Promise me. Promise me that you will always remain my friend."

"I promise," he mumbled. "Don't worry your head over that . . ."

23

CALVERT DeLong waited and wondered, with spring melting into summer and then fall. And then one day a new love came into his life.

"The Pacific?"

Horace DeLong nodded sagely. "That's how I see the future, my boy. Had Lincoln lived there would already be a hundred and eighty thousand black troops digging the Panama Canal. But it will come, and when it does I want DeLong ships on the Pacific. Calhoun has purchased land for me in a place called Oakland. Good harbor, good timber, good future."

Then, suddenly, he knew that his father was speaking of his future. Nothing had ever before so excited him. Day and night he thought of nothing else, seldom leaving the Brooklyn shipyard. Like a Columbus, he would take three ships on the long way to California. As the ship-building industry in California was in its infant stage, he had to carefully plan everything he would require to establish the new shipyard: men, equipment and materials. He was engrossed in making these plans at his father's shipyard when he was interrupted by a familiar voice.

"I understand the hermit seldom leaves his cubicle."

Calvert turned and gasped. "Laddie, where in the hell did you come from? Good lord, you do look marvellous."

Laddie grinned broadly. "Ah, how long I yearned to hear those words from your lips, but now 'tis too late. I've been refined and reeducated to the point where I only answer to Lawrence."

Calvert let out a bellowing howl. "Wherever did you pick up that ridiculous accent?"

"Really, now, dear chap." Then he giggled. "It is most absurd, but the only way that Lady Jane will have me."

"Oh?"

"That's why I've come down to your musty little office on this smelly waterfront, old boy. Your father warned us about your 'do not disturb' attitude, but you must join us for dinner and the theater and meet Lady Jane. She is charming, witty and very wealthy . . . and has talked me into becoming her spunky spouse."

"Well, well, well. This *is* news. And how is everyone else?"

"Fine, I assume. Theda and Laura were to return from France. I hope their crossing was better than ours. Horribly cold. How can you ever think of leaving on this voyage of your own in the dead of winter?"

"Because it is not the dead of winter in South America. When is this little party? I depart in just ten days' time."

"Friday next, and I'm counting on you. Until Theda returns I'm at a total loss to get Lady Jane introduced to proper society."

Calvert nodded. "I'll be there. I'll just about have all my work completed by then."

He suddenly thought of Laura. It wasn't that she had been totally out of his mind for the past eight months, but it suddenly dawned on him that he might never see her again. But there is no hope for us anyway, he thought. No hope.

He sat for a long time after Laddie left, carefully removing all thought of Laura from his mind. He would always love her, but soon—almost too soon—his life was to take a whole new course.

Then his mind went back to nothing but that course.

* * *

Calvert cursed himself for being such a forgetful fool. It was far too late to attend the dinner party and so he went directly to the theater. For a moment he stood outside the theater in confusion, thinking Laddie must have made an error. The posters proclaimed the play to be a DeWitt production of Edwin Booth in *Romeo and Juliet*. He didn't see how that could be possible, as the grief-stricken man had gone into immediate retirement after the assassination. And Calvert wondered if Booth's return to the stage hadn't proven to be a disastrous mistake, for there were no carriages arriving at the theater and the foyer was empty. A single usher stood with a forlorn face.

"I'm Calvert DeLong with the Dahlgren party."

"I was told we might expect you, sir. The house lights have just been dimmed for Mr. Booth's introduction. If you will step in and wait, I'll escort you to your seat at its conclusion."

Inside the auditorium was a different world. Every usher and doorman stood in the rear ready to rush down the aisles with monstrous baskets of flowers. Every seat was filled and had been for the past half hour, but the audience was as quiet as though they were all wax figures. It was as though they had come to take part in a tragedy and not to watch one.

The curtain began to rise on an empty stage. Unknown to any of them, Edwin Booth had made a subtle last-minute change. He was grateful that Theda DeWitt was helping him over the pressure of his financial obligations, but he would face the people without her introduction. If they booed him right off the stage, he would fully understand.

Alone, his shoulders hunched as though he was barely able to carry the burden of his humiliation, he started to walk slowly from the wings. It was as though everyone had stopped breathing at once; there was not a single sound. Then the silence was broken by the rustle of taffeta and a pair of gloved hands vigorously clapping.

Calvert's eyes were drawn to the box where the sound came from. He stared in utter amazement at the regally beautiful young woman. And as the rest of the audience immediately followed suit, he continued to stare. A thousand pairs of clapping hands were nearly drowned out by a thousand cheering voices, and still he continued to stare.

For Calvert there was no one else in the theater except Laura Dahlgren. She glowed with radiant beauty. He did not see the flowers being rushed down the aisles; he did not see Theda come from the wings to give comfort to the man who had broken into tears on the stage; he did not see Laddie lean forward and whisper in Laura's ear.

Then he saw her hands stop in mid-motion, and her head turned. Even in the dim theater he could see the blue of her eyes staring back at him. For a long time they were conscious of nothing but each other.

"It seems this will go on for some time, Mr. DeLong. Shall I show you up to your party now?"

Calvert nodded, but was suddenly afraid. He had made a promise always to be her friend and had conditioned his heart to accept that fact. Returning to the foyer so he could go up the grand staircase, he had a wild urge to go directly to the street and not give the wound a chance of being reopened.

"Here you are! Miss Theda's had me running all over town looking for you."

"Amos," Calvert roared, "how good to see you! No one told me that you were all back from Europe already."

"Just back this morning," Amos said gaily, "and most glad to be home. Miss Theda nearly took over the ship to make sure we got here by tonight." A twinkle came into his eyes. "Excuse me now, sir. I'll be going backstage to let her know that you've arrived."

Now he could not think of escape. Now he would have to turn and go up to the box. But as he turned he stopped dead in his tracks. Laura was floating down the stairs toward him, her arms outstretched, a worried frown creasing her forehead.

"I was afraid you were running out on me, Calvert DeLong."

"I can't lie to you," he said, suddenly grinning. "The thought crossed my mind."

Her frown softened; a twinkle played deep in her eyes. "You've crossed my mind a great deal while we were gone. I missed you."

"Thank you," he said, hesitating before he continued. "You have probably heard that you'll have to start missing me again."

"I've heard," she said lightly. "Betty tells us that you're taking Clint and Maggie. Anyone else that I know?"

He shook his head. Then he grew bold. "You, if you'd like."

She drew nearer to him. "Are you offering me a job, or something else?"

He stared at her incredulously. Her eyes were filling with dancing mirth.

"The something else," he stammered, "is what I have always wished to offer you. You know I've always loved you."

"I don't see how, the way I've treated you. But I've had time to think things out. I'm ready for that something else."

He looked at her in silence, neither aware that the ovation for Edwin Booth still continued. He searched her face in disbelief, but what he saw was truth and tenderness.

She touched his cheek gently with her fingertips. "I once wondered why some good friends of mine, Mildred and Marvin Carson, never said they loved each other. Now I know. Their love flowed back and forth so strongly that they didn't have to put it into words. They had respect and admiration and a comfortable feeling being with each other. That's love. That's what I now know that I feel about you."

"Oh Lord!" he burst out. "I'm due to sail on Monday."

Laura giggled. "Your father kept Aunt Theda well informed on that subject. I think you'll find that they've set the ceremony for two o'clock Sunday afternoon. Your mother has been doing all the arranging."

Calvert was stunned. "They certainly were very sure of themselves."

"Oh, Calvert, we'll just have to realize that we were surrounded by a bunch of romantics—the worst being Amos, though Aunt Theda and Laddie run good seconds. Well?"

"Well what?"

"Calvert DeLong, you big ape, do I have to propose to you?"

"I think you already have," he said in a trembling voice, "and my answer is yes, my darling."

With a heart that was at last calm and assured, she leaned close and kissed him tenderly. She felt no fear of the trip to California, because she would be with him. Neither was there any fear of the future, because she would be with him. It was not an overpowering love that she felt, but it was love, none the less, and she did not doubt that time would deepen and mature the feelings they already shared.

Happiness is a gift God has given mortals tŏ share with each other.

On May 13, 1867, Amos travelled to Fort Monroe to take his "Mister Jeff" home from prison. He would share his happiness and serve the man for the twenty-two remaining years of the proud man's life. Insisting on standing hatless in the cold at Jefferson Davis's funeral, he caught a chill. Amos died a month later.

After the death of Kitty in 1869, Theda officially adopted Kitty's son and shared the happiness of her remaining years with young Wilfred Jamison DeWitt. Clarence had indeed given her a gift in his grandson.

Laddie would have loved to share his happiness with his mother. His son, Oliver Lawrence Dahlgren, was knighted by Queen Victoria in 1889 for service to the Empire.

Happiness was also shared by the DeLong and Bell families in Oakland, each producing sons and daughters.

It took seventy-four years for Horace DeLong's dream to come true, even though the shipyard almost didn't survive the Depression years. On Monday morning, December 8, 1941, Dewitt DeLong knew he had to put his grief behind him. He could not change the fact that Ensign Harold DeLong would lie forever entombed within the U.S.S. *Arizona*. He had other sons and daughters and grandchildren to think about. He had been taught by a remarkable mother and father to have a deep love for family and country. He knew that they would want him to throw whatever DeWitt and DeLong money he possessed into building ships, great and small, that would become part of the greatest naval force ever put upon the water.

EIGHTH IN THE SERIES
FREEDOM FIGHTERS:

The Frontier War

by Jonathan Scofield

Driven by their lust for the great frontier, men and women—redman and white settler—mingled their blood on the prairies, mountains and valleys of the West, as Custer and his men of the U.S. Seventh Cavalry moved arrogantly towards the Little Bighorn.

Alex DeWitt and his brother, Buck, were rivals for the love of the beautiful, high-spirited Kelly, but stood together against the ruthless frontier traider, Barrow, who, with his wanton woman, plotted the betrayal of Indian and settler alike.

When the shadow of Crazy Horse, Warrior Chief of the Sioux Nation, loomed over all their lives, these proud and passionate people found themselves caught up in the West's most infamous massacre and its bloody aftermath—a fierce struggle for survival that shook and shaped a nation.

BE SURE TO READ
THE FRONTIER WAR
COMING IN OCTOBER
FROM DELL/BRYANS